D1180104

Lucy
Carmichael

Lucy Carmichael

Margaret Kennedy

RINEHART & COMPANY, INC.

NEW YORK

The lyrics from "Nice People" are quoted with the permission of Francis, Day & Hunter, Ltd.; and those from "I Ain't Gonna Grieve My Lord No More," with the permission of The Boston Music Company. The lyrics from "There'll Always Be an England" are reproduced by permission of Gordon V. Thompson Ltd., Toronto, Canada.

TO

Julia Davies

She was not an existence, an experience, a passion, a structure of sensations, to anybody but herself. . . . Even to her friends she was no more than a frequently passing thought. If she made herself miserable the livelong night and day it was only this much to them—'Ah, she makes herself unhappy.' If she tried to be cheerful, to dismiss all care, to take pleasure in the daylight . . . she could only be this idea to them—'Ah, she bears it very well.'

THOMAS HARDY. (Tess of the D'Urbervilles.)

CONTENTS

Lucy
Carmichael

Part 1

Lucy's Wedding

1

On a fine evening in September Melissa Hallam sat in Kensington Gardens with a young man to whom she had been engaged for three days. They had begun to think of the future and she was trying to explain her reasons for keeping the engagement a secret as long as possible.

"If my mother knows of it first," she said, "my father will be wounded to the quick."

John Beauclerc had only just learnt that he was to have a father-in-law. He had always supposed that Mr. Hallam, whose name was never mentioned, must be dead. But it appeared that he had merely left his family and was living by himself in a hotel at Budleigh Salterton.

"Can't you," he suggested, "write and tell him first?"

"That would wound my mother to the quick."

"You could tell her next morning, just when he was reading your letter. Then they'd know simultaneously."

"Ah, but the morning is a bad time with my mother. She is at leisure and able to listen to one. Fatal! She will instantly discover all the objections."

"But are there so many objections? I don't see—"

"Of course there aren't. None. But that is so dull. My mother believes that life ought to be tense and dramatic. She would prefer one's choice to be disastrous. If you had been born in the gutter,

3

or were tubercular and couldn't support one, she would be most sympathetic. As it is, I must choose a moment when she is involved in some other drama, late for an appointment, too frantic to listen. Then she'll say: Marry anybody you like but don't keep me now! You don't know my mother."

He agreed that he did not. He had only met Mrs. Hallam once and she had frightened him. He had fallen in love with Melissa during the summer holidays at a country house party, and their courtship, after their return to London, had been carried on outside her home. He had called for her in Campden Hill Square, where she lived, and taken her out to dine and dance, but she generally ran down the steps as his taxi drew up at the door. On the first occasion, however, she had not been quite ready, and he had been shown into a large dim room, full of flowers and engraved glass and Hallams, to wait until she came down. They were a formidable family. He was daunted by the suavity with which little Julian, who was at Eton, offered him sherry. He was chilled by the languid sophistication of Valentine, a schoolgirl sister. And the tense, haggard gaze of Mrs. Hallam terrified him out of his wits until he realised that she was not looking at him at all and that her thoughts were elsewhere. They were not, as he had at first supposed, scrutinising and condemning him. He was merely one of the procession which called nightly for Melissa. They were vague about his name and he was still disentangling himself from another John, a John Hobbes, when Melissa tripped in, wearing the flowers he had sent her. Mrs. Hallam's enormous eyes rested on these for less than a second, but in that instant he realised that pink carnations were a mistake. The odious Hobbes would, he supposed, have sent orchids.

He was soon to know better. During that first outing he picked up a great deal of useful information. Orchids would have been a worse mistake. She disliked conventional flowers. She had a friend who kept a flower shop and would make up an amusing corsage of sweet williams or nasturtiums, or would send something arranged for the hair, which Melissa preferred that summer. Yellow, orange, red or white blossoms would be welcome; blue and pink should be avoided. She did not tell him that her friend was inexpensive, but he soon discovered this, with considerable

4

relief. All his discoveries, indeed, were of a kind to raise his spirits, for he had been wondering how often he could afford to take Melissa out, and how he was to press his suit if he did not take her out. But it seemed that her tastes were unexpectedly simple. She drank very little. She would enjoy a country walk, a Promenade Concert, or an afternoon at Kew. By some miracle everything was made easy for him, since she had decided to marry him while still down in Hampshire and intended him to save up his money for their honeymoon. When John Hobbes took her out she cost him a pretty penny.

She had never talked very much about her family, with the exception of her elder brother, Humphrey, whom she adored. When she spoke of him her whole aspect changed: her eyes sparkled and she would begin to laugh. He was in Africa, among the French Dandawa, behaving very badly, said Melissa, with fond pride, earning no money and wounding both his parents to the quick. Having qualified as a doctor he had turned himself into a vet and was studying cattle diseases, simply for love of a black man called Kolo, king of a poor small tribe, to whom he had attached himself in Paris. In Kolo's country the cattle pined and died, and nobody knew why. The people were desperately poor, but the tribe was isolated, the disease did not spread to richer territories, and the French government was apathetic. Kolo, however, was not. By some means or other he had managed to educate himself and had scraped up the money to get to Paris and plead his cause. Official ears were deaf but he had made some valuable friends. A coloured American singer, struck by the force and heroism of Kolo's character, had offered money for research and Humphrey Hallam had undertaken the work. Melissa pretended to laugh at the whole enterprise, and called Dandawaland Humptopia, but John saw very clearly that she was consumed with anxiety lest the money should run out before any positive success had been achieved.

"If only Hump were at home," she now said, "the whole problem would be easier. There wouldn't be a problem. When he is at home everybody behaves sensibly. I don't think my parents would have parted company if Hump had been here."

"Why did they . . . what did they . . . I mean what was the trouble?"

5

"Oh, a magnolia tree."

"A magnolia tree?"

"Yes. My mother wanted it in the back garden and my father in the front garden. He was out when it arrived, and my mother put it in the back garden. So, when he came in, he said it was the last straw and went to live at Budleigh Salterton."

"You can't be serious."

"I am. That was exactly what happened. It isn't a legal separation. They are emotional gluttons, both of them. They gobbled up every sensation they could extract from marriage, and now they are seeing if separation won't provide them with a few more. I think they miss each other dreadfully. They have nobody to make scenes with."

Melissa broke off and mused for a while, her pretty eyebrows slightly lifted in distaste.

"Personally," she remarked, "I am an emotional ascetic. But if Hump had been at home he would have done something. He would have gone to Budleigh Salterton and been so intolerable that my father would have been obliged to come home to get away from him."

"But why Budleigh Salterton?"

"Oh, my father has a sort of romance about that place. He believes that the happiest years of his life were spent there as a child. Actually it was only three weeks, when he was recovering from measles. But, as he has never been happy anywhere else for longer than three days, I daresay he does feel attached to it. He gets rather bored there and loves an excuse for coming home and setting us all by the ears. He did that when my sister Cressida got married. And I suppose we must expect him at our wedding."

"You don't sound very . . ."

John checked himself and put it in another way.

"Which of your parents," he asked, "are you fondest of?"

The answer to this question was of some importance to him. Melissa had just described herself as an emotional ascetic and he feared that this might be perfectly true. There had been moments during their courtship when, in spite of his attachment to her, he had found himself wondering if she was capable of any strong feeling. She had revealed very little of her heart to him, and, though

6

she had said that she loved him, she had made the avowal in so cool a manner that he doubted if she knew what she was saying. He put his question therefore a little anxiously, and was rewarded by a smile of approval.

"I'm so glad," she said, "that you don't mind putting the preposition last. Jane Austen frequently did."

"Melissa! I asked a question. Of which are you fondest?"

"Now don't alter it just when I've said I like it. Which am I fondest of? Really, I don't know. For years I've been so perfectly exasperated with both of them that I might say I'm usually fondest of the one I'm not with."

This was not very reassuring. He watched her unhappily as she picked up a large straw hat which lay on the grass beside her. Her expression was pleasant but her voice had been chilly.

"I must go," she said, getting up. "Cressida is coming to supper."

"You're very fond of her, I expect," he pleaded as he scrambled to his feet.

She turned to him with an amused stare.

"How anxious you are that I should be fond of people!"

"I want to believe that you have a very sweet nature."

"Oh, but I have a very sweet nature. I like most people. I'd like everyone if I could. Dislike is so fatiguing."

"But do you really love anybody, Melissa?"

"You should know."

She gave him a glance, soft and ardent, which made him feel quite dizzy. When he had recovered she was walking quickly away across the thick summer grass. He rushed after her aware of people everywhere—people with dogs, people with perambulators, strolling couples, recumbent couples, and children playing organised games. He was obliged to walk sedately by her side through the alternate patches of sun and shadow, towards Notting Hill Gate.

"I wish . . ." he murmured.

"I know. But my mother is going to Italy soon, and I shall have the house to myself, because Julian and Valentine will be back at school. You can come to supper every evening, and we shan't have the whole of London looking on."

7

"Oh, Melissa! How did you know what I was thinking?"

"Ha! Ha! I'm Madame Leonore the celebrated clairvoyant. My crystal tells me that you still hanker for a list of the people I love."

"Yes I do. I want to know all about you."

"How dangerous!"

"I want to love them too."

"How ambitious! Well . . . there are three. But you only have to love two, because Narcissus came to a bad end."

"Hump?"

"Yes. And for years Hump was the only one. Till I was eighteen I could count the people I loved upon my thumb. But then I met . . ."

Melissa paused and smiled to herself before she finished:

"Then I met Lucy Carmichael."

"Oh! A girl! This girl who is going to be married . . . that you're going to be bridesmaid to?"

"Keep it up! Your prepositions beat Jane Austen's."

"She's no relation, is she? Just a friend."

"Umhm. Just an old college chum."

"What is she like? Is she pretty? Is she at all like you, I mean?"

"Not a bit. She is tall and slender, while I am short and dumpy."

"You are not. You aren't dumpy."

"I would be, if I wasn't as light as a bird. She has short, light brown, curly hair. Very attractive."

"So have you. I mean your hair is dark but it curls."

"I'm glad you think so. Lucy's nose is aquiline, not retroussé, and her eyes are grey. She has a very delicate skin, too pale, but that's easily remedied. I wouldn't call her pretty. When she is well and happy she is extremely beautiful. When she is out of sorts or depressed she is all nose, and dashes about like an intelligent greyhound after an electric hare. She has a natural tendency to vehemence which is unbecoming to one so tall, but under my influence she occasionally restrains it. She believes me to be very sophisticated—a perfect woman of the world. She admires my taste beyond anything and does her best to imitate me. She is incautious

8

and intrepid. She will go to several wrong places, and arrive at the right one, while I am still making up my mind to cross the road. She is my opposite in character. She is cheerful and confident and expects to be happy. She taught me how to enjoy myself. Until I knew her I had always been convinced that I must be destined for misery. I thought it safest to expect the worst. I suppose it was because everything in my home has always been so stormy and insecure; I was brought up never to expect anything to go right. Lucy forced me to believe that I might be happy. I don't expect I'd have had the courage to marry you, to marry anybody, if it hadn't been for Lucy."

"In that case," said John, "I shall have no difficulty in loving her."

"You will oblige me by trying to do so. She's not everybody's cup of tea. My mother is very supercilious about her, simply because her father, who is dead, was only a chartered accountant and her mother is a woman doctor in Surrey. In my mother's idiom, Lucy is 'a very ordinary girl.' And in some ways she is still rather childish. It is her ambition to be suave and *mondaine*, which she will never be. When she remembers this she undulates about with a remote smile. When she forgets, which is pretty nearly all the time, she prances along and roars with laughter."

"Did you know her before you went to Oxford?"

"No. We were freshers together and took to each other the first night, at dinner in Hall. I thought she was the only female in sight who didn't remind me of an earwig. She thought the same thing about me. So we went and sat in my room, and agreed how awful everything seemed to be, and I impressed her with my mulberry housecoat."

John also was immediately impressed by the mulberry housecoat, though he had never seen it. But he could and did imagine how it would become her.

"So after that," said Melissa, "we always went about together. We never accepted an invitation unless it was for both, and we made a very good team. When we arrived at a party everybody said: 'Here's Lucy and Melissa!' Or, if they did not, we would just look round the room, and at each other, and laugh a little, and go away, as if we had a much better party waiting round the corner.

9

One girl by herself can't do that. There is nothing more humili-ating than having to edge out of a crowded room when nobody has noticed one is there. Are you listening?"

"Oh . . . yes . . . yes . . ." said John, who was still mus-ing on the mulberry housecoat. "Er . . . is she clever?"

"Lucy? Clever? You do ask the strangest questions. Why, yes, I suppose so. As clever as she needs to be."

"What class did she get in Schools?"

"A second. She ought to have got a first, but she must needs go and fall in love during our last term, which made hay of her work. It was too bad of her, and entirely against our principles. We had decided not to fall in love till we had left college."

"But can people always decide whether—"

"Of course they can. There is no excuse for falling in love with an undergraduate. What sensible man wants to tie himself up so young? And where's the attraction of a silly man? Our men were all of them very superior men, ambitious men who meant to get somewhere in the world. We danced and dined with all the future prime ministers and attorney generals. We had a glorious time. But, at the end, Lucy had to go and spoil it all. She went to a party without me. I had a headache and cried off, but she had promised to go. It was a coctkail party, and she said she'd just look in for half an hour. She wasn't back at dinner time. She wasn't back at lock out. She had to climb into college over the garden wall at half past two in the morning, and I never did find out what she'd been doing all that time. I don't believe she knew herself. She'd met this man . . . at *least* he wasn't an undergraduate . . . he was staying in Oxford and came to the party; Patrick Reilly. You've heard of him?"

"You mean the explorer?"

Melissa looked doubtful.

"I wouldn't call him that. What has he explored?"

"Doesn't he go to places and write books about them?"

"M'yes. Have you read any?"

"I read the war one—about working with the French Re-sistance. I thought it pretty good. He must be a remarkable man."

"Oh? In what way?"

"He seems to have so many adventures."

"Quite. So then Lucy met Remarkable Reilly at this party and so then it was all over with Lucy."

Melissa led the way off the grass into the shaded avenue of the Broad Walk.

"That's all," she said flatly.

"But what kind of a man is he?"

"Haven't you seen his photographs?"

"What is he like to meet, I mean?"

"Oh, irresistible. One can't blame Lucy for a moment. A most elegant brogue, with just a touch of swagger and impudence . . . not offensive, you know . . . endearing! He rushes round having adventures just for the love of it. He's only got to be told, 'You can't do that there 'ere,' and he goes and does it, and gets away with it, and nobody minds, because he's the eternal boy. He's Mister Peter Pan."

"But is he *nice*?" persisted the patient John, plodding beside her along the Bayswater Road.

"Can you ask? No woman could ever resist a man like that."

A pneumatic drill in the road made further conversation impossible for several minutes. John stole glances at Melissa and when the racket had died away behind them, he asked why she was looking so sad.

"That," she said coldly, "is not the sort of question I care to hear."

"But you are looking sad."

"So what? I don't look sad in order to be asked what is the matter."

"I want to understand you."

"That's quite easy. I'm a very simple, obvious person."

"But if we are to live together . . ."

"Darling, you'll find me uncommonly easy to live with. I hardly ever have moods. I don't approve of them. I dote on equanimity. But, if a mood should overtake me, I expect that lapse to be pardoned and overlooked, like the hiccups. And if you want to understand it, think of the most obvious explanation."

An obvious explanation for Melissa's depression was already tormenting John. He could not quite allow himself to entertain it and stalked along beside her, keeping it at bay, until she suddenly began to laugh.

"No," she said. "No, no, no! I was not in love with Remarkable Reilly myself, and I am not marrying you on the rebound."

"Melissa!"

"How dare you think such a thing, after the description I gave of him?"

"I didn't know . . . I thought . . . you said he's irresistible. You said no woman could . . . then you really think he's a stinker?" cried John, brightening up.

"I've only met him twice, but I think he's bogus. He can climb the foothills of the Himalayas, and write about it as if he'd been up Everest. If he went up the Eiffel Tower I believe he'd write a book about it called *Parisian Escapade*, and there would be a waiting list for it at the libraries. No real adventurer has half so much façade. His talent is for blowing his own trumpet. We've all had adventures. I was machine gunned myself, at the seaside, when I was a little girl. And you fought from Normandy to the Rhine. If our adventures had happened to Reilly, people would be paying fifteen shillings to read about them."

Melissa's eyes flashed during this tirade, which was music in John's ears. But he felt obliged, in fairness, to point out that Reilly was talented as a writer.

"I suppose so," she agreed crossly. "But if I breathe a word in his favour it appears to cause you pain."

"Why . . . I could see you were very sad about something."

"Use your loaf. Consider what else I've told you."

He used his loaf, and by the time they reached Kensington Church Street he suggested that she had wanted Lucy to marry Hump.

"That's better. Always look for the obvious, when you're dealing with me. There is nothing subtle or mysterious about my nature. What else would a simple, natural girl like me want, when she has a brother and a friend?"

"Do they know each other?"

"No. They've never met. Hump has been in France and Africa ever since I knew Lucy. But they would have met sometime, and they're born for each other. If Lucy wants adventures she couldn't do better than go to Humptopia."

"I see."

But he did not see. Melissa might be disappointed at the collapse of a favourite scheme, but he had caught a glimpse of something deeper than disappointment in her face. She was profoundly miserable.

"Here is the tube station," she said, "and I think you had better go home, because we might run into my mother at any moment, on her way back from a tea party, and she might get ideas into her head if she knew how often I am meeting you."

"Come with me and help me to buy my ticket."

She laughed and crossed the road with him and stood beside him while he bought a ticket for Lancaster Gate. They then waited for a lift to appear. It took some time to do so, after the manner of lifts at Notting Hill.

"You're quite right," she said, interpreting his silence. "The disappointment over Hump is only a side issue. Go on chasing the obvious."

"You're sad . . . on Lucy's account?"

"Wretched."

"Because . . . because you think Reilly's a stinker? You think it's a frightful mistake?"

The hum of the rising lift ceased and the gates opened. Melissa nodded and turned away without a word. He saw that she was crying.

All that he had learnt of her forbade him to attempt any consolation. He stepped into the lift and sank downwards, deeply moved by her tears, painfully content—sure, at last, that his beloved had a very warm heart.

2

MELISSA HAD by no means told John the whole story. She had not said a word about Jane Lucas.

This legendary siren had for years provided a topic for conversation in Campden Hill Square. Melissa had never seen her, but for a short time, long ago, Jane Lucas had been married to the brother of Lady Skinner, Mrs. Hallam's closest friend. She had deserted him almost immediately, but her subsequent career had been followed in wrathful indignation by all the Skinner circle. As Melissa said, when discussing the matter with her married sister Cressida, they had been hearing of Jane Lucas, man and boy, ever since they could remember: how ugly she was, how wicked she was, how old she must be getting, and how slowly the mills of God seemed to be grinding in her case.

Her existence had been sharply impressed upon Melissa because she had been the indirect cause of a forfeited pantomime. Mrs. Hallam and some other ladies, wishing to tell Lucas stories in the presence of the nine-year-old Melissa, had taken refuge in the French language. *Et pourtant elle a du chien*, somebody had said. Melissa had been struck by the phrase. She lost no time in applying it to the Vicar's sister who bred Airedales; her father, overhearing, made a fine Hallam hullabaloo, and she was sent to bed instead of to Cinderella.

That Jane Lucas had been Patrick Reilly's mistress was scarcely a surprising piece of news; she had, in her time, been everybody's mistress. Mrs. Hallam disinterred and mourned over it as soon as the engagement was announced. She quite liked Lucy but she had never favoured the very close intimacy of the two girls and she was irritated that Lucy should marry first and marry so well. She could not repress certain little digs and passed on to Melissa all that she had gathered from Mrs. Knight, the wife of Patrick's publisher, who belonged to the Skinner circle. Poor Reilly had been infatuated with the woman though she was old enough to be his mother. She had very nearly driven him mad. All his friends had been in despair. And then she had run off with a jockey to Brazil which was why he was marrying Lucy. Only a very green, simple girl would take a man after Lucas had finished with him. Poor Catherine Skinner's brother had done the same, and had married a nice fresh girl, just like Lucy, on the rebound, six months before they had to put him away in an inebriates' home.

Melissa heard all this without much dismay. Her mother was bound to take a sour view of Lucy's marriage and something would certainly have been discovered to Reilly's discredit. If there were any truth in the story he would have had the sense to tell Lucy the facts. She refused to mourn over the probable shocks in store for her poor friend, and flippantly asserted that a past in Brazil could barely be rated as a past at all.

But she found it hard to retain her composure when she learned that the past had come back from Brazil, and had been seen, a week before the wedding, with Reilly in a night club. It was a fact. A certain Mrs. Otway had seen them there with her own eyes. The whole Skinner circle was agog with pleasurable indignation. Great fun for them all, Melissa had said, when her mother brought the story home to Campden Hill Square. But she had been obliged to run out of the room, immediately afterwards, in order to conceal her distress. She felt so miserable that she was driven to confide in Cressida, with whom she had not much in common save an alliance against the emotional onslaughts of their mother. She wanted Cressida to say that it was a great fuss about nothing. But Cressida put on matronly airs and looked grave.

"If she's all we hear," said Cressida, "and wants him back, she'll get him back. I don't think there's anything to be done."

"Mother evidently thinks I ought to warn Lucy; tell her she'd better refuse to marry him unless he promises never to see Lucas again. But how can I? Besides, don't you think it might all be one of mother's bogeys? Just think how often she's managed to frighten one?"

Cressida agreed. In Campden Hill Square an earache was always a probable mastoid and a small overdraft was described as bankruptcy. She had only escaped from this precarious atmosphere very recently but her placid young husband had already done a great deal for her nerves.

"I'll ask Alan what he thinks," she suggested.

Melissa demurred at this. She liked her fat brother-in-law well enough, though she shuddered when he referred to Cressida as Cress and to his unborn child as Little Buttinski. But she could not imagine that he would have anything useful to say about Lucy's affairs, and he might say something very coarse.

Cressida, however, did consult him and insisted upon retailing his verdict to Melissa.

15

"He says he can't see there's anything you can do, except watch how things go. When they come back to London, after their honeymoon, you'll be seeing a lot of them and if Lucas seems to be around you might drop a hint to Lucy. But he says, if you say anything now, it'll only cause a fearful stink and you'll quarrel with Lucy, and won't be able to be a good friend to her, later, when she might need it."

This was unexpectedly sensible and sensitive. Alan was a nice man in spite of his tap room limericks. Melissa took it to heart and travelled down to Surrey, the day before the wedding, in a tolerably composed frame of mind. But she was in no way reconciled to the marriage, Jane Lucas or no Jane Lucas. Reilly might be a celebrity, and he might be making a great deal of money, but he was not good enough for Lucy. Her own John was worth a hundred of him. Her own future, as the wife of an obscure chemist at a research station in Lincolnshire, was far more secure than Lucy's.

3

As THE train drew in at Gorling station she caught sight of Lucy rushing up and down the platform as though she expected her bridesmaid to fall out of the train and was preparing to catch her.

Half demented, mused Melissa, making a leisurely descent. A soldier, who had travelled in the same compartment, handed down her suitcase and hat box. Melissa had never lifted a heavy suitcase in her life. Somebody was always at hand to do this for her. Composedly she stood upon the platform awaiting Lucy's return charge. Up from the extreme rear of the train rushed the distracted Lucy, but when she caught sight of her friend she slowed down and adopted her undulating walk, hoping that all this unseemly galloping might not have been observed.

"Why," enquired Melissa, "were you looking for me in the luggage van?"

"I couldn't see you anywhere. You weren't here when I was."

"I should have been if you'd stayed here."

"Oh, Melissa!"

"Yes?"

Lucy blinked and confessed she had forgotten what she meant to say.

"You seem to be agitated."

"I'm fearfully agitated."

"Why?"

"I can't think why. I ought to be sending some telegrams and I can't remember what they're about."

"My dear Lucy. Let me take you home and give you aspirin."

"Wait till you see home," cried Lucy, seizing the suitcase. "It's a loony bin . . . full of packing cases and relatives."

"Don't do that! We'll get a porter."

"There never are any porters at this station."

"There will be if we wait. Are we in a hurry?"

"Well . . . actually I'm expecting a telephone call . . . at home."

A sudden glow infused Lucy. This call was clearly the only important event of the day. Melissa threw a glance at a porter and led the way into the station yard where a taxi obligingly appeared.

"It's odd how porters will always come to you," commented Lucy.

"They are like children and dogs, they know," said Melissa.

As they drove off Lucy remembered what she wanted to say.

"Oh, Melissa, I'm dreadfully sorry, but we've had to put you in Stephen's room. My uncle and aunt have the spare room and my cousin the dressing room. I wanted to put her in Stephen's room, but he kicked up such a fuss . . . he doesn't mind you having it, he likes you, but he won't have Joan in it. He has a black hatred of her because she used to bully him when we were little."

"I shan't mind Stephen's room."

"But it's revolting. He's picked a great hole in the wall above the bed and plaster falls out on your face in the night. You can't move it because it's a divan fixture; Mother did it out of a magazine . . . a design for a schoolboy's room."

"But where is he going to sleep, then?"

"In the garden. Unless it rains. But he could always use the marquee. He will not have his hair cut and he looks so awful. He's an impossible child. I can't think why Mother had him home; I can't think why the school let him come."

"Never mind. Tell me about the wedding presents."

"Oh, I don't remember. Thousands. Mostly salad servers. I had no idea getting married was so wearing. It's all very well for Patrick to say a conventional wedding is amusing. He'll only have to stand it for a couple of hours tomorrow."

"I should have thought he'd hate even that."

Lucy, anticipating, as she always did, some criticism of her lover, explained airily that it was just one of his poses. He liked to take people by surprise and his appearance in the rôle of a conventional bridegroom would astonish all his friends. His speech was to be a model of inarticulate ineptitude. He had been rehearsing it for a week.

Melissa thought this in vile taste and Lucy knew that she thought so, but was determined to brave it out, declaring that in some ways Patrick was a case of arrested development.

"Who," asked Melissa, "is responsible for seeing that he has the ring?"

"Gerald Clay. The best man. They're driving down from London tomorrow morning and they're going to lunch at the White Hart and leave Patrick's luggage there. Then, when I go to change, they'll nip back and Patrick will change at the White Hart. It's the only way, when our house is so full. Oh, Melissa! I am so sorry you've got to be a bridesmaid with Joan. Mother insisted. There's nobody to give me away but Uncle Bob, and she said it would be a slight if we didn't . . . but she will look such a lump. Oh, it's all hell."

The taxi turned into a suburban road and drew up at a house which Mrs. Hallam would have called very ordinary. Its name was Hill View and Dr. Gwendolen Carmichael's name was displayed on a brass plate above the door bell. Signs of the disorder prevalent inside were visible in the garden, which was littered with shavings and wisps of straw. Lucy explained that a good many wedding presents had been unpacked outside. She dived into the house, shouting for Stephen. When Melissa had paid the taxi, and joined her, she was storming.

"I told Stephen . . . he promised me . . . he was to sit right by the telephone just in case my call came through while I was . . . Stephen! Where is that wretched boy? Steee-vun!"

Mrs. Carmichael came out of the kitchen, carrying an armful of long stemmed roses. She was a short dark woman and there was no resemblance between her and Lucy. Everything about her suggested competency and common sense, from her neat cropped head to her neat black shoes. Her manner was ideal in a surgery, but in the home it was a little too detached.

"Stop yelling," she said to Lucy. "I've been listening for the telephone. Nobody has rung. I sent Stephen out with a message. Well, Melissa! How nice to see you again! How are you?"

"If a bride mayn't yell," complained Lucy, "who may?"

"Nobody may. Take Melissa into the garden and give her some tea. No . . . the telephone will not ring unanswered if you do. I'll be in the kitchen."

Lucy ushered Melissa through a living room, full of half unpacked presents, to a French window which led out onto a small lawn at the back of the house. Most of this was already covered by a marquee, put up for the morrow's festivities. Upon the remaining section Lucy's uncle, aunt and cousin were sitting round a tea table. Melissa had looked forward to meeting them, for Lucy's accounts of them had stirred her curiosity, and a first glance told her that these accounts had not been exaggerated.

Robert Rawlings was a swarthy bilious man who lived in the Midlands and had inherited a brickfield. He liked his women to be ignorant, inferior and dependent. In the masculine world he could not command much respect, for he managed his brickfield vilely. If he might not despise women there was no refuge for his starved vanity. He had opposed his sister Gwennie when she decided to become a doctor, prophesying that she would never get a husband. When she married her chartered accountant he deplored the money which had been wasted over her medical training. When the chartered accountant died, and she bought the practice at Gorling with her insurance money, he would almost have preferred supporting her and her children himself to perceiving that she could manage perfectly well without him.

He had married a sly, ferrety-looking woman who came up to

his standards in the matter of ignorance and inferiority. Their daughter had been taught nothing which might lead her to despise her father. Neither woman ever had sixpence to spend unless he was in a benevolent mood. But Joan, though occasionally sulky, really believed herself to be superior and fortunate because she lived at home and had nothing to do. She was a heavy girl and had inherited the Rawlings tendency to bile.

Social decency ordained that they should be present at Lucy's wedding, for there had never been any kind of quarrel, although the two families had nothing in common. Birthday and Christmas presents had always been punctually and conscientiously exchanged, the cousins had been exhorted to play with one another, and Robert had sent Lucy a very handsome cheque as a wedding present. In his way he was fond of Gwennie. But the invasion was a sore trial to Lucy, who had been floundering for twenty-four hours in a miasma of unspoken disapproval.

Now that she had the reassurance of Melissa's company she felt better. She introduced her modish friend and settled down to enjoy her tea, while the Rawlings family stared at Melissa and Melissa nibbled cress sandwiches. Their silence was gauche. Melissa's was not; she was practised in the art of saying nothing without discourtesy.

"Live in London?" barked Mr. Rawlings at last.

Melissa admitted that she did and said that it was nice to get into the country.

"Hmph! D'you call this country? I don't. Now we live in the depths of the country."

"Nicest of all," sighed Melissa.

"We think so."

Melissa turned courteously to her fellow bridesmaid and asked if she was not enchanted with the earrings which Patrick had sent them.

"They will be just right with our little hats," she suggested.

"If you ask me," said Joan, with a scowl, "nothing can stop those hats from looking ridiculous. I think they're awful. I'm sorry, but I do."

"Haven't spent a night in London for twenty years," ruminated Mr. Rawlings. "Can't stick the place."

"I can't say I'm keen on earrings myself," put in Mrs. Rawlings. "I can't think whyever he chose them."

Lucy had chosen them, as everybody knew, but the shaft was lost on her, as she had started up and was bounding into the house. She had heard the telephone ringing.

"Let's hope," tittered Mrs. Rawlings, "that he's vouchsafed at last. She's been like a cat on hot bricks, waiting for him to ring all day. Not at all the devoted bridegroom! I always say—"

But Mr. Rawlings, who had been noisily absorbing tea, interrupted her to demand whether Melissa knew this fellow Reilly.

"He sounds a rum sort of customer to me. How did she meet him? That's what we've never been able to discover."

"At Oxford," said Melissa. "He was staying with the president of St. Stephens and met Lucy at a party."

"Now that," said Mrs. Rawlings, "is what I don't like about letting a girl go to one of these colleges. You never know what sort of men she may meet."

"His books are very well known," suggested Melissa.

"Never read 'em," stated Mr. Rawlings. "I don't read much. I like a good yarn now and then, but I haven't time to read much."

"I've read them," put in Joan. "And so has Mummy."

"Oh, yes," agreed Mummy. "We aren't such country cousins as all that, Miss Hallam. We got them from the library, before the engagement or anything, just to read, you know."

"And didn't you think them very good?"

There was a pause. The Rawlings women did not like to praise anything belonging to Lucy. But neither did they wish to disparage a famous writer. Their lord took up the cudgels for them. A good writer, he said, might be a shocking bounder. Was Reilly a gentleman? That was all he wanted to know.

"Oh, yes," said Melissa, who would have called Caliban a gentleman rather than let Lucy down.

Stephen appeared in the living room window. He was tall for fifteen, taller than Lucy, and very like her, especially when his hair needed cutting. He brightened when he saw Melissa, whom he greatly admired, and called out a greeting to her. She returned it and asked if he wanted some tea. For a moment he did not reply; he was torn between hunger and distaste for Rawlings's company.

"Not just now," he said at last, and vanished into the house.

Mr. Rawlings asked if that boy was all there and if Melissa knew what Reilly's income might be. Mrs. Rawlings said, with a sigh, that authors make a great deal of money. Joan remarked that it was killingly funny to think of Lucy marrying one.

"Why?" asked Melissa, permitting herself a fleeting glance of astonishment at Joan's ankles.

"Well . . . I mean . . ." giggled Joan. "Lucy marrying a famous man . . . Lucy!"

Joan was genuinely astonished. She had never expected Lucy to marry anybody; she had always believed that her cousin was a freak. She had heard a bad end predicted for Lucy as long as she could remember.

The telephone call had been the wrong one. Lucy appeared dejectedly in the window, and Melissa, to save her friend from spiteful enquiries, jumped up, exclaiming that she must unpack. She ran across the lawn to Lucy and asked to be taken to her room.

"Hide me," she whispered. "Shelter me! I must recover my strength."

Stephen, who was never wanting in proper attention to Melissa, had carried her luggage up to his attic at the top of the house. Melissa had not seen it before and exclaimed at the view. Rank upon rank of hills stretched away, to a great distance, in the blue and golden evening.

"Très Claude," she said, leaning out of the window. "A light that never was on sea or land."

"What do you think of my relations?" asked Lucy.

"Museum pieces. You should cherish them, for nowadays people like that are getting quite rare. Especially Joan."

Lucy flung herself on the bed and picked some more plaster out of the wall while Melissa unpacked.

"I can't show you my trousseau," she said, "because it's all packed. I wouldn't anyway. It's a mess, except my tribute silk dress which you've seen. To begin with I hadn't enough money and didn't like to ask Mother for more. To go on with, I've been so flustered lately I've done everything wrong. To end up with, however rich and calm I was, I have no taste."

"You've avoided frills, I hope."

"I've avoided everything. That's the trouble. I've avoided large patterns and niggly patterns and bright colours and a cut that will date. Everything is so perfectly inconspicuous you can't see it at all, except for a scarf somebody sent me with Lucy! Lucy! Lucy! written all over it. Such luck my name isn't Maud. I mean: Birds in the High Hall garden . . . oh! one thing I have nice is an ankle-length moiré, raisin coloured. How exquisitely you do pack! All those shoe bags! How is Hump?"

Melissa gave the latest news of Hump as she took her shoes out of their neat bags. It was, as usual, lively. He was trying to make up a match between Kolo and a young coloured American called Mary Lou, who had suddenly turned up in the Dandawa.

"She isn't exactly black," explained Melissa. "She's high yellow. And she was sent to Paris to be educated and got a bee in her bonnet about going to Africa and working for her own people. She'd heard about Kolo—what a splendid person he is, so she came to look him up. She's got pots of money, but is rather fussy about bathrooms, Hump says. He likes her tremendously, though, and it would be such a thing for poor Kolo to get a really educated idealistic wife; he's so lonely, poor man. The only snag is that she's a violent Christian Scientist and may not approve of Hump. I don't know if they think cattle disease is error. Do you?"

Lucy had not been listening. She was wondering if the raisin-coloured moiré would be right for her first dinner, tomorrow night, with Patrick.

"Fancy Hump marrying a Christian Scientist!" was her comment when Melissa paused. "Is she pretty?"

"He isn't," said Melissa crossly, "and she's black."

"Oh? I didn't know they ever were."

"Who were what?"

"Christian Scientists. Black."

"She's American."

"Oh, I see. Of course they are."

"Black or Christian Scientists?"

"Both. I mean a lot of them. But who is Hump marrying? I didn't gather."

"Nobody. You didn't listen."

"I'm sorry."

23

Melissa took off her dress, hung it up, and began to work on her face. After a while Lucy asked, a little anxiously, if it was better for the man or the woman to be most in love. What did Melissa think?

"A woman who is rather selfish and bossy oughtn't to marry a man who adores her," suggested Lucy, "or she might get spoilt. She might have a lovely time at first, but at thirty-five she might start thinking her life had been wasted. I think a woman like that should marry a man she adores, and devote herself to his career. Don't you agree? An adoring man, who is always making a fuss of a woman and ringing her up, is very bad for a certain type of girl."

Melissa, perceiving the drift of these remarks, agreed that a man who rings up too often can be a bore.

Feet thundered up the stairs. Stephen, forgetting that Melissa now occupied his room, burst in upon them and stood staring in helpless dismay until sent about his business by Lucy.

"Go away," she stormed. "You horrible child! How dare you come in here? Get out!"

Apologising incoherently, he thundered off.

"He ought to be certified," wailed Lucy. "Rushing in here when you're naked."

"I didn't mind. I'm not naked. Do calm down."

"I can't calm down. I've tried. I can't."

"This time tomorrow it will be all over."

Lucy became very still, glowing with happiness until she looked almost incandescent. Then, without a word, she darted out of the room.

Melissa continued to unpack. She was still a little ruffled over Lucy's lack of interest in Hump. No doubt Patrick Reilly would think Humptopia small beer. He would take no interest in the Dandawa unless they were cannibals who had so nearly eaten him that he could write a book about it.

Her next visitor was Mrs. Carmichael who came to ask, with her usual brisk efficiency, if Melissa had all she wanted.

"Supper," she said, "is at half past seven. I've sent Lucy to bed. She's doing herself no good rushing about like this."

"My sister Cressida," said Melissa, "was just the same."

"I wish Patrick would ring her up," said Mrs. Carmichael. "He promised he would and she's upset that he hasn't."

She paused and looked at Melissa, who feared that yet another person was going to ask what she thought of Patrick Reilly. But she was spared this embarrassment. Mrs. Carmichael had formed her own opinion of her future son-in-law. It was no higher than Melissa's, but she was less anxious, because life had taught her that nothing turns out quite as we expect. Guessing Melissa's concern, she felt an impulse to reassure the girl. She crossed the room and picked up some books which had fallen off a shelf.

"I don't let myself worry about Lucy," she said. "I think that, whatever happens to her, she'll come through it all right. She's very . . . very true to herself, if you know what I mean."

Melissa nodded.

"She doesn't deceive herself. She is the more in love of the two. I think she knows it. I am not sure that she is going to be happy. But she will never deceive herself. And in the truth," declared Mrs. Carmichael, "there is always something . . . something that upholds us, however bitter it is, if we can only face it. At least . . . I've found that to be so. She may be sorry she married him, but she will never be sorry that she loved."

4

THE TELEPHONE rang at intervals all the evening, and Lucy kept peeping out of her room, expecting a summons. But no call came for her. At ten o'clock Melissa looked in to say goodnight.

"Has it been ghastly downstairs?" asked Lucy. "I'm a beast to have deserted you."

"Not a bit. I've been having fun. I've been subduing your uncle."

"You couldn't. Nobody could."

"Nothing easier, I assure you. Easy as robbing a blind baby. I've been listening with breathless wonder to his exploits."

"He never had any."

"Don't you believe it. He's got a clock in his house that has never lost a minute in fifty years. He's had ptomaine poisoning from eating anchovy paste."

"Have they all gone to bed?"

"They're just going. I hope you're as sleepy as I am."

"I'm horribly wide awake."

"Read a nice book. Read *Emma*."

"My books are all packed."

Everything that Lucy possessed had been packed for transference to her new home. Her room looked forlorn and bare. The bookshelves were empty and her treasured collection of Worcester china was gone from the chimney piece. Bright squares marked the walls, where pictures had hung. The chests and cupboards were empty too, save for the wedding dress and the going-away suit and all the finery that was to accompany them.

Melissa went to the wardrobe and looked into it. The wedding dress hung there, solitary and ghostlike.

"Dull, isn't it?" commented Lucy. "But one that tries not to be is worse. I'm going to dye it deep red at once, and turn it into a stately dinner dress. Brides at dances, whisking about in obvious wedding dresses, look so tatty."

"Deep red?" questioned Melissa.

"Patrick has given me some flat garnets. Haven't you seen them? They're on the dressing table."

"Oh, lovely!" said Melissa, inspecting them. "He *has* got taste!"

"Not naturally," said Lucy. "But he can do anything well if he wants to, you know."

Which exactly echoed Melissa's thought at the moment. She snapped the garnet case shut and waited for Lucy to speak again, aware that something important might be said.

"He's never fully given his mind to things," said Lucy finally. "He's just played about, and been such a success he's never really got down to anything. The one thing he's in earnest about is flowers."

"*Flowers?*" Melissa turned in astonishment.

"Rare flowers, that take a lot of finding. He knew a man who was paid by a millionaire to climb tropical mountains, looking for orchids. He'd rather do that than anything else. But there aren't many jobs like that going, so he started in to make money, meaning to go and hunt for flowers when he had some. Now he's got quite a lot, enough to live on for a long time. So we're going off to look for flowers. If we get poor he'll have to write some more books, but he needn't for some time."

"I never knew that!"

"Nobody knows, and you're not to tell anybody. He doesn't want all the newspapers saying that now he's going to hunt for flowers. There's always too much hullabaloo about what he does. He's getting sick of it and wants to cut it out. He says he's never had a real life. We're going up the Amazon, and we're not going to tell a soul."

"Oh, Lucy! What fun!"

"Won't it be?" said Lucy, bouncing on her bed till the springs creaked. "I'm learning botany like a horse."

Melissa's spirits rose, and for the first time she was able to hope that the marriage might be a success. She ran upstairs to her attic with a lightened heart.

Lucy immediately regretted her indiscretion. Patrick would be angry if he knew of it. But Melissa could be trusted, and all this unspoken criticism of him was becoming intolerable. Nobody really knew him; they only saw what was wrong with him—the exhibitionism which had made his fortune and from which he was trying to extricate himself. Melissa had stiffened when she heard of his intention to burlesque his bridegroom's speech. She was outraged at the implied carelessness towards Lucy. But if I don't mind, thought Lucy furiously, what the hell has it got to do with anybody else?

She checked herself, remembering that she did mind—not for herself, but for him. For his own sake she hoped that he would resist the temptation to pose and clown, but, if he could not, she meant to look as if she liked it.

She waited until the last creaking footsteps had shuffled off to bed, the last bath water had gurgled away, the last plug pulled, the last door shut. Then she slipped downstairs and dialled. She could not sleep until she had heard his voice. He had forgotten his promise to call her, but he did not know, probably, how much she needed reassurance, in this household which mistrusted him. He would be at his flat in London, correcting a late batch of proofs. He had said that he would have his work cut out to get them sent off before the wedding.

She heard the ringing of the buzzer, away there in London.

Brrr, Brrr . . . Brrr, Brrr . . . Brrr, Brrr. . . .

When he answered she would say: *Is this Wembley?* It was a catchword of theirs and the reply was: *No. It's Thursday.*

Brrr, Brrr . . . Brrr, Brrr . . . Brrr, Brrr. . . .

He could not be at his desk or he would have answered.

Brrr, Brrr . . . Brrr, Brrr . . . Brrr, Brrr. . . .

Could he be out? He might have gone down to the lobby to post his proofs.

"Have they answered?" asked the exchange.

"No," said Lucy.

"Hold on. We are trying to connect you."

Brrr, Brrr . . . Brrr, Brrr . . . Brrr, Brrr. . . .

The summons pulsed on through the empty flat. Lucy was sure by now that it must be empty, but she held on, in the hope that he had merely gone down to the lobby and would return before the ringing stopped. He was not in the flat. But this noise was there, going on among all his things, his books, his clothes, his letters, so that she liked to hear it, even if it was not answered. She tried hard to remember every detail of the room and saw it suddenly very distinctly in a clear, bluish light which was neither night nor day—saw it in a detail which memory could never have achieved. She noticed, for the first time, the checked pattern of a tweed cushion in the chair where she had usually sat when she was there. She saw a long envelope on the mantelpiece, leaning against the clock; she was sure that it had never been there before, and knew that it must contain the finished proofs. She saw the desk and everything on it and the telephone ringing and ringing, while the people in the room waited in tense silence for it to cease. *People?* She saw no people. She saw only the desk, the fireplace, the chair and the cushion.

The ringing stopped and the vision vanished as if a light had been turned off.

"We have rung them," said the exchange, "but there is no reply."

"Oh, that's all right," said Lucy wearily, wondering how exchange knew it was *them*.

But that, of course, was what the exchange always said. And there had been no people. The flat was empty. She had been the only listener. His proofs were finished and he must have gone out.

She returned to her room, sick and cold with unreasonable disappointment, for which she scolded herself. There was now less than a day to get through before she would be with him for ever. There were only fourteen hours. At this time tomorrow they would be in bed, in a strange room that they had never seen before.

Her thoughts swerved and galloped away, as though they had come to the edge of a precipice. She had no misgivings, but she did not want to imagine all that beforehand, apprehending that something vital and fresh might be lost if she did. She could picture more distant scenes in her life with Patrick, but the weeks immediately in front of her were lost in a golden mist into which, even in thought, she would plunge tomorrow for the first time.

She turned from it to survey the past, and to remember that first meeting at the cocktail party when she had been introduced to Patrick and he had flashed a conquering smile at her, and how, then, the smile had vanished, had been replaced by a glance of astonished enquiry, of delight, as if to say: *Is it you? At last, after all these years, is it really you?* She had been so much afraid that he looked like that at everybody. But they had not been able to part, and had dined together in a smelly little inn, and walked afterwards for hours among canals and gas works in a part of the town which she had never explored, until he helped her to climb over the garden wall into college. She had been afraid when they met by appointment next day. She had never dared to believe that it meant anything until he suddenly asked her to marry him. She had loved him from the first meeting, long before she knew that inner history, his disgust, his self contempt, his degrading infatuation for Jane Lucas, his halfhearted schemes for escape, for another life. She did not love him because she knew all this: she knew all this because she loved him.

Before getting into bed she pulled from under her pillow a small rag doll, dressed like a Highlander and called McNab, which had shared her bed since she was four years old. For a long time she had believed that McNab could think and feel, and some suggestion of sentience had clung to him when she had discarded her other dolls. His button eyes stared at her reproachfully and she had not the heart to thrust him away. Even after that fancy expired she felt a sort of disloyalty to the past in disowning him: he had shared the whole of her remembered childhood and until that was forgotten she was linked to him.

Very little of that childhood was dead to Lucy. She had enjoyed it so much and so many of her earliest pleasures still had power to enchant her. She could remember lying, as a very little girl, in long waving grass, looking up at the clouds in the sky, hearing a bumble bee close to her ear, and lapped in a vast contentment. She still knew that satisfaction when she lay in summer grass and watched the clouds. The flap of her bare feet on hot sand as she ran down to bathe, the dancing tingle, the shrill treble clatter of the waves, were as exhilarating now as they had been ten years ago. A robin whistling in the bloomy autumn dusk could always fill her with delicious melancholy, wood smoke always stirred some undefinable memory, and the view from the top of any hill was a miracle. Her heart still shivered with excitement at the soft rustle of a curtain rising on a stage.

She was the same person that she had been when she found McNab in her Christmas stocking. She had learnt much; her pleasures had expanded, but her enjoyment was of the same intense quality. Experience had merely opened new worlds for her and taught her how to use her natural capacity for joy.

McNab therefore had remained under her pillow and accompanied her to Oxford, though she had concealed him from Melissa. But from Patrick he could not be concealed, and he must be left behind, for nobody takes a rag doll on her honeymoon. Some portion of the past must now be relinquished. She decided to put him into an ottoman which was full of various oddments, still unpacked but selected for preservation. If ever she and Patrick became famous botanists McNab might become a relic and find immortality in a museum, among other historic dolls. He should have a label:

McNAB. RAG DOLL circa 1930. Formerly the
property of DAME LUCY REILLY O.B.E.

Tossing him into the ottoman, and slamming the lid, she
climbed into bed. If she could not sleep she could at least relax
and think of agreeable things. The present was too exciting. She
went a long way back and thought of summer days on the Cher-
well, the green shadows, the buttercup fields, and the splash of a
punt pole. But an unpleasant rhythm disturbed the memory. It had
been tugging at her ever since she came upstairs, though she would
not listen. Now it forced itself upon her.

Brrr, Brrr . . . Brrr, Brrr . . . Brrr, Brrr. . . .

By no effort could she escape from that dual pulse. The forlorn, unanswered summons rang on and on, through her thoughts,
through her drowsing, through her dreams.

5

MELISSA HAD wrought well. Mr. Rawlings told his women
next morning that she was a thoroughly nice, unspoilt girl. His
wife knew better than to disagree, but a faint murmur of protest
was wrung from Joan.

"Affected?" cried Mr. Rawlings. "Nonsense! She's perfectly
simple and natural."

"I thought she was frightfully affected last night," persisted
Joan.

"I'm not aware that your opinion was asked. You might do
worse than take a lesson from her. She's so interested in anything
one tells her."

"Depends on if you're a man or a woman," asserted Mrs.
Rawlings, rallying in defence of her young. "She'd listen to anything in trousers."

This did Melissa no great disservice. He smirked and told Joan
that a girl who listens intelligently is always attractive, before he
went off to find Melissa and tell her about his golf handicap.

His women adjourned to Joan's room where the sight of the bridesmaid's dress, laid out on the bed, did nothing to sweeten their tempers. It was primrose coloured and chosen to suit Melissa. They had protested but Lucy had been adamant, assuring her mother that no colour really suited Joan and that the shell pink, for which Mrs. Rawlings clamoured, would have been worse.

"I'll never wear it again, never!" mourned Joan. "A hideous rag I wouldn't be seen dead in. Honestly, Mummy, don't you think Melissa is sickeningly affected?"

"There's no other word for her," agreed Mrs. Rawlings. "You can see where Lucy's picked up all those airs and graces. I always said those posh friends would do her no good."

"When they came floating out to tea yesterday I nearly laughed. I nearly burst out laughing."

"I always have said, and I always will say, that Lucy needs her bottom smacked. She's so dreadfully conceited. Of course she's been spoilt. Nothing's ever been good enough for her. Such nonsense, sending her to this college, when she could have got a job and been off her mother's hands years ago. And now . . ."

Mrs. Rawlings was obliged to pause, for Lucy's marriage was hardly a retributive climax.

"Now," she said darkly, "it remains to be seen. Have you sewed in dress shields?"

"No."

"Well, you ought to do. You know how you perspire."

"I don't care. I'll never wear it again. I've said."

"When your father knows what it cost you'll get nothing more out of him for a month of Sundays. Sit down and sew them in now, do! There won't be time after lunch."

"I wish it was all over. I feel frightfully nervous. I don't know from Adam what I'm supposed to do."

"You do what the high and mighty Melissa does, and for goodness' sake hold yourself up. She's taking Lucy's flowers, though you're the one that ought to, being a relative. She won't be nervous. I asked her if she'd ever been a bridesmaid before and she said she'd lost count how often!"

"Three times a bridesmaid never a bride," quoted Joan in brighter tones.

Melissa had spoken no more than the truth. She had been walking up aisles behind brides all her life, ever since the age of three, when she had pinched a little train bearer in front of her. She knew all the ropes. She had already tried her yellow shoes in order to be sure that they were comfortable. She had practised a new way of rolling up her hair under the little hat. When she tripped into Lucy's room she looked so cool and composed that the atmospheric storm raging there abated a trifle.

Lucy's head and her veil seemed to have sworn an eternal feud. Repeated attempts to unite them had reduced her to frenzy.

"Look at me," she cried, "look at me! Nearly two o'clock and a head like a hearth brush! Why, Melissa! How lovely you look! I'm glad we settled on yellow."

"It is a success," agreed Mrs. Carmichael, who was also as near frenzy as her immense self control would permit. "And your hair is so nice. I do like it like that."

"But your hat!" returned the courteous Melissa. "I love the way it frames your face."

Mrs. Carmichael flushed with pleasure. Nobody had taken any notice of her hat, though the time which she had spent in choosing it had been as hard to spare as the money.

"Isn't it lovely?" said Lucy, looking rather ashamed of herself. "But this incarnadined veil, Melissa! I've pinned it on, and pinned it on, and pulled it off, and pulled it off!"

"It looks as if you had. Sit down! No . . . don't crush your dress all under you. That's better. Now put a towel over your shoulders . . . oh thank you, Mrs. Carmichael. . . ."

Melissa set to work on Lucy's roughened hair with a comb, and brought her curls to order.

"It's not my hair," wailed Lucy. "It's getting the veil to sit straight. I'm paid out for saying I wouldn't have a wreath. I thought a sort of vague cloud round my head would look nice, and it went perfectly well when I practised it. . . . Do hurry up! It's getting late and Patrick says if I keep him waiting he won't marry me. He says he'll give me ten minutes, and then walk out. Skewer it down with hair pins at the top first. Oh! There's Uncle Bob shouting! The cars must be there. Oh, do hurry!"

"It's finished. It's done. Look at yourself."

33

Lucy turned to the glass and saw the misty cloud, just as she had wanted it to be. She shook her head to see if the pins were firm.

"You angel! You genius!"

A peremptory bellow was heard below:

"Joan! May! Gwennie! Miss Hallam!"

In renewed panic Lucy thrust them from the room, imploring them to be off, since she could not set out for the church until ten minutes after they did.

"And if Patrick tries to walk out before I get there, sit on his head. Oh, Mother, what *is* it?"

"I was just looking to be sure I have my latch key."

"You won't *need* a latch key. Patrick and I will get back *first*. The head waiter will open the door and after that it will *stay* open. Do go! Tell Uncle Bob I'll come down in seven minutes. *Seven!*"

She drove them downstairs. There was a little commotion as they went out with Mrs. Rawlings, Joan and Stephen. Car doors were slammed in the road. A silence fell upon Hill View, in which Mr. Rawlings could be heard clearing his throat impatiently, in the hall.

Lucy put her watch on the dressing table and sat down to wait for seven minutes. She spent the first three of them in remorse for having been so sharp with her mother. There would be no opportunity now to apologise. They might not be alone together again for weeks.

She snatched up a pencil and pad and scribbled hastily:

> My dearest, darling Mother, I love you more than tongue can tell. You know that, don't you? Every year I live I come to understand more what you've done for me. You are the best mother anybody ever had. God bless you, Lucy.

This note she took into her mother's room and put it on the pillow, just under the counterpane. Tonight, hours after she had gone, it would be found, when Mrs. Carmichael went to bed.

A particularly loud *harrrrmph!* in the hall reminded her of her Uncle Bob and the seven minutes. She rushed back to her room for her bouquet, gathered up her skirts, and rustled downstairs.

Mr. Rawlings had never been fond of Lucy, but he was touched by her appearance as she came down to him. He was a sentimental man—her bridal white, with its poignant associations, transformed his tiresome niece. She was a virgin, tender, young and lovely, by whom he must now act a father's part. He handed her and her flowers into the waiting car with affectionate care and when he had taken his place beside her he patted her hand.

"I wish," he said huskily, "that your father could have been sitting here now, Lucy. I wish he could have seen you."

Lucy smiled at him abstractedly and asked what time it was.

"Ample time," he assured her. "We shall be there at two thirty-five precisely. Five minutes late is correct."

Lucy smiled again and looked at the familiar houses slipping past. A couple of turns brought them to the road where the church was. Cars were parked along the kerb. Here was the awning and the red carpet and the crowd on either side of it. Everything flowed on. The car stopped, and Uncle Bob was out, and she was out, and a camera clicked. She was rustling up the red carpet to the porch where open doors gave a glimpse of yellow dresses, and white clad choristers, and her mother's worried face peering over somebody's shoulder. The easy flow of events jerked to a standstill, for this was wrong. It was quite wrong that her mother should be hovering about in the porch. She should be in the front pew. How stupid! And how badly Melissa was made up! Surely she had not looked like this at the house—the rouge standing out on ashy cheeks and startled eyes staring under the little hat? *Melissa's eyes!* So horrified. . . . And Mother clutching at Uncle Bob. Something was wrong.

"What?" boomed Uncle Bob. "*Not here?*"

"Lucy darling . . . there's a little delay. . . . Patrick isn't here yet."

Her mother was saying this. Melissa had come up and taken her arm.

"Stephen has just run round to the White Hart."

"Never heard such a thing in my life! Inexcusable!"

"Has anybody gone for him? Has anybody gone for him?"

This was from Aunt May, who came darting down the aisle and pushed Joan's hat straight.

"Shouldn't have let her come. Shouldn't have let her arrive till he was here. Why didn't you—"

"Stephen's gone."

"Never heard of such a thing. Keeping Lucy waiting. . . ."

Lucy interrupted them all in a loud voice which startled them, so that they turned and stared at her.

"No, that's all right. He never knows what the time is."

"And how long have we got to stand here?" asked Uncle Bob indignantly.

"I shan't stand. I shall sit."

She rustled into the last pew and beckoned Melissa to come and sit with her. Mrs. Carmichael joined them, biting her lip, but Joan and Mrs. Rawlings remained, popeyed and whispering, by the font. The church was full of whispering and rustling and people turning to stare. Canon Ryder, who had been waiting at the chancel steps, now came down towards them and Mr. Rawlings hastened to meet him amid a covey of choirboys, who, in a panic, had decided to get into the chancel. He turned and waved them away, exclaiming indignantly:

"Go back, you boys! Stay where you are! Go back I say!"

Lucy giggled, though she was furious with Patrick. When she had forgiven him, when he had apologised properly, she would describe this scene to him and he would laugh. But it was too bad of him.

Running feet were heard outside. Stephen appeared, crimson and breathless.

"He's not at the White Hart. He's never been there. They never arrived there at all."

The church became several degrees colder.

"Must have been held up on the road."

"Their lunch was ordered for one o'clock."

"They'd have telephoned . . ."

Among all the voices there was one saying it now:

"An accident. . . ."

"A motor accident. . . ."

"They were coming in Reilly's car. . . ."

". . . Serious . . . or they'd have telephoned. . . ."

The church pillars wavered and swung like curtains in an icy fog.

"Lucy! Put your head between your knees! Melissa! Press her head down between her knees."

Relentless hands pressed Lucy's veiled head between her knees and held it there much longer than was necessary. A fainting bride, she thought, should be allowed to sink backwards gracefully; she should not be treated like a sick school child. But at last the pressure slackened and she sat up. A babel of voices asked if she was all right and a man's hand appeared over her shoulder with a glass of water.

"I'm quite all right," she stated. "What had I better do?"

Nobody seemed to know. Mr. Rawlings was talking about the police and telephones and enquiries concerning accidents on the Kingston By-Pass. All sorts of people were making suggestions. The whole congregation were now pushing up to the west end of the church.

Melissa's cool voice cut through the clamour.

"I think," she said, "that we should take Lucy home."

Several voices disagreed. Mrs. Rawlings pointed out that Patrick might still arrive at any moment. Surely it would be better to wait a little longer. An old lady called Miss Betteridge, a patient of Mrs. Carmichael's, was telling everybody that Patrick had probably gone to the wrong church. There were three churches in Gorling. He might be waiting at any of them.

Lucy came out of her pew, pushed through the gaping choir-boys, ran out of the church and down the red carpet, and jumped into the car before anybody could stop her. She wanted to get home before they told her that Patrick was dead. One part of her knew it already and had nearly fainted, but the whole of her mind had not yet caught up with the idea.

The party in the church had been so much taken aback by her sudden exit that nobody followed her. She sat alone in the car while the crowd, which had never seen a wedding like this before, surged up against the windows. Cameras clicked and flashed. Miss Betteridge came bustling out of the church and thrust her head into the car.

"St. Barnabas," she said, "or St. Nicholas . . ."

She was pushed away by Mrs. Rawlings, who came up with Lucy's bouquet which she poked into the car onto Lucy's lap.

"You forgot your flowers. You left your bouquet behind."

"Isn't it awful!" said the voices round the car.

"A head-on smash . . ."

"The Kingston By-Pass . . ."

"The Portsmouth Road . . ."

"Pore thing!"

"Looks ghastly, doesn't she?"

"Isn't it awful?"

"Excuse me . . . if you'd just tell him to drive to the other churches, just in case—"

"Oh, get in, get in!" cried Lucy. "Get in, somebody else beside me. I don't have to go home alone, do I? Get in, Aunt May. Get in, Miss Betteridge. Tell him to go home."

They got in and the car slid forward.

"But you can't have a reception now," exclaimed Aunt May. "It's impossible. . . ."

Lucy leant back and shut her eyes, dropping into a queer little doze, while their voices ran on like a couple of babbling brooks. . . . So when we got into our pew I looked round . . . where is he? I said . . . thought he must be lurking behind a pillar. . . . Most unfortunate, but he'll turn up, you see, my dear . . . I never thought for a minute . . . Lucy was actually arriving. . . . It came over me all of a sudden . . . take a cheerful view of things . . . all those cameras! It'll be in all the papers! Here we are! Lucy! Lucy! Here we are!

The car had stopped at Hill View and the head waiter from the caterer's was holding the house door open for the bride and bridegroom. Lucy pushed in past him and ran up to her room, where all the bookshelves were empty and the walls patchy with squares where pictures had hung. She stood for a moment, looking about her.

"Patrick is dead," she said aloud.

It must be so. If he was alive he would have come, or sent some message. But the fact still meant nothing at all to half of her mind. She sat down on the bed to wait for something else to happen.

38

There were sounds below. Everyone else was coming back. People called to each other and doors banged. Uncle Bob was telephoning noisily. Mrs. Carmichael came up to Lucy and sat down on the bed beside her.

"There is nothing we can do till we get news," she said. "Uncle Bob is telephoning to the police."

"So I hear."

Mrs. Carmichael took Lucy's hand, exclaimed that it was very cold, and brought sal volatile. Then hesitating, her lips twitching a little, she forced herself to say:

"Would you . . . wouldn't you . . . hadn't you better . . . take off . . ."

Lucy rose. The veil was unpinned, the dress stripped off and returned to the wardrobe. Her new dressing gown was packed in a suitcase marked L.R. She put on the old cotton kimono that she had worn the night before.

Melissa tapped at the door, put her head in, and glanced meaningly at Mrs. Carmichael, who hurried away.

"Come in," said Lucy. "What's happening downstairs?"

"Everybody seems to be rushing about."

"What's the time?"

"Ten to four."

"Only that? I thought it must be about six."

"Shall I stay? Or would you rather be alone?"

"Oh, stay. I'm quite all right. I mean, I'm not really upset yet. I suppose I haven't taken it in. I know Patrick must be dead, but I don't really believe it. I feel rather sleepy."

Melissa sighed and turned away to look out of the window.

"You know it too?" asked Lucy quickly.

"Oh, Lucy . . . I'm just not thinking . . . till we hear more."

"What else can have happened?"

"We're bound to know what's happened soon."

"What are you looking at down there?"

"There's an old lady in the marquee, all by herself, eating ices."

"I expect that's Miss Betteridge. She came back with us."

"Who is she?"

"Some belonging of Mother's. *Melissa!* When you came up just now, and Mother went out, was there news?"

"Mr. Rawlings wanted her."

"To tell her some news?"

"I don't know," lied Melissa.

Lucy was quiet for a while and then she said:

"You've changed your dress. You got that cotton at Elliston's last year."

Melissa agreed. She had brought this old cotton dress with her in case her services might be required for moving furniture or washing up. Immediately on her return from church she had changed into it, foreseeing much practical work ahead of her, as soon as the family should have come to its senses. There was a room full of presents to be packed up and returned. There were a thousand things to be done. She had made up her mind to stay for a day or two and see Mrs. Carmichael through the worst of it. She could be of service there, though there was nothing to be done for Lucy. Her capacity for envisaging disaster had its useful side.

"What's the time?" asked Lucy again.

"Four o'clock."

"They'd come and tell me, wouldn't they, as soon as any news came?"

"Oh, yes."

"What will happen to all that food?"

"I expect the caterers will take it away."

"Yes, but where will it go then, I wonder. Who'll eat it? Will anybody eat it?"

Mrs. Carmichael returned, looking as though she came to execution. She dismissed Melissa with a nod and sat down beside Lucy.

"So it's true," said Lucy, studying her mother's face. "He's dead. He's been killed."

"Oh, no. No . . . not that . . . no. . . ."

"He's *not?* Is he hurt . . . is he . . . ?"

"No, darling. He's perfectly safe. Quite all right, as far as we know."

A faint pink suffused Lucy's pallor. It swept from her throat to her forehead. She came to life.

40

"Oh, Mother! If he's all right . . . what does anything matter?"

"Dearest . . . I'm afraid he must have changed his mind. He didn't come because—"

"Changed his . . . you mean about the wedding?"

"Uncle Bob rang up Mr. Clay's house. He wanted to find out what time they started and he couldn't get any answer from Patrick's flat. To his great surprise, Mr. Clay answered. He was at his house, and he was perfectly astonished when he heard what has happened. He thought the wedding was cancelled. He said that Patrick rang him up before eight this morning to say that they wouldn't be going . . . that the wedding was cancelled. Of course he thought we knew. He couldn't believe we'd heard nothing."

"But he's sure Patrick is all right?"

"Why . . . there's no reason now to suppose there's been any accident. He never started."

"But why? Why? He loves me. If he is all right why didn't he come?"

"We don't know, dear. We must wait until we get the explanation."

Lucy took a little while to comprehend it, but her immense relief had reduced all other facts to insignificance.

"I thought he was dead," she kept repeating. "That's why I nearly fainted. I thought he was dead. But he's not."

Mrs. Rawlings burst in, tapping at the door as she did so. She made significant grimaces at her sister-in-law. Lucy rose.

"If there is more news," she said, "I'll go down and hear it myself."

"Oh no . . . no . . ." chattered Mrs. Rawlings. "Let your mother go. Be a brave girl and stay here till—"

"No. I'm tired of people coming up and shooting off bad news at me like minute guns. If Uncle Bob has found out anything more, he can tell me himself. Nothing can upset me very much as long as Patrick is safe."

"But it's the most awful thing that ever happened!" cried Mrs. Rawlings as soon as Lucy had left them. "He's jilted Lucy. He's walked out. Mr. Clay has been round to his flat and talked to the porter."

"Did Bob ring Mr. Clay again then?"

"No. He rang Bob to say the porter says Patrick went off in a taxi to Euston Station at nine o'clock this morning."

"I can't believe it! It's impossible. He couldn't treat Lucy like this. There must be some explanation. . . ."

"You never did know very much about him, did you?"

"Some message must have miscarried."

"Bob says you ought to have made more enquiries about him. Bob says—"

Lucy reappeared.

"Uncle Bob," she said, "has told me about Mr. Clay and the porter and the taxi and Euston. I've got it into my head that the wedding's off. Patrick must have gone to Ireland. So please everybody go away and eat ices with Miss Betteridge."

"Miss Betteridge?" said Mrs. Carmichael, looking puzzled.

"She's the reception," said Lucy. "And she's all alone in the marquee. Go and look after her. I want to go to sleep."

When they had gone she locked the door and lay down. Any connected train of thought eluded her. In this overpowering relief it was confusing to be aware that everything was not all right. Patrick was not dead. He had not been burned to cinders under a blazing car. He was not lying in the Kingston mortuary. He was alive, somewhere or other, breathing and talking and walking about. But there was to be no wedding, no future. Life had stopped.

She fell into a stupor in which confused impressions jostled one another. Again and again Melissa's face confronted her—the shocked, questioning eyes, the rouge on haggard cheeks. *Melissa's eyes!* Disaster had begun with Melissa's eyes. Familiar houses slid past, and Uncle Bob shouted at the choirboys: Go back, you boys! Go back. Through the open doors yellow dresses were mingled with white surplices. *Melissa's eyes.* "Put your head between your knees, Lucy." "Go back, you boys!" "Not at the White Hart." "Isn't it awful?" "A head-on smash." "You forgot your bouquet." *Melissa's eyes!*

The afternoon mellowed to evening. Evening sank to dusk. People came sometimes to her door and tapped and called to her gently, but she did not answer. She did not hear them. She lay in an echoing tunnel, unable to wake up or fall asleep, harassed by a multitude of voices, jostled by impressions which would not congeal into thoughts. Whenever she drifted towards oblivion those eyes popped up, and a shudder went through her whole body.

At last this nightmare subsided. She emerged from the tunnel into solitude, silence and night. Sitting up she switched on her bedside lamp. She wondered what time it was.

Her watch lay on the dressing table where she had put it when she was timing her seven minutes. When she remembered this she remembered the note which she had written, years ago, and left on her mother's pillow. It must be retrieved.

She darted across the landing, but she was too late. Mrs. Carmichael had found the note. She was holding it in her hand as she lay upon her bed, shaken with the harsh agonised sobs of defeat.

"Oh, Mother . . . oh, Mother . . ."

Lucy sat by her and put a timid hand on her arm.

"I came to get it . . . I put it there when I . . . I didn't mean . . . I'd forgotten about it. . . ."

"Lucy! Lucy! I can't bear it."

"I ought to have remembered . . ."

"Oh, Lucy . . . my precious . . . Oh, I mustn't cry like this. It's no help to you. And I'd have died, oh, I'd have died gladly, rather than let this happen to you. . . ."

"Oh, no, Mother, darling Mother, don't be so miserable. I shall be all right. I haven't quite taken it in yet. But I shall get over it. People seem to get over things, don't they? I don't know how, but they do. Ordinary people . . . I'm very ordinary, so I expect I shall do what they do. I don't know how, but I shall . . . I mean it's the likely thing, I suppose, isn't it?"

Mrs. Carmichael continued to sob. She was at the end of her endurance. Lucy sat beside her and presently continued in the unemphatic voice of exhaustion:

"I've got you. I've got a reason for trying to get over it. You've worked so hard, and done everything to give us a happy life, it would be too unfair if it was all to be disappointment. Look, Mother . . . wouldn't you like some tea? I'll bring you up a cup of tea, shall I?"

Without waiting for an answer Lucy went down to the

kitchen. A fearful crash met her ears as she opened the door. Stephen stood in the middle of the room staring with stunned horror at a lot of broken china on the floor.

"I was getting you some tea," he stammered. "You haven't had anything to eat since lunch. I thought you might like it. But all the things fell off the tray. It's all spilt."

He looked at her hopelessly and humbly.

Several sentences rose to her lips; the Crown Derby cups! The last straw! Wretched child! But her anger collapsed like a kite which falls for lack of wind. She was too much exhausted to scold or even to feel very much irritated. She knelt down in silence and began to collect the broken pieces.

"I . . . I can't tell you how sorry I am. I wanted to do something for you."

"I know, Stephen. Never mind. Get a cloth and we'll wipe up the spills."

He helped her to clear up, glancing at her from time to time in an awestruck way. Her gentleness really alarmed him.

"Tea was a good idea," she said. "I'd like some, and I'm sure Mother would. We'll make some more and take it to her."

"I'll boil another kettle."

He lighted the gas again and collected some other cups. It occurred to Lucy that he must have spent a tough day, and that tomorrow he must go back to school.

"What have you been doing all the afternoon?" she asked.

"Running errands for Melissa. I've been with her mostly. We've been pretty busy . . . er . . . clearing up things . . . food and things."

"Didn't the caterers take it away?"

"Most of it. But they left a lot."

He pointed to a side table loaded with bottles and plates of sandwiches. Lucy suddenly realised that she was hungry. She sat down and began to eat, watching Stephen as he laid another tray. Her own disaster was still too enormous to be understood. She could more easily perceive the implications for her mother and Stephen. But it was so much a habit with her to see him through a mist of irritation that he seemed, in this moment of detachment, quite strange and queer.

44

His wedding present had surprised and embarrassed her. Without consulting anybody he had drawn out his War Savings and bought a little string of pearls. She had not liked to take it from a person with whom she was always bickering. But now the explanation flashed upon her: He had been trying to fill their father's place. All her friends had these little pearl strings, given to them by their fathers on their eighteenth birthdays. She had none because she had no father. Stephen was not particularly fond of her but he wished to be thought of as a man and to act a man's part. That was why he had offered to give her away in church, a suggestion which she had repelled with noisy scorn.

And now he was probably wondering if the man of the family ought not to go after Patrick, seize him by the collar, and haul him to the altar. He might do something quite frantic unless prevented.

"I think," she said, "that the sooner all this business is forgotten, the better, don't you? It would be very undignified for us to make a fuss of any kind. I'm sure Father would have thought so. If Mother consults you, I hope you'll say that."

Stephen started, not merely because she had guessed his intention, but at a note in her voice, a steady coolness, which he had never heard before. Nobody had.

"After all," she continued, "it may be some time before we know . . . all the explanation. Aren't you hungry? These smoked salmon rolls are very good."

He took one, still eyeing her nervously.

Mrs. Carmichael peered into the kitchen. She had thought Lucy gone rather long and had come to see what was happening.

"Come and join us," commanded Lucy. "We're eating."

"I'm afraid I broke—" began Stephen.

But Lucy interrupted him.

"If Stephen could open one of those bottles, I believe it would do us all more good than tea. Could you, Stephen?"

He assured them that he could, though he had never opened a champagne bottle before. Taking the pliers he set to work. He became very much flustered and Mrs. Carmichael made a movement to take the bottle from him, but Lucy checked her. For once Stephen must be allowed to do something which they could not.

"Try the smoked salmon," she advised her mother.

"We had it for supper," said Mrs. Carmichael. "We ate up a lot of the food at supper time. But still . . ."

Pop!

They hastily thrust teacups at Stephen, which he filled. A little champagne had lodged upon the ceiling but on the whole he had acquitted himself very manfully.

"Tomorrow," remarked Lucy, when she had drunk two cups, "is going to be unbearable. But now is not so bad."

They all felt that. For a moment they were able to detach their minds from tomorrow. They were weary and famished and the champagne did them good. They became quite animated.

Mrs. Carmichael remembered the first night of the war, when she and her husband, having finished an improvised blackout, went out into the warm September night to see if any chink had been overlooked. They were in despair. They expected immediate air raids to demolish London. They were facing separation. But, as they strolled in front of their house, they had met a neighbouring couple, out for the same reason, and the four, with linked arms, patrolled the street, filled with a sudden unaccountable exhilaration, laughing and talking nonsense. *Now we are for it*, they had thought, and found a mysterious tonic in their mutual predicament.

Alone in her room upstairs she had despaired. But now, sitting with her children round the kitchen table, she recovered her fortitude. The Carmichaels were certainly for it, but Lucy's gesture, in thus assembling them, made their misfortune bearable. The same hilarity, a tendency to giggle at nothing, rose in her that she remembered on that other dire September night.

If Patrick were dead, thought Lucy, we couldn't be doing this. We couldn't laugh. Which proves . . . something or other. I'm too tired to puzzle it out now.

A horsewhip, thought Stephen. But I haven't got a horsewhip. Could I buy one? *Sir! You are a coward and a cad!* But Lucy says Father wouldn't . . . I believe I'm drunk.

"Not nearly so bad as Munich," observed Mrs. Carmichael hazily.

"What isn't," asked Lucy, "this?"

"No. September nineteen therry nine. Nine-teen-thirty-nine. Nothing has ever been so bad as Munich. We all said so, walking up and down the street."

"Who walked up and down the street?"

"Your father and I and the Gunnings. Next door to us. You must remember them. They kept rabbits."

"Well, well," said Lucy. "Did they have any money?"

"I expect so. He ran away in 'forty-one with a lady warden. Why?"

Her children sang:

"They've nice habits
They keep rabbits,
But . . . they've got no money . . . at . . . all!"

"Everybody had money before the war," stated Mrs. Carmichael with tipsy solemnity.

"Lots and lots of money," agreed Lucy.

"And lots and lots of rabbits," said Stephen.

"Even the rabbits had money," proclaimed Lucy. "Rich people's rabbits had lots and lots of money, hadn't they, Mother?"

"No," said Mrs. Carmichael, after reflection. "No, I never heard of a rabbit having money. Don't be silly, dear."

Stephen's crowing laugh rang through the kitchen.

Joan, who was peeping at them through the door, rushed up to report to her parents the meaning of this scandalous commotion: "They're sitting down there in their dressing gowns, drinking champagne out of teacups and laughing their heads off."

6

WEDNESDAY'S NEWSPAPERS informed Mrs. Hallam of the scene at the church and explained a telegram she had had from Melissa postponing her return home. There were photographs of Lucy sitting alone in the car, and paragraphs from reporters, who had interviewed a great many people in order to amass a very small quantity of information. But it was clear that Patrick Reilly had vanished on his wedding day and had jilted his bride.

On Thursday Mrs. Knight rang up with more news. Her husband, alarmed for Reilly's reputation, had been to see Clay and learnt facts which Clay had not felt obliged to divulge at Gorling. Patrick had certainly gone off with Mrs. Lucas. The porter of the flats knew her well by sight; she had often been there. He told Clay that he saw her go up to Mr. Reilly's flat on Monday night and had not seen her come out again until the pair of them emerged at nine o'clock on Tuesday morning and took a taxi to Euston.

On Friday Melissa came home, pale, silent and steeled against unfriendly comments. For she had forgotten that her mother could always rise to a real occasion, and possessed a great deal of genuine feeling. It was the littleness of life which irked Mrs. Hallam and caused her to magnify minor crises and to invent delicate situations where none existed. When tact and sympathy were really wanted she was in her element. Melissa was received with so much kindness, so few questions were asked, so much distress on Lucy's behalf was apparent, that she soon found herself telling the whole story.

"It's quite clear," she said, "that he never meant Lucy to go to the church. He thought she knew it was off. She got a letter on Wednesday which made that obvious."

"Oh? He did write?"

"Yes. It was posted from Euston. She showed it to us. She . . . oh, Mother . . . she's so gentle and sensible and considerate . . . it's really worse than anything. I found myself wishing she'd be unreasonable and scream the house down. Well, he evidently thought she'd had a telephone message, early on Tuesday, putting the wedding off and saying he'd been taken to a nursing home with a bad attack of malaria. He said it was the only message he could think of at the moment, but the truth was that he realised he couldn't live without Mrs. Lucas."

"Did Lucy know about Jane Lucas?"

"Oh, yes. He'd told her. But she didn't know Mrs. Lucas had come back to England. He didn't apologise, which was just as well.

He said Lucy was well rid of him and he hoped it wouldn't be long before she knew it."

"That's true enough," said Mrs. Hallam, "but not the sort of consolation one can offer now."

"Plenty of people think they can," said Melissa grimly. "You wouldn't believe what tactless, insensitive . . . anyway, he isn't as bad as we thought. Somebody must have bungled the message at his end, because it certainly never reached Gorling."

"It was that devil of a woman. She probably undertook to send it and didn't. It would be just her idea of a joke—to let the marriage go on."

"But, Mother, he'll find out."

"She won't care. But how did Lucy take it? Did she realise it's final?"

"Oh, yes, I think so. There was a bad moment yesterday. We were in the garden and Mrs. Carmichael came out and said: 'There's been a mistake.' It was only about returning some wedding present, but Lucy"—Melissa's voice shook—"Lucy jumped up, all alive and glowing and joyful. She thought he'd come, that it was *all* a mistake. Oh, that was the worst moment."

"Oh . . . oh . . . how piteous!"

"She is, Mother. She's so . . . so bewildered and . . . and docile . . . doing whatever anybody suggests . . . and a little apologetic all the time, you know: as if she hated bringing so much trouble on everybody. You can't imagine . . ."

Mrs. Hallam could not. A memory flashed into her mind of Lucy as she had been three years ago when they first met. There had been a cold snap and everybody was skating when Mrs. Hallam went to Oxford for the day to see Melissa. They had gone to meet Lucy on Port Meadow which was frozen and flooded; she had come skimming over the ice to greet them, curls and skirts blown back, her grey eyes full of guileless interest in Melissa's mother. She had been so sure of her welcome, poor child, and obviously unconscious of any carping criticisms which might be brought against her, and her middle class background.

"But what is she to do now, Melissa? What are her plans?"

"I suppose she must get a job of some sort."

"Yes. But she ought to get away for a time. Away from Gorling. It's such a small place; it must be most unpleasant."

"Oh, it is. We went into the town yesterday and half the people we met dodged into shops, so as not to have to speak to her because they didn't know what to say. The other half had the impertinence to come up and sympathise. A person who has been publicly humiliated is such a pariah."

Mrs. Hallam then suggested that Lucy should come to Campden Hill Square. She was herself going to Italy, and the two girls could have the house to themselves. She outlined this plan with great enthusiasm, unaware of the dismay with which it was received.

For Melissa had been fortifying herself during these appalling days by visions of all the fun she would have with John as soon as her mother was despatched to Italy. That would be impossible if Lucy were in the house. It was no moment in which to confide her own engagement to her unhappy friend and, in any case, nobody could have fun with Lucy before their eyes.

She told herself that she had John to consider and that she had no right to spoil his happiness. For the moment she had been through enough for Lucy. She had coped with the Rawlingses. She had packed up wedding presents. Was there never to be an end to it? No . . . she would not have Lucy.

She gave a non-committal answer and, as soon as she was alone, rang up John to discuss festive meetings while her mother was in Italy. But John, who had also read the newspapers, would talk of nothing but Lucy and assured her that he was expecting to see very little of her, just now, as he realised that Lucy must come first.

"What plans you do make for me," complained Melissa.

"I know how fond you are of her, and I'm sure she needs you more than I do. I was wondering if she'd be coming to you when your mother goes away."

"Oh, you were, were you?"

"What's the matter?"

"Fatigue. A good man's love is so strenuous."

"I don't understand. Are you cross about something?"

"Oh, no, no, no! I'll meet you this evening as usual."

"Melissa . . . what have I said?"

"He for God only, she for God in him," she snapped, and rang off.

She repeated to herself that she would not have Lucy. John need never know that the invitation had been suggested. He need never know that she was not the angel he thought her.

But someday he would find out. He was bound to do so unless she took upon herself the lifelong task of adopting his principles, his standards, his considerate scruples. Being herself rather selfish she had sometimes wondered whether marriage with so unselfish a man might not ruin her character. But now she saw that the boot could be on the other leg.

After tea she rang up Lucy and invited her to Campden Hill Square.

7

RICKIE HAVERSTOCK was one of the amorphous, musical young men with whom Lucy and Melissa had experimented during their first year at Oxford, while they were perfecting their technique with future prime ministers. They had discarded most of these callow swains, but Rickie refused to be shaken off. He escorted them to concerts, conducted them in madrigals, played his own compositions to them, and fell in love with Melissa, who never thought of him except as a joke.

He intended to marry her as soon as he should be earning £800 a year. This would not be for some time, but he was untroubled by any fear of rivals, who might forestall him, since he had no imagination whatever. He had not discussed the matter with her; he wished to marry her, so he assumed that she must wish to marry him. He sent her Christmas cards, kept her photograph beside his bed, and boasted about her to all his acquaintances. So far as he was concerned she had been put away in camphor till he was ready. But, having occasion to visit London, he naturally wished to unpack her and look at her while he was there.

Her dismay was considerable when he rang her up and announced that he was coming to tell her all about the marvellous job that he had got. She hedged and protested, but he was so insistent that she was at last obliged to invite him to supper. Lucy, she told him, would be there and no mention must be made of Lucy's engagement because it was off. That Lucy should be there did not surprise him. She always had been there. He hardly realised that they did not live in the same house. And her engagement made no impression on him, whether on or off, because he had never heard of it.

A whole evening of Rickie's exuberance and Lucy's pallid silence was more than Melissa could face. She decided that John should make a fourth. After supper she would take him into the garden sitting room; as soon as Rickie had got well away on the piano. Lucy could stay and listen, which would be tough, but not more tough than anything else in Lucy's life just now. She so plainly did not care in the least what she did, or with whom she talked, that she might as well be abandoned to Rickie.

He arrived in high feather, ten minutes too early. They heard him coming up the hill humming the *Trumpet Voluntary*, to which fanfare he expected, someday, to escort Melissa out of church, while executing it in person on the organ. The event was still so distant that he had not yet troubled to consider how he was to be in two places at once. Bursting into the room, he told them exactly how long it was since they had seen him, accepted a glass of sherry without a word of thanks, and began to describe a concert he had attended that afternoon, carolling his favourite passages and spilling a good deal of sherry into the piano. They could only get him to stop by asking about his new job.

"Well," he said, settling down to it, "as you know, it's in Ravonsbridge, in Severnshire."

They had not known, but he gave them no chance to say so. He rushed on. It was a marvellous job. He had got his own orchestra to conduct. He was junior music director at the Ravonsbridge Arts Institute. When old Pidgeon died, Dr. Pidgeon, the composer, he would become senior director. As it was, he could do pretty well what he liked, because old Pidgeon lived in Severnton and hardly ever came over to Ravonsbridge. All the real work was done by Rickie. Everybody knew that. Hayter, the executive director, a splendid person, had said as much: "We all know who really does the work," he had said. Which was pretty good evidence that Hayter would back Rickie for the senior post when it fell vacant. Pidgeon, of course, conducted at concerts. But Rickie rehearsed the orchestra, which was jolly good, considering, and at present he was busy on Fauré's *Requiem*. Surely they must remember it? Those marvellous semitones: Ta-tum! Ta-tum! . . .

At this point John was shown in, grinning broadly, for he had been warned what to expect and had heard these ta-tums as he came upstairs. Lucy was introduced and the grin was replaced by an expression of respectful concern which Melissa thought tactless. Also she could detect a trace of surprise in the occasional glances which he turned on Lucy as he drank his sherry. His thoughts were perfectly apparent. Was this the beauty—this lanky listless creature with her sharp nose, her dull hair, and eyes fixed in the astonished stare of recent shock? He had come expecting to like her, and was repelled.

Rickie continued to tell them about Ravonsbridge. As Melissa led the way downstairs he explained that the local millionaire, old Matthew Millwood, of Marsden Millwood Motors, had built and endowed the Institute because he wished to turn Ravonsbridge, his home town, into the "Athens of the West." He described the theatre, the concert hall, the art gallery and the view over the Ravon valley.

"And you'll like the staff," he assured Melissa. "You'll find them jolly nice to work with. They're such a friendly lot."

"I?" exclaimed Melissa, in astonishment.

"Yes, that's what I've come to tell you about. There's a marvellous job going at the Institute which will suit you down to the ground. But you must hurry up and apply, because the appointment is going to be made early next week. But I must explain more about the place first, or you won't understand—"

"But, really, Rickie . . . I—"

"Besides the music school there's an art school and a drama school, with first rate people running all of them. Old Angera, the art director—"

"Rickie! Do help yourself to chicken!"

"Oh? Sorry! He's so good, many people think his classes better than the Slade. And Thornley, who'll be your boss, is a well known playwright."

There was a fractional pause, while Rickie put some food into his mouth, and Melissa turned to Lucy.

"Didn't you have a school friend who works there?"

Lucy, after a slight hesitation, said yes. Bess Turner, who had been at Gorling High School, was now junior librarian at Ravonsbridge.

"How does she like it?"

Again there was a pause. The length of time which Lucy took to answer any question was beginning to get on Melissa's nerves. It was as though anything said to her had to be decoded before she could reply. At last she said:

"I think so. But she seems to stand in great awe of the Millwood family. Don't they order everybody about rather a lot?" she asked Rickie.

"Good old Bess," exclaimed Rickie, with his mouth full. "She sings in my choir."

Lucy decoded this and displayed a trace of surprise.

"Bess sings?"

"Rather. She has a voice like a peacock, but she's very reliable on her leads."

"Are you short of singers?" asked Melissa.

"Oh, no. But it's the thing to do. All the staff are supposed to sing in the choir and all that. Take an interest in all the activities of the Institute. Why, I went on in the crowd in Thornley's *Julius Caesar*, and shouted: Rhubarb! Rhubarb!"

"You didn't really shout rhubarb?" exclaimed Melissa. "I thought nobody actually did. But who insists on all this hearty activity? The Millwoods?"

"It's part of the Ravonsbridge tradition."

"You mean that this motor magnate—"

"Oh, not old Matthew. He's dead. It's his widow that runs the place. Lady Frances, and her daughters. But they don't really count for much. The big noise is Hayter and he's grand. Absolutely first class. The council just eats out of his hand. It was his idea to use the buildings for these summer festivals, and they've been an immense success. Now I happen to be on pretty good terms with Hayter, and if I drop a word to him about you, Melissa, I think he'd see you got the job."

"But, Rickie, I don't want a job."

"Oh, you must want a job like this. The minute I heard it was going I thought: What an excuse to get Melissa here! It's assistant dramatic director, to work under Thornley. The Frog, Miss Frogmore I mean, and Miss Paine train the students. But Thornley wants a subscrub to look after rehearsals, while he's off judging drama competitions. Sheila Doe, who used to do it, got married suddenly. They want a girl with a degree and some stage experience. She's expected to take classes in English literature as well. I told everybody I knew a marvellous girl, who'd be just right for it. She's got a degree in English, I said, and she was simply marvellous as Maria in *Twelfth Night*. I told Hayter and he said it didn't rest with him. The council makes the appointment. But the council is merely the Millwoods, and they do what he tells them to, and if you apply I'm sure he'll put in a good word for you. And that," concluded Rickie happily, "is what I came to say."

Having thus delivered himself, Rickie attacked his supper, unaware that Lucy and Melissa were both shaking with laughter and that John was crimson with rage.

As soon as she could control her voice, Melissa began to assure him that she did not wish to leave London. He was not easily quenched. He repeated all that he had already said and added, as an inducement, the suggestion that he and she would be able to spend all their free time together. But at last he understood that she was serious. Her refusal so mortified and astonished him that he said little more for the rest of the meal.

Not much passed between the others. John was outraged at the impudence of the whole idea. Melissa and Lucy had to do what talking there was, and reminded one another languidly of a performance of *Comus* in Worcester Garden and how Sabrina, played by a girl whom they particularly disliked, fell into the lake instead of rising from it.

"The Provost of Oriel had to fish her out," mused Melissa, "and I believe he got pneumonia. It was very sad."

55

"I wasn't there," stated Rickie, gloomily disposing of the topic.

When they went upstairs for coffee Melissa commanded him to play. His normal response would have been a Bach Fugue, played very loud and rather too fast. But he was feeling miserable and wanted this fact to be known. He sat down at the piano, sought a suitable vehicle for despair, and began to sing.

"Home no more home to me—"

"Oh, no," cried Melissa, starting up. "Not that, please, Rickie! It's too sad."

"I'm feeling sad," Rickie informed them. He went on.

"This," whispered Melissa to John, "is the final horror."

"What is it? It's a good tune."

"Mmhm . . . Vaughan Williams . . . but very malapropos."

"Cold blows the winter wind over hill and heather;
Thick drives the rain and my roof is in the dust."

Rickie mourned a lost childhood through six long verses. They both stole a glance at Lucy, but she did not seem to be listening. She stood at the window, looking out into the Square and apparently sunk in some kind of inward debate.

"Spring shall come, come again, calling up . . ."

"Nearly over," murmured Melissa. "The moment he stops I shall insist on playing rummy. Back me up."

"He sings rather well."

"Yes, he does, curse him!"

"Fair the day shine as it shone on my childhood;
Fair shine the day on the house with open door.
Birds come and cry there and twitter in the chimney . . .
But I go for ever and come again no more."

"And now let's play rummy," cried Melissa.

But Rickie was sulky and said that he hated cards. He was going to sing them Lully's *Bois epais*. Melissa was obliged to be really uncivil before she could get him away from the piano. He then said that he was tired and would go home to bed. He must catch a 73 bus from Kensington High Street to Richmond. Melissa might walk over the hill with him to the bus stop. This she refused to do and when Lucy, turning from her post by the window, offered her company instead he was not very gracious.

He could not, however, refuse it and they set off together as soon as she had got a coat.

Rickie would not talk. He strode along with his shoulders hunched up, humming Lully.

"*Je ne dois plus voir ce que j'aime . . .*"

He was not used to disappointments. The little that he asked of life had always fallen into his lap.

When they were halfway over the hill Lucy spoke.

"Do you think I could apply for that job?"

"At Ravonsbridge? You?"

"I have the same qualifications as Melissa."

He did not think she had at all the same qualifications.

"They want somebody permanent," he said. "Aren't you engaged or something?"

"I was, but it's off."

"Oh, yes, I remember. Melissa told me."

"So I've got to get a job, and I don't want to be a schoolma'am. I'd like a job in the country."

Rickie peeped for a moment over the prison walls of his own depression and perceived that Lucy seemed to be in low spirits. She never used to speak in that flat, weary voice. He recalled Melissa's warning and surmised that Lucy must have taken a knock. He reflected gloomily that they were both in the same boat. And then a new idea occurred to him.

"Of course," he said, "if Melissa really won't take it, you would be better than nobody. We could talk about her."

"We could," agreed Lucy with a faint smile.

"And she'd come to see you."

"I'd ask her."

This was worth considering. Also he remembered a drawback which he had put out of his mind when urging Melissa to come. There was a great shortage of comfortable accommodation in

57

Ravonsbridge; in fact there were, he knew, no rooms to be had at the moment. The women's hostel was full, and if Melissa had come she would probably have had to go as a paying guest to Emil Angera, the art director, who had a half-witted wife and lived in such squalor that nobody stayed there for longer than a term. This would not have been good enough for Melissa, but it would do for Lucy very well.

"It's not a bad idea," he decided at last. "I really can't think of anybody better, if Melissa won't come."

"To whom should I write?"

"To Poole . . . to The Secretary, The Arts Institute, Ravonsbridge, Severnshire. State your qualifications and send copies of any testimonials you may have."

"I can get those from the Prink and my tutor. And I have a stage one too . . . one vacation I worked as assistant stage manager for the Bradstowe Rep."

"Splendid. Well . . . you send them along. And I'll speak to Hayter and get him to support you on the council."

"Thank you, Rickie."

"You don't by any chance, play the bassoon, do you?"

"No. Why?"

"I'm short of bassoons. But you could learn. You'd better start learning right away. I'll borrow one for you; they're expensive. It's really providential," said Rickie, who was growing quite enthusiastic. "Because one couldn't ask Melissa to play the bassoon, could one? She's so sort of fairy like."

"Where does one live?"

"Wherever one can. But I can get you lodgings with the Angeras. He's the art director . . . he's a refugee; very interesting chap. But his wife is English."

"Look, Rickie! There's your bus. Run!"

Rickie ran, with a hasty goodnight.

Lucy turned and plodded up the hill again, her hands plunged in the pockets of her loose coat. She decided to write to Ravonsbridge that very night. It would be better than a school. And of all her friends, perhaps Bess Turner would be less of a trial than any. She was a nice old donkey, completely good natured and without a spark of imagination. The things about her which used to irritate

Lucy did not signify now. She thought it funny to call anemones annymoans and a telephone a tephelone; but her comment on her friend's disaster would be soothing.

"I say, Lucy! What sickening luck! I mean, how perfectly sickening. But you've got your trousseau and you're sure to marry somebody else, you're so pretty, and then you'll have two trousseaux. I mean, there's a bright side to everything, if only you can see it. But I expect you're still feeling awfully sick about it, and it's easy for other people to say cheer up. Have a peppermint!"

Lucy felt that she would rather be with stupid and insensitive people than with a friend like Melissa, who was feeling away on her behalf and hating it. Sympathy was like a reverberator, like a looking glass, in which she was perpetually confronted with the spectacle of her own wretchedness.

Pain swept over her—such a tempest of grief and desolation as seemed more physical than mental. It was sheer feeling, in which thought played little part. Every limb ached. Nothing could help her. All was hostile—the pavement upon which she planted her weary feet, step by step, the quiet houses, the vast and cloudy sky. Her footsteps rang in an empty universe.

Je ne dois plus voir ce que j'aime.

She had got used to these spasms. They came on suddenly but after a while they went away again. There was nothing to do, when they seized her, save walk about until the anguish slackened and exhaustion, beneficent apathy, took its place.

When she came to the Square again she went down the other side of the hill to the Bayswater Road, where arc lamps burned among the trees and the noisy traffic roared past her to the west. She paced for half a mile under the flickering tree shadows, and then, knowing the crisis over, turned homewards. She had forgotten how tired she was. By the time that she again reached the Square she almost shrank from the effort of climbing the hill.

She paused for a moment, leaning against the Square railing, and a sly voice murmured, close to her ear:

"Good evening! Where are you baound?"

Since the age of fifteen she had been able to deal with such prowlers, but tonight she had not her wits about her. She turned puzzled eyes upon the shadow by the Square railings.

"I beg your pardon?" she said vaguely.

The leer vanished from his face. With a muttered apology he walked off.

I frightened him, she thought, as she began to toil up the hill. I frighten everybody, even the corner boys.

The party had been such a failure that Melissa and John could not recover from it, even when they were alone. They laughed a little over Rickie, but they did not enjoy their tête-à-tête as they had expected. Presently they heard Lucy come in. She put her head in, for a moment, to say that she had letters to write, and went upstairs to her room. But her presence was felt by them, even after her slow footsteps were heard no more. They could not forget that she and her sorrow were in the house, and secretly each of them wished her away. They were ashamed of the wish but it was there. At this period of their lives they had a right to be gay and lighthearted. Before them were all the sober years of marriage, when they must often endure disagreeable evenings and be worried about their friends. This was their spring and Lucy was making it seem like autumn.

"Anyway," said John, snatching at a cheerful suggestion, "perhaps there'll be a chance now for Hump!"

Melissa laughed. "I've no hope that Hump will marry Lucy now. He wouldn't want to. Who would? You didn't think her at all attractive, did you?"

"Well . . . not this evening. But she's unhappy. When she gets over it, perhaps—"

"When she's got over it she'll be a different person. She won't be my Lucy. Hump would have adored my Lucy. But she's gone. She's gone for ever . . . and . . ."

Melissa could not finish. She laid her cheek for a moment against John's shoulder.

Part 2

The Lump

1

(Extracts from Lucy's letters to Melissa.) Oct. 4th.

I saw my fate 10 miles away, as I was coming in the train up the Ravon valley. What is that unsightly *lump* on the top of that hill? I wondered. Can it be a building? Who could have done a thing like that on purpose?

The train wound up the valley and the hill with the Lump on it kept disappearing and re-appearing, and each time it was nearer, until I realised what it was—the Ravonsbridge Institute. I suppose Matthew Millwood had the Acropolis in mind. But he didn't find anyone to build him a Parthenon. It is just a great lump of masonry, and it dwarfs the town, which is a nice little old country market town, going up a steep hill from the Ravon valley, with an early Perpendicular church on top, which must have been a pretty landmark before they went and put the Lump on rising ground just behind it.

The station is in New Ravonsbridge, which fills the whole valley and is hideous. I'll never go down there if I can help it—miles and miles of nasty little houses built for the workers at M. M.M. So I got a taxi and came to Angera Heim. He is the baldest man I ever saw. His wife says his hair all fell out in one night in 1940 when France capitulated. He was interned here and thought Hitler would win. I can't imagine what he looked like before; his

61

head is so enormous that it looks top heavy even without hair. His nose is the shape of an electric light bulb and he has Jewish eyes—i.e., dark and mournful as if he'd been persecuted for centuries, which he has, I suppose, and has learnt to expect the skinny leg of the chicken. He is 37.

He opened the door when I arrived, clutching a frying pan in his hand, I can't think why, for he can't cook. And he looked at me very, very sadly and said: "Zis is terrible!"

It was, rather, because they had made no attempt to get my room ready, though they knew when I was coming. Mrs. A. is The Bottom as a housekeeper. She is an apple-cheeked little ninny with humble brown eyes and a blue plastic hair slide in the shape of three daisies. They have a baby which she calls "baby" and he "ze child." It is a dribbly object; I wish I was a womanly woman and could think it sweet.

Well so I cleaned this room I am to have, for the first time in its life, and wrote home for some bed linen as the A.s have not got any—their other pair is at the wash. It's not a bad room; a big attic with a view east over Slane Forest, which stretches all the way between here and Severnton. And at about 9 we had a meal in the kitchen: tea, stale Swiss roll, 5 sardines, 4 tomatoes, and some cold porridge. Why this house should reek of cooking I cannot think. Nobody cooks. Mrs. A. said forlornly that she had tried to get kippers but there weren't any so Mr. A. said of course there were, but the fishmonger is anti-Semitic.

So we sat and he told me how much he hates England and how unkind we were to intern him in 1940, and how insensitive and stupid all the British are, and what hell Ravonsbridge is.

He says that Lady Frances Millwood, the founder's widow, knows nothing at all about art, and simply uses the Institute to give jobs to her pets, and that the Council of Management all toady to her. All the directors are hopelessly second rate, except himself, and it is an insult for him to have to work with them. He mentioned that Mr. Thornley, my boss, is sore because he had a little friend for whom he wanted the job. At 10:30 having said something nasty about everyone on the staff, we went to bed without washing up.

Next morning I went up to the Lump. It's not so bad when

you get close up to it—rather stately. It's the site that is wrong. There are 2 big quadrangles of Cotswold stone. I saw Mr. Hayter first, the executive director and the *Eminence grise* who got me the job, if Rickie is to be believed. I think I shall like him very much; he gives himself no airs, though he seems to be the big noise here. At first I thought he looked surprisingly young, quite a boy, but when he sits down you can see he's going thin on top, and you think his wrinkles are smiles until he isn't smiling. He was very agreeable and talked to me a lot about my work and everything. I got the impression that he doesn't expect me to get on very well with Mr. Thornley, but hopes I'll stick it, because he feels the place is going down hill and he's anxious to get young blood in. I felt he was just a little apologetic about the level of the Institute drama.

So then he took me to the theatre and introduced me to Mr. Thornley, who is dapper and dignified, with a quiff of white hair on the top of his head and, my dear, a monocle with a black ribbon! Altogether he looks quite as distinguished as he obviously thinks he is. And I realised I'd got off on the wrong foot, because I ought to have gone straight to the theatre, and not to Mr. Hayter's office at all. I didn't know. Nobody told me. Mr. Hayter's office was the first place I came to. Mr. Thornley spent half the morning explaining to me that Mr. H. is junior to most of the directors and that his job is the *business side*. There does seem to be an awful lot of jealousy.

We went to the theatre where I was permitted to watch Mr. T. rehearsing some students in *She Stoops To Conquer*. Mr. Hayter may well apologise, and I can quite believe about Rhubarb! It's that sort of tradition. To call it *ham* would be to insult nice food which we don't often get.

But it seems that Mr. T. is the author of that play, *His Eminence Is Detained*, which every amateur society has to act. You must have been in it yourself, some time or other. I have twice, once at school and once at a Village Institute. So he is called H.E. behind his back.

In the afternoon I went to tea with my old school chum, Bess Turner. She works in the library, which is really lovely. It not only has every book anybody could want but a very rare and valuable

63

collection made by Matt Millwood and presented to the Institute on his death. The head librarian is a sweet old tortoise of a man called Mildmay, a great bibliophile, who used to buy books for Millwood. He has promised to show me all the treasures sometime. He didn't say anything nasty about anyone, perhaps because he never comes out of his library, and hardly knows the names of his colleagues.

Bess tells me everybody *loathes* Angera and I'm not to believe a word he says about anyone. She says it is particularly mean of him to be always crabbing Thornley, because Mr. T. got him the job here, and is a very good friend to him—always making the peace when Angera is silly and quarrels with people.

This letter is so sour I think I had better finish it. I had meant it to be sparkling with wit and humour but it hasn't turned out that way. I'm not sorry I came, and I think that Slane Forest looks most enticing. I mean to explore it.

Oct. 15.

I seem to be settling and have got upsides with the work, which consists of running errands for Mr. T. and taking classes in English literature. I get on very well with Mr. T., who has quite forgiven me for going to Mr. Hayter first. He may be sore about my appointment, but he is a gent, and doesn't take it out on me.

I have not met my lady patroness yet. I imagine her exactly like Lady Catherine de Bourgh. She has gone away to superintend the confinement of a daughter. It appears that she does this every autumn. She has 4 daughters, 3 of whom are married and have autumnal babies in rotation, so Ravonsbridge gets a holiday from Lady Frances in October.

She is also the mother of Charles Millwood, of whom we all speak with bated breath, though we never see him because he despises the Institute and never comes near us except to a general meeting, which he has to do because he is our president. He is a director at the M.M. and is always just flying to America. Bess sat next to him once at a tea party, at Cyre Abbey, where they live, 6 miles off, in Slane Forest. The staff are asked out there in a drove, occasionally, and are fed with buns. No . . . I invented the buns. But I daresay it's true. And pray Bess, what was he like? Oh,

64

says Bess, her eyes popping, he's TERRIFIC! Why? What could he have said to you? Nothing. Not a word. For which Bess is profoundly grateful, as she would have died if she had been expected to talk to him. But he is said to be frightfully good-looking and frightfully brainy (Bess's language, not mine) and stinkingly rich (my language). Which *is*, I suppose, rather terrific.

You have asked me, more than once, what the Ravonsbridge Institute is for. My dear, it's no use asking, for I don't know, unless it is to provide Bess and Rickie and me with three square meals a day.

I have read a little book explaining what it was meant to be for: a Memoir of Matthew Millwood which all the staff are supposed to study. It gives a short account of his career with 2 photographs. One is of a solemn young man in the 80's, with his hair in a cowlick, sitting beside a potted plant. This was *before* he became a millionaire, when he was just a town boy and his father kept a hardware shop in Market Square. The other is *after*: a snapshot of a stocky old man on the lawn at Cyre Abbey, snapping his fingers at a dog; his face is completely obscured by a panama hat.

It seems that he was a clever boy and wanted to go to Oxford, and would have gone, if his father hadn't had a stroke so he had to stay in Ravonsbridge and run the shop. But you can't keep a good man down, so he went into partnership with Marsden who had a small factory, down by the bridge, round about 1900. They made sewing machines and mowing machines and then they made motor cars and then they made millions. The M.M. works now seem to extend for miles and all the new town grew up round them. And he bought Cyre Abbey and eventually married Lord Ravonsclere's daughter.

But, says the Memoir, he always regretted not having the opportunity to read more, and hear more music and learn to know good pictures from bad pictures. So he built the Institute, so that Ravonsbridge should have the best of everything in art and culture. His idea was that no Ravonsbridge boy, kept at home as he was, should have to eat his heart out, thinking of all he was missing. The best was to be on his doorstep. It was to be a privilege to live in Ravonsbridge, and people of culture from all over the world were to flock to it.

There were to be first rate concerts and plays and lectures, and schools for painting, music and drama, where the citizens could study these things. For townspeople or workers from M.M. the fees are nominal, though students from elsewhere pay.

He built it and endowed it handsomely and presented it to the town and died a fortnight after the opening ceremony, leaving Lady F. to carry out his great project; and she, unfortunately, knows as much about art as my Uncle Bob does.

And anyway, Ravonsbridge doesn't happen to want art and culture. Nobody ever comes to the concerts, plays, etc., and nobody uses the library. Except, of course, at the festivals, and they have nothing to do with the Institute. The buildings are hired out during the summer vacation for a nice sum, which helps to check the drain on the endowments. During the rest of the year concerts and plays are given by the students, which are not worth going to. We get no outside talent: it wouldn't be worth anyone's while to come here.

As for the schools: the music school has collapsed. There are no full time students. Rickie and his aides, Harry Dent and Mrs. Carstairs, give music lessons on various instruments to anybody who wants them, and Rickie conducts a very bad amateur orchestra at rehearsals. Occasionally Dr. Pidgeon, our senior director, turns up from Severnton, tells everybody how hopeless they are, and conducts contemptuously at a concert.

The drama school isn't as bad as I thought at first. Mr. T.'s productions are the bottom, but the students get quite good voice training, etc., from Miss Frogmore and Miss Paine, and they do seem to get jobs when they leave us—not often on the stage, but semi-educational jobs. It's quite an efficient concern, in its way, and we have 20 resident full time students. Mr. T. is an amazing man. I never met anybody so pleased with himself or so sure he knows all about the drama. He's written a lot of plays for amateurs, and what he really loves is travelling round and judging at amateur dramatic competitions, and lecturing. He knows nothing whatever about the professional stage. But he is rather an old pet and doesn't pinch the students' behinds and I can see why Lady F. appointed him.

The art school is her lucky strike; and that's not because she knows about pictures, apparently, but because Mr. T. got her to appoint Angera, who is really first rate, and seems to be an inspired teacher.

Angera improves on acquaintance. He can be very nice when he forgets his grievances. He's quite the most interesting person here . . . I mean to talk to. But he is horribly moody. Sometimes he is quite embarrassingly affectionate to Nancy (we are on Emil-Nancy-Lucy terms now), fondling her in front of me till I don't know where to look. And then he will snarl and sneer at her, till I want to hit him. In her shoes I should go mad. And I suspect him of being slightly lupine; he looks at one, well . . . you know, the way foreigners do. Still and all, I find I'm getting to like them both in a way. In fact, I'm getting to like everybody, in a way.

The only person I don't like better is Mr. Hayter, whom I started by liking best. I have this feeling that he wants to set me against Thornley. Whenever I meet him he asks how I'm getting on, as if he hoped I'd criticise. And he smiles too much.

Oct. 20th.

My dear, I must write at once to tell you: I've met Lady Frances! Not really like Lady Catherine de Bourgh though quite as formidable. She bounced into the theatre this morning, wearing wellingtons and a sou'-wester, as it was pouring with rain. She has a fleet of cars at Cyre Abbey but I expect they were all busy taking sick people to hospitals and voters to polls and lecturers to village institutes. If ever you see a Millwood car it is always going on some public errand.

She is tall and bony and stern and rather lame, with a beaky nose and piercing dark eyes and an abrupt voice. She asked me a million questions about how I was getting on, and if I'd got a bassoon yet (how on earth did she know I was learning the bassoon?) and ended by saying I didn't look very well and she would send me some vitamin tablets. I can't think why I didn't resent her impertinence more.

She wanted a detailed account of my English classes. I don't think I've mentioned them yet, have I? It's a dull topic. I give them twice a week for the drama students, and any burghers of Ravonsbridge, or M.M. workers, who take an interest in English literature. They are, needless to say, a flop. The students are supposed to come, but most of them cut it as often as they can; the ones who don't are those dreary girls you get in every drama school who can't act for toffee and think to make up for it by knowing what Shakespeare really meant. Of Ravonsbridge burghers I have 7: the assistant of Orson the chemist, who wants to be a writer, and thinks this will help, though he doesn't know what he wants to write about. A Mrs. Beasly, who tells us about her psychic experiences during the discussions. A Mr. Cottesmore, who has a thing about Kipling. Mr. and Mrs. Chick, from the lower town, who are rather pathetic; he is a clerk at the goods station and they are solemnly crazy about culture and are teaching themselves French on a gramophone. Miss Foss, a tiny little old lady who is on the council and comes to every Institute activity but never utters. And Mr. Meeker, stone blind, a retired schoolmaster, who knows much more about literature than I do and is a standby in discussions. I tried to express my gratitude to him once, for his kindness in coming, and he said, rather snubbingly: "I wish to support our Institute."

No M.M. workers have ever turned up.

While all this was being extracted from me, Lady Anne Chadwick came in, who is Lady F.'s sister and very like her. Same costume, same rather Spanish handsomeness, but softer and less emphatic. Imagine, in fact, an early and a late *Domingo Theotocopouli*. Ha! My dearest creature, pray do not start! Where did I pick up all this culture? From Emil, who talked like an angel for hours the other night, explaining to me about composition lines, and the influence of Italy and Spain, respectively, on Greco's art. On any subject outside art he is liable to be second rate and woolly. Foreigners are strange: so much more cultured than we yet hardly educated at all. I happened to quote: "Know then thyself, and seek not God to scan. The proper study of mankind, etc." and he was much struck, and wouldn't believe it was not by Byron. He is quite certain we have only 2 poets: Byron and Wilde, who were both driven into exile by British hypocrisy. "Unser Shakespeare" doesn't count as British.

Where was I before this digression? Oh yes, Lady Anne. She had come to a council meeting; the council is quite a family affair.

68

And, said she to me, apropos of my lectures: "But do the Poor come?" Oh! I felt I was at Rosings!

Nov. 1st.

You say I tell you all about Ravonsbridge but nothing about myself. There is nothing to tell. I am quite well, though always a little hungry, owing to Nancy's horrible cooking. I am making progress with the bassoon. On Sundays I explore Slane Forest on a bicycle or go to read to Mr. Meeker who is blind and has nobody to read to him. I am quite all right, only my hair is falling out. Do you know of a good tonic?

Mr. Meeker lives in the new town, where I said I'd never go. He lives with his son, who is a doctor there, and he went to school, in his youth, with Matthew Millwood. Their fathers kept neighbouring shops on Market Square. He got to Oxford and has been a poorly paid schoolmaster all his life, while Matthew, who didn't, made all these millions. I asked him what Matthew was like, and he said: "Not merely the most lovable man I ever met but the most lovable I ever heard of, or read about." I was astonished; I didn't know anybody lovable could get so rich.

But I got the same impression from the Mildmays (Librarian), with whom I had tea the other day. Mrs. Mildmay is very amusing, though crippled with arthritis; she talked a lot about the Millwoods and the Ravonscleres, a little, I think, to the disapproval of Mr. M. who didn't like to discuss his patrons with one of the junior staff. She is a flippant old thing and made me laugh a great deal. But you know, I think they are both very fond of Lady Frances and admire her; and it's plain they adored Matthew Millwood.

Mrs. Mildmay says all the Ravonsclere women are the way they are because of their mother—old Lady Ravonsclere, the Reforming Countess. She used to pray with her maids for an hour every day, and always got up at 6 a.m. and never spent more than £20 a year on her clothes. She brought up her daughters to believe that it is not only wrong, but very vulgar, to waste time in pleasure or spend any money on themselves. They were Earl's daughters; God had given them rank and wealth in order that they might do good, and they must never forget it.

69

Lady Frances was, it seems, rather a problem daughter; she took up women's suffrage and insisted on going to prison, which Mrs. Mildmay says was probably a good deal more luxurious than anything she was used to at Ravonsclere Castle. But she settled down when she met Matt Millwood on a committee for the improvement of rural housing. They fell in love while poring over plans for septic tanks.

I told them about Lady Anne's question: Do the Poor come? which had convulsed me. Mrs. Mildmay said that was the whole trouble. Lady Frances has spent her whole life working for the Poor and now there aren't any—not as there were when she was young. Most of the things she fought for have been won: votes for women, sickness insurance, old age pensions, etc. And now, as a general rule, the workers in M.M. eat more than she does, their women dress better, and a lot of them have television, which she has never heard of. She can't get the hang of this new world. She thinks of the Institute as a scheme for keeping the Poor out of the public house by acting Shakespeare at them.

I have an idea that the Mildmays don't like Mr. Hayter. Mr. M. said it is a pity the younger staff are encouraged to criticise the senior directors, and I'm sure he had Hayter in mind. And incidentally I learnt the truth about the "little friend" of Mr. Thornley's who was, according to Emil, after my job. She was an elderly spinster, who once worked for Thornley and is now on the rocks, and, being the kindest of men, he wanted to do her a good turn.

Bess is quite right. One shouldn't believe a word Emil says. I ventured to ask them a little about Terrific Charles, because Emil is always particularly scabrous about him. An instance: a draughtsman at M.M. had a very pretty wife, who is said to have caught Charles' eye. A rival firm offered the draughtsman a much better job and he departed to London. Gossips said that Lady F. had arranged it all so as to put harm out of Charles' way. But Emil knows better. He has it that Lady F. knew nothing of the matter. Charles, he says, arranged it because an intrigue in London is much easier for him than one in Ravonsbridge. I apologise for the squalor of this, but it shows you what a *cloaca maxima* Emil's mind is, the moment he gets off Greco. He's the oddest mixture.

Well, the Mildmays didn't speak up for Charles as much as I'd hoped. They say he really is clever; he got the Ireland or the Hertford, I forget which, at Oxford, and Mr. M. said: Oh, a promising young man! Very promising! He has everything in front of him. So Mrs. M. said: Yes. The only thing he needs is something behind him. And then she muttered something that sounded like: One good kick in the pants. She looks such a meek little old invalid, but she has a devilish eye. Mr. M. coughed reprovingly. I don't think they like him—not, I'm sure, on account of squalid little mutterings about employees' wives, for I don't suppose they've ever heard them. But I think they are hurt by the despisery he shows for the Institute and the town, when his father was such a good citizen. Whenever there is an election his mother makes him stand as Liberal Candidate, and he always forfeits his deposit. Mr. M. said that's not surprising when he is so little known in the district. He never shows up at any local functions, and ignores his father's old friends. I know he has never once taken any notice of Mr. Meeker, who would love an occasional chat with him, for his father's sake.

A letter from you has just arrived. What on earth has my mother been saying? I have not been ill. But my hands and feet went numb. I couldn't feel anything in them. So Emil said I had pernicious anaemia and would die. I pointed out that people don't die nowadays; they take liver extract. But he wouldn't have any of that. He insisted, with gloomy relish, that liver extract kills more people than P.A. does. So I floated off to the doc. who said I wasn't anaemic, it is merely polineuritis, if that is how you spell it. So I said what is that? So he said, oh nothing at all, just numb hands and feet. So I said: For the rest of my life? So he said get plenty of sleep and lots of fresh air and it will pass off.

Well, I pay 7/1 a week, at least the Institute pays 3/3 of it, for National Insurance and I really thought I ought to get some of it back, so I said: Won't you give me some medicine please? So he said, oh yes, what medicine would I like? I said prussic acid, but that didn't go down well, because this doc. never had a patient who made jokes before. He got into a flap that I might be mentally deranged and it seems that he wrote to my Ma, who wrote back

71

and gave him a flea in his ear for not giving me Vitamin B injections, which are expensive, so he doesn't prescribe them but just asks patients what medicine *they'd* like, which shuts them up. So then he gave me injections and it has passed off. It was a sell for him, her being a doctor too!

Nov. 12.

What do you mean . . . why don't I go out more? There is nobody to go out with, except Rickie, and a little of him, as you know, goes a long way. And why do you keep asking if I've met Charles Millwood yet? You can't have grasped the first thing about Ravonsbridge if you think I'm ever likely to, or that he'd take me out if I did. Do get it into your head that I am only one step above the Poor.

Anyway, I'd rather be alone. I get on all right with everybody here, but I couldn't care less about anything or anybody, so now you know. *I'm quite all right*, except that I don't sleep very well and I'm going bald, like Emil, probably for the same reason: Nancy's catering.

Dec. 8th.

I am sorry (a) not to have written for so long, (b) that my last letter was cross.

What good news about Hump! I'm so glad he has at last spotted the carrier fly. But what is an ichneumon parasite? Is it the carrier, or something he means to import that will kill the carrier off?

And it surely must be good news that Kolo is marrying the High Yellow heiress? She must really have something to her, to be leaving civilisation and American plumbing to live in the Orchard Bush. She must be violently in love with Kolo, for I cannot believe it's very nice there. It will be a great standby for her to have somebody there like Hump, with whom she can play Toscanini on her Victrola. In a novel there would be complications: one knows what would happen next as one knows tomorrow is Sunday. But real life is less inevitable.

Nothing happens here except that Mad Ianthe has come home. She is another Ravonsbridge Worthy. You see, Canon

Pillie, who is the incumbent of the church, is always called "poor Canon Pillie." Why poor? Because he has a mad stepdaughter called Ianthe Meadows, who is always disgracing him. To me she sounds like a perfectly sane show-off, but she manages to set Ravonsbridge by the ears. When the town gets too hot for her they send her away for a while to an uncle in Yorkshire.

Emil says she is frustrated, but that means nothing. He is a howling cad about women. You must know that all our sex is divided into three classes.

(I) The select and, I hope, small class which has had the good fortune to be loved by Emil. These are described, with a smirk, as fulfilled.

(II) The larger class which doesn't want to be loved by Emil. These misguided creatures are subdivided into: (a) *Nymphomaniacs*, (b) *Lesbians*, (c) *Frigid*. I think, and trust, that I am now relegated to group c.

(III) The unfortunate masses whom Emil does not love. These are *frustrated*. They may be married and mothers of ten, but they have missed the highest experience life can offer. If you give one little moan of protest, when he tells you all this, you will be accused of British prudery and British hypocrisy.

So when he says Ianthe is frustrated he merely means he doesn't think her attractive.

You say in your last that I can't really like him. Well, I do, though he often annoys me. Why? Why does one like anybody? I don't know. At his best he is first rate. And he has done rather a lot for me: I have really got round to understanding rather more about painting, and enjoying it, through talking to him, and it has been a helpful occupation. So I'm grateful to him.

Well, Ianthe turned up at one of my lectures on Donne, and I nearly lost the thread, I was so much consumed with curiosity as to who she could be. She is most striking; a dead white face; very lovely, rather crazy, dark blue eyes, black bangs, and an enormous scarlet coat, like a bell tent. Like nothing I'd yet seen in Ravonsbridge.

At discussion time, before anyone could bring up Kipling or spiritualism, she asked if she might recite her favourite poem of Donne's. I said yes. I should have known better, for it was one of *those* poems and my audience had decamped before she had finished. I had naturally touched but lightly on them in my lecture. Oh . . . you'll want to know which. It was the one about the ghost in the middle of the night. She said it beautifully. No point missed.

So then she grinned and said: "That's what's called making a party go." I asked who she was and she said: "I'm poor Canon Pillie's stepdaughter and I'm ma-a-ad! I've been away for six months in a loony bin." She hadn't. She'd only been in Yorkshire.

Since then she has rather attached herself to me, and I can't help liking it for she is amusing in a breathless, scatty sort of way. She is rather like something out of a Marx Bros picture. She is a very good mimic; she can imitate anybody's voice. I was on a ladder on the stage, fixing some lights, when the voice of Lady Frances rose up from the dark stalls. "Miss Carmichael! I can see *right* up your legs! Go home and put on sensible knickers." I was furious. I quite thought it was Lady Frances and was just about to hand in my notice.

Dec. 15th.

What a honey you are to want me at Campden Hill Square for Xmas, and how kind of your mother to send that message! My dearest M, it's very, very good of you to invite this skeleton to the feast. But I think I ought to go to Gorling and make merry with my poor Ma and little Brother. It's going to be so madly gay I can't wait, though we needn't Hark the Herald in *that* church.

Mr. Meeker has found "a objick in life" for me, to quote old Annie the Scout. What objick? *To run this Institute!* Me!

You see, I went to him in rather a flap because I'd been to tea with the Chicks, the cultured railway clerk and wife who come to my lectures—my only link with the new town besides Mr. Meeker. Terrific high tea with sausages and Mr. Chick quoting Shelley rather in the style of Mr. Wegg. "Life like a dowm of many coloured glass, Miss Carmichael, stines the white ridiance of eternitee!"

I said why shouldn't we have a poetry reading evening at the Lump? And was told by the Chicks that the Lump had been taken

74

away from the town by "Lady Millwood" who wastes all the money putting on plays and concerts that aren't worth going to. Well, that's true. They aren't. But it made me feel a little uncomfortable to think I'm taking the town's money and giving so little for it, though the Chicks say they like my lectures. Somehow I'd always thought of myself as employed by Lady F. and if she's satisfied why worry?

I pointed out that the town elects the council, once every five years. Why do they keep on electing Lady F. if they don't want her? But it seems that Mrs. Meeker says she's going to get the Lump back for the town if it's the last thing she does.

Now Mrs. Meeker is Mr. Meeker's daughter-in-law, and she is misnamed Grace, for she is quite the most disagreeable woman I've ever met. She lets me in when I go to read to Mr. M. and sniffs at me as though to suggest she knows I'm up to no good, but never utters, except that once she told me my lectures would be worth listening to if I'd been sent to work in a factory instead of to college. She has hair like an O-Cedar mop and a pale face full of sharp features, and she is on the Town Council and full of good works, and quite sure that everybody else is full of bad works. Having to live with her must be hell. But I believe Mr. M. is quite fond of her, though he laughs at her. He says she's the most innocent creature in the world, and will bark like Cerberus in defence of the People's rights, but any crook can throw her a bone with a nice name like *Justice* or *Democrat*, and she'll be off yapping after it while he gets away with the loot. And that has happened so often she's got sour.

The idea of Grace as my boss gave me quite a turn. So next time I went to Mr. M. I asked him what he thought. Isn't it this town's fault that it's got such a dud Institute? He said yes it is. Will they ever bother to get a different council? He said he didn't suppose so. Very few are even interested enough to grumble. So then I said: Need I worry? Hoping he'd say: Of course not.

But no! He gives me to understand that he'd simply love to have me worry. He sits in his blue spectacles, stroking a cat that's always on his lap, and urges me to worry. I said I've worries enough already. Said he: No. I don't think you've any. That's your trouble.

Which is perfectly true. When nothing matters any more one

75

has no worries. I suppose he thinks if I could get into a flap about anything, even the Lump, it would mean I'd started to think *something* mattered. He's a fly old bird. He doesn't know a thing about me except my voice.

Well, but, I said, wasn't Matt Millwood crazy to wish a thing like this onto the town? He said no. If Matt had lived, he'd have carried it through and got the town interested. He wasn't a starry-eyed dreamer. He didn't put a big theatre and concert hall in a small town without making plans to fill them and attract good artists. He'd have got motor coach lines from Birmingham and Bristol, and a variety of restaurants at different prices, so that people over a wide area could find it easy to run over to Ravonsbridge and dine and do a show, as they do at Stratford. And he'd have known which people in the town to get hold of, to help him, because he was friendly with everybody. He'd have got Chick onto organising poetry discussions. And there's a young Welshman at the Works now, who has an amateur dramatic society which puts on very good shows; Mr. M. is going to take me to see one. He says that's just the sort of man Matt would have roped in.

When he talked like that I did see that a lot could be done. A wonderful job for someone, I said. Whereat the objick was thrown at my head. After an interval of cat stroking he said: Why not for you?

Me? Lucy C.? What could I do?

Anything you like, says Mr. M. You're that sort of person. Matt Millwood was another.

Now Melissa, don't start sending me telegrams to tell me not to. Lady Frances can worry about the Lump. Mrs. Meeker can worry. But if ever you catch me worrying about anything in Ravonsbridge you may put me into a straight waistcoat. My objick is to keep my hair on and not lose any more. I said so and read T. S. Eliot to Mr. Meeker until sniffed off the premises by graceless Grace who wanted to lay the table because Mr. Hayter was expected to supper. He, I may mention, seems to be exempt from her general disapprobation, which shows you what a smooth man he is. I believe he could get onto slap and tickle terms with the Furies.

But I rather wish I had known Matt Millwood.

76

Dec. 24th.

Damnation! I can't go home for Xmas. I have got shingles. What do you know about that? I didn't know anybody my age could have them, but they can for I have, or something of the sort.

It came on at a horrible party they have at the end of term, after a most depressing Nativity play. The Millwoods, the staff, the students, etc., all have to have an *agapemone* in the assembly hall, and sing carols and dance Sir Roger, etc.

I felt so ill I could hardly crawl through it and when I got home I was very rude to Emil who was being spiteful about Thornley's Nativity play. I had a *crise de nerfs* and screamed at him, and we had a most disgusting brawl and next day I was all out in spots. Also a temperature. The doc. prescribed Antiphlogistine, but I felt too ill to put it on and lay in my attic for 3 days wishing for nothing but death. Till "Lo and Beholes," as Annie the Scout used to say, who should appear before me but Lady Frances! She had heard of the shingles and came storming along to reform them, in the good old Ravonsclere way. She declared that my attic was much too cold and uncomfortable and that I wasn't being properly looked after, which I wasn't. Poor Nancy can't look after herself, let alone anybody else.

Within two hours I'd been whisked away to the Women's Hostel, which was nearly empty, owing to vacation, and put in charge of Miss Plummer the matron, who is an excellent nurse, though nosey. She is one of those women who say: "Ah! I understand young things." And hopes for confidences. She says people of my age never get shingles unless they've had a fearful nervous shock, and then she looks at me invitingly. Wouldn't she get a turn if I told her my life story? But I must say this place is like heaven, after Angera Heim; so clean, so warm, and the food so delicious. And here I am, on Xmas Eve, for the whole holidays! It serves me right for having rather dreaded the idea of going home and facing Gorling.

Dec. 31.

A happy New Year, and all that sort of thing.

My Xmas was full of drama but I haven't felt up to writing about it till tonight, while I'm waiting to hear midnight strike.

On Xmas morning the Plum was in my room and we heard a car drive up and she rushed to the window and let out a shriek: MISTER MILLWOOD IN HIS RAVON ROADSTER! Terrific Charles at last! Out she rushed, and out of bed I popped, Antiphlogistine poultices and all, to get a dekko at this fabulous young man. But he'd gone into the house by the time I got to the window, so I admired the Ravon Roadster. In a couple of seconds he emerged. And I'll say, right away, that as far as I could see he does look like the complete answer to the Maiden's Prayer, and I am sorry that we move in such widely different circles.

"E'en in our ashes live their wonted fires."

I'll tell you who he is a little like: that man David produced when Martin couldn't come, when we all went to Stratford on Avon. You remember we both admired him, but you said he had sensual lips, which was rather hard on him, because it turned out a wasp had stung his mouth and the swelling hadn't gone down. We saw him at a concert later on, and he had quite an ascetic mouth really. But we always called him Sensual Lips, because we didn't know, or had forgotten, his name; and for a long time he was our standard of manly beauty. Terrific C. is the same type: tall, dark, patrician. Very like his Ma. You said Sensual Lips was élancé, which impressed me very much and I've always wanted to say it about someone myself, and if it means what I think it means, Charles is too.

A face was goggling at him from every window in the hostel but he never turned a hair and got into his Ravon Roadster and drove off in a very dashing manner. I nipped back to bed. Presently Plum comes in with hothouse grapes and freesias from Cyre Abbey and a kind little note from Lady Frances, wishing me a happy Xmas and saying how sorry she was I couldn't be at home. Cried I: Did Charles bring them? Plum's eyebrows went up at my impudence. She said Mister Millwood has brought them because Lady F. probably didn't care to take her chauffeurs away from their families on Xmas day.

After this excitement I felt suddenly very flop. I suppose it's because I'm not well. I get quite interested and amused and excited for about 5 minutes and then . . . poof! I go flat like a burst balloon, and realise I'm not really interested. I felt more depressed than you can imagine, until a big box of candy arrived, from dear Thornley, and some tulips from the Mildmays, all with such kind messages. And in the afternoon Emil came with a little Christmas tree he and Nancy had decorated.

This is exactly like the Angeras. You can starve in their house. But over an unnecessary and imaginative thing Emil will take endless trouble. He must have spent hours doing this little tree. It was charming. And he led off with a handsome apology for his part of our brawl. He said: I am a fool and ungrateful. Thornley is my best friend here. But I am jealous of him, because he is happy here and contented, and he is doing the best work of which he is capable, and I am not.

While he was there, Ianthe came with a bottle of gin, and she was very nice too; she didn't show off at all. They both laid themselves out to be nice and the Plum came in and we all drank the gin, with some orange juice, so I didn't have too bad an Xmas after all.

I am much better now. Nearly well. It is midnight. The bells have just rung out.

Happy New . . . oh I said that. Oh, Melissa!

2

COUNCIL MEETINGS took place on the first and last Mondays of each term, at two o'clock in the afternoon. Lady Frances came in from Cyre Abbey. Tish Massingham, her eldest married daughter, came from Gloucester. Lady Anne Chadwick, her sister, came from Bath. Meeting in a café on Market Square they would lunch frugally and settle in advance any matters of importance which might come up at the council, upon lines already suggested to Lady Frances during her many confidential discussions with Mr. Hayter.

On the first Monday of the spring term Tish was late, and her mother and aunt, waiting impatiently in Betty's Bun Shop, decided to order their meal without her.

"Don't bother with your spectacles," commanded Lady Frances. "I can tell you what there is. Baked beans or Welsh Rarebit. Which for you? Beans?"

She beckoned to a languid waitress and ordered one beans, one Welsh Rarebit, two rolls and butter, and two coffees.

"I'm sure that child has curvature of the spine," she said, as the girl slouched away. "I wonder . . . oh! There's Tish. Why is she decked out like that?"

Tish had merely put on a hat instead of the dingy head scarf which she generally wore. But she had a coat of black and white check in a loose cut which was unfamiliar to them.

"She's not going to have another baby?" speculated Lady Anne, peering at the approaching Tish through the steamy window.

"Certainly not. I expect it's the fashion."

This was said with considerable scorn, and poor Tish, when she joined them, had to defend herself for her moderate finery. She was going, after the meeting, to a sherry party given by Mrs. Meeker, whose acquaintance she had made at a Gloucester conference on juvenile delinquency. This sounded dreary enough to be permissible, though eyebrows were raised at Mrs. Meeker's name, for she was greatly disliked by all the Millwood faction.

"One must be civil," conceded Lady Frances. "But do listen to our news. Aunt Anne says Mr. Morgan is dying; she's heard he can't last a week. Such a good thing it's the Lent term."

Tish perfectly understood the connection. Mr. Morgan was the Socialist Member for Ravonsbridge, put in by all that rabble across the river. If he were to die there would be a by-election in which family honour required that her brother Charles should stand as the Liberal candidate, since few people could better afford to forfeit the deposit put up for running. All resources must be mobilised in his support, including those of the Institute, which was never very busy in the Lent term.

"No play," remembered Lady Frances, biting into her leathery Welsh Rarebit. "Some of the students might be available. And I must get hold of the younger staff: Mr. Haverstock, Miss Turner and Miss Carmichael."

Nobody asked if her intended recruits were Liberals. She assumed that if they were not they would say so. She respected the consciences of people who disagreed with her, but had no compunction for those who were too timid to speak up.

"How is Miss Carmichael?" asked Lady Anne. "Is she quite recovered from the shingles?"

"Oh, quite. But I must get her away from the Angeras. I must find her something more comfortable."

"You think she's a really nice girl?" persisted Lady Anne.

"Oh, very. So quiet and sensible. A little slow. She takes rather a long time to answer, when you speak to her. Why? Have you heard anything against her?"

Lady Anne had. During the vacation she had learnt of Lucy's story, from a friend in London, and she now told it, with the comment that it might not have been Lucy's fault.

"We-ell," objected Tish, "no sensible girl would try to drag a man to the altar who was so obviously unwilling. Unless of course . . ."

Lady Frances frowned.

"She came here immediately afterwards," she said.

Something in her tone made it clear that Tish had forgotten herself. The suggestion in her *unless of course* could not possibly, in the circumstances, apply to Miss Carmichael, and should never have been made in connection with her. It was typical of a certain vulgarity which Lady Frances occasionally deplored in all her daughters and which puzzled her, for she had given them the same upbringing which she had received herself. They said and thought things of which she would have been incapable. She did not realise that they suffered from social uneasiness, whence most vulgarity springs. She herself never did. All her principles were founded upon an unshaken belief that earls are superior to commoners. This belief her children could not share, though they wished to do so. The spirit of the age had got at them and they could not be perfectly certain that they were better than anybody else. From their uncertainty sprang these lapses.

"It explains her clothes," said Tish. "I always thought her unusually well dressed. Everything new, you know, and everything matching: bags and scarves and shoes. Of course, she's wearing out her trousseau."

"Oh!" cried the other two. "Poor girl!"

This practical detail touched their rudimentary imaginations and forced them to realise a little of what Lucy must have suffered.

"She must have a lot of character and courage," said Lady Anne, "to put it all behind her and come away to work here."

"Yes," agreed Lady Frances. "One respects her for it. And the fewer people who know this story the better; to have it dogging her must be very painful. It must go no further than our three selves. You understand, Tish?"

Tish agreed, rather sulkily.

"It explains a lot of things," went on Lady Frances. "I had wondered why an apparently healthy girl should look so wan and listless, and speak in that tired voice. It had struck me she must have had some great trouble recently. But I must get her away from those sluttish Angeras. That place isn't fit for a pig to live in."

"They can't make ends meet without a paying guest," Tish reminded her.

"Ah. They would take that big house, though I warned them not to. But Mr. Haverstock could go there."

"Poor Mr. Haverstock," expostulated Tish. "Why should he?"

"It would be no hardship to him. I'm sure he never washes. His fingernails are always as black as my shoe. Or that new curate, Mr. Finch, might go there, and Miss Carmichael could have those nice rooms in Sheep Lane, where Mr. Finch lodges now. I'll suggest that to Canon Pillie."

"Does Mr. Finch have black fingernails?"

"No, but he writes plays."

Having come to this conclusion Lady Frances paid their bill, made enquiries about the waitress's spine, was snubbed, and led the way out into the Square.

"Don't turn round, and step out," said Mr. Garstang to Mr. Thornley, as they picked their way up Church Lane. "The Amazon host is behind us."

Both men broke into a brisk pace which was almost a trot. They too were on their way to the council meeting and they did not want to meet the Millwoods sooner than they need.

"And you will back me up, won't you?" panted Thornley.

"Angera ought to be on the council, and now that there's a vacancy we must say so. It's only right for a man of his distinction. And if we don't secure him, who will we get? Somebody with a name who never comes, or a nonentity who never speaks up. Of what earthly use are Coppard and Miss Foss? We want someone who will occasionally stand up to . . ."

He gave a jerk of his head to indicate the ladies behind.

"Spedding comes and speaks."

"Yes. But he's not the type . . . if we wanted a solicitor, why couldn't we have had Corfield? Solid man who does all the solid family business, and his father before him. I can't think how we ever came to elect Spedding. He's a stranger to the town, only been here four years, and takes all the shady cases that Corfield won't handle."

"He was elected down in the Bun Shop."

"I know. Everything is done in the Bun Shop. Look how they wished that washed out young 'un on me last term, when I wanted the job for poor old Minnie Andrews! Not that I've anything against Lucy. But surely I might be allowed to choose my own assistant?"

"Isn't she Haverstock's best girl?"

"No, no. Nothing of the sort. The council meetings are a farce, nowadays."

Garstang laughed. He thought the Institute very small beer and was amused that Mr. Thornley should take it all so seriously. He had himself been on the council for many years. He was an elderly bachelor and an authority on church brasses.

He was still chuckling when they reached the council room where they found Mr. Hayter, Colonel Harding, who was the chairman, Mr. Poole, the secretary, a stenographer to take down the minutes, and Miss Foss, the daughter of old Canon Foss, who had succeeded her father on the council, had attended every meeting for seven years, and had never been heard to say a single word at any of them. But she belonged to the town as completely as did the market clock and was unfailing in her support of Institute activities.

"Coppard coming?" demanded Thornley, as he took a chair at the end of the table.

The question was unnecessary. Coppard, the headmaster of Severnton Grammar School, was never free at two o'clock on a Monday afternoon.

The Millwood women clattered in, removed their galoshes, hung up their mackintoshes, and greeted everyone, including the stenographer, with appropriate graciousness. Lady Frances took a seat beside the chairman and told him to begin. It was two o'clock and they need not, surely, wait for Mr. Spedding.

Hayter, however, was determined to wait for Spedding whose support he needed over the first item on the agenda paper. So he discovered a draught and took such a long time to locate it that another five minutes elapsed before Poole could be told to read the minutes. This he did, very, very slowly, and Garstang, who saw through these manoeuvres, nearly laughed. Poole was an inconspicuous young man, who had been appointed on Hayter's recommendation.

Mr. Spedding arrived just as the minutes were being signed. Hayter deftly dealt with an agenda paper which Colonel Harding was holding upside down. He turned it the right way up, and the Colonel read out:

"Election to the council."

And sneezed. The vacancy had arisen because old Mr. Hutchins had died on New Year's Day and the Colonel still had the cold he caught at the funeral.

"Any suggestions?" he asked, when he had blown his nose.

Spedding immediately spoke up.

"I believe," he said, "that local feeling would be in favour of putting Mrs. Meeker on the council."

"Mrs. Meeker!"

The cry was unanimous. Even Miss Foss contributed a faint squeak.

"I don't propose her," Spedding hastened to add. "I merely thought I ought to mention it. She's a prominent town personality, very active in all sorts of ways, and . . . and popular . . ."

He paused tactfully. Everybody present detested Mrs. Meeker, and he knew it very well.

"Popular in certain quarters," he concluded.

"But impossible on a committee, surely?" exclaimed Mr. Garstang. "If you say it's a fine day she bares her teeth at you and says: I challenge that statement! What do you think, Lady Frances?"

"She'd never do," said Lady Frances. "She would import politics into everything. This Institute is nonpolitical. Let's hear some other suggestions."

Spedding bowed. He had expected nothing else. His task had been to mention the lady's name and to give the council no excuse for ignorance of public opinion. To fellow citizens, who might demand indignantly why Mrs. Meeker was not on the council, he could reply that he had done his best. He was not sticking his neck out.

Thornley was opening his mouth to suggest Angera when Hayter forestalled him with a diffident plea that the staff might be more fully represented. There was some feeling about it. Hints had been dropped. Not, of course, that there was any complaint that Mr. Thornley did not adequately convey the staff point of view. But some of the other directors were sensitive about their prestige.

"I quite agree," said Lady Frances. "I hadn't known there was this feeling, till Mr. Hayter mentioned it. And when we have so very distinguished a man as Dr. Pidgeon on our staff, I certainly think we should ask him to join us."

"Pidgeon!" exclaimed Thornley. "Why, I don't believe he cares twopence about his prestige. And I'm sure he'd never come to meetings. I think we should have Angera."

"So do I," said Garstang.

But the Millwood ladies looked doubtful.

"He's such a silly man," complained Lady Anne.

"He hates the Institute and he hates us," said Tish. "He goes about saying so. He hates England."

"I would prefer Dr. Pidgeon," said Lady Frances, who did not much care for Angera.

But the obstinate Thornley insisted on proposing him, and Garstang seconded the proposal. The four ladies and Spedding opposed it. Hayter abstained. On a further vote Dr. Pidgeon was elected.

"Treasurer's report," wheezed the Chairman.

Mr. Spedding was the Treasurer and his report was not stimulating. The Institute, in spite of its lavish endowments, was losing

85

money. The Christmas Nativity play showed a deficit of £37. 5s. 9d.

Smaller than usual, thought Mr. Garstang, drawing pictures of crabs on his blotting paper. Perhaps, as the collection of props grew larger, poor Thornley did not have to lay out so much on wings and haloes and beards. But if every treasurer's report which Garstang had heard read out in that council room had been super-imposed and photographed, he did not believe it would be blurred, and nobody seemed to be taking it much to heart.

"There aren't enough late buses," said Tish. "People from Gloucester and Severnton can't get back."

"If the town itself would turn up, it would be something," said Mr. Garstang. "But I suppose they can't be bothered to climb the hill. Very natural. They've their own amusements. Their cinemas and radios. Why should they climb this hill on a beastly night to hear an indifferent performance of Beethoven when they can hear a much better one by their own firesides? . . . If they like Beethoven, that's to say."

Spedding caught Hayter's eye.

"There are some things they haven't got, that they would climb the hill for," he suggested. "They've no really good dance hall, and no chance of building one, just at present."

Hayter cleared his throat.

"Should I, do you think?" he suggested to the chairman, "read that letter of Adamson's in this connection? We'd put it in Other Correspondence, but perhaps I'd better read it now."

Colonel Harding had no recollection of the letter but he nodded, and a letter was forthwith read out from a cinema proprie-tor in the new town, with whom Lady Frances had had a brush over the banning of a picture. He wrote to enquire if the great hall at the Institute would be available at any time during the spring for a Bebop Contest, and upon what terms he might hire it.

"What insolence!" exclaimed Lady Frances, adding reproach-fully: "You never told me about this, Mr. Hayter."

Hayter looked modestly down his nose. Some things were told to Lady Frances before the meeting, and some were not. Had she heard of this letter it might not have been read, and he wished it to be read.

86

"Bebop might not be very suitable here," said Spedding. "But the fact remains that the hall and theatre are not often used in the Lent term. If they could occasionally be hired for some form of . . . er . . . popular entertainment it would bring in a nice little sum of money and need not, of course, interfere with the Institute performances, which would always have prior claim."

"But, Mr. Spedding," cried Lady Frances, "you don't understand. This Institute was not built as a profitmaking concern. We are not interested in nice little sums of money. That was not my husband's intention. . . ."

A shadow of grief crossed her face as she thought of poor Matthew dying, holding her hand and whispering of his hopes for the Institute. In a gentler voice than usual she tried to explain those hopes, as far as she had grasped them, to this common little man.

Spedding bowed again. He could have told her that the town had some right to ask why its property was being so inefficiently managed. He could have told her that the terms of the bequest, which he had been at pains to study, allowed a wide interpretation of the uses to which the buildings could be put. But he was not sticking his neck out. If she preferred to run up deficits upon performances which the town did not enjoy, and which were notoriously poor in quality, that was all right by him. It was for the town to decide whether or not she was carrying out the founder's intentions.

Nobody had any further comment to make. Poole was instructed to write a snubbing letter to Adamson in the name of the council. And the chairman went on to the next item:

"A letter from the British Council. . . ."

3

SNOW CAME in from the east, over the Cotswolds, over the Severn valley, silting through the forest ridges of Slane, driving level on a wind so cutting that nobody went out, if they could help it, except the Millwoods, who were herded by Lady Frances to church. They had it all to themselves. Charles was obliged to read both the lessons, which he did with gloomy distinction, and, after the sermon, he had to hand the offertory bag to his mother and his youngest sister, Penelope. There was no hymn. The organist and the choir had blenched at the blizzard. In a shuffling silence Lady Frances pushed a pound note into the bag. Penelope, whose allowance was measured by Ravonsclere austerity, put in half a crown. Charles added his own pound note and then took it up to Mr. Ladislaw, who laid it on the altar. Then, returning to the Millwood pew, he knelt down, was blessed, and repaired to the vestry. It was his duty, as a churchwarden, to count the contents of the bag and to enter in a little book the statement that £2. 2s. 6d. had been received for foreign missions. This task did not take long, but the women did not wait, and when he reached the church porch they had disappeared into a flurry of snowflakes.

"Do you think," murmured the rector, who was peering out behind him, "that anyone from Cyre Abbey will come to Evensong?"

There was a flicker of hope in his voice. If the Millwoods did not come, nobody would; he could rattle through the service, cut the sermon, and return to his warm parsonage. But the worse the weather the more likely it was that Lady Frances would insist upon coming to church. She believed that poor Mr. Ladislaw would be discouraged at having no congregation.

"I don't expect so," said Charles, reassuringly. "We have a lot of people coming this afternoon, all the people from the Institute who are going to canvass for me. They can't go till the six o'clock bus."

The rector looked despondent. He said that no buses were running between Cyre Abbey and Ravonsbridge. The drifts at Slane Bredy had stopped all motor traffic.

"They won't be able to come," he suggested.

But Charles knew better. If his mother had told them to come they would come, though they had to walk the whole six miles. And if there were no buses, he himself would probably be forced to drive them home in the station wagon, since Sunday, like Christ-

88

mas, was a day when the Millwood chauffeurs could not be taken from their families.

"They'll come," he stated. "They'll get here somehow."

"Wonderful enthusiasm," commented the rector.

Charles made a non-committal noise and set off to face the wind. He did not believe that enthusiasm was bringing these wretched people out of Ravonsbridge on their only free day. He felt none himself. He believed Liberalism to be a lost cause. He was only standing because the fatigues of a by-election were less to be dreaded than a disagreement with his mother. He did not expect to poll more than a hundred votes, and, to get as many as that, he would have to make pleasant faces at people, an art to which he did not take naturally. Platform oration troubled him less: nor did he suppose that any other Liberal candidate might hope to do better. If somebody must be obliged to cast the pearls of progressive moderation before this herd of swine, intent upon self destruction and only divided in its choice of precipices, he might as well see to it that a thankless task was performed with ability and distinction. The swine should not say that the Liberals were unable to put up a first class man.

He fought his way across the park to the luncheon table where, over a meal of cold beef and junket, he heard his mother's plans for the campaign. The staff in the kitchen were eating a hot joint; the Cyre Abbey servants always ate better than their masters. Lady Frances thought it only right and proper that they should; people in that class, she would explain to her family, expect a hot meal on Sundays. Had she been the Spartan queen, whom she so much resembled, she would have referred to it contemptuously as "slaves' food." A well bred person, to her way of thinking, eats as little as possible on Sundays in order to allow a day of rest to the Poor.

"Our people," she said, "had better canvass the new town in couples. Mr. Haverstock had better go with Miss Turner. She'll keep him to the point. Otherwise he'll merely sing to them."

"Won't he want to go with Miss Carmichael?" asked Penelope. "Aren't they engaged or something?"

"I don't know what you mean by or something," reproved Lady Frances, with a frown. "It's a vulgar, slipshod phrase and I can't bear it. I've told you not to use it before. No. They are not engaged. We thought they were, when we appointed her, but it turns out not to be so. No . . . poor girl. . . ."

"The one with shingles," remembered Charles.

"Yes . . . poor girl. . . ."

Charles scowled. He hated poor girls with sad stories, and he could detect some calamitous history in his mother's manner; there were far too many of them in her employment, gallantly supporting bedridden parents or bastard babies. And against this one he had an especial grudge; she had caused him to be dragged from his bed and sent into Ravonsbridge at an impossible hour on Christmas morning. He had never seen her, and he never wanted to see her. While his mother told them how well Miss Carmichael seemed to be shaping he wondered why all poor girls should fall into two types: the brave, bright blondes, and the damply despondent brunettes. The brunettes were the more unappetising, the blondes the more fatiguing. Not that he ever saw very much of them, but he was obliged sometimes to offer them bread and butter when they came to Cyre Abbey for patronage and advice at tea time. On the whole, he thought, the brunettes were the worst, and decided that Miss Carmichael must be one of those sallow passionate girls who are deceived by villains and refuse to send their triplets to an adoption society.

"Now dear, if you've finished," said his mother, "I've put a lot of literature I got from headquarters on your desk in the library. You'd better go up and look it over before these people come."

Charles was hustled upstairs and presented with a great deal of very dull material, including a list of jokes, sent in by the local association, which might raise a laugh in a Ravonsbridge audience. His spirits sank as he looked them over. The recommendations sent by headquarters struck him as having been written by half-wits or morons. He could have stated the Liberal case better himself while still in the kindergarten. But he remembered that he must try not to talk above the heads of his audiences. A tendency to do this was, he believed, his chief defect as a public speaker. It was not easy to scramble down to the mental level of the people whom he must convince, and he had found, by experience, that a tacit assumption of equality never flattered them as much as it ought.

After a while he thrust the pamphlets aside and turned to a

more congenial task—an answer to a letter which had been sitting on his desk for several days. He pondered for a while and then began to write rapidly:

Madam,
(*Monument to Dickon Salter*)
I regret that I am unable to offer any support whatever to this project. Nor can I refrain from comment upon certain inaccuracies in the pamphlet which accompanies your letter.

(1) The Ravon has nothing to do with a bird. It is a corruption of the Celtic word *Avon*, or *Afon*, meaning a river.

(2) Dickon Salter was not hanged upon Gibbet Hill in 1357. He was hanged in the courtyard of Severnton Castle, in 1349.

(3) Gibbet Hill was called Carlings Hill until 1735, when it took its present name from a gallows erected there for the execution of Bob Mantrip, a highwayman.

(4) Dickon Salter was not a Ravonsbridge citizen. According to the Cyre Abbey records he came from Norfolk.

(5) There is no evidence whatever that he "led the common people in an age long struggle against privilege." He led a band of robbers which infested Slane Forest for ten years and pillaged the common people on their way to Severnton market. In 1348 he sacked and burnt Slane Bredy, a hamlet which was then entirely populated by swineherds. It was the common people who eventually united to catch him and deliver him to justice.

(6) He could not have been hanged for burning Lord Ravonsclere's haystacks, for there was no Lord Ravonsclere in 1349. The Ravonsclere title dates from 1688. I think that the author of your pamphlet here confuses Dickon Salter with William Salter of Ravonsford, who was convicted of arson, and transported to Botany Bay in 1825. The haystacks in this case belonged to Sir Harry Knevett of Slane St. Mary's.

(7) The reference to "unjust taxes" is obscure. I infer a further confusion with Richard Shotter, a cordwainer, who, in 1602, led the burgesses of Ravonsbridge in a successful demand for exemption from certain tithes. But Shotter was not hanged; he was subsequently elected Mayor of Ravonsbridge three times. There is a monument to him in the Parish Church. He amassed a large fortune but had a reputation for starving his apprentices. . . .

Penelope looked into the library and asked if he had finished, as his canvassers were due by the three-thirty bus.

"There are no buses," he assured her.

"Who says there are no buses?"

"Ladislaw told me so, at church."

"Charles! Why didn't you say so at lunch?"

"It didn't occur to me. Look Penelope . . . do you happen to know who"—he studied the letter he had received—"Grace Meeker may be?"

"Oh, Charles, how can you ask? She's that awful woman who has got onto the Town Council. Why? Has she been writing to you?"

"Yes. She's raising money for a monument to Dickon Salter on Gibbet Hill. She believes that he was hanged there for protesting against unjust taxes laid upon the common people by my ancestors. She assures me that the time has now come when our townsfolk dare to pay tribute to a local martyr. The monument is to have a raven carved on it and a pretty strong reference to servile chains."

"What cheek!" commented Penelope, without much interest.

Charles wished that there could have been someone at Cyre Abbey who might have appreciated the scholarly broadside with which he meant to demolish Mrs. Meeker. Penelope was very stupid. And his mother, though she shared his interest in local history, would have wondered at him for writing such a letter and asked what good it could do. The desire to score, especially off an inferior, was not characteristic of the Ravonscleres. Perhaps it came from the plebeian Millwoods.

Penelope had gone to the window and was looking out.

"Here they are," she said.

He joined her. The snow had ceased to fall, the wind had dropped, and the sky was a little lighter. Up the wide avenue a party of people was trudging towards the house, each figure picked out and isolated against the white vacancy of the unbroken snow, which presented no background to absorb, group or soften them. Animated units, they advanced, with that appearance of drama which so often permeates a snowy scene.

"There must have been a bus," said Charles. "How like a Breughel they look, especially Miss Turner. Who is the girl in the red coat, coming along behind the rest?"

"Oh, that's Ianthe Meadows. And the tall girl with her is Miss Carmichael."

"Ianthe? She's not coming?"

"Oh, yes. Didn't you know? Mamma thought it would be good for her to have something to do."

Charles went back to his desk and sat down.

"In that case," he said, "the whole thing is off."

"What is off?"

"This tea party, as far as I'm concerned. I shall stay up here as long as Ianthe is in the house. Mamma must be mad."

"But Charles—"

"Just because we are all sorry for Canon Pillie, nobody is allowed to say that that girl ought to be shut up. After that Hunt Ball, to which Mamma insisted I should take her—"

"But Charles—"

"I've made up my mind. I'm never going to have her wished onto me again, in any capacity. Mamma knows how she behaved at the Hunt Ball."

"Yes, and for that very reason she thinks it's a good idea to invite Ianthe here; just to pass it over, I mean, as something too childish and silly to notice. She says all Ianthe wants is to attract attention and she'd think she was a heroine if she was banned from Cyre Abbey. It's a much better snub to invite her here with all the Institute people."

Charles saw the point of this and reflected that though the

Ravonscleres did not enjoy snubbing, as he did, they were adepts in the art of it. But then he shook his head.

"Not when I'm in the house," he said obstinately. "I never wish to live through a more ghastly evening than I did at that ball. You'd better go down and tell Mamma I shan't show up at this tea party."

"Charles," said Ianthe, as she stumbed through the drifts beside Lucy, "will probably hide when he knows I'm coming. He doesn't like me very much."

She waited for Lucy to ask why, but Lucy would not oblige her, and merely said that she had never met him, though she had seen him from a window at the Hostel and thought he looked élancé.

"Come again?" exclaimed Ianthe.

"Élancé," repeated Lucy boldly.

"Oh, Lucy! You do use elegant expressions. What a thing it is to be an educated girl! Well, his mother made him take me to a Hunt Ball once, and he was so obviously reluctant that I got fed up and decided to create a little excitement. So I whispered to one or two people that we'd just got engaged. In five minutes it was all over the room. Oh, my dear! The sensation! He couldn't make it out, till someone congratulated him, and I must say he's no gent, for he denied it. I've never had such fun in my life! Poor Charles!"

All this was perfectly true—an unusual state of things where Ianthe was concerned. But Lucy never thought of believing it and said:

"I wonder he's asked you to canvass for him."

"Oh, that's Lady Frances. She thinks it more dignified to ignore my girlish pranks. Besides, some sensible occupation will be so good for me, you know. Look Lucy, let's sit on this log for a minute, and wait till all the others are in the house. Then we can make our entrance."

"Not me," said Lucy, quickening her pace. "You stay behind and make an entrance if you like. I'm not stopping you."

"I'm sick and tired of being all by myself. What I need is a nice friend who'll be a good influence over me. If only you'd be nice to me I should be much more normal."

94

"I am nice, but I'm not going to be dragged into any exhibitionism. If you don't behave yourself this afternoon I'll drop you."

"Oh, I'll behave. I promise! I'll be just like Bess Turner. You wait. Everyone will be perfectly astonished at my good behaviour. . . ."

"Do hurry up. They're all waiting for us at the door. They won't ring the bell till we catch them up."

"Oh, aren't they cows? Aren't they just like a flock of cows at a gate, waiting to be milked? They're simply terrified. They think a butler will open the door and they aren't used to butlers. But Lady Frances will probably open the door, because it's the butler's day out. All the servants at Cyre Abbey sit on their fannies while the Millwoods do the work: it's *noblesse oblige*, you know."

They joined the waiting mob and Rickie timidly rang the bell. After a long pause a cross looking woman in a green overall opened the door and admitted them into a hall littered with dog leads and wellingtons, where they removed outer wraps and snow boots. Then, clustered shyly together, they were ushered into a room full of chintz chairs, where Penelope received them and abruptly commanded them to sit. Her mother, she said, would be down in a moment.

Poor Penelope's natural gaucherie was not lessened by the thought of the scene probably going on upstairs between her mother and Charles. She sat on a low chair, revealing two inches of navy woollen knickers under her short tweed skirt, and tried to entertain them by asking gruff questions of each in turn. Even Rickie was so much subdued that he merely said the choir was rehearsing the St. John Passion Music without trying to hum any of it. Ianthe alone made an attempt to rescue the conversation. She talked easily and pleasantly about their bus ride and the snow drifts. A stranger, hearing her help Penelope out, might have been pardoned for supposing that she was the earl's granddaughter and Penelope the country bumpkin. Occasionally she threw a side glance at Lucy as if to ask if she was not behaving well.

After ten awkward minutes Lady Frances appeared. Her face told Penelope that Charles was obdurate, but its anxiety gave place to disappointment when she counted her visitors. She had expected

95

to see twice that number. Where, she asked, were all the others? Had not a notice been put on the Institute board?

Who was to tell her that her staff was mainly Conservative, while the great majority of the students were Socialists? Nobody liked to do so, except Robin Barlow, one of the dramatic students, who was not, indeed, a Liberal, was without any political convictions, but who hoped for Millwood patronage. He had no objection to letting her know how undeserving some of his fellow students were, but she cut him short with:

"What a pity! Well . . . the chosen few must work all the harder."

Spreading a large map of the town on a table she arranged them in couples and gave to each couple an assignment of streets, for house-to-house canvassing. They were not, she said, to be daunted by a Labour poster in the window. They were to knock on every door and argue on the doorstep as long as they possibly could. If they called between six and seven in the evening they would catch people at supper.

Ianthe suggested that they might canvass the people in the cinema queues. This was the only independent suggestion made by anybody and Lady Frances looked pleased, both by the idea and by such proof for her theory that rational occupation was all that poor Ianthe needed. As time went on proceedings became more and more of a discussion between Lady Frances and Ianthe, in which the girl seemed to be answering for the rest of the party. The surprise which she had prophesied was visible on all sides, for nobody had ever heard her talk so sensibly before, and her appearance at the bus stop had caused a good deal of dismay.

At five o'clock they were led into the dining room for tea and Lucy gleefully observed that there were buns. She would have to make the most of the buns in her account of this trip to Melissa, in order to make up for the disappointment over Terrific Charles, though his absence was so strange and so uncivil that it really made a better story than his presence, however impressive. She could not imagine what had happened to him, for he was apparently in the house, and she nearly made herself giggle once or twice by inventing fantastic explanations for it. But it never occurred to her

96

to believe that he was hiding from Ianthe; to disbelieve Ianthe had become a reflex action.

Before the meal was over, however, he appeared—brought down by a belated reflection that he would be giving Ianthe more consequence by staying away than by coming. But he was in a vile temper and showed it. Lucy, now able to scan him at close quarters, decided that she had never met a less attractive young man.

"He walked here and he walked there," she would quote in her letter to Melissa, "fancying himself so very great. I wish you had been there, my dear, to give him one of your sets down."

For a few minutes she was possessed by an impulse to set him down herself, and had it on the tip of her tongue to ask if he would not say something inspiring, something that might encourage them to go through fire and water for him since, as yet, they had only been through snow. But her anger flickered and failed, as all emotions had a habit of doing nowadays. She sighed and drank her tea and thought that nothing really mattered.

Before they left the table he pulled himself together and muttered a few sentences about gratitude for their help. He spoke a little about the Liberal cause, very mournfully, so that everyone felt all lost save honour; and they sat staring gloomily at their plates until Robin asked him what they were to say about Marshall Aid.

To this subject Charles had given a good deal of thought for he had travelled about Europe, during the past year, and had observed its workings in several countries. He replied with some animation, describing what he had seen, and Lucy was just upon the point of granting him intelligence when Lady Frances interrupted him to make a fuss about their bus. If they were to catch it in the village they ought all to be off.

Robin replied with a suggestion that they should first find out by telephone whether there would be any bus to catch. Rumour had it that the late buses were to be cancelled, owing to the snow drifts, and Robin did not intend to walk home, even in the sacred cause of his own career. His companions thought him very bold: none of them would have dared to use the Cyre Abbey telephone. But they were glad enough when the rumour was confirmed and

Lady Frances announced that they must all be driven home by Charles in the station wagon.

"But if the bus can't get through," said Lucy, as they stood about in the hall waiting for their conveyance, "how can your car go?"

Lady Frances explained that Charles would not take the bus route, through the narrow valley, but go the straight way over Gibbet Hill which would probably be free from drifts. The night was clearing and the clouds had parted when Charles brought the wagon to the door. Down the steps they crunched, slipping in the snow. Ianthe got in first and took the rearmost bench with Robin, where she could continue a decorous flirtation which had sprung up between them during tea. For Robin was taking a day off: as a general rule he was considered to be the property of Wendy Howell, who played all the leads in the drama school productions, but who had refused to come this afternoon on the grounds that she was a Communist. All the others climbed in after them, leaving the front seat, beside Charles, empty: Lucy, however, was detained for a moment in the hall by Lady Frances, who told her that new lodgings had been arranged for her next term, in Sheep Lane.

"But I don't want to leave the Angeras," protested Lucy, "and another landlady might object to my bassoon."

"Mrs. Sparkes won't. She's stone deaf and a very good cook, much too good for Mr. Finch who is there now. You'll have a sitting room and a bedroom. Much more peaceful. Think it over. Goodnight."

Lucy ran down the steps and jumped into the seat beside Charles. The car set off cautiously along the avenue. She was so much engrossed by this suggestion of new lodgings that she scarcely noticed the honour of her position. The rooms in Sheep Lane certainly sounded very nice: but she did not like being ordered about in this way. Yet it would be foolish to refuse a good arrangement merely because Lady Frances was peremptory; and Emil had been going through a lupine phase just lately, catching hold of her and kissing her, not behind Nancy's back, but in a jocular manner before Nancy's face, which was unfair and difficult to repel. But what would poor Nancy do without her?

She sat revolving all these questions while Charles pushed

warily through the drifts. Conversations and smothered giggles sprang up on the benches behind them. . . .

They nosed through the avenue gates into the silent village street where all the roofs were white, and light from an open door threw an orange patch on the snow. Then they took the long, lifting road up the hill. The valley and the shadowy woods and the white roofs fell away. Slane Forest, chequered in black and white, came into view under a fitful gleam of moonlight, the bare ridges rising like blanched ghosts of familiar hills, very beautiful and strange.

All white under the moon, thought Lucy—all England under the snow, which has fallen so silently everywhere, making all places look alike, and all the places where I have been, on Oxford and Ravonsbridge and Gorling and London, and where I am now and where he is now, living his life at every moment away from me, for ever away from me, and with no thought of me. . . .

She shivered a little and Charles asked if she was cold. She assured him that she was quite warm and asked hastily if this was Gibbet Hill where Bob Mantrip, the highwayman was hanged. Charles said that it was and commended her for not confusing him with Dickon Salter, as some people did.

"Oh, that mangy Robin Hood!" exclaimed Lucy. "But he was in 1350! I was thinking of him, coming through Slane Bredy in the bus."

"What a lot of local history you know!"

"Old Mr. Meeker tells me. He knows a lot of local things."

"Meeker?"

"He's the father-in-law of Mrs. Meeker, who is on the Town Council. He's blind, and lives with them."

"It's a pity he doesn't teach local history to his daughter-in-law."

"Oh, you mean the monument? He does, but she never listens. Have you seen Mr. Finch's pamphlet?"

"Oh, Finch wrote it, did he? You mean Canon Pillie's curate?"

"Yes. And he's written a play about Dickon Salter. He sent it to Mr. Thornley and wanted the Institute to put it on, but it was really too silly. Mr. Meeker says he's mixed Dickon Salter up with at least three other people."

Charles decided not to post that letter. He had supposed himself to be the only person in Ravonsbridge well informed enough to have written it. And he asked for more about Mr. Meeker.

"He went to school with your father," said Lucy. "I think they were great friends when they were boys. Did your father never mention him?"

Charles reflected and remembered that his father had sometimes spoken affectionately of "Harry Meeker" when recalling old times.

"Blind?" he said, thoughtfully.

"Yes," said Lucy. "He was a schoolmaster, away in the north, till he went blind. Now . . . Oh, I suppose they look after him all right, but he's very lonely. He has nobody to talk to. He loves talking about your father. He'll want to know everything about my visit to Cyre Abbey today. I've promised to go in tomorrow and tell him about it."

And what will she tell him about me? wondered Charles. That I made a surly exhibition of myself.

For he knew that he had behaved badly all the afternoon. He said quickly:

"I'd like to go and see him, as soon as this election business is over. I didn't know he'd come back to Ravonsbridge."

"Oh, if you would!" cried Lucy turning to him. "He'd be over the moon. You can't think how pleased he'd be."

She beamed at Charles, almost ready to forgive him for his bad manners, in her pleasure at the proposed treat for Mr. Meeker.

A nice girl, decided Charles. Not a damp brunette. Not even a bright blonde. A cut above most of the poor girls with sad stories. But not exciting.

They slithered downhill and crunched into Ravonsbridge market square, where the snow was all furrowed into blackened ruts. Charles drew up and everybody got out, thanking him and calling out farewells to one another and dispersing to their scattered homes. Lucy, Ianthe and Robin clustered together for a moment, talking in low voices. Then they came back to the car, just as Charles was starting up.

"We're all going into the Swan for a bracer," said Lucy. "Do come with us and have a drink before your drive back."

He hesitated, and then got out, hardly knowing why he did so except that he wanted to give her something pleasant to tell old Harry Meeker, who would be glad to hear that Matt's son put on no airs, and took bracers when invited. He was really anxious to modify the impression of insolence which he knew he must have given, and to make amends to this nice, dull girl for having, in imagination, saddled her with triplets.

Ianthe led the way across the Square into the Swan, which was full of Sunday night conviviality. Room was respectfully made for them when Charles was seen, and many heads were furtively turned to stare at the four handsome young people, as they sat at a low table with a rum apiece. Robin hastily paid for all the drinks, knowing that the girls would later re-imburse him for their share; money was short among the students and Dutch treat was the rule at such parties. But they did not want Charles to pay; he was their guest.

Lucy and Ianthe made a striking couple. By Ravonsbridge standards they were very well dressed and their poise was remarkable. Robin was, in this company, on his best behaviour. The rum warmed them. Conversation became unexpectedly easy.

Quite like old times, thought Lucy. She had not been to a party at the Swan before. But a year ago, less than a year ago, she had often sat with Melissa, smiling at agreeable young men, secure and gay, aware of being looked at with admiration and interest. Two pretty girls and their escorts! Two pretty girls who never knew, never knew that time rushes on to the spring, to the summer, to the end of everything. And then, after the end of everything, time went on until now . . . here were two pretty girls and their escorts.

But Ianthe is not Melissa, she thought, and I don't really like her much, and we would never have dreamed of going out with a boy like Robin, nor would we have had much to say to Charles Cross Mouth. And my heart is aching all the time. All the time. But, even after the end of everything, one goes on doing the same things, in a kind of parody, because there is nothing else to do.

She laughed a little too loudly at some joke of Robin's, for the rum was taking effect. Charles, she could perceive, thought them all very provincial. His real friends, she supposed, must be among those people whose pictures she saw in the *Tatler*, in that world to which the Hallams did not quite belong but into which Melissa might possibly marry. I suppose he's only happy among the Nobs, she thought.

In this she was mistaken. Charles despised the provinces but he was not really happy among the Nobs. The Ravonscleres were, in their superb way, as provincial as the Millwoods. They devoted themselves to Severnshire, ignored the *Tatler*, and thought many of the Nobs rather vulgar. On both sides of the family there was a vein of idealism which Charles had inherited in a degree just sufficient to make him discontented in any kind of society.

He glanced at his watch and said that he must go. Lucy smiled at him over her glass and thought that nothing really mattered.

4

ON THE Saturday before the election Lucy and Ianthe bicycled over to Slane St. Mary's, an outlying forest hamlet which had not been canvassed, and which burdened the conscience of the local organisation.

The day was mild and balmy. Spring had come with a rush on the heels of the thaw. Though patches of snow still lay on shadowy corners of northward slopes, the crocuses were out in the cottage gardens. The tapestry of forest trees had lost its uniform brown; beech, oak, chestnut, ash, elm and larch—each had now a particular tint as the sap rose and the buds began to swell.

Slane St. Mary's was difficult to locate. They rode all over the forest, trudging up steep hills and skimming down narrow lanes to hidden valleys. In the end they found it by accident; they saw a cluster of thatched roofs in a hollow below and went down to ask the way.

"This is it!" called Lucy, who was talking to a woman by a garden gate.

It was a strangely quiet place. Thin threads of smoke rose straight into the air from the chimneys above the thatch. A cock crowed from time to time. All the men of the place were out at work, but the women listened civilly, so civilly that they might never have heard of the changed world beyond the forest ridges. They called the young ladies "ma'am" and thanked them for the pamphlets. One old crone even dropped a curtsey. But there was no way of knowing how they would vote.

"No bus comes nearer than Slane Bredy," said Ianthe, as they wheeled their bicycles along the rutted lane. "I believe they'll vote for anyone who sends a car to take them to the poll. How on earth do they do their shopping? Hullo? Is this where wold Squoire lives?"

They had come to two rusty gates, half off their hinges, and were looking down a drive at a mouldering Elizabethan house.

"Yes," said Lucy. "Mr. Meeker was talking about it. It used to belong to the Knevetts, but they've taken the roof off, to save taxes, and all gone away."

They pushed a gate open and went down the weedy drive to get a closer look at it. Once it must have been lovely but, in its decay and neglect, it was not pleasant to see, and not sufficiently ruined to be romantic. The windows were dirty and broken, and an old bathtub was propped up against the porch. Both the girls felt cold, as they surveyed it, though they stood in sunshine. Something of its desolation affected them. Lucy felt sadder and Ianthe madder than they had felt a few minutes before.

"Once," said Lucy, "they enclosed the people's grazing land and the people were angry, and some ricks were burnt, and some men were sent to Botany Bay. When the Knevetts rode through the village the people used to shake their fists and mutter curses. And now . . ."

The distant cock crew, faint and shrill, triumphant in the quiet morning. He was echoed by Ianthe, who crooned in a soft, high chant:

"They've all gone away! All gone away! The roof's falling in and they've all gone awa-a-ay!"

In the silence, a loud noise came from the degraded house. Ianthe screamed and clutched Lucy.

"Oh . . . oh! There's a ghost inside. It heard me. It'll come out!"

"Don't be silly. It's only some plaster falling."

"No, no, they haven't all gone away. They're inside still. I'm frightened."

"I don't wonder. You frightened me. How did you manage to make your voice sound so horrible?"

"I'm very good in mad parts," said Ianthe complacently. "Let's go round and see what it's like at the back."

"I'm not sure I want to. I think we'd better get away."

"Now it's you that's silly."

Ianthe propped her bicycle against a wall and set off round the house, followed by the reluctant Lucy. For there was really something malign about the place, a chill which could not be shaken off, an expectant silence, as if invisible people were awaiting some inevitable catastrophe. Lucy remembered afterwards that she had known something bad would happen if they stayed there.

Yet at the back it was attractive. They found a mossy terrace, looking onto the remains of a garden with shapeless overgrown yew hedges. It was out of the wind and the sunshine was almost hot. Repelled, yet fascinated, they sat on a low stone balustrade and ate the sandwiches they had brought with them.

As they ate they amused themselves by imagining the Knevett family, inventing names and characters for them through the long centuries. A curious sharpening of perception, in both of them, made these pictures very real, so that they almost believed in their fantasy, and more than once they threw half scared glances over their shoulders at the house behind. Very rustic and boorish these Knevetts must have been, they decided, shut away behind the forest ridges, secluded even from the urban amenities of Ravonsbridge. Ignorant, arrogant—lagging always behind the manners and morals of the age, they had ruled the little hamlet in the hollow with an absolute power against which there could have been little appeal.

The wicked lord! thought Lucy, when Ianthe wandered off to explore the garden. Lord Ravonsclere did not hang Dickon Salter. But Sir Harry Knevett did send another Salter to Botany Bay. The wicked lord is a folk character and his name is of no consequence. He was real once, and he is remembered, and curses come home to roost.

The thought of all this unexpiated evil oppressed her. She

could not detach herself from it or shake off the creeping melancholy which had weighed her down ever since she pushed the
gate open. Miserable as she had often been during the past months,
she could not remember any moment when her courage had sunk
lower. At the side of the terrace an almond tree was in blossom,
lovely against the dark yew. Soon it would be spring. The leaves,
the flowers, would come out, while she stayed where she was. It
had been natural that the leaves should fall, those leaves which had
seen the time of her happiness; winter had but reflected the desolation in her heart. But it was strange, strange and cruel, that this
other spring should come, in which she had no part. She had again
the feeling, first encountered when she had plodded over Campden
Hill, of isolation and rejection.

If only it had been for a woman he loved, she thought sadly.
For she had often felt that her sorrow would have been easier to
bear if that were so, and if she had been able to think of Jane Lucas
as another woman. But she could never picture her rival at all, save
as a black mist which had enveloped Patrick and snatched him
away—an abyss which had swallowed him up. He had told her very
little about his former infatuation, but he had spoken of it with
bitterness and disgust, as an association in which love, as Lucy
understood love, had played no part. Jane Lucas was a vice which
he thought to have shaken off and which had reclaimed him; she
was as impersonal as a brandy bottle or a hypodermic syringe. Lucy
could not imagine her; but the idea of his degradation struck her
forcibly in this rotting place, so haunted by black thoughts.

A step on the terrace roused her. An extraordinary creature
had emerged from among the yew hedges, a lunatic with wild black
hair in which a few celandines were tangled. It swept up the terrace in a frenzy of anxiety, exclaiming:

"Where is the beauteous majesty of Denmark?"

Ianthe's talent was phenomenal. She peopled the terrace with
a king, a queen, a whole court, as she drifted from one to another,
begging for counsel, dropping hints, swerving aside, nodding mysteriously. The horror which had crazed her was plain, her inability
to tell it was piteous. Every word, every snatch of droning song,
had, for her, some other import; she believed that she was telling
the secret, though sometimes, assailed by confusion and doubt,

she would pause, shake her head, and craftily bid them mark what she would say next. Not a word, not a gesture failed in effect, until she called imperiously for her coach, sank in curtseys to the sweet ladies, and swept from the terrace.

A moment later she appeared again, pulling the celandines from her hair.

"Well?" she asked.

"Ianthe! It was . . . it was tremendous. I've never seen anything like it before."

"I bet you haven't."

Ianthe sat down on the wall and began to eat a celandine. She was always eating things; anything she picked up she would nibble and chew.

"The singing was so frightening," said Lucy. "How did you manage to get it just that much out of tune? It's generally so bad; the Valentine song is such a jaunty little tune and they plod through all the verses, looking so embarrassed. Can you do the next bit?"

"No. I'm not sure of the lines."

"How would you do: Rosemary, that's for remembrance?"

"Oh . . . terrified. I wouldn't linger wistfully . . . the way they do. She didn't want to remember. She went mad so as to forget. I should fling the thing away as if I'd picked up a snake."

"That's what I think. But she's supposed to give it to Laertes."

"And why pray? Why should she always have to deal those flowers round as if it were a hand at bridge? I shouldn't."

Lucy pondered and then said:

"I can't imagine why you don't go on the stage."

"I can only act mad parts."

"Oh, nonsense. If you worked hard, there are heaps of parts you could act."

"I'd hate to work hard."

"They'd have to be a bit morbid, of course. But I can't wait to see you do them. Why don't you go into the drama school?"

"What? With the Frog? Not for Joseph!"

"But we're putting on *Hamlet* in the autumn. I can't bear to think of that little pink pig of a Wendy playing Ophelia when you're in Ravonsbridge."

"Honey pie! Would H.E. or the Frog ever let me play it?"

"You can't have a gift like this and just do nothing with it."

"Too much trouble," said Ianthe, chewing a piece of moss. "I act when I feel like it. To go on, night after night, when I don't feel like it . . . no, thank you!"

"Oh," cried Lucy. "Then I despise you. I really despise you. When I think. . . . Oh, I'd give anything to have such a talent."

She had often wished that she had some marked gift, or some vocation, to which she might devote her life. It would have helped her through these months. But she had none.

Ianthe scowled. She wished to be admired, not scolded. Her performance had excited her; the strangeness of the afternoon had roused a devil in her which was inseparable from her genius.

Hitherto she had failed to impress Lucy, and knew it, and accepted the fact. Their relationship had been the sanest, the most friendly, affair of the sort that Ianthe had ever known. Never before had she become so intimate with anyone without deceiving them; she had told a few romantic tales to Lucy, had been openly disbelieved and laughed at, and had agreed to laugh at herself. She knew that their friendship depended on the maintenance of this integrity, and that she herself had never been happier than she was now. But some devil goaded her to experiment; to find out how much she could make Lucy believe if she really tried.

"If you knew everything about me," she retorted sullenly, "you wouldn't be surprised at anything I do. I . . . I had a fearful shock once . . . I don't believe I shall ever get over it."

"Saw something nasty in the woodshed?" asked Lucy unkindly.

Ianthe's fearful shock was usually on those lines, though she never told exactly the same story twice. But in view of Lucy's callous incredulity she decided that perhaps she had better not have been raped at a tender age. She would think of something perfectly new. A striking episode popped into her mind, of which she had never yet made use, though she had always meant to do so. Sometime last year she had seen a picture in a newspaper of a girl, a bride, sitting alone in a car. People crowded round and peered at her. The bridegroom had not turned up. She had forgotten, perhaps had never troubled to learn, names and details, but she had immediately pictured this girl as herself.

She hesitated for a moment, but only because she would have liked to think it out a little more. Then she said:

"No. It happened three years ago, in Yorkshire. Nobody in Ravonsbridge knows, except my family of course. You must please not tell anybody. . . ."

In a low and trembling voice she began her story.

Lucy at first sat rigid. She thought that Ianthe knew the truth and was laughing at her. But a wild burst of sobbing bewildered her. It seemed so real. In spite of the acting which she had just witnessed on the terrace, it convinced her.

"But . . . why didn't he come?" she asked in a low voice.

Ianthe had not made up her mind about this, so she did not answer.

"Was it . . . another woman?"

"Oh, no . . ." gasped Ianthe, making up her mind. "No. Not as bad as that. He was dead. Killed in an accident. . . ."

Not as bad as that! thought Lucy, staring at her. Why . . . she couldn't have loved him, then!

"How soon did you know?" she asked.

"They came and told me . . . in the church. I went out and got into the car. It was waiting outside. All the people kept staring at me through the window."

But if she's lying, thought Lucy, how does she know what it's like? Oh, this is a nightmare!

"Where did you wait then?"

"Wait?"

"In the church . . . before they told you?"

"Oh, at the Chancel steps."

"They let you get up there! When he hadn't come! Who was there? Was it a big wedding?"

"Oh, yes. Crowds."

"Bridesmaids, I mean, and all that?"

"Oh, yes . . . I had four bridesmaids."

"What did they do?"

"I don't know."

"But didn't anybody do anything? I can't picture it at all."

"I didn't notice," said Ianthe, who found this catechism rather chilling. "When a frightful thing like that happens, you don't notice details. You don't notice other people."

"Don't you?"

"I expect they were rushing about and making a fuss," conceded Ianthe, realising that this was probable.

"I expect they were."

"I fainted. I remember the clergyman catching me as I went down."

"You seem to have managed it all very gracefully."

Lucy's dry voice told Ianthe that her story had failed. It was disbelieved. She looked up, ready to admit that she had been lying, and to laugh it off. Confess I had you fooled for quite a long time, she would say.

But Lucy's face, blanched, almost withered, with disgust, silenced her. She realised that she had made some dire and irretrievable mistake and that their friendship, such as it was, had come to grief. There would be no more laughter.

Lucy felt quite sick and bewildered. She was sure now that Ianthe knew nothing and had intended no malice. It was pure chance which had played this grotesque trick on them. Or perhaps it was not fortuitous; reflecting on the episode afterwards, she came to believe that her own name, seen for a moment and forgotten, had subconsciously influenced Ianthe and caused her to select this story rather than another.

But the sense of outrage was the same, however it had happened. She had thought that she knew all that she must endure. She had struggled with loneliness, with humiliation, with anguished memories, with spasms of wild longing to see Patrick, just once; she had plodded through the dreary days and faced the nights when Melissa's eyes, floating on the darkness, came to murder sleep. She had got used to it. She had learnt to bear it. But for this ludicrous parody of her own suffering, this exploitation of truth, she had not been prepared.

Unconsciously, she had always clung to dignity as her sole possession. She had asked for no pity, made no lamentation, and had endured each moment as it came, waiting patiently for release, because she believed that in all circumstances there must be some right way in which to think and act, which can lift them into a kind of beauty. But now it was as if the value of feeling itself had been cheapened; as if this tainted creature had made her own experience false, so that she could never again be free from Ianthe's grimaces. *Melissa's eyes,* she thought, snatching at truth, intolerable, healing truth. But she could not see them any more.

She sat on the parapet, stiff, white and bitter, looking, so Ianthe thought, as if she belonged to this ruined house. *As I shall sit,* mused Ianthe, *when I act my next mad part. I'll freeze everybody to stone, if I can manage to look as she does!*

After a while they rose and went in search of their bicycles. Lucy looked back at the house as they pushed the gate open again. She had a sudden vision of its daimon; a little, old, cold, sly thing with no nose, utterly stupid and immensely powerful. They had lingered near it too long and it had put a spell on them.

They rode back to Ravonsbridge and parted with scarcely a word, each considerably the worse off for that afternoon's work. Lucy banged into the Angera kitchen and tried to make herself a cup of tea. With the clumsiness of misery she managed to scald her hand. Her agonised yelp brought in Angera who was unexpectedly kind and clever. He bandaged her hand, gave her brandy, and made her lie down in the sitting room while he brought in tea. He was in a very good humour that afternoon.

"Poor Lucy," he kept saying, as he ministered to her. "Poor little Lucy!"

"Not so little," she said, when she had drunk the tea and felt better. "That's the trouble. Poor women shouldn't be tall."

"That is true. Pathos is for little tiny women. How is your hand now?"

"Throbbing a bit, but better. Where's Nancy?"

"She has gone out with the child."

He sat on the sofa beside her and explained his good mood.

"Imagine! Today I have sold a picture. A party came to see the school and they have bought a picture."

"Which one?"

"Of bomb damage in Severnton."

Angera was fond of painting bomb damage.

"What will you do with the money?" asked Lucy, trying to show interest and pleasure.

"I shall give it all to Nancy. It's she who needs money, not I."

He put an arm round Lucy's waist.

"At Easter," he continued, "I shall take her to Leamington Spa."

Who cares? thought Lucy drearily.

"Why Leamington Spa?" she asked.

"She is always vishing to go. She says it is beautiful."

"She should know," said Lucy drowsily. "It looks dull from the train."

Angera might be as bald as an egg, but his caresses were expert. She submitted to them and wondered if she liked them.

"I shall take her," he said grandly, "to an expensive hotel in Leamington Spa."

Lucy suddenly pushed him away and got up.

"You're quite good at it," she said, "but it's no use. I don't like it."

"You think I try to seduce you?" he asked derisively.

"No. I know it's only slap and tickle. I don't think you'd ever be really untrue to Nancy. I think you love her."

"I also think so. But what then is the harm of slap and . . . and . . . what did you call it?"

"Slap and tickle. No harm in the world, I suppose. But it doesn't do me any good. If it did, I'd thank you for it. If getting drunk could do any good I'd go out and get pickled." Lucy's voice rose and shook. "But nothing . . . nothing . . . nothing. . . ."

"Ach, poor Lucy!"

Angera jumped up, his eyes bright and compassionate.

"You are very bad tonight?" he observed.

"Yes."

He was, she knew, curious about her past and had often asked impertinent questions. But he did not do so now. He balanced on the edge of a table, staring at her with unusual friendliness.

"Nothing," he suggested, "is lasting for ever."

"I suppose not."

"Listen, Lucy. I have something to tell you. You won't listen because I behave always so stupidly. You think I don't have any sensible ideas. But I have been in moments as bad as yours, if you can believe that."

"Yes, Emil, I can believe that. Worse, I should think."

"And I have seen how one must bear them, though myself, I'm not doing it, because I'm a fool."

He paused, trying to arrange his words.

"One must think: life is like a river and it is taking me places. All the time. Every day. Always somesing new, some new place, and each day I say: what is this place I've come to? And sometimes it's very bad. Other times not so bad. And next day I say: Goodbye bad place! Goodbye sweet place. My life is taking me on. So! We can't stay in the good places. We need not stay in the bad places. We must go on and always make ourselves interested, and we must not fight this river. For life . . . life . . ." said Emil, his dark eyes blazing, "that is everything. The river that carries us."

"Old Man River," said Lucy.

"How? I said nothing of an old man!"

"I know. I think I see what you mean, Emil. You mean we mustn't think any place, good or bad, is the last place?"

"That is what I mean. If we think that, the river doesn't go any more."

"I see. Well, thanks. I believe I'll go to bed, now."

She climbed upstairs to her room and knelt for a long time at her open window, looking at a young crescent moon which had risen over the long humped hills of the forest.

Emil's kindness had calmed her. He was not often kind, but when he did feel sympathy he accepted and expressed it as easily as he did the impulse for a bout of slap and tickle. He did not feel himself to be divided from the object of his compassion by some superior immunity.

His philosophy of Old Man River did not impress her, but it could not be written off as nonsense, for it had apparently brought him through wreck and disaster, through the stagnation of internment, in fairly good shape. He was a good artist and an inspired teacher, he did his share of work in the world, and his recurrent silliness was not, probably, a product of his misfortunes; he had been born with it.

Mr. Meeker, she remembered, also had an Old Man River. He

had said that every experience of any value can be translated into the language of a religious experience. This phrase conveyed nothing to her, but it must mean a lot to Mr. Meeker, who was blind, lonely and dependent, yet managed to be cheerful.

Life, mused Lucy, is not a river. It's a race course, where everybody rides his own little bit of nonsense. If you can't find a bit of nonsense of your own, to take you over your fences, you're done. You can't offer yours to anybody else, and theirs are no good to you.

I can't find a mount. I had one. I thought it was noble to be brave. But that wasn't a stayer. Nothing is noble. I'm done.

At last she went to bed and fell asleep at once, without having to dodge *those* eyes, which generally popped up when she began to grow drowsy. They were, as she discovered later, gone for good. The physical reverberations of shock ended at a moment when she believed herself to be defeated. In time she came to look back upon that day at Slane St. Mary's as a turning point. In twenty-four hours she had grown much tougher, and very far removed from the vulnerable creature who had come to Ravonsbridge in the autumn.

5

Rickie pushed the hair out of his eyes, raised his baton, and hummed a line of recitative:

"*And all the more they cried out saying:*"

"CRUCIFY HIM!" yelled the Ravonsbridge choir.

Lucy, who did duty as a soprano when she was not playing her bassoon, thought that she must have injured her larynx, but Rickie was not satisfied. He rapped on his music stand and stopped them.

"No, no—that won't do. You're a mob, remember, out for blood. I want more of a howl. Now again . . . *They cried out saying:*"

Nobody howled. The choir was gaping at Robin, who had put his head in at the door and was making faces.

"Results?" cried somebody. "Not out already?"

"No," said Robin. "Only grapevine telegraph. We're getting a good many votes. That's what they're saying, down in the market place."

He vanished.

"I say," spluttered Rickie, "I say! How marvellous! Well, let's get back to it."

But his choir was by now out of hand. Everybody wished to be in the market place. Only Rickie would have tried to hold a practise on election night. All over the room people were jumping up, stampeding for the door. The quadrangle was full of groups making for Church Lane, the lights, the hubbub of Market Square.

"But the results won't be out for hours," cried Rickie piteously. "You can't want just to go and stand—"

"Yes, we do," said Lucy, seizing his arm. "Come along!"

He capitulated and came along. In Church Lane they met more news.

"They're saying Millwood will get in."

"Oh, no," cried Millwood's supporters in unison. "That can't be true."

"How could they possibly know, anyway?" asked Lucy. "They've only just begun the count."

"Everyone in the Square is saying it. A lot of people said they'd voted Liberal when they came from polling."

The Square was packed with faces all staring hopefully up at the town hall where the count was going on. Every window was lighted and open. People leant down and called to friends below. The Swan was a furnace of noise, sucking people in continually and pouring them out. Singing burst out and died down. Sometimes two or three songs were going on at once.

The Institute party, arms linked, pushed their way into the throng. Voices all round told them that Millwood was going to get in, but only Rickie believed it, because Rickie would believe anything.

> "As long as England means ter you
> What England means ter me . . ."

"There's Mr. Hayter. He always knows everything. Ask him! Hi! Mr. Hayter!"

> "The people's flag is coloured red,
> It sheltered oft our martyred dead . . ."

"Who's going to get in, Mr. Hayter?"

"Hallo, Haverstock! Hallo, Miss Carmichael! Why . . . your guess is as good as mine."

"Oh, no. You know everything. What's your guess?"

"I guess that Pugh will get in and the Tories will be very angry with you-all."

"Us Liberals?"

"I shouldn't be surprised if you-all turn out to have done a very nice bit of work."

Hayter sketched a mock salute and vanished into the crowd.

"He means," deduced Bess, "that we've got more votes than anybody expected."

"And the Tories will think they'd have got them if it hadn't been for us," said Lucy.

"Ianthe got them," said Robin, close behind her. "Where is she? Lucy! Where's Ianthe?"

"I don't know."

"I thought you two were inseparables."

"No-no. . . ."

"Look! There's Mr. Finch waving a red flag."

"I didn't know he was a Communist."

"He's not really. He's just silly."

"Where's the difference?"

A violent pushing and swaying nearly carried them off their feet. The crowd was trying to make room for a car which crawled towards the town hall.

"Take care! Take care! . . . What is it? . . . It's a car. . . . Who is it. . . . Who . . . Lady Frances! Lady Frances! Millwood! Millwood! Boo! Boo! Hurrah! Yah! Hurrah! Millwood."

The Liberals yelled themselves hoarse as Lady Frances stumped up the town hall steps. She was not an interfering old woman just then. She was a heroine—their candidate's mother, a leading figure in the drama. They felt utterly loyal to her.

115

"How proud she must be!" cried Bess sentimentally.

"What of?" asked Lucy.

"*Him!*"

"We don't know yet, do we?"

"How much longer will it be?"

"Hours and hours."

"Oh, my pore feet!"

"Oh, look at Mrs. Meeker! Look at her hat!"

"Where?"

"In that window ossipite."

"Window what?"

"Opposite, Rickie. The girl is trying to be funny."

Darling Bess, thought Lucy, darling Rickie! How fond I am of them and what fun this is! Oh, I haven't had such fun for ages!

A rocket went up from Institute Hill and broke into a shower of stars. All faces turned up.

"Oh, Lucy! Don't you wish Melissa was here?"

"No. Not particularly. Why?"

"She'd enjoy it so much."

"Would she? She hates crowds."

"Look, Lucy! There's Ianthe, upstairs at the Swan. She's waving to us."

"Who's she with? Who's the man with her?"

"Mr. Angera."

Lucy turned and caught a glimpse of Ianthe and Emil leaning out of an upper window at the Swan. She was surprised at such a juxtaposition, and a swift alarm darted through her mind, as though she had seen a lighted cigarette smouldering on a petrol drum. I hope Emil has the sense to keep off slap and tickle, she thought. She remembered that they had both behaved very prettily when they met at her bedside on Christmas Day; but that, even at the time, she had felt to be a lucky accident. They had been in their best moods and she had been there to restrain Ianthe. For the first time since the breach at Slane St. Mary's it struck her that, since nobody else in Ravonsbridge could force Ianthe to behave, there might be some obligation . . . but no! She was not Ianthe's keeper.

"Oh, Lucy! Didn't you say you'd had a letter from Melissa?"

"Yes. But all about Hump."

"Who's Hump?"

"Why, Rickie! Her brother!"

"I didn't know she had a brother."

"Rickie! How can you! She's always talking about him."

"Not to me. What are you laughing at, you girls?"

"Oh, Rickie!" giggled Bess. "You are priceless!"

"He's a vet in Africa, Hump is."

"So what?"

"So he's looking for a fly!"

"Just one fly? Just one little fly in the whole of Africa?"

Lucy's answer was drowned in a roar, for the Returning Officer had appeared on the balcony to announce the results.

Pugh was in by a greatly reduced majority. The Conservatives were disappointed and the Socialists not nearly so triumphant as they said they were. Both were furious with the Liberals, who went to bed that night with feelings of unmixed satisfaction, for they had never expected to get their man in.

The Institute party went back to Rickie's rooms where they drank beer, sang silly songs, and acted charades until two o'clock. Lucy's vivacity surprised them all, and Robin asked Bess what could have happened to her.

"She's just the same as usual," said Bess in surprise.

"No, she's not. We always thought she was one of the quiet ones."

"Oh, rot! She's always ragging."

"We've never seen her ragging before."

"Oh, well, I suppose the election bucked her up."

"Let's hope it lasts," said Robin, half determined to date Lucy sometime.

But next morning she had regained her customary pale composure and rated him so sharply for cutting a class that he changed his mind.

I<small>F</small> <small>ONLY</small> he had his father's voice, thought Mr. Meeker sadly.

He had already listened to Charles on the platform, for, though he had voted Socialist, he had gone to the Liberal meetings in order to hear his old friend's son speak. And he had been disappointed. The young man spoke well enough; he made good points and he made them with clarity and common sense. But his voice conveyed no warmth, no friendliness. It was, so Mr. Meeker was obliged to decide, a conceited voice—the tone of a man who is anxious to make himself understood by his inferiors. Many times, in the course of his life, had Mr. Meeker heard a good cause ruined by that sort of voice.

If Matt Millwood had addressed his fellow men in such accents he would probably have sold kettles in Market Square all his life, until put out of business by a competitor who could sell a kettle more genially. Marsden, with his little factory, would never have taken a chance on a young fellow whose every word suggested patronage. Matt's voice had not been very loud, yet it had always secured attention. His Severnshire accent, which he never lost, had been an advantage. Midland business men, investing capital in the first M.M. company, felt him to be one of themselves, not a stuck-up chap from Eton.

But platform speaking, Mr. Meeker remembered, is not quite a fair test. Matt himself was not at his best when addressing an audience; he was too deliberate and slow. Shyness can sometimes sound like conceit. A friendly chat might reveal quite other qualities in Matt's son. For this call was, surely, proof that young Charles had a good heart, and the letter, in which he had asked if he might come, was a model of civility. Grace might sniff and point out that it had taken him three years to find out that his father's old friend had returned to Ravonsbridge. The fact remained that the boy came as soon as he did find out.

Lucy had described him, after her tea party at Cyre Abbey. Matt Millwood had been fair, short and thick set, but his son would seem to take after the Ravoncleres—tall, dark and slender; Lucy had declared that he would be very good looking if he could be rid of his scowl. But she had never seen him without it, during the whole election campaign. Had a chip on his shoulder? suggested Mr. Meeker. A chip! Lucy had cried. Say rather a plank. A whole timber yard.

Listening to that voice, Mr. Meeker could believe it. The visit languished, and the pleasure of getting that nice letter was probably going to be the best part of it. They had nothing very much to say to one another until Charles remembered a question he had meant to ask. He knew that his father and Harry Meeker had been weekly boarders at Severnton Grammar School, but that they had come home for week ends. He wanted to know how, in those days before bus transport, they had travelled the twelve miles across Slane Forest.

"We walked," said Mr. Meeker. "We came home on Saturday afternoon, and went back on Monday morning. We had to be in school by nine. I was a slow walker, so I started at five. Matt, he was a quick walker, never started before six. He generally caught me up at the top of Severnton Hill."

"Nowadays," said Charles, "you'd have been driven in a motor coach, at taxpayers' expense. I don't know what modern schoolboys would say at having to walk twelve miles before breakfast."

This annoyed Mr. Meeker. He thought it smacked of an attitude of mind which he privately termed the Bootstrap Boloney. He had observed that many people in easy circumstances have a sentimental enthusiasm for those who pull themselves up by their own bootstraps, and extract from this the precept that hardship is good for the character. He particularly objected to the bootstrap legend in connection with Matt Millwood, because it was grossly inaccurate. Matt had not raised himself from the gutter. The hardware shop had been a prosperous little business and the Millwoods respected citizens of the lower middle class. There had been plenty of enterprise and romance in Matt's life without any nonsense about bootstraps.

"We walked," he said testily, "because we liked it. We didn't have to. We could have spent our week ends at school. But we liked to go home and get a taste of our mothers' cooking. And as for the young people nowadays, I believe they walk a great deal. They go out in herds on Sundays, all over the forest and the Welsh hills. Only they call it hiking."

"You had breakfast before you started?" asked Charles.

"Yes. But we got hungry enough before dinner time. So your father—you know how he was always inventing contrivances—he made a sort of thermos, before such things were ever heard of. He got a big tin and lined it with several thicknesses of felt, and it had a metal flask of coffee inside and a couple of eggs boiled hard. They stayed hot for several hours. We used to have a snack on the hill before we went down to school."

Mr. Meeker stroked the cat on his lap and saw, with that inward eye still left to him, the bank where they used to eat, and Severnton below in the morning mist—the red roofs, the smoking chimneys, and the great bulk of the Cathedral crouching like some huge animal in the midst of the town. He added:

"Your father was very fond of singing. He knew hundreds of songs. When he overtook me on the road he always struck up to let me know he was coming; generally some song about eating or drinking. *Little Brown Jug* or *The Silver Tassie* or *When We Are Married We'll Have Sausages For Tea!* I'd hear him and think: Hurray! Grub!"

Mr. Meeker broke off for a moment, thinking how green the grass had been, how fresh the sunlight, how young the heart, when Matt came singing along the road, singing like a lark in the glory of the morning.

"Once," he said, "a carriage and pair went past me in the forest. Lord Ravonsclere's—I could see by the arms on the panels. Out early, I thought. When I got to our corner I looked back for Matt. He wasn't anywhere in sight. I waited. He didn't come. I couldn't think what had kept him. He'd never been so late. And just when I'd given him up, I heard his voice come singing up the hill from Severnton, the one way I hadn't been looking. He'd been in that carriage. It was old Lady Ravonsclere, your grandmother, only she wasn't old then, going to catch an early train. She saw this young lad on the road with his satchel, and stopped and

120

offered him a lift into Severnton. That was her way. Matt, he'd have liked to go on the box with the coachman, but she took him inside with her to ask him about his soul. That was her way, too. They had the Holy Catechism all the way to Severnton. She put him down at the bridge, but he wasn't going to leave his mate with no grub. So, as soon as she drove off, he started back up the hill to meet me. She little knew she'd been driving her future son-in-law."

There was a long pause. Charles had hardly listened. He was remembering something which had happened a very long time ago, when he was a little boy. The words *The Silver Tassie* had brought it back to him. His father had come home one cold night in tearing spirits, full of triumph over some achievement, and his mother had brought in a little silver cup of mulled wine, urging Matt in her grave, earnest voice, to drink it, lest he should have got a chill. She must have been very beautiful in those days, thought Charles, with a faint surprise. And his father, laughing, protesting, had taken the cup, raised it and bowed to her, and hummed something about a silver tassie and a bonny lassie. Whereat his mother's severity had melted into a momentary glance of delight and rapture; she had blushed and besought him not to be so silly, with a glance at little Charles among his bricks on the floor. "Silly?" cried Matt, "not a bit. I'm not silly, am I, Charley my boy?" Charles had said no, and asked who the bonny lassie was. "Who d'ya think?" Charles suggested Ida, an apple cheeked nursery maid, which made them both laugh. It had all slipped from his mind, years ago, and only now, when he recalled it, did he identify the bonny lassie.

It struck him that his father had had everything life can offer to a man. He had not only married Lord Ravonsclere's daughter but he had captured her heart and had been completely happy with her.

Mr. Meeker, afraid that his reminiscences had bored his guest, changed the subject and asked questions about Charles' war experiences in North Africa. The visit seemed to be flickering out when Charles exclaimed, with more energy than had appeared in his voice before:

"I wonder very much what my father would have done if he'd been in my shoes!"

So, thought Mr. Meeker, now we're getting to the timber yard.

There was plenty of it. Charles considered that there was no future at all, in England, for a young man in his shoes. Brains, wealth and family were no longer of any importance. His Liberalism forbade much hope of a political career. His position as a director in the M.M. was a sinecure, since all that he might do was to turn out cars for export. The whole plant was concentrated upon the production of certain models for which there was a lively overseas demand. Matthew Millwood had never been content unless he was trying to do something new; he would have suffocated had he been obliged to do the same thing over and over again.

Matthew Millwood had invested his money out of the country; he had dammed rivers and built railways in regions which needed capital. Charles might not do this. He might not even take more than five pounds with him on a visit to New York, unless some Jack-in-Office thought his journey necessary. In practice he could of course go where he liked, but in theory he must ask leave before earning dollars.

Matthew Millwood had endowed and governed hospitals. These were now all taken over by the State. He had built a town for his workers. Charles might not build a house, although New Ravonsbridge was seriously overcrowded.

"I can't," said Charles, "think of a single thing my father did that he would have been allowed to do, if he'd been alive today. Enterprise was the breath of life to him. I don't think he cared much for money, as money, do you?"

"No," agreed Mr. Meeker. "I don't. He liked starting things. He liked finding the answer to difficulties."

"That home-made thermos you spoke of," said Charles, "that was typical. I can imagine him ruminating over a way to keep coffee hot: 'Let's see . . . a liddle flasssk . . . and a liddle bit of . . . felt' till he'd worked it out. But this country has no use for a man like that nowadays. I ask you, who knew him so well, what would he have done in my shoes?"

"We-ell now . . ." pondered Mr. Meeker, "we-ell . . ."

Matt could not ever have had a chip on his shoulder. Had he found one there he would have removed it and used it to wedge a rattling window. But it was difficult to see him in postwar Ravonsbridge.

"He wouldn't have liked it very much," admitted Mr. Meeker. "But I think he'd have found something to do, because that was his way, you know."

"What sort of thing?"

"Why . . . for one thing, if he was here now I don't think there'd be this distrust between the two towns. It's bad, and it's getting worse. I think he'd have tried to tackle it and seen to it that the people up the hill and the people down here got together more. And he'd have known what a lot of . . . of quiet looting is going on. Your father wasn't an intriguer, but he always knew what was going on. He knew because he liked people, and was interested. And though he was so sweet tempered, he had a good deal of pugnacity. When he was around, a certain type of person didn't get away with things very easily."

"I don't see what he could have done."

"Oh, he'd have been around. He'd have managed to know what was going on. He'd have been in on a lot of activities, and he wouldn't have minded how Parish Pump they were, and he'd have known who's on the make, and who's two faced, and who's well meaning but soft headed, and who's a good ally in a scrap."

"I daresay. But would anybody have listened to him?"

"Oh, I think so. There's a big breakup going on, here and everywhere. New people running things, who haven't got all the experience they might have; and the old lot, who have experience, not always co-operating as they ought. And a lot of little things left lying about, don't you know, for the wise boys to pick up because it's nobody's business to look after them any more. It's a golden age for chisellers."

"Bound to happen when everything is handed over to the State."

"No. Not *bound* to happen. But likely to happen. Why now . . . there's Grace, my daughter-in-law. She's on the Town Council, and she's got very high ideals, but she just doesn't know what a new fire station ought to cost. I think, if your father had been around, she wouldn't have been able to help knowing how the Council was done over that deal."

123

"Some of them must have known," said Charles.

"Oh, yes. I'm afraid some of them must have known. But not poor Grace. She didn't mean to waste rate payers' money, you know. Now your father, he'd have got on with Grace. I think he'd have liked her and respected a lot of her ideas. And sometime or other, when they were judging vegetable marrows at a cottage flower show, he'd have managed to tell her a thing or two about fire stations, though she mightn't have been aware of it. But when the estimates came up . . . well . . . Grace would have been wise to it."

Charles made no comment. If Mr. Meeker was suggesting that he ought to go and judge vegetable marrows with Mrs. Meeker, there was no comment to make. Ravonsbridge had elected that odious woman to lay out its cash, and Ravonsbridge could foot the bill.

"And then," said Mr. Meeker, after a moment's hesitation, "there's the Institute. That was very near to his heart."

"I know it was," said Charles, rising to go. "But I'm afraid I can't feel any enthusiasm about it. To my mind it was a hopeless scheme. It could never have succeeded."

"Perhaps. But it's a valuable piece of property, Mr. Millwood."

"Completely wasted."

"At present . . . yes. It could be more useful to the public than it is. Or it could be exploited by private individuals, for their own profit."

"Not very likely," said Charles, "while my mother is above ground."

He took his leave. Mr. Meeker came courteously with him to the door and stood there while his guest went down the garden path. At the gate Charles turned and made a gesture of farewell to the tall old man, standing up so straight in the doorway. It was not returned, and he remembered that Mr. Meeker was blind.

Part 3

Melissa's Wedding

1

LUCY MOVED to her new rooms in Sheep Lane at the end of term, and remained in Ravonsbridge during the vacation. Stephen came to spend his holidays with her, for their mother had gone on a long promised visit to some cousins in Canada and the house at Gorling was let. But neither Rickie nor Mr. Finch, the curate, went to the Angeras'. Rickie stayed where he was, and Mr. Finch declared that he would prefer to live "among the people" in the lower town. Lucy's attic was eventually occupied by two art students for whom there was no room at the boys' hostel, an arrangement which was agreeable to the Angeras and, indeed, to everyone except Lady Frances, who thought that Mr. Finch would never get rid of his silly ideas if he was allowed to go and live down the hill.

During the vacation Melissa came to spend a couple of nights in Ravonsbridge. She had not seen Lucy for more than six months; she was upon the point of announcing her engagement to John Beauclerc, and she wanted her friend to know of it in advance. Also there was a delicate point to discuss; in their Oxford days they had agreed that the first to be married should be attended by the other as a bridesmaid; this, to Melissa's mind, was no longer desirable. She could not ask Lucy to follow her to the altar so soon after the fiasco at Gorling. She was sure that Lucy would not wish it, but she did not know how to phrase that assumption in a letter. It was the sort of thing which could only be settled, in half sentences, during a conversation.

Unhappy memories smote her as the train drew into the station and she caught sight of Lucy waiting for her. Lucy was not rushing about any more; she stood calmly by the exit, clutching a large handbag and looking, thought the shocked Melissa, at least forty-five years old. They met, smiled, and went out to find a taxi. Lucy explained that they would go first to the Swan, where she had taken a room for Melissa, and then for a tour of the Institute. Stephen, she said, had gone to Gloucester for the day, but he would be back for supper, which they would have in Sheep Lane, and he was delighted at the thought of seeing Melissa again.

As she talked, Melissa watched her and tried to define the change. A certain roundness of face and limb was gone, and a bloom, the last soft bloom of childhood which had lingered late with Lucy and had been there a year ago. But more than these had been lost. Lucy could, Melissa thought, have lived to be a very old woman and have still kept a certain quality, a sparkle of the eye, a note in the voice, which would always have been young and would infallibly have captured attention. Now it was extinguished. She was like a handsome unlit lamp, pleasant enough to behold but easy to overlook. And this change had come about since they parted; during those dire first weeks, when she had been in London, she had burnt with a flame so tragic that nobody could have overlooked her. Now she was just one of those nice girls whom everybody likes and nobody remembers.

The taxi raced through the new town and crossed the bridge. Melissa decided to take her fence immediately. Any long discussion of her present happiness must be avoided, and arrival at the Swan would give them an early opportunity to change the subject.

"I have a piece of news about myself," she said, "that won't wait another minute."

Lucy looked at her and said quickly:

"You're going to be married?"

"Yes. To John Beauclerc. You met him once at supper."

"That night Rickie came? I remember. Oh . . . very nice! I rather wondered then . . . Oh, Melissa! I did think he was very nice. I am so glad."

Lucy asked all the right questions, with just the right amount of pleased interest. Before they reached the Swan she had learnt that the engagement would be announced in May, the wedding was planned for July, and that John had found a little house in Lincolnshire.

"July . . ." she mused. "Oh . . . I do hope I shall be able to come. But we're putting on *Twelfth Night* and I might not be able to get away. I might be able to dash up to London, just for the day, but I shan't know till the last minute. I know Mr. Thornley will be nice about it if he can."

Which told Melissa that she perfectly understood the bridesmaid quandary, and was not expecting to officiate. So that was settled and when they reached the Swan they were able to talk of something else. But she reverted to the topic again for a moment when, in Melissa's room, she once more watched the unpacking of those familiar shoe bags. She said that poor Rickie would probably drown himself in the Ravon. Melissa laughed and refused to take Rickie seriously.

The Institute was closed for vacation, but they went to see the theatre and amused themselves with the light switches while Lucy described the Nativity play, which she had been too ill to do when it was produced. They then went to the art school, in the north wing of the second quadrangle.

"I don't know if we can get in," said Lucy, as they went. "It may be locked, but it's generally open, as Emil often works there in the vacation."

"Will he be there?"

"No. He'll have gone home for tea, but I hope he's left the door open. Oh good! He has. Come in."

The stove in the big studio was lighted and a great many empty beer bottles stood about everywhere.

"He must be working quite hard," said Lucy. "I never knew such a man for beer; when he's working really hard he sluices beer down his throat with one hand and paints with the . . ."

She broke off to stare in amazement at a half finished picture on an easel.

"Is that his?" asked Melissa.

"Yes," said Lucy slowly. "It . . . it must be."

"It's extremely good. The hands are wonderful. But I wouldn't care to live with it. Oh, Lucy! Is it Ianthe?"

"Yes. I never knew he was . . . but how did you guess?"

"She's so like your descriptions. Your letters are good, you know, Lucy."

They both studied the portrait and Melissa again commented on the hands. Lucy had not hitherto perceived the oddness of Ianthe's hands. Though vivid in gesture they were, in repose, very ugly, mere bunches of limp fingers which did not look capable of holding anything or doing anything.

"No allure at all," said Melissa. "Not for men, anyway. I see why she has to live in two places. In Ravonsbridge she can talk about her beaux in Yorkshire, and in Yorkshire she can boast of Ravonsbridge conquests."

"I hadn't thought of that," said Lucy.

"Well, do the boys here ever take her out?"

Lucy shook her head. She had never known Ianthe to have a date, and Robin's admiration had been short lived, for Wendy had reclaimed him almost instantly.

"It's odd," said Lucy, "for really she's very good looking and amusing, when she likes to be."

"Not odd at all. Men don't like neurotic women. They're scared of them. That's why Hedda Gabler had to marry old Tesman."

"It's queer you should mention Hedda Gabler," said Lucy. "For I was thinking the other day how well Ianthe could play that part. How do you come to know more about her than I've found out in six months?"

"The picture tells a good deal. Look how she's standing outside that door planning to go in and make somebody jump. By herself she's nothing . . . she's an empty icebox. She has to make people jump in order to be sure she exists. She can't feel. Neurotic people can't."

"How do you know all this about neurotic people?"

"A man called Armitage, a medical friend of Hump's; he's a neurologist. He was talking about girls with nervous breakdowns because of unhappy love affairs. He said nobody with a real love affair gets a nervous breakdown; they go haywire because they haven't had any love affair at all, and couldn't—they're so wrapped up in themselves."

"Well, anyway," said Lucy, "if Emil is painting Ianthe he isn't pinching her, which takes rather a load off my mind. He's perfectly sexless when he paints. Venus of Milo or a coal scuttle, it's all the same to him. In the art school he's a different man . . . never silly, never lupine. Really he makes one feel he's a great man, when he's on his job."

"And how much of that does Ianthe understand, do you think? I expect the poor girl thinks she's got a man at last."

"Then she'll have a rude awakening. 'Tomorrow I finish, thank you very much. I shan't need you any more because I now paint a portrait of Miss Foss.' "

"And what will Ianthe do? Fire off a gun, like Hedda Gabler?"

"Probably. But everybody is used to that."

"Even Hedda fired off one too many," said Melissa, turning to examine some of the students' work.

They then went to the library and Melissa was introduced to Mr. Mildmay. He gave them a warm welcome and displayed all his especial treasures. On their way to Sheep Lane they caught a glimpse of Mr. Hayter going into his office, and in Market Square they met Miss Foss. Everybody came up to Melissa's expectations, and she felt that she knew exactly what they were like; they emerged intact from Lucy's letters. And this seemed strange to Melissa, because she was quite sure that not one of them could have the least understanding of Lucy or any means of knowing what Lucy was like. If the lamp should ever be lit again, Ravonsbridge would get a shock.

But on the next day Lucy appeared to be in much better spirits. They went with Stephen into Severnton, and she kept smiling to herself, as the bus drove through Slane Forest, as though she was thinking of something very pleasant. She seemed to be on much better terms with Stephen than formerly. Melissa had noticed it at supper the night before. She had stopped scolding him and treated him as though he were grown up. He, for his part, treated her with an anxious, almost protective, care, which was rather touching.

On arrival in Severnton Lucy announced that she had some

shopping to do and despatched the other two to look at the Cathedral without her. They spent half an hour admiring Norman pillars and peering at tombs and trying to identify the Pentecost window. And then they went into the cloisters, which led to the Chapter House where the whole story of the Bible was carved in high relief round the walls. Melissa had got as far as the Drunkenness of Noah, that great topic of the Middle Ages, when Stephen abruptly exclaimed that he wanted to consult her. She turned and saw that he was swallowing rapidly.

"You know all about women," he said. "I mean, you are one. I want to consult you about Lucy."

Melissa smiled and sat upon the Dean's throne, beckoning Stephen to sit beside her.

"You see . . . I . . . I've been seeing Patrick Reilly."

"Oh? When?"

"About a fortnight ago."

"Does Lucy know?"

"Oh, no. You see I thought I ought to thrash him."

"And did you?"

"Partly."

"How do you mean . . . partly?"

Stephen explained that he had been determined to thrash Reilly for months but had not known where to find him. At last a gossip paragraph in a newspaper informed him that Reilly was in London and that he lunched, more often than not, at the Black Tulip.

"So I went to London and I went to the Black Tulip," said Stephen. "I'd meant to take a horse whip, but I didn't know where to get one, and anyway it was an awkward sort of thing to carry about. I said: Is Mr. Patrick Reilly here? And they must have thought I was a guest, for they took me to his table and he was there lunching with a lot of women. I'd meant to tell him to come outside with me, but when I saw him I felt so angry I suppose I lost my head. I went up to him and slapped his face and said: Sir! You are a coward and a cad."

"You didn't!" cried Melissa, enraptured. "Well? Then?"

"Then all the waiters rushed up and M. Benoit . . . you know . . . the manager—"

"Don't I know him! He's a lamb. Well?"

"So Reilly's nose was bleeding. But he was really very nice about it, Melissa. He said: This gentleman and I have something to discuss; can't we go somewhere more private? So M. Benoit was marvellous. He made it all seem quite ordinary and natural, so everybody stopped staring and went on with their meals, and he took us up to his office."

"Darling Benoit! He would."

Melissa was very fond of Benoit and he was very fond of her and always came forward to welcome her in person when her young men brought her to the Black Tulip. She was the kind of girl he liked to see in his restaurant—*très bien élevée, très comme il faut.* He knew that the Reilly clientele might desert him at any time for some newer haunt; and he knew that loyalty often goes with good manners.

"So we mopped up Reilly's nose. And then he asked how Lucy is."

"He *dared?*"

Stephen had always supposed that Melissa was a sweet gentle girl. Her blazing eyes quite alarmed him. He explained hurriedly:

"He . . . he did it quite nicely. And he was really very nice to me. I mean, he said he quite saw why I had to hit him, only he said he thought honour was satisfied. And you know, Melissa, he's very cut up about it all. He explained some things I'd never understood. He'd never meant her to go to Church like that. He didn't know about that till afterwards. He'd thought she'd had a message . . . he didn't exactly say so, but I think it was that . . . that woman . . . who promised to send the message and didn't."

"I'd always suspected that," agreed Melissa.

"He's left her, you know."

"Has he? Did he say so?"

"Yes. He left her when he found out what had happened, and he's never seen her since. So then he asked, rather hesitatingly, how Lucy is. And I said: She's quite all right, thanks."

He paused, and Melissa nodded approvingly.

"So then he said if there was ever anything he could do for her would I let him know. So I said yes I would. So that's what I wanted to ask you. Do you think there's anything he can do for her?"

"No, I don't. Nothing."

"You mean, you think she's quite all right?"

"I think her heart is broken."

"But that's it," cried Stephen. "I think so too. And I can't bear it. I sometimes wish she'd start calling me a frightful child as she used to do. You know what I mean?"

"Yes. I can't bear it either."

A guide led a party of tourists into the Chapter House. His scowl reproved Melissa for perching on the Dean's throne, so she rose, in some confusion, and fled with Stephen into the cloisters. They paced round two sides of them before Stephen spoke again:

"I've heard," he said solemnly, "I mean I've read, that women are very constant."

"We're generally supposed to be fickle," said Melissa.

"Well, look at all the books and poetry there is about girls who will go on loving the most awful cads! Look at that girl . . . er . . . Sollwig . . . she's supposed to be very touching. Nobody writes poetry about a man who will go on loving a frightful woman. They think *he's* cuckoo. What I mean is . . . do you think Lucy still loves him, in spite of everything?"

"It's quite possible."

"Because . . . he did ask if I thought she might like to see him."

"Stephen! You mean—"

"I think he'd marry her, if she still—"

"But you can't want him to!"

"It's not what I want. It's what she wants."

"What did you say?"

"I said no. But he gave me his address. I could tell him to come. And since I've been here, these holidays, I've sometimes wondered if I oughtn't to tell him to come. If she forgives him, does it matter that we can't?"

Melissa reflected and then asked how Reilly was looking.

"That's another thing that worries me. He looks a lot older and . . . and thicker. I think he'd been drinking. But it might be only lunch. Only . . . he does look rather a mess."

"Oh, Stephen! She ought to marry somebody nicer."

"What's the use of saying that, if she doesn't want anyone

nicer? Think of all the times she must have prayed he'd come back! Melissa, do you remember the time when Mother said: There's been a mistake. And Lucy jumped up . . ."

"Oh, don't. I remember. But he'll only break her heart again. He's a heel."

"She has the right to choose which way she'll break her heart, hasn't she? If I thought she was getting over it—"

"Oh, I don't know. I don't know. I'll think it over and tell you later."

They met Lucy at a café for lunch and both of them were struck by her unwonted elation. It was even more marked than it had been in the bus. Something of the old glow had really returned and it was soon apparent that the explanation lay in her handbag into which she peeped importantly from time to time. Stephen caught Melissa's eye and telegraphed an enquiry. But she shook her head. She could not think what had happened.

Towards the end of the meal Lucy ordered Stephen to go and get his hair cut, with something of her old imperiousness. She and Melissa would meet him in the lounge of the Crown Hotel for tea. He winked gleefully at Melissa and obeyed. Melissa almost began to believe that Lucy must have met Reilly while they were in the Cathedral and be concealing a new engagement ring in her bag. But this revived flicker did not quite warrant so dramatic an explanation as that.

The two girls wandered round Severnton examining the shop windows, and Melissa declared that the clothes exhibited were much more attractive than any to be seen in London. She bought herself a summer cotton and urged Lucy to do likewise, but Lucy said that she had no money. This was nonsense; she had, Melissa knew, just received a quarter's salary and she had cashed a cheque in Ravonsbridge before they started that morning.

When they grew tired of walking they went and sat in the lounge of the Crown, though it was a little early for tea. There was a comfortable sofa in a corner upon which they subsided; Lucy peeped into her mysterious bag and Melissa observed provincial life.

"Cool!" said Melissa suddenly. "Look! County! Real moth-eaten County!"

133

"Where?"

"That toothy girl in tweeds who just came in; you should have seen all the bowing and scraping. She's sitting by that potted palm over there."

Lucy looked and said:

"That's Penelope Millwood."

"What? The daughter-at-home?"

Melissa studied Penelope eagerly and said: "She does, doesn't she?"

"Does what?"

"Let us know she wears woollen knickers."

"These sofas are so low."

"You and I can sit on them without making poppy shows of ourselves, and we're only poor middle class girls. Think of all the advantages she's had!"

"Control yourself," said Lucy. "A greater thrill is on its way. Terrific Charles has just come through the swing door."

"No! No!"

They sat breathless while Charles advanced and stared about him. His eye swept their sofa, became blank, as he hesitated and bowed slightly, and then continued the search for his sister. Having discovered her behind her palm he went to join her.

"Well," said Melissa, "are you burnt up like Semele? What did that gaping sort of salutation mean?"

"He doesn't know who we are," said Lucy. "He thinks we're Severnton belles he's met at a Hunt Ball."

"Oh, nonsense! You worked for him like a black. You gave him a drink at the Swan."

"I don't remember that he's ever looked at me."

"Ho! I think he should have come and talked to us."

"He'd never dream of it."

"Where are we?" asked Melissa getting up. "At Rosings? In the shades of Pemberly?"

She crossed the lounge and ordered tea from a porter by the door. She looked at nobody, but everybody in the lounge looked at her, as she floated back to her sofa and came gracefully to rest upon it. Charles asked his sister a question and Penelope craned round her palm to stare at them.

"She says," opined Melissa, "that she's never seen me before but that you are one of the Institute minions."

A few seconds elapsed during which Charles fidgeted.

"He's wondering," continued Melissa, "whether he ever thanked you for all your hard work. Did he?"

"No."

"He will, in a minute."

She began to time it on her wrist watch. Before the minute was out Charles rose and approached them. He wanted, he said, to take this opportunity of thanking Lucy for the noble work she had done for him during the election. Lucy smiled and introduced Melissa. The two girls sat side by side on their sofa looking up at him. The Lucy-Melissa battery, though it had been out of action for nearly a year, was as effective as ever. Charles shifted uneasily from one foot to another.

"I believe," said Melissa sweetly, "that you might be able to tell me about the Pentecost window. I couldn't find it."

He began to explain that it was hidden behind scaffolding, and she interrupted him to suggest that he would be more comfortable if he sat. The chair which he would be permitted to use was pointed out to him. By the time that he had taken it his spirit was thoroughly subdued. He stayed talking to them as long as Melissa chose and was then pleasantly dismissed. He went back to Penelope wondering who Miss Hallam could be.

Melissa, impeccably well bred, talked to Lucy about stained glass until tea trays, brought to both parties, ended the incident. Then, as she poured out Lucy's tea, she murmured:

"Hoity-toity! What airs to be sure! I'm not a rich woman, as Annie the Scout used to say, but I'd give half a crown to see that lofty top knot brought low."

"You ruffled it a little," said Lucy.

"You helped. It takes two to do that sort of thing."

"You caused quite noticeable emotion, Melissa. I'd never have believed it . . . he was almost human."

"Oh, I daresay he's human. I expect he conducts a stately love life in some lofty region beyond our ken. Where was he raised? Not Eton, I think?"

"No. Winchester."

"I'm not surprised. Anything can come from Winchester. In college I suppose."

Melissa pondered and then exclaimed that this must be the Millwood who was in college with Hump.

"Why didn't I realise that before, Lucy! He must be the Eel!"

"Is that what Hump called him?"

"It's what everybody called him. You see, this Millwood had a very peculiar method of getting into bed. Still has, for aught I know, if he's that Millwood. He doesn't tear the sheets apart to get in; he likes to stay all neat and tucked up. So he sits on the pillow and slowly inserts himself. Everybody thought it highly diverting. Crowds collected to watch him do it."

Lucy, enraptured, wondered if this ritual was still observed in some august alcove at Cyre Abbey.

"Well, so a friend of Hump's called Pattison caught a lot of eels one day. He'd meant to cook and eat them, but they looked too horrible. And up came Hump, who'd been out running, and dashed up, you know, all panting and dishevelled in shorts and a singlet, and Pattison called out: 'Hi! Hallam! Where does a man put unwanted eels?' And Hump never paused, he dashed past, shouting: 'In Millwood's bed.' "

"And did they?"

"Yes," sighed Melissa disapprovingly. "Hump is very crude sometimes. Hump thought it was funny. He said Millwood got into bed as slowly as usual until his toes touched the eels . . ."

"Ha! Ha! Ha!"

"Dear me," expostulated Melissa. "What a coarse laugh some people have! Some people are as crude as Hump."

Lucy blushed, aware that everyone in the lounge was looking at her. But she continued to giggle for the rest of the afternoon over this simple joke.

Stephen, with a close-cropped pate, joined them and they had a merry tea. The evening passed delightfully until Lucy took Melissa back to her room at the Swan to help with her packing. For Melissa was leaving by a very early train in the morning.

"Melissa!"

Melissa looked up from her shoe bags. Almost . . . almost the

136

old Lucy was sparkling at her. What is it? wondered Melissa. Is it . . . can he . . .

"I'm going to be selfish," said Lucy, "and give myself a treat. You see, I mayn't get off in July, so I want to give it to you now, for I must see your face when you see it. Your wedding present," she explained, fishing in her bag, "I got it in Severnton today. I saw it there last week, in a tray in a junk shop, and I did love it so, but of course . . . and then I remembered it in the night and thought: Melissa's wedding present. But oh, I was so much afraid it would be gone! But it wasn't."

She handed a grubby little box to Melissa. Inside, lying on cotton wool, was a ring—an intaglio on a pale green stone.

"Hold it up to the light," commanded Lucy, "and you'll see. It's a cupid riding on a dolphin and waving his little hand. I don't know what the stone is, and I didn't like to ask in case the man in the shop might start looking at it and find out it was really good, for I think it must be, it's so lovely: Do you see his little hand? And his wings?"

"Yes," said Melissa, looking at the ring through smarting tears.

So this was the secret! Nothing for herself at all, only for me, thought Melissa. And that's how she spent all her money! But I mustn't cry . . . I must be delighted. She's waiting for me to be delighted.

"Oh, Lucy, it's perfectly lovely. I never saw anything quite like it. I know I shan't have any other present quite so nice. I can't wait to show it to John. . . ."

But the sparkle was fading and disappointment was pushing Lucy back into her lonely path. She had seen Melissa's distress and guessed the cause.

"I knew you'd like it," she said flatly.

Then she gave Melissa a warm hug, as if trying to console her and to apologise for their ghastly predicament.

"We'll be here with a taxi at eight o'clock," she said, "and take you down to the station. Goodnight. . . ."

For some time afterwards Melissa could do nothing but scold herself for her want of self command. But then a more cheerful thought occurred to her. She argued that if so small a thing could, even for a short time, have so marked an effect, there must be great reason for hope. Time and Lucy's own nature might heal the wound.

Next morning, at the station, she found an opportunity to take Stephen aside and beg him not to send for Patrick Reilly.

"If he comes of his own accord," she said, "we can't help it. But don't let's send for him. I believe she will get over it. I believe she will, in time, get over it completely, without any help from anybody."

2

"I shall never get over it. Why should I?"

Thus Rickie, when the fact of Melissa's wedding had at last been got into his head.

"People do," said Lucy, "I can't think why."

"Not unless they want to. I don't want to. I can't face life without Melissa."

"It's no worse for you than for other people," said Bess, in whose library they had assembled for a mid-morning cup of tea. "Everybody has their troubles and they get over them."

Rickie helped himself to two lumps of sugar and said that people who get over things can't have suffered very much.

"Oh bosh! Look at Lucy. She's had the most sickening luck. You know she has. But she's been sensible and looked on the bright side, and now she's quite all right again."

Bess rose and took a cup of tea to Mr. Mildmay in his little room. There was a pause while Rickie stared at Lucy and Lucy digested this astonishing description of herself.

"I know you had a bad time," said Rickie at last. "But I can't believe you were ever as wretched as I am."

"Oh, Rickie, I think I was."

"You might have been at first and then you must have thought you'd never get over it."

"No. I thought so at once. It was the first thing I thought. At least . . . I didn't think it. I said it. I said it to my mother. She

138

was crying. I suppose I wanted to comfort her, but, when I said it, I knew it was true."

"My mother is dead," he reminded her gloomily. "I have nobody. I always thought Melissa would take her place."

Lucy made a sympathetic noise but hardly heard him. She was lost in amazement, recalling that strange announcement which she had once made at her mother's bedside. How had she come to say such a thing? She had never thought it strange before, but now she found it mysterious and inexplicable—a prophetic utterance, proceeding from no connected chain of thought, no effort of will. Reason and determination had come much later. This had merely been a statement of perception.

"I said it," she repeated in a puzzled voice. "I suppose I'm like that lady in Gide's novel; I can't know what I think till I see what I say."

"Then you're crackers," said Bess, returning. "Sensible people think before they speak."

"I know they're supposed to. But I sometimes wonder if the most sensible things we say have much to do with thinking."

A reproachful groan from Rickie recalled them to his predicament. He still wanted to know why he should not drown himself in the Ravon.

"No reason on earth that I know of," snapped Lucy. "If you do it's because you do. If you don't it's because you don't."

She rose and added that they ought all to be getting back to their work.

"Work!" cried Rickie. "How can I? When I'm feeling like this! I hate the thought of it."

"You can't hate the thought of it more than I do," said Lucy. "This term has been hell, ever since Ianthe joined drama school. How I could ever have been so crazy as to suggest the idea to her beats me. But hell or not, I work, and so must you, Rickie."

"Is she no good at it?" asked Bess.

"She's frightfully good. But she's properly knocking the drama school to pieces. She has caused the Frog to quarrel with H. E. Frog wants her in *Twelfth Night*, and he won't have her in the cast because she's a first termer. So we've all split into a pro-Ianthe party and an anti-Ianthe party, headed by Wendy."

139

"Which are you, pro or anti?"

"I don't know. She ought to be Viola, if talent counts. But she's so spiteful. She's put the others up to staring at poor Wendy's legs, whenever she comes on. Well, they are terribly bandy, you know. She ought never to wear tights. But we never noticed it till darling Ianthe joined us. Come along, Rickie! Back to hell!"

But Rickie declared that he could not work.

"I'll go for a walk," he decided. "And tonight I'll come to Sheep Lane and sit with you, Lucy, so that I shan't be quite alone."

Lucy had a lecture to prepare and did not relish this suggestion. But she was really sorry for him and felt that perhaps she had been a little unsympathetic. So she assented and thereafter discovered that she was to enjoy very few evenings to herself. He came every night to Sheep Lane and remained there until she threw him out. Sometimes he sat with his head in his hands, moaning feebly. At other times he entreated her to say that Melissa might yet change her mind.

He was not mentally deficient, but various circumstances had impeded his maturity. He had been an only child and his widowed mother had spoilt him.

Music is the least educative of the arts; it may lead its votaries to a better world but it teaches them little about this one. Living only for music he had existed in a harmonious dream. Now, in his mid-twenties, he was not only confronted with a major disappointment but had become belatedly aware of many hard facts which should have been digested ten years earlier. It was nobody's business to look after him. Nobody cared a pin for him and his troubles. His dinner must still be earned though his discoveries appalled him. He announced them one by one to Lucy, as they burst upon him, and finally, upon a Sunday evening, he came to the conclusion that a loving God would never have allowed him to be so unhappy.

"I've lost my religious faith," he declared. "That's a simply frightful thing to happen to me just now."

"But you always knew he allowed other people to be unhappy," Lucy pointed out. "And that never worried you."

"Well, naturally. I didn't think about that much. If I had I suppose I'd have lost my religious faith before. Do you believe in God, Lucy?"

"I don't know," said Lucy. "I only know I can't talk about Him. If I do I always feel I'm saying something false . . . not quite what I mean. . . ."

"For me, personally, it's the end if I can't put my trust in God any more."

For some days after that the Institute saw nothing of him. He lay upon his bed in his lodgings, much to the annoyance of his landlady, who could not get into his room to clean it and reported that he groaned and created up there, fit to be heard down in the new town. His students, already restive, became rebellious. There was talk of an appeal to Pidgeon, to Lady Frances; but Hayter, who always knew what was in the wind, staved off such a catastrophe by promising to tackle Rickie himself. He did so, at first kindly, then severely, but with little success.

Lucy's kindness and patience with Rickie were well known, so Hayter sent for her and asked her advice. Could any steps be taken to cheer Rickie up?

"Nothing, unless he was asked to conduct at Covent Garden," said Lucy, "or got some of his own compositions on the air."

She was surprised to see that Hayter took this suggestion seriously.

"You think a broadcast might do the trick?"

"It would send him up to the stratosphere. He'd forget Melissa in a week. He's always posting his songs to radio artists and it's a shame they never get taken. But I suppose it's all a matter of luck."

"H'm," said Hayter. "I think we might attend to Rickie's luck a little. These songs . . . are they any good?"

"Oh, quite. I mean they're very like good songs, only a little too like, so you keep feeling you've heard them before."

"Are they for men or women?"

"Men, I think. They're too sentimental for women."

Hayter laughed and explained that he could pull some strings. He knew of several singers who would do him a good turn in exchange for his kind offices at festivals. He thought he might persuade somebody to give a Haverstock recital in the autumn, not, he hastened to add, at nine thirty in the evening, but at some less distinguished time of day. He would see Rickie at once and dangle this carrot before his nose.

Lucy thought him so kind to take all this trouble that she stifled a carping distaste for the atmosphere of string pulling in which Hayter seemed to thrive. He was really very good natured, she decided, and there were no justifiable grounds for the faint distrust which he always inspired in her. Only a cynic would say that he was too nice to everybody—that his quick grin and friendly laugh were employed too frequently to give any indication of his real character. What if he were not perfectly sincere? A great many people, she reflected, are not only insincere but disagreeable into the bargain. It was rather hard on a man to dislike him because he was always pleasant.

In the warmth of her repentance towards him she accepted a cigarette and a drink before going back to the theatre. And when he asked how *Twelfth Night* was getting on she told him it was going to be terrible, and told him why. Before she was half through her drink she had said much which might be construed as criticism of Mr. Thornley.

"But will it be so very much worse?" asked Mr. Hayter blandly, "than our productions usually are?"

Lucy pulled herself up and resolved to say no more. She began to perceive how it was that the executive director always managed to know everything, and, as she rose to take her leave, a fresh instance of this omniscience considerably startled her.

"Let's hope," she said, "that you'll all settle down better now that Miss Meadows has gone."

"Gone?" cried Lucy. "Where? When? She hasn't gone away from Ravonsbridge."

"I heard she went back to Yorkshire this morning."

"She can't have! She was in school yesterday. She said nothing about going away."

"I may have been misinformed. But, if it's true, it may be just as well for the drama school."

"A godsend," agreed Lucy. "The drama school is no place for her."

"Nor the art school either," said Hayter, opening the door for her, "though I admire Angera's portrait tremendously, don't you?"

"Oh, but that was done in the vacation," said Lucy. "She had no chance to upset the art school."

"Or the art school to upset her?"

Lucy started, glanced at him, and met a very sharp look. He certainly knew everything—knew what a snub Ianthe had got from Emil when her portrait was finished, knew of the spiteful vendetta which had gone on between those two ever since.

Nor had he been misinformed concerning this latest event. On returning to the theatre, Lucy discovered everybody whispering in corners. Ianthe was gone. There had been an explosion of some kind on the previous night. Somebody had heard her sobbing in Mr. Thornley's office. Somebody else had seen H.E. marching her out of the Institute and home to the rectory. Nobody had actually seen him putting her into the train that morning but a belief prevailed that he had done so.

Mr. Thornley's aspect forbade any questions. Neither Miss Frogmore nor Miss Paine could elucidate the mystery.

"The most promising pupil I ever had," mourned Miss Frogmore. "Such a wonderful voice! She'd have made the school famous. Now, I suppose we shall have to lose her to the A. D. A. It's too bad of H. E. From the start he did nothing but discourage her and now she's gone."

"It's my belief," said Miss Paine, who inclined to the other party, "that he had no choice. I expect she's been spinning one of her yarns. Probably accused Robin or Peter of making a pass at her."

This would have been so like Ianthe that neither Lucy nor Miss Frogmore could quite reject it.

"Even if she did," protested Miss Frogmore, "he needn't have made such heavy weather of it. He could have snapped her head off . . . but to send her away . . . what do you think, Lucy?"

Lucy did not know what to think. She never liked thinking about Ianthe, for the memory of Slane St. Mary's could still make her wince. And she felt a little guilty over the breakup of their friendship; if Ianthe had told any other lie on that sinister afternoon she would have been able to forgive it. Her anger and repulsion were the consequence of an accident.

"Perhaps he didn't send her," she suggested. "Perhaps he just annoyed her, and she went off in a huff."

"Then why is he looking so black about it?" asked Miss Paine. "I'm sure she did something outrageous."

Lucy was sure of it too, really, but she could not try to think what it was. The pieces of the puzzle lay on the table before her— Hayter's broad hint, Ianthe's grudge against Emil, and Thornley's drastic action—but she would not put them together or speculate on the nature of the lie which Ianthe had probably now told.

"I'm afraid it's too late to save *Twelfth Night*," she sighed. "We'll never pull them together before the opening. What a foul term it's been! Between Rickie and Ianthe my work has gone completely to pot and I expect I shall get the sack."

She spoke lightly, but she really did feel uneasy when, after a disastrous opening, Lady Frances came storming in from Cyre Abbey to know the reason why and to confer with Mr. Hayter. That conference lasted for close on three hours, as all the staff were uneasily aware.

Nobody could pretend that the drama school had not disgraced itself. Even Mr. Thornley was obliged to refer to *Twelfth Night* as "one of my few disappointments." The Ravonsbridge *Echo*, always tepid about Institute productions, came into the open with a frankly hostile notice. It seemed inevitable that some heads must fall and Lucy supposed that her own might be the most expendable. Her lectures had suffered from the demands made by Rickie, and she could not feel that she had contributed anything to the work in the theatre.

To her surprise, the idea of leaving Ravonsbridge was extremely unwelcome. She did not like it much, but she had got used to it, and her heart sank when she thought of going somewhere else and starting all over again. Tears rose to her eyes when, crossing the quadrangle from the theatre to the canteen, she saw Lady Frances stumping back to her car, respectfully escorted by the executive director. *He* looked cheerful enough, as cheerful as a cat with a saucer of cream, thought Lucy. And the smile he flashed at her was particularly sunny. But there was no trusting his smiles. He had probably been signing her death warrant.

She did him less than justice. From the post mortem which

had been held, during that three hours' conference, only one person had emerged with enhanced credit and an assured future. Mr. Hayter who knew everything, knew nothing save good of Miss Carmichael.

"It's not only her work in the drama school," announced Lady Frances to her family at lunch. "She's a really useful, loyal member of the staff. Just the sort of girl we want. Mr. Hayter discovered her, you know, and I can't be too grateful to him. It seems that she's been endlessly kind to poor Mr. Haverstock. He thought he was engaged, you know, and then found that he was not, and really, Mr. Hayter says, he might have quite gone to pieces if it hadn't been for Miss Carmichael. Between them they got him to pull himself together, and he's quite all right again now."

"But who wrote that disgraceful notice in the *Echo*?" asked Tish, who was lunching with them. "Does Mr. Hayter know?"

"He says it's some young man in the gas works, who does journalism. Basil Wright, I think he's called. But the *Echo* has a perfect right to criticise, Tish. The newspapers must say what they think. *Twelfth Night* is very bad, and Mr. Thornley ought to be much more ashamed of it than he is. And he's been very tiresome about Ianthe, I gather. It was so nice that she wanted to work steadily at something, but he seems to have discouraged her so much that she gave it up. Miss Carmichael has had such a very good influence on Ianthe. I think we are extremely lucky in Miss Carmichael. I think, and Mr. Hayter thinks, that she will be perfectly capable of taking on the theatre when Mr. Thornley goes."

Charles, who never attended when Institute chatter was going on, came out of a reverie to ask why Thornley was going.

"Oh, he isn't going just yet," said Lady Frances. "But I feel it might become advisable. His heart isn't really in the Institute nowadays, you know, and that is why the productions have fallen off so much. He has so many outside interests. He's always away, lecturing and judging drama competitions. He might prefer to give up all his time to this outside work. He might want to retire."

That Mr. Thornley should ever want any such thing seemed unlikely to Charles, but it was clear that his stock had fallen.

"He's very tiresome on the council meetings," said Tish. "He never pays any attention to what Mamma says. Mr. Angera, you know, resigned at the beginning of this term; he'd taken offence over some ridiculous trifle. He's always resigning. We wanted to give him a good fright—accept his resignation and force him to eat humble pie. But Mr. Thornley went off then and there and got him to apologise while the council was sitting, so we were forced to overlook it."

"One wouldn't have Miss Carmichael on the council," mused Lady Frances. "She wouldn't expect it."

Thornley's days were numbered. For years he had spent half his time lecturing up and down the country without any protest from Lady Frances. *Twelfth Night* was not very much worse than his other productions. But if Hayter wanted him out, out he would go. Charles, who rather liked the old fellow, felt an impulse to protest, but thought better of it. Hayter must either be allowed to rule the roost or be flung out neck and crop. Thornley would go, and the enigmatic Carmichael would get his job. For enigmatic she had seemed to Charles, ever since that curious encounter in Severnton. Not a poor, nice, dull girl with a sad story at all, but one half of a most disturbing combination. He had thought about her several times and had decided that she was neither poor nor dull. And now, if she was really making for Thornley's job, he doubted if she could be nice.

"Perhaps," said Penelope, who was also remembering Severnton, "Mr. Haverstock will marry Miss Carmichael, if this other girl has jilted him."

"Oh, I hope not," cried her mother. "He's not nearly good enough."

"Good heavens no!"

Charles said this with so much vehemence that all his family were startled. Tish began to laugh.

"I don't believe you even know her by sight, Charles! I don't believe you'd recognise her if you met her in the street."

"Oh, yes I should," said Charles. "She . . . has a very pretty friend."

At which even Lady Frances laughed.

TURNING A CORNER on their way from the Underground station, Rickie and Lucy were confronted unexpectedly by the church, the awning, the red carpet and the little crowd.

"What are you hanging back for?" asked Rickie. "It's quite time we went in. Come along."

Lucy came along, thankful for his company. If he had not, in a sudden wave of heroism, decided to attend the wedding, she might never have got herself into the church. She was braced for an ordeal inside, but she had not supposed she could be put out by so small a thing as a red carpet. She settled her big hat on her curls and sailed into church beside Rickie, looking more serene than she felt—looking indeed like everybody else. The moment of panic was behind her. She was in the dusk and rustle of the nave, where a flower garden of summer hats turned this way and that on a tide of soft music.

"Bride or bridegroom?" whispered somebody to Rickie, who was so much interested by the discovery that the music was *Jesu Joy Of Man's Desiring* that he took no notice.

"Bride," stated Lucy.

They were put into a pew which was some way back. Rickie, although he had lost his religious faith, immediately knelt down and buried his face in his arms. Lucy also knelt. She thought it bad manners to enter a church without doing so. She shut her eyes and launched a command into vacancy:

Make Melissa happy! Make Melissa happy! Make Melissa happy!

When she sat up she saw that somebody in the pew just in front was making faces at her. Lucy grimaced back, recalling the name with difficulty: Sylvia Stoner—Oxford—looking years older and much smarter than she had looked when she was cycling frantically down St. Giles' with a lot of books falling out of her basket.

Rickie was taking an unconscionable time over his prayers and making himself conspicuous. Lucy stared round and recognised other Oxford faces. Everyone looked older and smarter. But then they were all wearing their best clothes, and most of them had been exhausted by Schools when she last saw them.

A plump, eupeptic looking young couple bustled up the aisle —Cressida and fat Alan, who had a baby now, which they must have left at home. Rickie sat up at last, his face fixed in an agonised grin which he meant to keep up during the whole ceremony in order to prove that Melissa's happiness was more important than his own. But it flickered a little when he looked at the white and silver *Order of the Service* which had been handed to him. Proceedings were to end with the *Trumpet Voluntary*.

Lucy studied one and wondered if hers had looked so impressive. Had she had any? She could not remember. It was probable that she had; all that sort of thing had been done very correctly at her wedding. But what, she wondered, had become of them afterwards? Had people taken them home? In how many houses were they lying about now, tossed away with Christmas cards and other undestroyed rubbish—those hymns and psalms for Lucy Angela Carmichael and Patrick Reilly?

She craned round the forest of hats in an attempt to catch sight of John Beauclerc. He was invisible, but he must be there, by now, waiting for Melissa.

Mrs. Hallam, competent and graceful, walked up the aisle nodding at friends. Julian followed her. It could not be long now. Melissa, at home, had waited the prescribed ten minutes, and must have started for church. What a pity Hump could not be there! That must be the one bitter drop in Melissa's cup. Where was he at this great moment? In the Orchard Bush, whatever that was. Lucy pictured a vast apple orchard, and a man in a pith helmet crawling about looking for a fly, "just one little fly in the whole of Africa."

"Pum, pa pum-pum!" hummed Rickie, unable to keep silence while Bach was going on.

She nudged him and he shut up, blushing.

Oh you Hump, stop crawling and looking for flies! Think of Melissa. Pray for Melissa. For, next to John, she loves you better than anyone in the whole wide world.

Hump turned and ran towards her, not a man in a pith helmet, but a boy who had just won a race—a schoolboy in shorts and a singlet, whose photograph had stood on Melissa's mantelpiece all the time she was in Oxford. It was an enlargement of a snapshot taken at Winchester. The tensity and strain of the race were still upon him; his head was thrust forward and his mouth was grim. But in his eyes was the dawn of exultation. He ran towards her and dashed past her shouting: *In Millwood's bed!*

The music faded. The agitated rustle of suspense was rising. Heads were constantly turned towards the door. Unseen events were taking place out there in the sunshine. Everyone knew that the bride had arrived.

The organ pealed, the choir burst into song, and the congregation surged to its feet.

"Praise, my soul, the King of Heaven!"

Ah now! There was John! There he was with his kind, slightly worried, young face; he had stepped into view with a very tall, very fair, best man. He was up there, waiting for Melissa, while the choir paced onwards, two by two.

"Praise Him, praise Him!" sang the altos.
"Praise Him, praise Him!" chanted the tenors.
"Praise the everlasting King!" rumbled the basses.

Rickie gave a convulsive gasp, for Melissa was coming now. She passed them slowly in her misty white, touching and grave, upon her father's arm. Her lovely little head was bent beneath her veil and yet she was steadily offering to the world's view her resolution, her hopes, her love. A stir of emotion, a strange compassion, accompanied her passing, as of wind blowing over a field of corn. The receding choir was singing softly:

"Father-like He tends and spares us;
Well our feeble frame He knows . . ."

Behind her walked Valentine, elegant and collected in white organdie with green ribbons. There were no other bridesmaids. If she could not have me, thought Lucy, she would have no other friend.

"Angels in the height adore Him!
Ye behold Him face to face. . . ."

Now they were at the chancel steps and the choir had filed into their stalls. John had stepped forward to join his bride. All the actors in the drama had taken their places:

"Dearly Beloved, we are gathered together here in the sight of God . . ."

The entry of the bride is the most moving moment of any wedding—the moment at which all hearts are touched. The poignancy subsides as the ceremony proceeds. Lucy found herself growing calmer as the vows were taken, the troth plighted, and the ring placed on Melissa's finger. This was very like other weddings; John Standish and Melissa Mary were just another couple after all. They were saying the things which everybody said. She found herself able to observe details and studied with interest the mysterious Mr. Hallam, whom she had never seen before. He was handsome, grey haired and distinguished. But she decided that he had a very ill tempered mouth.

Once or twice she glanced round to see how Rickie was bearing up. He held his grin firmly in place, even through the most solemn parts of the ceremony, and joined loudly in the psalm when the bridal pair went up to the altar.

During the address the congregation sat in reverent boredom while marital advice, after the modern hole-and-corner fashion, was whispered into the ears of John and Melissa. Lucy hoped that the parson was not saying anything very stupid, because Melissa would not want to feel flippant at such a moment. An arch smile hovered upon his silly old face. Perhaps he had known Melissa in childhood and was recalling her infancy in some unwelcome way. She remembered that Melissa, in a moment of extreme unreserve, had confessed to having been called Pudding until she was seven years old. There were, she complained, a few odious people, mostly very old, who kept up the habit. Was this one of them? Was he adjuring John to be kind to dear little Pudding?

It was over at last and another hymn took the bridal party into the vestry. The congregation broke into loud chatter and the choir struck up Parry's *My Soul There Is A Country*. Mr. and Mrs. Hallam, Julian, Cressida, and Alan hurried out, followed by a lot of odd looking people who must be Beauclercs. Sylvia Stoner leaned over the pew to ask how Lucy was, much to the annoyance of Rickie, who wanted to listen to the Parry. Everyone felt that the holiness was now over, and was glad when the choir stopped singing.

As usual they took a long time in the vestry. But the buzz of conversation at last died down and the church was once more galvanised to attention.

The *Trumpet Voluntary* blared out. Everyone was on his feet. Out they came, down they came—John so transported that he took no notice of anybody, acknowledged none of the nods and smiles to right and left of him; Melissa securely tucked under his arm, her veil thrown back and her face sparkling like a morning in May. Behind them came a triumphant grinning mob of Hallams and Beauclercs. Tara! Tara! shouted the trumpets. And they were gone out into life, into the sunshine.

"Lucy! I *am* so glad to see you," cried Mrs. Hallam. "I'm so glad you could come. How *well* you're looking and what a *success-ful* hat! Humphrey! This is Lucy Carmichael! Melissa's *great* friend. Come and talk to her."

Her meaning eyes reminded Mr. Hallam of circumstances which he was all too unlikely to forget. They had already shaken hands with Lucy and Rickie when the procession of guests filed past them, but this was at a later stage of the reception, when they were at liberty to notice individuals.

Mr. Hallam bowed in a courtly way and drew Lucy aside to tell her how much he admired the intaglio ring. It had been shown to him the moment he arrived from Budleigh Salterton. A most beautiful ring, he repeated, and so clever of Lucy to have found it. Did she know anything of its history? He was interested in gems and thought that the stone might be a flawed emerald.

While he talked he was covertly examining this girl who had been jilted at the altar. How could she have got herself into such a scrape? There was nothing wrong with her that he could see. She seemed to be a nice girl, a pretty girl—quite a lady. His meditations were as clear to Lucy as if he had shouted them at the top of his voice.

Cressida and Alan came up. Oxford friends greeted her brightly. They were all emphatically kind and cordial and they all praised her hat as if surprised that a girl in her situation should still be capable of choosing hats. Encouragement, applause for the good face she was putting on things, beamed in every eye. She began to wish heartily that she had slipped away from the church and cut the party.

She had never before faced a crowd of people who knew her story. Nobody at Ravonsbridge, except Bess, had heard the exact details. Nor had she expected such a thing to be remembered on an occasion like this. She had supposed that all attention would be concentrated upon Melissa. She would not have come, had she known that her appearance would cause all this excitement. But she had longed to kiss Melissa just once, so she had trooped with all the others along the Kensington pavements, and stood in a queue in the foyer of the hotel, and reached Melissa at last only to catch a small spark of dismay in her friend's greeting. Melissa's eyes always told the truth. She should not have come.

John was sent to talk to her and he pumped her hand up and down a great many times and said that she must come and stay with them as soon as ever they were settled in Lincolnshire. He was saying this to everybody but he said it six times in succession to Lucy because he was so sorry for her. He, like everybody else, was determined to remember her trouble just when he had every excuse for forgetting it. There was to be no escape. Where she was known she must take it about with her like a label which nobody would allow her to remove. She had thought that she would remember long after everyone else had forgotten, but it seemed as though things might turn out the other way. She herself could now go for days at a time without any painful recollections, while to all these people she was permanently an object of compassion.

The cake was cut. Mr. Hallam made a graceful speech, John a manly one. Lucy sought refuge in a corner with Rickie, who was grinning steadily over successive glasses of champagne. She suggested that they might now slip off, but he insisted upon grinning it through, so they stayed, and ran out upon the pavement, and saw Melissa rush laughing through a storm of rose petals, and followed her car a little way until it turned a corner into Kensington High Street.

Rickie was staying the night with his aunt at Richmond and Lucy had got a room in a small Bayswater hotel. They strolled together into Kensington Gardens, their heads buzzing with champagne, and sank into two deck chairs. It was a broiling afternoon. Rickie's hair hung into his eyes and the carnation in his buttonhole was sadly wilted. He still wore his grin, but after sitting for a few minutes he realised that it was no longer necessary and exchanged it for a look of noble exaltation.

"He's a . . . dam fine fellow!" he announced solemnly.

"Umhm!" agreed Lucy drowsily.

"He's . . . worthy of Melissa."

"Nobody could be that. But I can just forgive him."

"He made a dam fine speech."

"Yes. I liked the way he spoke. Nice and simple."

"I couldn't have made a speech like that. I mean . . . it's easier to give Melissa up to a man who can make a dam fine speech like that."

"Oh, Rickie! You have had a lot of champagne!"

"I know. But I would if I hadn't. Think he made a dam fine speech, I mean."

Lucy leant back and shut her eyes. The heat was unendurable. She wondered what she should do with herself for the rest of the day. A cinema would be stifling. To wander about the Gardens alone in this hat would be to invite unwelcome attentions. But the lounge of her hotel, her airless bedroom, were repulsive alternatives for a poor girl all alone in London in a great big hat.

"Lucy!"

"Umhm?"

"We've got very friendly, haven't we?"

"We always were."

"Yes, but just lately . . . what we've both been through has brought us together, hasn't it?"

"Um. . . ."

"I shall never forget . . . helped me . . . don't know what I should have done . . . admire you tremendously . . . respect you frightfully . . . think you're marvellous. . . ."

She completely lost the thread of it, dipping into a short nap, and returned to the surface to hear him say:

". . . could be very happy. Nothing takes the place of first

153

love, of course. But respect and affection and common interests . . . they're a very good basis, don't you think?"

"Umhm."

"The only difficulty is the housing shortage in Ravonsbridge. But your digs in Sheep Lane are really large enough for a couple."

Lucy sat bolt upright, wide awake. He was asking her to marry him. He was suggesting that they should mutually pour balm into one another's broken hearts.

"Oh no, Rickie, I couldn't. I'm very sorry. I couldn't."

"But it would be a great shame for you to be an old maid, Lucy. You're so nice. You ought to be married."

"I couldn't agree with you more. But—"

"You think it's wrong to marry a man you . . . you can't love as much as the first one?"

She hesitated. Did she? She thought not. A very nice man who offered to rescue her from being poor Lucy might some day be welcome. Yes. She hoped to marry, though she did not suppose she could ever marry for love. The possibility of marrying somebody who was not Patrick had become credible.

"I'm very sorry, it couldn't be you, Rickie dear."

"But why not?"

It was impossible to tell him why not without hurting his feelings. She said:

"You'll fall in love again yourself one day. I'm sure you will."

He was sure that he would not. They wrangled about it until Rickie, glancing at his watch, discovered that he ought to set off for Richmond. He struggled out of his chair, assured her that his offer would remain open, advised her to think it over, and departed, humming the *Trumpet Voluntary*.

Lucy went to sleep again and slept until the chairman woke her up with a demand for threepence. Then she set off through the blistering heat towards the Bayswater side of the Gardens. The solitary evening in front of her was so depressing that she almost regretted her refusal of Rickie. He would have been company and she was growing tired of solitude. She was very fond of him in a way. But no . . . she meant to get more out of life than marriage with Rickie could supply. She was quite astonished to realise how much she still hoped to get, what fun she expected to have.

Part 4

The Ravonsbridge Hamlet

1

THE INTAGLIO ring had been an undoubted bargain but it had cost a good deal more than Lucy could afford. When she had paid for her wedding hat, another absurd extravagance, she found that she had nothing upon which to live during the summer vacation. Her mother was still in Canada and Stephen had an invitation to Scotland. So she volunteered as a holiday land worker and spent August on a farm in Shropshire.

The life, though pleasant, was strenuous. As she wrote to her mother, she had not time to think a thought from dawn, when she rose, to dusk, when she plunged into another night of dreamless sleep. Hours of leisure there were, but during these she simply sat, digested the vast meals provided by the farmer's wife, and listened idly to the wireless. In a very short time she regained most of the pounds which she had lost during the past year, her cheeks grew rounder and her nose less sharp. She returned to Ravonsbridge in September with a fine sun tan and scratched from wrist to shoulder by corn sheaves which she had been imprudent enough to carry in a sleeveless dress.

The Institute was still closed but she came back early because she wanted to prepare her lectures for the autumn term. She was looking forward to them with considerable zest; her intellect, though it had been quiescent at the farm, had not been starved. It had enjoyed an interval of refreshing repose and was now active.

She wrote three papers with which she was really pleased. It was agreeable moreover to be welcomed so warmly by all her Ravonsbridge friends. She had never expected to enjoy this return so much.

One morning, just as she was finishing her breakfast in Sheep Lane, Mr. Thornley knocked at her door. In an agitated voice he asked if she could possibly come with him at once to his office, and if she was free for the day.

She hesitated. During the vacation her time was her own, and she had meant to take a day off in Slane Forest. It was the anniversary of her ill-fated wedding day, and, though she could think of it with far less pain than she had once supposed possible, its reappearance in the calendar had made her feel rather low. She wanted to be by herself in the open air.

"I know it's a favour," said Mr. Thornley. "But I badly need your help. The fact is," he went on, almost shyly, "I . . . I'm going abroad almost immediately. . . ."

"Oh!" cried Lucy. "*His Eminence?* It's been chosen?"

For she knew all about the drama festival.

Yes, his play had been chosen, and not only for Geneva. The three winning groups had been invited to go upon a short European tour; they were to visit Nancy, the Hague, and Copenhagen. And Mr. Thornley had been invited to accompany them as lecturer on the British Amateur Drama. He was beside himself with innocent gratification.

But he would not be back in Ravonsbridge till November and all his work at the Institute must be delegated. Miss Frogmore was still away on vacation. The production of *Hamlet* must be put in hand; it could not be postponed until his return because the theatre must be free in December for the Nativity play. The casting and rehearsing must all be turned over to Lucy, since Miss Frogmore would have her hands full with the students' classes. He could only get back himself in time to put the finishing touches. Lucy, he was sure, could manage. He would have postponed the production till the spring term if Robin had not been leaving at Christmas. But Lucy was so capable. He had every reliance on her.

By this time she had capitulated and they were hurrying together to his office while he poured out instructions, encouragement, and joyful self-congratulations. His excitement over his coming trip was so great that he could not think continuously of *Hamlet*. He was particularly looking forward to Nancy. He had always wished to visit a French university town. And after all, Lucy had been at Ravonsbridge for a year. The production estimates would have to be worked out with Hayter, who would tell her how much she might spend. But she would have no difficulty. Hayter was always very co-operative about that sort of thing. Angera's sets must be put in hand, but she could trust Angera to do the thing properly; anything he sent in would be all right. The theatre in Copenhagen, the theatre in which the British groups were to play, was said to be a very fine one. All these small countries had such good architecture. The props list and the wardrobe list she would find in the *Hamlet* file. He believed that all the props were there, had been there when the play was last given, five years ago, though he had a notion that Yorick's skull might be missing. Had he mentioned that one of the judges at the drama festival had called *His Eminence* "the ideal play for amateurs"? All nonsense, of course; but still, it did give good sound acting parts to— Why! Now he remembered that skull was missing. It had vanished during the run and the children had had to make do with a turnip. Of course, he knew Geneva well. He had been there twice before. There were to be some immediate rehearsals before the party left England, and that was why he must go to London at once. If possible he wanted to get off that very afternoon. There were some reports which Lucy must have ready for the council meeting; he was sorry to have to cut it, but it could not be a very important meeting as Lady Frances would also be away. Marion, the daughter who had married a Scottish laird, was expecting a baby in October. Of course, in casting, there would be the usual shortage of men. Rosencrantz and Guilderstern must double with the grave diggers. He had always done that. And Polonius with Osric. Lucy must do as she thought fit. He left it entirely in her hands. If she cast Peter Sykes for Horatio she couldn't have him for Laertes. She would have no Laertes. She must decide which part had to suffer. It was always the way; too few boys in the school and too many girls who would never be any earthly good, but had been despatched to Ravonsbridge because they were stage struck.

It was impossible to get Robin to speak verse as if it was verse, but she must not worry about that unduly, for there was nothing to be done.

Lucy listened in a silence which was partly enforced, for she could not have inserted a word had she wished, and partly diplomatic. She had not the slightest intention of letting Robin play Hamlet; she knew whom she was going to cast for the part, but instinct warned her to hold her tongue. To listen, to agree, was the best course until she had hustled Mr. Thornley out of Ravonsbridge. At every other sentence he was assuring her that she could do as she thought best, and she meant to take him at his word. But it would be very dangerous to let him guess, at this stage, the excitement this permission had let loose. If she could, without actual dishonesty, allow him to believe that she meant to take all his advice, he was much more likely to go that afternoon. And she could hardly wait to see him gone—to get the Ravonsbridge Theatre to herself, just at this moment when all her energy seemed to have returned to her.

"As for the girls," he said, "that's simple. Wendy and Ruth. There is nobody else, now that Jill has gone."

Some risks had to be taken, and Lucy thought it better to let him know that she did not want Wendy, who was growing much too big for her boots. It would be very good for Wendy, she suggested, to be left out of one production.

Thornley was inclined to agree, but reminded her that Ruth could not play Gertrude and Ophelia.

"Kitty wouldn't be bad as Gertrude," said Lucy. "She has so much . . ."

Voluptuousness was the word which occurred to her but she feared that it might shock him.

"Warmth . . ." she continued. "And she can make up to look middle-aged better than any of them. She really is a good actress."

"I know. I'm fond of Kitty, and she has worked so hard. She deserves a leading part. But that accent!"

"She's been working at it all the summer; she went to a phonetics specialist, and she's greatly improved. She'll still say, 'The Queen caraouses . . .' but I've heard as bad on the West End stage. She's back in Ravonsbridge; if you could just find time to . . ."

This was an astute suggestion. Mr. Thornley was certain that he could not find the time, and that he would be content with Lucy's decision. But could Ruth manage Ophelia?

"Ianthe . . ." murmured Lucy.

"Ianthe's in Yorkshire," he said hastily. "She's left the school."

"If she came back—"

"I should be sorry. She'd really very much better stay in Yorkshire. There's no question. . . . You must see what Ruth can do. You must decide as you think best."

Lucy deftly changed the subject and launched such a battery of questions upon minor points that he thought he should never catch his train. All the positions and movements, he assured her, had been worked out by him years ago. She would find them in his interleaved copy of the play and on diagrams in the *Hamlet* file. Every step, every gesture was marked and she need alter nothing. (Oh, needn't I? thought Lucy.) If she had the players coached according to his notes by the time that he got back in November, he could supervise the final rehearsals.

"But if I should want to alter anything?"

"Oh, alter anything you like, my dear. But I don't think you'll want to. I think you'll find my notes can't be bettered."

They lunched on sandwiches as they went through the reports she was to prepare for the council, and in the middle of the afternoon he rushed off to pack and catch his train. His parting remark reflected his frenzied state of mind:

"I'll send you a wire from Geneva to tell me how it's getting on."

Lucy collected her armful of files and, before returning to Sheep Lane, slipped for a moment into the dark, silent theatre. Fumbling with the switch-board she turned on all the available lights—battens, floats and spots. Then, looking out into the dim auditorium she announced:

"You're going to see something!"

On her way home she called first at the rectory, for Ianthe's address, and then at the post office. A telegram had to be composed which should not reveal too much to the postmistress.

After some cogitation she wrote and despatched the following message:

> His eminence gone away and I am the local
> Basil Dean stop Where is the beauteous
> majesty of Denmark query In the bag
> come right home Lucy

Not for an instant did she hesitate to bring Ianthe back to Ravonsbridge. She knew nothing of Thornley's reasons for wishing the girl away and thought him prejudiced. She believed that she could get Miss Frogmore's support and she was sure that such a performance as Ianthe would give, as Ophelia, must convince him, on his return, of her right to the part. All that she had against Ianthe was forgotten or set aside. The Ravonsbridge *Hamlet* was now all important and must not be allowed to suffer because she had quarrelled with her former friend.

Caution had never come naturally to Lucy and she flung herself into this task with all that vehemence which had been but temporarily suspended. She was determined to get a production which had room in it for Ianthe's talent. None of Thornley's old stuff would do. The rest of the cast must be galvanised; they must be made to feel that this was not merely another student production, but a unique and important event. They must all do better than they had ever done before. Everything must be new and fresh and vigorous. Technical shortcomings might look after themselves if only the atmosphere of poetry could be created.

After a hasty tea she sat down to study Thornley's script. It was, as she expected, like a plan for a walking tour. He always kept his players travelling—partly because he seldom directed people experienced enough to stand still. They were never allowed to say more than three lines upon the same spot. There were not many chairs at Elsinore, but Hamlet was kept busy, during most of his soliloquies, sitting on them, one after the other, in relentless rotation. And Rosencrantz, inevitably, sat astride a chair, facing the back—no Thornley production ever omitted this most unnatural proceeding, except the Nativity play, which had no chairs. But nobody was going to do it in a Carmichael production.

At six o'clock a reply from Ianthe arrived:

The croaking raven doth bellow for revenge
arriving Ravonsbridge tomorrow you are a pet
Ianthe

It was a relief to Lucy, whose only fear had been lest Ianthe should refuse her olive branch. She decided to meet Ianthe's train, if she could, and enjoin discretion; they had better keep their plans secret until Miss Frogmore returned. A very little persuasion would secure her approval, for she had a high opinion of Ianthe's work and had wanted to cast her as Viola. With Miss Frogmore behind them they could let pink pig Wendy know that she was not indispensable.

Having studied Thornley's notes, **Lucy** began to work out her own ideas. Immediately she perceived **that** he really did know what he was doing, that her own inclinations were too static, and that she had a tendency to leave people in the same place for ever. The longer she worked, the more her respect for him revived. The magnitude of the task began to be apparent to her. There were even moments when she wondered if she ought not to follow his directions. But there was no room for anything like Ianthe in his *Hamlet*, and Ianthe she must have. The world must see what she had seen that afternoon upon the terrace of Slane St. Mary's.

She was quite sure that she could get what she wanted if she had time enough—if she could proceed on a system of trial and error. But this might impair her authority with the students. Not all of them would obey her as they obeyed Thornley; here, too, she perceived that she had underrated him. He was mild and equable, but his authority was unquestioned. He could always make them do what he wanted. Could she?

She hoped that she could. Robin, who could, if he liked, give a lot of trouble, would be on her side. He would be so glad to play Polonius that he would do his very best for her. She knew that he had been dreading this production. He disliked tragedy. He could not speak verse. His gifts were for comedy, though he was not a Shakespearean actor at all. As Polonius he might hope to give a creditable performance, but his Hamlet would be dire and no one knew it better than he did. She decided to be very artful. She would not tell him immediately of her plans; she would give him Polonius as a reward for co-operative behaviour.

Towards midnight she discovered that she was hungry; she had forgotten to get herself any supper. She paused to brew some coffee and remembered that at this moment last year she had been sitting with her mother and Stephen in the Gorling kitchen, drinking champagne and laughing like an idiot. Ever since Mr. Thornley's appearance at breakfast she had been too busy to tell herself what day this was. She was too busy, now, to do so for long. She swallowed her coffee and went back to her notes.

2

MARION'S BABY kept Lady Frances in Scotland throughout October. She chafed at so long an absence, unable to believe that the Institute could get on without her. She had proof that it could not. Had she been in Ravonsbridge, Mr. Thornley would never have been permitted to abandon his post in so flagrant a manner. The council should have recalled him, would have recalled him, if she had been at the meeting. But in her absence they had tamely assented to his unauthorised jaunt and there was nothing to be done save pickle a rod for him when he came home. Meanwhile the *Hamlet* rehearsals must be going on with nobody to direct them except poor Miss Carmichael. She wrote urgently to Charles and Penelope, commanding them to go and find out what was happening in the theatre.

Charles declared that he was too busy, but Penelope looked in on a rehearsal one evening and came back to Cyre Abbey with a very long face.

"It's awful," she told Charles, during dinner. "I don't know what Mr. Thornley will say when he comes back."

"He won't have a chance to say anything much," said Charles. "Mamma will do all the talking."

"Yes, but I really don't think I'll tell her how awful it is. It'll only worry her and she's worried enough about Marion. She can't do anything."

"What is so bad about it? It can't be worse than it was five years ago."

"Oh, it is! Miss Carmichael doesn't seem to know in the least what it ought to be like. She can't ever have seen a production of *Hamlet*. And who do you think Ophelia is? Ianthe!"

"No. Not really?"

"She is. That shows you. And you know that bit where she's supposed to be mad and hands all the flowers round? Well, she doesn't. She buries a bird instead. At least . . . I gather it's a bird. She says: *Farewell my dove!* Is that in the book?"

"Yes. I think it is."

"I never heard anyone say it before. Well, you can't see this bird or the flowers, they're all imaginary. Mr. Thornley always had real flowers, so you knew what they were. And she never takes the least notice of anybody. She comes on looking completely mad."

"Oughtn't she?" asked Charles.

"Not so mad. She's got this bird and these flowers in her apron, supposed to, and she says it's a bier, and goes to a sort of altar where the King says his prayers in another scene, with steps up to it, and she puts the bird down and arranges the flowers round it and sings over it. I mean she's talking to the bird when she says: Here's fennel for you, and here's rue for you, and all that. I should have thought everybody knew she had to hand the flowers round to the King and the Queen and Laertes. You really don't know if she thinks it's the bird or her father!"

"Who is Hamlet? That boy with the eyelashes?"

"Robin? Oh, no. He's only Polonius. That's another thing. She's got in a Hamlet from outside."

"Outside Ravonsbridge?"

"Outside the Institute. He's a Welsh boy from the new town and he's in the Works. That's why they have to have the rehearsals so late; he can't come till after six."

"Is he any good?"

"I only saw him in part of the graveyard scene. He's all right, but he's got a Welsh accent. But he does it quite properly; he picks up the skull and says: *Poor Yorick* and everything. It's rather ghastly, though. He does it too much as if it was really a skull. I mean it's not a nice idea to think you've picked up a real person's skull, especially somebody you knew. It seemed worse, because he had a yellow pullover."

"My dear Penelope! What do you mean?"

"I mean when they're all dressed up perhaps it won't seem so real. The horrified sort of way he held it made you wonder if it smelt or something."

"He sounds as if he might be rather good," mused Charles. "What's his name? Do you know?"

"I've forgotten. Miss Frogmore told me he'd won a prize for declamation at an Eisteddfod. But that's Welsh. And he runs an amateur dramatic company down in the new town or something like that. And Miss Carmichael went to see one of their shows and admired him so much she got him to play this. But I'm sure Mamma won't approve. I mean, it's rather a cheek of him to run this dramatic company when there is the Institute."

Charles advised her not to disturb their mother by reports of this kind. He pointed out that such innovations could not have been attempted without Hayter's approval. His curiosity was roused. He did not often go to the Institute but he was obliged, a few days later, to look in at Hayter's office in order to sign some presidential letters. He took the opportunity to ask a few questions.

Hayter explained. Owen Rees was the son of a coal miner, over in the valleys beyond the Welsh border. He had been in the M.M. works for some years and was a personality in the lower town. There was no question but that he was a gifted actor and his little company, largely drawn from the M.M. workers, had staged some striking productions. Miss Carmichael had escorted old Mr. Meeker to see one of them and had been greatly impressed. She had thought, and Hayter agreed with her, that efforts might be made to bring all this talent and enthusiasm into the orbit of the Institute. If Rees could be induced to take the part, many M.M. workers would come up the hill to see him, for he was very popular.

She had asked Hayter if it would be possible, since Rees was obviously far superior to any of the students, to include him in the cast without enrolling him in the school. Hayter had obligingly looked up the provisions of the constitution and discovered that guest actors could be invited at any time. Rees had jumped at the chance; he had always yearned to play Hamlet and he was not, so

Hayter declared, afraid of all that poetry. Also the invitation had gratified public opinion in the lower town. The production was causing more stir than anything done by the Institute for a number of years. There were even enquiries from the mining valleys whence Rees came; parties were coming in motor coaches for the first night.

"And does Mr. Thornley know of all this?" asked Charles.

Hayter looked demure and said that it had been difficult to get in touch with Mr. Thornley. But Miss Carmichael had consulted himself and Miss Frogmore at every point. There was no doubt that she was a most enterprising girl. She seemed to have put new life into everybody. Mr. Millwood really ought to look into the theatre and see them at it. Miss Meadows would be rehearsing that evening, and she was worth watching.

Charles would have liked to do so, but he flinched from the furore which his appearance always caused at any Institute function. He would have smothered his curiosity and gone home if he had not met Angera in the quadrangle.

"You are coming to see the rehearsal?" suggested Emil. "I also. Tonight it is Ianthe."

"Shouldn't we disturb them?"

"Ach no. Everybody is going, the whole Institute. One goes every night."

"But I'm . . . I turn up here so seldom, they might be excused for thinking it an intrusion."

Angera realised that a Millwood in the audience might create self-consciousness.

"We can go to Miss Frogmore's little box," he said, taking Charles by the arm. "Nobody can see us there."

Charles yielded. They went into the theatre and climbed the stairs to Miss Frogmore's box.

"For myself," said Angera, as they went, "I am the most enthusiastic for this Owen Rees. He is a true artist. For Ianthe . . . but you will see. I am curious to know what you will think."

"And Miss Carmichael's production?"

Angera paused in the corridor outside the box and burst out laughing.

"Ach, poor Lucy! It is not production. All the time she is saying: Now that's wrong. I have made a mistake. . . ."

"She's no good at it?"

"You will see. All the time, nothing but mistakes. Yet imagine, these children are acting one million times better than they have ever acted before. All these mistakes, but she is not stupid I think."

He opened the door of the box upon a shrill hullabaloo. Laertes, on the stage below, was battering at the gates of Elsinore, accompanied by a chubby mob. Lucy had been obliged to use all the extra boys as guards and the insurgent Danes were played by the stage struck girls.

Her voice rose from the auditorium:

"No, no! Stop! That's all wrong! I'm so sorry!"

Laughter went up, from the stage and from all parts of the house. Charles peered out of the box for a moment and saw her standing in the stalls. Her face was dirty and her hair was wild. The house was full of people who had come in to watch.

"You," she said, pointing to Claudius, who was down stage, "oughtn't to be there."

"It's where you told me to be."

"I know. I made a mistake."

There was more laughter. But it was, Charles realised, affectionate and friendly. It ceased as soon as she spoke again. They might laugh but they were taking her seriously.

"Get up on the throne," she commanded. "Get up there as soon as you've said: *The doors are broke!* And sit there waiting for anyone to dare touch you. You can say: *Divinity doth hedge a king* . . . much better up there."

"O.K.," said Claudius.

"And you, Laertes, rush in . . . *Where is this king?* . . . see him waiting for you on his throne and pull up short. Checked by seeing him there. Then turn and tell the mob to get out."

"O.K.," said Laertes.

"And you, mob, don't all shout: *No, let's come in!* Only the ones behind, who can't see, shout that. The front ones start pushing out almost before he tells them to, when they see the king. Kitty . . . don't clutch Alec from behind. Throw yourself between him and the king. Now! Again. . . ."

166

The scene proceeded.

"Every time," whispered Angera, "poor Lucy must make a mistake before it is right."

"It's right now," replied Charles. "It's very good now. I like your set, Angera. Who's that girl?"

"Kitty. She speaks badly, but she acts with the whole body. This I find so rare, in England."

"She does. One can believe she's infatuated with Claudius. Laertes is pretty bad. . . . "

"There is nobody good for the part. He can't speak. At the grave he is good, also I think in the fencing. . . . Ach now! Attend!"

The clamour off stage had begun again. Charles felt, though he could not see, a wave of excitement go over the house. Kitty, sitting on the steps of the king's throne, half rose, but Claudius restrained her, with a hand on her shoulder. They watched Laertes as he turned to meet his sister.

Charles had once entered an empty room in an old house—the Manor House of Slane St. Mary's, before the Knevetts left it, to encounter a sense of unearthly cold and horror. He knew that something had taken place there, was still taking place, and it would, in another moment, be revealed to him. He had rushed out, and had never been able to speak of it to anyone.

The same kind of chill stole over him now as Ianthe stumbled down the stage, seeing nobody, her head bent crookedly over the burden in her sacking apron. Not that he recognised her immediately. He did not say to himself that it was Ianthe until she reached the little shrine down stage, and laid her pitiful burden upon the lowest step. He scarcely felt her to be human; she was a vision which might have appeared, had he stayed in that room. His only fear was that she might speak, and tell what she knew. That fool Laertes was begging her to speak, calling her rose of May, dear maid, and sweet sister. But she made no answer until, pointing at the step, she exclaimed in a raucous chant:

"They bore him barefaced on the bier . . ."

The king stirred uneasily on his throne. But the hunted mind had slipped away from its pursuer and she was muttering now of a wheel and a false steward. She fumbled with her flowers to deck the bier. There was a moment's piercing terror on the word: *Remembrance!* She cowered, flung memory from her, and rambled on, the horror modulating into an overwhelming, an endless grief. Tears rolled down Kitty's cheeks and Laertes relaxed from his stiff pose. Only Claudius watched, intent for a betraying word. None came. She sang the last dirge very low, and almost sweetly; then, with the same shambling step she withdrew, her head always bent a little sideways. But at the door she turned and straightened her neck. She seemed to become aware, for the first time, of other mourners. A look, not sane, but of extreme tenderness, stole across her wan features. In a changed voice she exclaimed:

"And of all Christian souls I pray God . . . God be with you!"

In the next moment she was gone—to her death.

After a short silence, applause broke out and Lucy's voice could be heard exclaiming:

"Shut up! This is a rehearsal!"

"Well!" said Charles, turning to Angera. "I couldn't have believed it. How is she in the nunnery scene?"

"Very good. There is always, even at the beginning, a little look . . . something queer . . . too much gentleness, too much obedience . . . it's not healthy. One feels this girl might go mad."

"I'd always thought her . . ." Charles checked himself.

"Oh, she is a nasty girl," agreed Angera. "But she has a gift. One can't deny that. Only . . . she is not artist."

"What? I should have thought—"

"I know. But wait till you have seen Rees. He is artist. He has not any colossal gift. He has talent only, but he is artist."

Charles remained in the box until the graveyard scene was over. He found himself unable to form any opinion of Rees; everything was an anti-climax after the shock produced by Ianthe. After a time he found himself rebelling against the memory of her. He turned to Angera, who was watching him, and nodded before Charles could speak.

"You see? She is not artist. She doesn't fit. She is a firework simply; somesing marvellous but all by itself. She has no *mesure*, no conscience. She can shatter, but she cannot raise the soul . . . she has no light to bring. One is spellbound, but then one rejects her."

168

"I believe you are right. What a pity! She should make the production, and I think she'll ruin it."

"Poor Lucy," agreed Angera. "It's a very, very big mistake. So big it has been worth making. These big mistakes, they make one think. I have an idea that all Lucy's mistakes will be like that."

3

CHARLES MISSED the opening night. He had to go to London for some weeks and thence to Scotland, for Lady Frances had overtasked herself in the care of her daughter and was too unwell to travel home alone. She had been advised not to travel at all but she thought that nonsense. She had had sciatica before, and though she could not walk without pain she still walked a good deal more than many women of her age who enjoyed perfect health.

So she was hoisted into a sleeper at Stirling and travelled south in considerable agony.

On arrival at Cyre Abbey she refused to go to bed though she was unable to sit at the dinner table. A tray was brought to her by the breakfast room fire and there Charles joined her when he had finished his own meal.

"Penelope has been telling me about the play," she said. "I'm so afraid I shan't see it; I don't think I really can get into Ravonsbridge just now."

"Was it a success?" asked Charles eagerly.

"Oh, yes," said Penelope vaguely.

A description of any sort was hard to get from her, for she was unobservant and had no command of words. But, when questioned, she did allow that the theatre had been fuller than usual. On reflection she added that it had been quite full and that a lot of people had not been able to get in. She could not say whether anybody from the Works had come. A lot of rough noisy people had come who stamped and cheered when Mr. Rees made a speech and sang Land of My Fathers in Welsh, which sounded weird.

"Those must have been the miners from his home village," said Charles.

"He made a speech? This actor?" asked Lady Frances.

"They shouted till he did," explained Penelope. "Mr. Thornley made a speech first of course, but they went on shouting till Mr. Rees made a speech, quite short, just thanking everybody. It was rather cheek, in our Institute."

"Did Thornley get back?" asked Charles.

"Oh, yes. And he'd been able to improve it a lot. It was much better than the rehearsal I saw. They'd changed all that weird business about the dead bird. She handed the flowers round properly —Ophelia did, I mean."

Charles expressed some concern for Ianthe. He thought it hard that she should be made to change that scene.

"Oh. She wasn't in it."

"What? Why not?"

"I don't know. Ruth Hilliard did it. She was much better."

"What can have happened?" lamented Charles. "Were there many other changes?"

Penelope thought not and gave him the programme.

"Produced by F. Thornley!" he read. "I call that a shame. Miss Carmichael did all the work. She found Owen Rees."

Lady Frances agreed. She was furious with Mr. Thornley and intended to tell him that all his outside work must, in future, be dropped. As for unfairness to Miss Carmichael, Mr. Hayter was coming out to Cyre Abbey next morning, and he would be certain to give an unprejudiced account of the facts.

Charles was not so certain of this. He expected that Hayter's account would damage Thornley, and it did. Lady Frances could find no excuses for Thornley when she told the story to her children at dinner time.

He had come back a week before the opening and had cavilled at everything done by poor Miss Carmichael, in a most unreasonable way. For Miss Carmichael had done nothing without first consulting Mr. Hayter and Miss Frogmore, and Miss Frogmore was very much put out. As for Mr. Hayter he was really distressed; Lady Frances had never seen him so much distressed. He kept insisting that he ought to take full responsibility and that he had never dreamed that he would be getting Miss Carmichael into trouble when he encouraged her to pursue her own ideas. They had been, in his opinion, excellent ideas, and he had never supposed that Mr. Thornley would object to them. The invitation to Owen Rees was perfectly in accordance with the provisions of the Institute, and the play had been a great success—the greatest success ever known in the annals of the Institute. There had been notices in the local press and at Gloucester, Severnton, and several neighbouring towns. It was playing to crowded houses. For the first time in years the lower town was taking some interest in an Institute production. That was, undoubtedly, because Owen Rees was in the cast.

"I told Mr. Hayter," said Lady Frances, "that I should have sanctioned the invitation if I had been here. It would have pleased your father; he would have been delighted that a young man from the Works should play such a part as this, it's exactly the sort of thing he had in mind. I shall tell Mr. Thornley so. And in any case, if he objected, he should have been here to say so, not in Switzerland."

"But did he try to throw Rees out?" asked Charles.

"No. I don't gather that he went as far as that. He must have realised it was too late. But I got the impression that he was not at all pleasant to Mr. Rees and would treat him as if he was a student. Mr. Rees is an experienced actor. Naturally he resented it."

"And Ianthe? What happened to her?"

"She resigned the part in a huff, when Mr. Thornley insisted she must play it differently. Her understudy played it. He would have altered a great deal more, but there wasn't time. He had to let most of it stand. I asked Mr. Hayter if he thought it ought to be called Mr. Thornley's production, and he said no. He says a lot of people are indignant about the programme and think it most unfair. But he says Miss Carmichael has behaved very well; she has not complained at all. As soon as Mr. Thornley came back she handed back the reins to him and never said a word when her work was undone. But, as I said to Mr. Hayter, that's not the point. Has she, or has she not, been fairly treated? There has never been unfairness in our Institute before, that I know of. She had all this work thrust on her and she should get the credit, especially when it is such a success. We must set this right."

Charles felt that his mother was being manoeuvred into so violent a prejudice against Thornley that he made some demur. Hayter, he suggested, might not know all the facts. Miss Carmichael might have used Thornley's notes.

"I shall ask her that," said Lady Frances. "I'm going to get to the bottom of it. I'm going to hear all sides. Before I see Mr. Thornley I'm going to send for Miss Carmichael and hear her version. I shall have her out to tea on Sunday."

"Couldn't you make it lunch?" asked Charles. "I'm out to tea on Sunday."

"You mean you'd like to be there, dear?"

Lady Frances was surprised and pleased. She had always wanted Charles to take some interest in Institute affairs. But she pointed out that there were no buses out from Ravonsbridge on a Sunday morning. Perhaps, however, Miss Carmichael had a bicycle.

"I'll drive in and fetch her," said Charles. "If she has to come out here, on her only free day, she'd better come in comfort. And I can drop her in Ravonsbridge on my way to my tea party, in the afternoon."

He was praised for his unselfishness, at which he scowled.

"Miss Carmichael," he said, getting up, "is a very . . . she is a talented and distinguished member of our staff. She is not a scullion from the Institute canteen. I think she should be treated with courtesy."

He stalked off to the library, leaving his women to stare at one another.

"How very odd of Charles!" exclaimed Lady Frances.

"I think he's smitten," muttered Penelope.

"Smitten?" repeated Lady Frances with distaste.

"Oh, Mamma, you know perfectly well what I mean. I think he's in love with her."

"Nonsense."

"It's not nonsense. I've thought so ever since that time we met her at the hotel in Severnton. I told you . . . when she was with her friend."

"I thought it was the friend who made such an impression on him."

"She did. But ever since then he seems to have got this absurd idea that Miss Carmichael is . . . well, superior to the other girls at the Institute. And she did look different, that day. I hardly recognised her. Well . . . you know how different the servants look when you meet them on their day off?"

"Overdressed? Very much made up, you mean?"

"No-no." Penelope could not honestly say that. "They were both very simply dressed. It was their manner. It was so . . . so . . . easy and cool. Charles went and talked to them and they treated him as if he was an equal."

"So he is! Don't be such a snob, Penelope!"

"But Mamma, you know he's not. I'm sure you'd have been surprised yourself. They treated him as if he was nobody."

Lady Frances could not believe it. Such a thing was impossible in Severnshire. She told Penelope to telephone to Miss Carmichael at the Institute with the news that Charles would call in Sheep Lane on Sunday morning at half past twelve and bring her out to Cyre Abbey for lunch.

"And that," said Lady Frances, "will give her plenty of time to get to church first."

Lucy believed that she was in the dog house. She did not realise that cold meat and junket at Cyre Abbey was an unusual distinction and thought that she was going to be put on the carpet for her misdeeds. Penelope's curt instructions over the telephone annoyed her, nor was she mollified by the fact that the Eel was calling for her, presumably in his Ravon Roadster. In a belligerent mood she took especial care over her hair and make up; a good appearance might not impress Lady Frances but it would strengthen her own morale. When she heard the roadster draw up in Sheep Lane she sailed out deedily, determined to stand no nonsense from the Eel. Should he sulk at having to fetch her she would pay him out by asking after his old school chums, Hallam and Pattison.

But he greeted her with less stiffness and more cordiality than she could have thought possible, making quite a fuss of her, tuck-

173

ing a rug round her knees, and saying all that Penelope ought to
have said about his mother's illness, their regrets at having to bring
Miss Carmichael out to Cyre Abbey, and her kindness in coming.
He could be a charming Eel if he liked. She felt all the subtle flat-
tery of haughtiness when it chooses to be cordial, and she was
really concerned to know that Lady Frances was in so much pain.

As soon as they were out of Sheep Lane he said such warm
things in praise of the play, which he had now seen, that she was
completely melted. He also told her of the rehearsal he had witnessed, and asked who had thought of the business with the bird.

"Ianthe did," said Lucy. "And I was very sorry it was changed."

"And that she was out?" asked Charles.

Lucy hesitated and then said:

"I'm miserable for her sake. It was a dreadful blow to her. And
I feel so guilty at having asked her to come back and play it. But
. . . the play was better without her."

"That's what I thought, amazing though it seemed," said
Charles. "She was brilliant. And the understudy was quite bad
really. But—"

"Ruth's badness did less harm to the play than Ianthe's bril-
liance," interrupted Lucy. "Ianthe knocked the play to bits. She
wasn't right in it. She seemed to be made of quite different material . . . something isolated, that didn't fit in."

"I came to the conclusion that her performance was a stunt,"
said Charles. "It wasn't art. It knocked me over at the time, and
afterwards I disliked it."

"That's just it. It was something quite different from what
Owen did, or even Robin and Kitty. It didn't add anything. I'd
never been so clear about the real art of acting until I realised that
Ianthe hasn't got it. She imitates so well that she can give you the
sensations the real thing would have. I always thought that was
acting. But afterwards, when you remember it wasn't real, there is
something impure about it. Now an actor, even if he's second rate,
if he has any true art, adds something to the real thing. I don't
quite know what. But it's intensely interesting."

"Put it this way," said Charles, "and it might apply to all art.
Behind the real thing there is a blueprint . . . the design of that
thing which is laid up in heaven. Which is much more real than

174

our vulgar conception of the thing. Any art gives you a hint of that other reality. An actor, giving you a drunken porter not only gives you a drunken porter, a common object, but a touch of *the* drunken porter, devised by the Immortals. So that the common object becomes infused with greatness."

"Yes . . ." said Lucy, pondering. "Yes."

"So it was really a relief to you when she went out?"

"Oh, I can't tell you what a relief! Because Owen Rees was getting desperate. I think he'd have gone out if she hadn't. And stupid people thought he was jealous because she attracted so much attention. But he was quite right. And yet, you know, I had believed she would make the play."

"Did Mr. Thornley alter very much, besides that?"

"Very little. He had to work day and night to get poor Ruth coached for the part."

"Then allow me to say that I think your name should have been billed as producer."

Lucy flushed. She was growing tired of hearing this. The question of credit had never occurred to her until she saw Thornley's name on the programme. She then realised that she had always thought of the production as her own, and was both angry and disappointed. But some of her adherents were making such a case of it that she had grown impatient.

"Oh, that doesn't matter," she said hastily. "I'd much rather people shouldn't say that. It spoils all one's pleasure in the play's success . . . it's so petty."

"Perhaps I ought to warn you that my mother believes that there has been some injustice. That's why she wants to see you."

"Who can have given her such an idea?"

"Hayter," said Charles, watching her closely.

"Then he was talking through his hat," cried Lucy hotly. "I'm perfectly certain Mr. Thornley never intended to pinch my credit. He thinks of all the Institute productions as his: from his point of view this one was. He left me all instructions, and I merely had to carry them out—and I had no business to ignore them as I did. If I'd let him in for a dire failure, he would have shouldered the responsibility and billed himself as producer just the same. He wouldn't have saddled me with the blame. He has a terribly good opinion of himself, but he's not a mean man or a jealous man."

All lingering suspicions of Lucy's sincerity were stilled in Charles' mind. She had evidently not set Hayter on. She was not involved in the intrigue against Thornley. He ventured on his next question.

"I do long to know—I won't tell anybody—but did you and Mr. Thornley have a scene when he got back?"

"Oh, terrific! But I'd asked for it. I deliberately went against his wishes, and planned to have everything so far ahead, when he got back, that he wouldn't be able to alter it. And I did. I got my way over nearly everything, and what's more he got me out of the scrape with Ianthe—my big mistake. He had every right to be furious, and I was very meek and apologetic, because I knew he couldn't do much. But after the first night he apologised and kissed me and gave me an inscribed copy of *His Eminence*. There aren't any hard feelings between us now. In his way he's very, very generous."

And so are you, thought Charles, liking her better for every word she said.

His warning was useful to Lucy during luncheon. She was put through a brisk cross-examination and took care to do the utmost justice to Mr. Thornley. She explained that she could never have undertaken the production without his notes and spade work, which was perfectly true. Very often she had reverted to his methods, discovering her own to be at fault.

"Then you don't think," asked Lady Frances bluntly, "that your name should have appeared with his, as co-producer?"

Lucy was cornered.

"I'd have liked it," she admitted. "But truly I don't think it worth any fuss. I mean . . . credit in the Institute . . . well, it's not like the professional stage where one's living depends on it. Everybody knows what one's done. The credit ought to be communal. . . ."

Lady Frances looked pleased, and a smile crossed her pain-racked face. It occurred to her that Matt would have liked this girl. When she rose, to hobble upstairs for her afternoon rest, she gave Lucy a little push which was almost a caress.

"I don't wonder you get people to do what you want," she said.

176

"I must see this play of yours if I have to go on a stretcher. Now I must lie down. Goodbye, my dear, and thank you for coming. Charles will take you home."

Penelope helped her out of the room. Charles and Lucy, left alone, smiled at one another.

"You got over that stile very well," he commented. "You don't have to hurry back, do you? Come and see the gardens."

There was not very much to see at that time of year. Lady Frances had patriotically dug up everything she could during the war, planting cabbages instead of roses and potatoes in the herbaceous borders. The lawns had run to seed for hay, and shortage of labour had since delayed any extensive restoration of the old magnificence. But the afternoon was fine and the young couple strolled along the neglected paths contentedly enough, talking of Matthew Millwood, concerning whom Lucy was always eager to know more.

"You must see the glass houses," said Charles. "They were one of his pet hobbies, so we kept them up all through the war, because my mother couldn't bear to let them go. We used to shiver round a small oil stove while all our fuel allowance went into the orchid house furnace."

He led the way round the lake, and explained how his father had come to have this hobby.

"When my father bought Cyre Abbey they were in charge of a Scotch gardener who treated him very contemptuously, as an upstart who had never seen anything rarer than a potted geranium before. My father wouldn't have minded that if the man had known his job—but he didn't think the goods justified such airs. He told the man one day that he could grow better orchids himself, and proceeded to do so."

Lucy laughed and said that Mr. Meeker believed Matthew Millwood could have done anything in the world, if he chose.

"Not in these days," grumbled Charles.

And offered his chip for her inspection, just as he had offered it to Mr. Meeker. Lucy listened politely. She longed to ask him if there was really anything which he violently wished to do and could not. He spoke of experiments which he might not attempt, but he did not strike her as much of an experimenter. He complained that his Liberalism forbade all hope of a political career, but she could not imagine him as a Liberal minister, even though the electoral tide should turn. It seemed to her that his situation was ideal for a young man who believed himself destined to do much but who preferred to do as little as possible.

His lament and her silent comment were still going on when they reached the glass houses. He opened a door for her and they passed from the bracing afternoon into damp warmth and a forest of camellias. She stared at the rosetted trees and tried to admire them, but she never could care for glass houses. The rich mouldy smell stifled her.

They strolled through the blossoming aisles of two more houses and came at last to an inner one, where the temperature was tropical, and the famous Cyre Abbey orchids stunned the beholder with a fantastic variety of colour and shape. She duly marvelled and wondered if they had been beautiful in the lands from which they came. Here they were not. But, in the Himalayas, so Patrick had said—Patrick, who was so very different from this peevish Charles! For oh, she thought, she did like a man to be deedy and high spirited; that was why Patrick had charmed her and why stories of Matt Millwood were so captivating. *I can't . . . I mayn't. . . .* Here was Charles still keeping up his low spirited grumble, when his father would have discovered a dozen grounds for saying *I can . . . I'm going to. . . .*

"What a lot you know about orchids!" commented Charles, when, for the third time, she had identified a blossom without referring to its label. "Are you a botanist?"

"I . . . I was interested in botany at one time," said Lucy.

She had been several times to the orchid house at Kew with Patrick, and a sudden memory of him came back to her now, a clearer picture than she had had of him for many months. He had stooped over a spray of flowers and then looked round at her, saying something about the Amazon.

Poor Patrick!

A wave of sorrow and pity went over her. She never now wanted to see him again, but she was sad because she knew that he would never go hunting for flowers, that he was not a Matt Mill-wood, and that his high spirits during the months of their engagement had been deceptive. She no longer loved him but she was filled with that compassion which is the fruit of love and which survives it, when love has been untainted by bitterness. In all her troubles she had never felt bitter towards Patrick, had never wanted him to suffer, and now she found herself wishing quite passionately that he might fare well, and ever well—that he might find freedom.

She lifted her eyes to Charles, who was asking her some question. He thought that he had never in his life seen such beautiful eyes, though he could not put a name to the light which shone in them. The turn of her head, her smile, and this luminous tenderness of her glance, made him feel quite giddy; they tingled through his nerves like a shock. His question unanswered, he led the way through the orchid aisles. The other man, he thought, must have been a botanist. Though why he should call this shadowy individual *the other man* he did not immediately realise.

He took her back to Ravonsbridge. It was a silent journey. Lucy was thinking of Patrick, caught up in a mood of sharp recollection which could sadden but had no longer power to wound her. Charles was wishing that she would look at him. He wanted to see those eyes again. The memory of that glance made him thirsty, as though he had had one sip of some celestial drink which had then been snatched away. He *must* have more of it.

He was to get no more. When he had set her down in Sheep Lane he drove off, feeling quite parched. Nor could he see how he was ever to slake this thirst. There was little prospect of seeing her again save in a crowd. She would not be invited to Cyre Abbey. And if he took to haunting the Institute, if he invited her to come out with him, the whole of Severnshire would gossip. To see her again was just another of those things which he was not to be allowed to do.

Unless, of course, she should leave Ravonsbridge. If she went to London, if she were to be offered a much better job in London, they might meet in comfort. Such a thing would not be impossible to arrange. His name need never appear in the transaction. He had obliging friends and the barest hint would produce, in due course, some attractive and unexceptionable offer to Lucy—some work, he supposed, in connection with stage production.

But there was a flavour of intrigue about such a ruse which would never blend with the pleasure of looking into Lucy's eyes. Her candour was her great charm; he could not simultaneously enjoy it and impose upon it. Nor could he imagine how he was to phrase even the barest hint so as to escape the inference that he wanted to smuggle the girl out of Ravonsbridge in order to seduce her.

Marriage never occurred to him as a remotely possible solution. He did not intend to marry. Some years earlier he had been rebuffed by a very lovely girl, augustly connected, who had queened it in the set which he then frequented. Common sense should have warned him not to address her without emphatic encouragement. This he never got, but, having a very good opinion of himself, he persisted, and then chose to regard his rejection as a humiliating snub. He suspected, with some truth, that people were laughing at him; a certain self consequence in his manners impaired the popularity which he was otherwise well qualified to command. Dislike of meeting her, and she was to be met everywhere, began to embitter his social life. He retired to sulk in Severnshire, where he was bored but where he was certain to be treated with deference. His vanity had been more severely wounded than his heart, but Lady Flora still set his standard for a wife—the kind of wife whom he believed himself to deserve. Lucy, unabashedly middle class, fell as far below that standard as she soared above his requirements in a mistress. Such a girl could have no place in his life. He must forget about her eyes.

4

"Mr. hayter! Might I speak to you for a minute?"

Any customer less cool than Hayter might have been intimidated by Lucy's aspect when she made this request. But he was all accommodating cordiality. His cigarette case was out in a moment, and his enormous, efficient lighter. A comfortable chair was pushed forward and enquiries were made after Lady Frances.

"You were lunching out there yesterday, weren't you?"

"Yes," admitted Lucy. "I thought she looked very ill. And she seemed to have got hold of some very stupid ideas about the play —that I had quarrelled with Mr. Thornley and that I was dissatisfied with the programme. And I understand that she got that impression from you, Mr. Hayter."

She looked accusingly at the executive director, who shook his head in a puzzled way, and denied having ever suggested such a thing.

"Then what did you say?" demanded Lucy.

"She asked me if I thought it was fair that your name should be omitted from the programme. I said I thought it unfair. I'm sorry. I had to say what I think."

"She asked you? Who can have first put the idea into her head then?"

"I can't imagine," said Hayter, with perfect truth.

They stared at each other. Lucy wondered if he was a liar. He wondered who on earth Lucy's pigeon at Cyre Abbey could be. He had gone out there the very moment her ladyship got back and was immediately asked about that programme, before anybody else at the Institute had had a chance to say a word. By some means, Carmichael had got in with her story first. But how? Carmichael might look simple but she was a very, very clever girl. She had got the Millwoods eating out of her hand and yet had managed to keep on good terms with old Thornley. However things fell out, she was sitting pretty. But what was she after now?

"I know you didn't mean to give a wrong impression," said Lucy, doubtfully. "But, as a result of what you told her, she sent for me first, before Mr. Thornley, which wasn't a very good idea."

Hayter smiled and refused to agree that there could be any harm in this.

"We did talk a good deal about you," he admitted, "but I don't think we said much about recent happenings. I really don't remember that we did. We were talking of the future. In confidence, I'll tell you that she wanted my opinion. You see . . . it's a question of Thornley's successor, when he retires. Your work this autumn has impressed everybody. You only need a little more experience. I think we all hope you'll eventually get a chance to run that theatre."

"I shall have had masses of experience," said Lucy, "by the time Mr. Thornley retires. I shall be at least forty."

Hayter laughed.

"Unless he's run over by a bus," she added, and was surprised by the sharp look she got.

"That might happen," he agreed. "Or Mr. Thornley might be lured from us by work which interests him more. He has so much to call him away, nowadays. If that should happen, should you care to stay in Ravonsbridge?"

She meditated, and realised that she might enjoy it. The work was beginning really to interest her, and if ever she got an opportunity of trying out her own ideas it might absorb her. But the students and the drama school were not the chief attraction; she wanted to follow up her friendship with Owen Rees and other cronies in the lower town. She wanted to interest Ravonsbridge in its own Institute. She tried to explain this to Hayter.

"I quite agree," he said nodding. "That aspect of the theatre has been neglected and it's very important. But I think Lady Frances intends to make a lot of changes. This is absolutely in confidence, for I don't know if she's discussed it with Mr. Thornley yet. She wants to separate the theatre from the school. Miss Frogmore can take over the school. For the theatre she would eventually like a young producer who would work very much on the lines you've indicated—putting on shows in which local talent could be supplemented by the students. And then she thought she might get some distinguished London producer as titular senior director, who would visit us, from time to time, and keep us in touch with the outside world. Now . . . would you care to take on the theatre? There would of course be a larger salary, since less would have to be paid to a part time senior director."

Lucy thought it sounded a delightful idea and sighed. For she was sure that Mr. Thornley, when it came to the point, would never be lured out of Ravonsbridge. She said so.

"Oh . . . I don't know," laughed Hayter. "The traffic gets more dangerous every day."

There was a pause. Lucy was quite unaware that she had been sounded. Hayter was wondering how far *he* had been sounded. Had she come to him in order to find out how the land lay? If so, she had forced him to put several cards on the table without revealing any of her own. What if she now took all this to Thornley? And why had she come at all?

She had come to scold Mr. Hayter for making mischief, but she realised that he had managed somehow to elude her. She rose to go and he came with her to the door of his office. He stood looking after her as she crossed the quadrangle to the theatre, and admitted to himself that he did not understand her. If he could have read her mind at that moment he would have saved himself some anxious moments, later on, by packing her off with Thornley. But honesty will always be a little mysterious to a rogue.

The wretched, petty business of the programme was not yet to be forgotten, as Lucy discovered when she got back to the theatre. Mr. Thornley had just heard of it for the first time, from the malicious Emil, and he was in a state of miserable consternation. It had never occurred to him that he ought to have billed her as co-producer and he was deeply shocked when Angera accused him of unfairness.

"I don't know why I didn't think of it myself," he told Lucy. "If I had, of course I'd have put in your name. You did so much of the work. Why didn't you mention it to me?"

"Because I never thought of it either," said Lucy unhappily. "You know what Emil is. Please don't worry about it!"

"It's the last thing I'd ever want to do. . . .".

The telephone rang and Lucy answered it. Penelope Millwood's voice barked an abrupt demand for Mr. Thornley. He took the receiver, in so courtly a manner that Lucy nearly laughed, and assured it that of course he would—he would be at Cyre Abbey in half an hour, and how was Lady Frances?

"She's too unwell to come in," he explained, as he hung up. "She wants me to go out there. I expect she wants to know all about the play. If your ears burn, Lucy, you'll know why."

"I was out there yesterday," said Lucy quickly.

He was astonished and looked it.

"She wanted news of Ianthe," explained Lucy, "and she asked a good bit about the play."

This was partly true. Lady Frances had asked after Ianthe.

But it was so evasive that Lucy felt guilty and more than ever uneasy at this atmosphere of intrigue which seemed to hang round them all.

Mr. Thornley, however, was satisfied. He was flattered by this early summons to Cyre Abbey and looked forward to describing his triumphs in Geneva. He had not the faintest foreboding of the rod in pickle which was waiting for him. As he put on his overcoat and scarf he said:

"I'll tell you what, Lucy! You shall do the Nativity play this year. You shall be billed as sole producer. I shan't be here for it anyway, as I'm going North before the end of term, on a lecture tour. You deserve a production of your own, my dear, and you shall have it."

And he went off gaily to the slaughter house.

Lucy had a fit of quiet hysterics. The Nativity play! What hell on earth! Bloody angels, bloody shepherds, bloody star, God Rest You Bloody Gentlemen! PRODUCER: L. CARMICHAEL.

What could L. Carmichael do with a Nativity play? Such things might be bearable when staged by believers, but as a form of drama they stank. Could she make it Chinese and put Our Lady on a lotus? Or modern? A gypsy's baby born in a stable? Was there no escape from those corny angels and Wendy in a blue mantle? But nothing would make it real, thought Lucy, when so few of us believe in it. In the Middle Ages, or even now in a church, it might have real beauty because it has truth both for audience and actors. In the Ravonsbridge theatre it can be nothing more than an orgy of sentimentality. It will have to be done very straightforwardly and simply, just for the sake of a few people, like Miss Foss and Lady Frances, to whom it does mean something. L. Carmichael mustn't try to be clever.

And the joke of it was that Lady Frances would probably also regard it as a most satisfactory amends. She and H. E. would sit nodding over it in perfect agreement. For Lucy had no more idea of the rod in pickle than he had. She had never had any reason to suppose that his absences from Ravonsbridge were regarded as unlawful. He had been going off during term time for years, though never abroad before, and never for quite so long.

At lunch time she told her news to Miss Frogmore, who

laughed over the Nativity play but looked thoughtful when she learnt that their superior had been summoned to Cyre Abbey. Miss Paine, too, said: *Oh!* when she heard of it, in a very meaning way. There was a strange tension in the air. It flashed across Lucy's mind that they had both been told of the changes which might some day take place, and had both been asked if they were willing to stay.

In the middle of the afternoon Mr. Thornley returned looking very crestfallen. He reported that Lady Frances seemed to him to be very ill indeed, and that it had been impossible to discuss anything with her.

More he would not say to young Lucy, but he was angry and greatly distressed. Never, in all his years at the Institute, had he received such a dressing down. He would have resigned on the spot had he not ascribed the whole outrage to the effects of sciatica. Lady Frances was clearly not herself. So he did not take his scolding seriously or suppose, for a moment, that he need cancel his lecture tour in December. Long before that she would have recovered and apologised. But it had been a most disagreeable interview and he had not been offered lunch.

A good many people looked in upon Mr. Thornley and Lucy before the end of the day. One errand or another brought Mr. Hayter, Miss Frogmore, Miss Paine and Mr. Poole. Perhaps they were expecting to hear that Ravonsbridge must now look for another senior drama director. If so, they were disappointed. Mr. Thornley had felt the rod. But he had not resigned and he had no intention of resigning. He was not the man to quarrel with an old and valued friend over a few sharp words, spoken, obviously, in pain.

5

TRADITION had decreed that the Nativity play should end with *Adeste Fideles*, sung by the cast and the audience in chorus. Applause, curtain calls or the *King* were felt to be unseemly.

Lucy observed this custom but she introduced certain improvements. It had struck her, when she watched the performance a year ago, that the four verses took too long; the devotional poses of the crowd on the stage became constrained and stiff. And in front the shuffling silence, unrelieved by applause when the curtain fell and the lights went up, gave a sense of anti-climax.

She decided that Bethlehem and the manger should fade more gradually from the sight. During the first verse she brought her stage lights down slowly till all was darkness save for a spot on the raised platform where Wendy knelt beside the manger. The singing crowd on the dim stage below was thus merged with the singing crowd in the auditorium, until the curtains fell together at the end of the second verse. The third and fourth verses were sung only by the audience as the house lights came up gradually. By this means she hoped to engineer a less abrupt return to the everyday world.

The effect was successful and the audience, moved, continued to sing fervently beyond the fallen curtain, while on the stage a secular bustle had already broken out. Angels, kings and shepherds scrambled up from their knees. Wendy, kicking the manger out of her way, jumped down from her platform. A low buzz of conversation drowned the distant strain of pious song. Their spirits, depressed by the synthetic reverence of the performance, were inclined to rebound into noisy flippancy.

On the last night, the night of the Institute party, they were particularly obstreperous. Lucy was afraid that they might be heard out in front. She emerged angrily from the wings to drive them to their dressing rooms.

"Get off!" she whispered to Robin, who was dancing a samba with Kitty. "Don't make such a hell of a noise."

But Robin, for once, was intractable. He was leaving Ravonsbridge and had secured an engagement with a well known repertory company. He did not have to obey Lucy any more. He snatched Melchior's turban from his head and thrust it onto hers, exclaiming:

"Last time I wear this corny old tile!"

"Oh, you little brute. My hair was all tidy for the party."

"Darling! I can't wait to see you all dressed up. Kitty says you've got a most marvellous dress."

186

"Ssh! Get off! They're still singing out there."

"Aw! They're nuts!"

"*Venite adoremus!*"

Penelope Millwood, singing in the stalls, gave a nudge to Tish and indicated the box where their mother was sitting.

"*Venite adoremus!*"

Tish looked up and saw to her astonishment that Charles was there between Lady Frances and Lady Anne.

"*Venite adoremu-us Do-ominum!*"

Rickie sawed the air majestically with his baton and frowned at the double basses, who were behind the beat.

"I never knew Charles was coming," said Tish, as soon as the last note died away. "White tie and tails! Is he coming to the party? Wonders will never cease!"

Neither of them could remember when Charles had last deigned to attend either the play or the party.

"There's an attraction," murmured Penelope.

"No! Who?"

"I shan't tell you. Just keep your eyes open and see if you see what I see. Mamma insists I see what isn't there. . . . No . . . we're not to go yet. We're to stay till Mamma comes down and then all go across to the hall together."

The theatre was already nearly empty. Tish sat down again with a sigh of relief, for her shoes hurt her. It was another tradition that everybody should dress up for the party. In former days all the men had come in white ties, but now very few of them possessed tail coats and only the senior staff wore the festive uniform. The women put on long dresses. Tish had driven over in the red lace which had done duty for ten Institute parties in succession. Lady Frances wore her equally famous black velvet. But Penelope had a comparatively new dress of taffeta in an aggressive shade of blue.

"They never used to let the curtain down in the middle of *Adeste*," complained Tish. "Was that on purpose or an accident?"

187

"I expect it's Miss Carmichael. She's producing."

"I think Mr. Thornley did it better."

"He's gone, you know."

"What? Gone where?"

"Left Ravonsbridge. He's resigned."

"Good heavens! I never knew that."

"Mamma only heard of it today."

Lady Frances came into the stalls, calling them to join her. Tish, as she limped in her tight shoes up the gangway, was still exclaiming over the resignation of Mr. Thornley, and Penelope was scolded for having gossiped.

"Tish would have heard tomorrow at the council meeting," protested Penelope.

"And it shouldn't be discussed before then," said Lady Frances. She turned to Tish and added: "Yes, it's true, I'm sorry to say. Mr. Poole got the letter today. Mr. Thornley has written to the council resigning immediately."

"I suppose he'll tell us why, tomorrow."

"He won't be there tomorrow. That's the whole trouble. He's away. He has gone off to give some lectures, in spite of all I said to him when I got back. When I heard he really meant to go I came in, last week, and repeated what I'd said. I told him that I wouldn't have it, and that he must choose. If he wants to stay here he must give up all his outside work. He seemed to be utterly dumbfounded. But now he has made up his mind. He's written resigning. . . . Oh! They're turning off the lights. We must go. Come along. Where is Charles?"

Charles had vanished. They called to him in vain, peering round the darkened house. And then he suddenly emerged from the pass door leading to the stage. Penelope again nudged Tish.

"You've been on the stage?" marvelled Lady Frances. "What for?"

"Thought I'd like to congratulate them," muttered Charles.

"How silly . . . they're all changing. You can do it at the party. Come along, dear. . . ."

"Was there anybody on the stage?" asked Penelope as they came along.

"No," said Charles.

The stage had been perfectly dark and he had barked his shins on the manger.

"You've got dust on your trousers," said Tish.

They followed their mother out of the theatre into the quadrangle. It was a fine frosty night. Orion and the winter constellations spangled the sky. Voices and laughter echoed across the stone court. The hall windows glowed with festive light and little groups of people were going up the steps.

Charles lingered for a moment to look up at the snapping stars. He was ashamed of the impulse which had driven him on to the stage in the hope of catching Lucy for a moment's conversation. He would see her at the party. He must be content to see her there—and to dance with her in due course, for civility dictated that he should dance with the Institute girls. The hard hall lights would shine down on them, and the gambolling students would jostle them, but he would have her in his arms for a few minutes and with that he must slake his intolerable thirst.

In the ladies' cloakroom the Millwood women disposed of their sensible evening wraps. Lady Frances stumped off to the hall to greet her guests but Penelope and Tish lingered before a glass to put a very little powder on their noses.

"But Mr. Thornley will be coming back next term anyway?" suggested Tish.

"No. I don't think so. He says he isn't prepared to give up some important engagements he's got next term."

"But who will do his work?"

Penelope gave her sister a push and indicated a row of doors. One was ominously shut, and, as the cubicles behind these doors had no ceilings, it was probable that every word they had said must have been overheard. Tish made a grimace of dismay. They hurried out of the cloakroom and paused in the corridor just outside to discuss their indiscretion.

"It'll be all over the Institute now!" lamented Penelope. "I never noticed anybody in there, did you?"

"No," said Tish, "or I'd have held my tongue. They were very quiet and we'd been in there some minutes. Perhaps it wasn't anybody. Perhaps the door just happened to be shut."

The cloakroom door, opening suddenly, bumped Tish in the

back. Ianthe swept into the corridor, nodded coolly to them both, and went into the hall.

"Ianthe!" cried Penelope. "The very worst person. It would be her. She'll tell everybody. She's livid with Mr. Thornley because of *Hamlet*. Oh, Tish, what shall we do?"

"Nobody listens to her, so it doesn't really matter," said Tish. "What a sight she looks in a strapless dress. Far too thin. Nothing to keep it up over. And black too! At her age!"

They went into the hall which was already crowded. A small dance band was assembling on the platform, behind a hedge of holly. At the other end of the room was a long buffet table loaded with tea, coffee, lemonade and an abundance of sausage rolls. A good many Millwood and Ravonsclere connections had come in from all over the county. Most of the council were there, all the staff, and a selection of Ravonsbridge worthies. Mr. Hayter, who was growing a little too fat for his dress clothes, was being tactful and active. He perceived that the eye of Lady Frances had lingered enquiringly upon a strange young man in a yellow pullover, and he immediately introduced the newcomer. The pullover was explained. Mr. Owen Rees was one of the Poor. Lady Frances received him very graciously and told him how sorry she was that she had never seen his performance in *Hamlet*. Her sciatica had imprisoned her at Cyre Abbey.

Rees had dress clothes at home, but he had decided not to put them on for this party. He had been in two minds about coming. Though he had enjoyed acting at the Institute he was anxious not to be too closely associated with the Millwoods who were "the bosses." But Lucy had sent a personal note with his invitation card, begging him to come and assuring him that all his colleagues in the *Hamlet* production would be very much disappointed if he did not. So he came, only half ready to be genial and on the lookout for patronage, which he intended to resent.

He gave a taciturn reception to the graciousness of Lady Frances and eyed the elegant Charles, who was presently beckoned up to talk to him. They got on very badly. Owen could not endure Charles' voice, and Charles, full of genuine admiration, felt himself rebuffed. The Class War lay between them, though they had much in common, were both extremely fond of poetry and both

190

infatuated with the character of Hamlet. Actually each was meditating an imitation of the other, when he got home.

Angera joined them, smiling a little at their obvious discomfort, and asked Owen if he was enjoying the party. Owen replied
impatiently:

"I came on account of Lussi. I thought she wass going to be
here. She iss the only person here I want to see."

Which was exactly the case with Charles.

Lucy was, all this while, in the girls' dressing room at the
theatre, changing for the party, while the others removed their
greasepaint. She threw off her smock, made up her face, and
changed her shoes and stockings. Then she took from its hanger
a sheeted dress which she had brought up with her before the performance. As she settled the skirt about her hips a gasp went up
from all her young companions.

"Oh, LUCY!"

She had never worn it in Ravonsbridge, had never worn it anywhere, for it was intended for those very distinguished parties to
which she might have gone as Patrick Reilly's bride. It was made
from a rich brocaded silk, given to her as a wedding present, in a
pink so pale that only the rosy shadows of its folds proclaimed the
hue. She had felt a sudden impulse to wear it, though it was far too
good for such a party. No suitable occasion was ever likely to occur
in her life now, and it was stupid to let the lovely thing rot, un-
worn and unadmired, year after year, in her wardrobe. Also she
needed to free herself from the miasma of the Nativity play by
some daring gesture of this sort.

The girls crowded round her, admiring and unenvious, since
none of them could have carried it off.

"Where did you get it?"

"What's it made of?"

"I never saw anything so smashing."

"Is it an heirloom?"

"No," said Lucy. "It's Chinese tribute silk. That's what the
person said who gave me the stuff. But don't ask me what it means,
for I don't know."

"It makes you look like royalty!"

"Yes. It's like one Princess Elizabeth has. The same neckline."

"Don't dance with Rickie in it, for heaven's sake."

Lucy smiled and sat down at a glass to rearrange her curls. That unreliable beauty, which could so completely desert her when her spirits were low, was in full strength. None of them could stop looking at her. Ravonsbridge had already experienced some of the surprises which Melissa had forseen, should Lucy recover, but this was a new one.

A pounding came at the door. Robin's voice was heard bellowing a demand to see Lucy's smashing dress. He was told that he could not come in, that he would see it in the hall, but he would not go away. He kept shouting through the door:

"Wanna see it now!"

The other boys, who were waiting about in the passage to escort the girls to the party, joined in:

"Wanna see Lucy! Wanna see Lucy!"

The band struck up and a few bold couples took the floor. But the party hung fire until the contingent from the theatre arrived. Ianthe sat between her mother and her stepfather and refused to dance. She would have refused to come at all, if she could have been sure that her absence would be noticed, for she hated everybody in Ravonsbridge. But now she was not sorry that she had come. That little piece of news which she had overheard in the cloakroom had changed the evening for her. Mr. Thornley was going away!

As long as I'm in Ravonsbridge, you'll behave yourself.

It was quite true. She was afraid of him, and of nobody else, in this abominable town. She turned to look at Angera, insolently at his ease among a group of his students, and smiled to herself.

But then, in a fresh paroxysm of bitterness, she wondered whether anybody would believe that he had ever done more than paint her portrait. She had told so many stories and set so many people by the ears. They would merely laugh at her.

A robust and cheerful voice broke in upon her reverie. Miss Plummer had stopped to speak to Mrs. Pillie and was now saying, with facetious dismay:

"Ianthe not dancing! Dear, dear!"

"She isn't feeling up to it," bleated Mrs. Pillie, who lived in terror of what Ianthe might do next.

"Feeling seedy?"

Miss Plummer's tone invoked the cupboard full of laxatives which she kept at the hostel and pressed upon students who indulged in the vapours.

"I'm a good deal better than I was," said Ianthe, gently, "I'm nearly well again. Only dancing makes me breathless."

As she spoke a vista of ideas opened before her.

"Ought to see a doctor," suggested Miss Plummer, running an experienced eye over the emaciated shoulders sticking up out of the strapless dress.

She moved on and Ianthe's sombre gaze followed her. The Plum was a joke among the Ravonsbridge students. She liked to say that she understood young things and was perpetually frustrated by being given so little to understand. Ruth, Wendy and Kitty would never ask for so much as an aspirin, far less for counsel in their love affairs. The poor old Plum was said to be starving for a heartbroken girl whom she might mother, or a nice rich scandal with which she could sensibly deal.

But she was not a fool. She was not likely to believe all that she was told. Her weak point was her faith in her own insight. A carrot of vague ill health and unhappiness, dangled before her nose, might lead her down strange paths. Should she believe herself to be astutely getting the facts out of a reluctant confidant, she might swallow a good deal.

And she doesn't like Jews, remembered Ianthe. She's madly anti-Semitic. And she doesn't like Emil. Not that I shall say anything against him, not ever, not ever! Oh, Miss Plummer, don't ask me! I can't tell you. I couldn't ever tell anyone. But she's so awfully clever, she may guess why I had to go away in a hurry in the summer, and why I've never been quite well since. And she'll mill it over in her mind and look for somebody she doesn't like, to fasten it on to. She shall say it was Emil. And Mr. Thornley won't be here.

A procession was coming into the hall. The band, which had paused in the dance music, caught sight of it and struck up a lively

193

march. All the young people from the theatre were arriving, led by Robin and Lucy. Two and two they came, their hands held high, in the royal manner. Everyone paused and stared. Somebody clapped. The applause was taken up, partly in congratulation to the players, and partly from pleasure at the agreeable sight. Robin led Lucy to the chair in which Lady Frances was sitting. He bowed low, Lucy, in her lovely dress, swept a court curtsey, and they passed on, making way for the next couple. The other guests cheered and clapped. The party flashed into life and gaiety.

Lady Frances was delighted and bowed with a beaming smile to each couple as it passed before her. Her ideas of fun were not highly developed and the dreariness of former Institute parties had not troubled her much, but she did perceive that this one seemed to be unusually nice. She thought: *If Matt had been here it would always have been like this.* All warmth, all gaiety seemed to have fled from Ravonsbridge, from the world, when Matt died. She toiled on as best she could, trying to carry out his wishes through the desert that life had become without him. But nobody helped her much.

Her eyes followed Lucy, who was now dancing. She greatly admired the dress—such a pretty modest dress, she thought, with a proper neck. She could not bear these vulgar dresses, with no tops, that all the girls seemed to wear nowadays, even nice girls at Hunt Balls. The costliness of the material did not strike her as extravagant; she thought it an economical dress. It would wear for ever and Miss Carmichael need never get another. Lady Frances had a pretty accurate idea of a cottager's budget, but was extremely ignorant where the middle classes were concerned.

She wished that Matt could have seen this pretty girl. He liked pretty girls. He used to call me a bonny lassie, she thought, though I'm sure I never was, but I liked it. Oh, Matt! Oh, Matt! When will this weary life be over? When shall I get to you again?

"I don't need to use my eyes very hard," murmured Tish to Penelope. "I hadn't realised . . . I'd always thought her, well—not plain, but quite ordinary. But fancy a girl like that having a dress like that! It's absurd . . . and ridiculous to wear it here."

"If he wasn't so underhand," said Penelope, "I shouldn't think so much of it. If he said he admired her, I mean. But he never mentions her if he can help it. I've noticed. He goes out of his way not to say her name, if we're talking about the Institute. He's carefully not looking at her now! About the only person who isn't."

Tish saw that this was so. Charles had turned his back on the dancers and was talking to Mr. Mildmay.

"You don't think it's serious?" she cried.

"I think he's very badly smitten."

"Not Charles! He's so fastidious."

"Yes, but she *is* striking, in a way. One sees . . ."

"Still . . . he couldn't want to . . ."

"I wouldn't be too sure, Tish. If he's as badly smitten as I think, there isn't anything else he could do, is there?"

Tish reflected. They both knew that Charles was no Galahad, though they hoped that their mother did not. But something about Lucy, they knew not what, forbade them to class her with Charles' other fancies. It was just possible that he might want to marry her.

"I wonder if he knows!" breathed Tish. "I don't think he can. I'm sure it would put him right off."

"Knows? What? Is there something against her?"

"Why, yes, there's something he really ought to know, if he's in any serious danger of being caught. Not exactly her fault I suppose, but very putting off."

Tish and Penelope moved into a window embrasure and Lucy's history was retailed.

"I should have thought it must have been her fault," exclaimed Penelope. "I mean, a man doesn't treat a perfectly respectable girl like that."

Tish was inclined to agree; she had always wondered if Reilly failed to turn up because he had already got what he wanted—a view which had its supporters in Gorling. To both the sisters the story brought Lucy down to the level of those girls whom Charles might think he need not marry. But the possible consequences of telling that to Charles disturbed Tish, who had more experience than Penelope.

"Perhaps it's as well he doesn't know," she murmured.

"But of course he ought to know," cried Penelope. "You don't want her for a sister-in-law, do you?"

"No. But if he thought . . . that he didn't have to respect her . . . one might be responsible. . . ."

"She can look after herself, I should think! You're very anxious to save her from Charles. Don't you see that it's a case of saving Charles from her?"

"No," said Tish, more firmly. "Supposing it wasn't in the least her fault? I'd rather he married her, than run the risk of . . . of causing evil, and doing damage to an innocent person. We mustn't say anything, Penelope."

"You're as bad as Mamma!"

"I sometimes try to be as good as Mamma."

Neither sister thought it likely that Lucy would be able to refuse Charles, either as a lover or a husband.

"I oughtn't to have told you," said Tish. "Mamma would be furious. She'd say it was gossip. I say! What is Ianthe doing?" She looked round anxiously. "I don't see her."

"She was sitting with the Pillies and looking like a tragedy queen."

"She isn't now. Oh, I see her! She's all right. She's down by the buffet with Miss Plummer."

Lucy danced and danced. She was enjoying herself enormously. Her pink skirts flew out, she smiled at everybody, and was applauded for everything that she said. She would not have danced with Charles at all if she had not paused to speak to Lady Frances. For he, though he knew exactly where she was at any moment, also with whom she was dancing, could not bring himself to the vulgarity of cutting in, and there was no other way of approaching her. But his mother beckoned to her, as she danced past, and detained her for a few minutes to praise the Nativity play. When she turned away he was at her elbow with his murmured request.

Nobody dared to cut in on Charles. He had Lucy to himself for the greater part of a foxtrot, and she was very soon aware of the fact that she was, in Melissa's phrase, "causing emotion"—not the lighthearted admiration which had emanated from all her other partners, but that anguished agitation which by Melissa's creed, and her own, must never be deliberately excited unless it could be

196

returned. To cause avoidable unhappiness was, in their eyes, to behave like a bitch.

The discovery astonished and perplexed her. She wished that somebody would cut in and take her away. Charles said nothing. His face was blank. He held her lightly and steered her adroitly through the crowd. But the emotion which she was causing seemed to flow all over and through her. She could not pretend to herself that she entirely disliked it. If her conscience would have allowed her to do so, she would have enjoyed it very much. She reflected, as she had reflected before on like occasions, that it must be fun to be a bitch. But, since she was not, she must take steps to quench this ardour. She must not dance with him again, and it would be as well if she put him off a little by romping noisily with Robin. Both Melissa and she were adepts in the art of making themselves a trifle unattractive if kindness and commonsense made that necessary.

When the band stopped they were near the buffet. Charles, who was determined to retain his monopoly, thrust her into a chair beside Miss Plummer and plunged into the crowd by the table to get her some refreshment.

She leaned across Miss Plummer's massive torso to greet Ianthe, who might by now be supposed to have forgiven the Ophelia fiasco. She received a pale and tearful smile.

"She's not feeling any too well this evening," explained Miss Plummer mysteriously. "In a minute or two I'm going to take her home and tuck her up."

Ianthe murmured a protest and was informed that Bedfordshire was the place for her.

At this moment Charles returned from the fight round the buffet and called to Lucy.

"Miss Carmichael!"

Lucy turned, in affronted astonishment.

"Would you rather have tea or coffee?"

She asked for coffee and he resumed the struggle.

Miss Carmichael! From a man who emanated emotion like a power station. To Lucy's way of thinking it was fantastic. At Oxford she had been Lucy to everybody; even at Ravonsbridge nobody called her Miss Carmichael except a few old sweets like Mr. Mildmay. It had never occurred to her, after that friendly afternoon at Cyre Abbey, after she had listened so patiently to all his grievances against life, that they were not now Lucy and Charles. Does he have to? she wondered. Would everybody faint if he behaved like an ordinary man? Why should there be this divinity doth hedge a Millwood? Miss Carmichael! Keep your distance my good girl! Good heavens, what would Melissa say? Can't keep his feelings to himself and calls me Miss Carmichael. If the gulf between us is all that wide I needn't worry about his feelings.

She was really very angry. When he brought the coffee she smiled upon him and indicated the chair by her side. She need not, she felt, put him off by romping with Robin. He was not at all in danger of forgetting that she was just one of the Institute girls. She took more pains to amuse and interest him than she had ever before taken, aware that curious eyes were watching them, all over the hall.

There was a flourish from the band and a long cadenza. As the first bars of the *Blue Danube* pulsed out, Charles whispered: *Please!* She tossed the last shred of scruple from her, looked him in the eye, and stood up with him. She loved waltzing. She adored the *Blue Danube*. He was a superb dancer and he had called her Miss Carmichael. Let him look out for himself!

They took the floor and for several minutes danced there quite alone, for the rest of the gathering was unable to do anything save stand and watch them. They were worth watching. Their waltzing was extremely good, and Lucy's rosy skirts, swinging wide, demanded an exhibition dance. Both were in a reckless mood and this fact was apparent to everybody. Round and round they went, amid a tempest of excitement and speculation. Among all the onlookers only two watched them calmly. One was Rickie, who merely wondered how it was that he had not yet danced with Lucy himself. The other was Miss Foss, who thought it was part of the entertainment.

The senior staff, the Pillies, and all the Millwood tribe thought that Charles had lost his head and that Miss Carmichael was putting herself forward in a regrettable way. The junior staff wondered how soon Lucy would be sent packing. Emil Angera rejoiced in so un-English a scene. Owen Rees was disgusted; he had not liked

198

that curtsey, and now he was convinced that Lucy was sucking up to the Millwoods. Ianthe decided that a dramatic exit upon the arm of Miss Plummer must be postponed until a more propitious moment. Miss Plummer hoped that poor damsel was not losing her heart to Mr. Millwood and had understood that a waltz did not mean anything. Robin and all the boys thought it a pity Charles had come to this party. Wendy and all the girls sighed over the magic wrought by tribute silk. Everybody thought that there had never been a Christmas party like this before.

Hayter watched Lady Frances and came to the conclusion that gold medals awaited a man of action. He seized Bess Turner, ignored her cries that she could not waltz, and swung her out upon the floor. They were joined, almost immediately, by Tish, who had plucked Canon Pillie from his chair and by Penelope with Mr. Mildmay. The Millwood faction rallied from all sides. They might not be able to waltz but, by stumbling about the floor in couples, they could put an end to this ambiguous pas de deux. The swinging pink skirts vanished in the jostling crowd and the incident was over.

Lady Anne crossed the hall and sat down by her sister. With Ravonsclere bluntness she asked if Charles was in love with that "gairl."

"Penelope thinks so," said Lady Frances tranquilly. "But I never saw anything of it till just now. It rather looks as if he was."

"Of course, she's very pretty."

"She's beautiful," said Lady Frances. "And I don't think it was her fault that they danced alone in that conspicuous way. The others were stupid and hung back. I think she was quite right to go on; it would have looked foolish to stop. I was a little annoyed . . . but not with her."

"You like her?" hazarded Lady Anne.

"I like her very much. Charles isn't happy or contented, you know. To fall in love and get married might be very good for him."

"Married?"

"I don't see why not, if they like each other."

"But, Fanny . . . her background isn't at all the same as his."

"Not as different as Matt's and mine were. And anyway," said

Lady Frances, "there is too much background about Charles. What he needs is more foreground."

Amazed at her own fanciful wit she laughed a little. Lady Anne, who was even more matter of fact, could not imagine what she meant, unless it was a reference to those shocking rumours which the family had been so sedulous to keep from her ears. If she had known of them, she would not, surely, have made a joke of it.

The *Blue Danube* swung to its final chord, releasing Charles and Lucy from an embrace which had become a penance. They were furious with themselves, aware that they had created a sensation, and deeply regretting it. As Lady Frances rose, and gave the signal for *Auld Lang Syne* which should end the party, they broke asunder with scarcely a civil word. Charles took refuge with the Millwood clan, unable to understand how, after all these circumspect weeks, after remembering to call her Miss Carmichael in the hearing of Miss Plummer, he had so given himself away. And Lucy, buried among the dramatic students, refused to exchange glances with any of them. Such a vulgar, poky, tattling place as this Institute I never did see, she thought, as she crossed hands with Rickie and Alec. They have the minds of imbecile infants. They'll be writing CHARLES LOVES LUCY on the walls next.

But her conscience told her that it was all her own fault for dancing with him again. How could she have been such a fool? Because she had been so happy, she supposed, as she sawed her arms up and down and yelled about cups of kindness. Because she had forgotten the danger of being in tearing spirits. It was so long since she had been in tearing spirits. So I've been through all that, she mourned, all that misery and loneliness, and learnt no sense at all. I thought unhappiness was supposed to make us nobler and wiser. It hasn't changed me a bit. Not a little bit.

Part 5

Second Spring

1

EARLY in the Lent term Lucy wrote to Owen Rees and asked if they might meet sometime as she wanted to consult him. Knowing him to be touchy she did not summon him to the Institute but left to him the choice of time and place. She did expect, however, that he would give a little thought to her convenience, and was surprised when she received a curt summons to meet him at six o'clock on the following afternoon in the New Café Bar, next door to the Odeon. It was a long way for her to go, and he could much more easily have caught a bus from the Works up to the Swan. He said that he was very busy but could give her a few minutes, if it was important. Altogether, the tone of his note was slightly disagreeable, but she could not believe that this was intentional. They had been such good friends in the autumn. She told herself that he had no knack for writing notes.

She had no sooner met him, however, then she realised that something was amiss. He was quite changed; she hardly recognised the tousled enthusiast in a yellow pullover with whom she had worked so eagerly during those unforgettable weeks. He wore a pin stripe suit, his hair was oiled, and his eyes were hard. For the first time she felt that there was, after all, something a trifle inferior about him.

He bought her a drink and asked how she was and answered her questions about his forthcoming production of *Outward*

Bound, but he never really smiled. She began to wonder why she had assumed that he liked her. She must have done something to offend him, but what it was she would probably never find out, because Owen was one of those people who always baulk at the responsibility and exertion of a showdown. He would take offence and cherish mistrust but he would never make the effort to state his case, in order to clear up a misunderstanding; his grievances must either be nursed in silence or made the text of mere unconstructive abuse.

She thought it better to ignore his ill humour; he might forget it when he heard what she had to say. But she felt slightly annoyed with him, since she had come, full of good will, to do him a good turn. She sat silent for a few moments, gazing round the garish café, and trying to recapture her self confidence.

A little brown man came in and stared hard at her as he passed their table. Before going to one of the high stools at the bar, he nodded to Rees. His entry seemed to cause some stir; everybody evidently knew him and the group at the bar greeting him noisily. Lucy asked who he was.

"Adamson," said Owen. "He owns this joint."

"Oh . . . I think I've heard of him."

"You're bound to do. He runs the fun fair down by the gas works, and the Odeon, and several cafés besides this. And now he's collared the Old Drill Hall, where I put on my shows. It's a headache for me, for he's doubled the rent, knowing there isn't another hall."

This gave Lucy her opening.

"That's what I wanted to talk to you about," she said. "You see, Mr. Thornley has gone. He resigned at Christmas."

"I *had* heard that," said Owen.

"And I'm carrying on till they get a new senior director."

"Why? Haven't you got Thornley's job?"

There was so much hostility in his voice that she opened her eyes.

"Not exactly," she said. "I'm still only junior director. I'm not nearly experienced enough yet for the senior job."

"Aren't you?"

He conveyed immense astonishment.

"Oh, come off it," said Lucy. "You know I'm not."

"I'd have thought not. So how come Thornley went?"

"Oh . . . He wanted to give all his time to his other work."

"Huh!"

She stifled an impulse to ask what *Huh!* meant. Everybody means the same thing by that sort of noise. He did not believe that Mr. Thornley had left for the reason stated, and she felt reluctant to discuss the matter further with him, because it troubled her. That Mr. Thornley should have gone away without a word of farewell to herself, to anybody—should have vanished from Ravonsbridge in the course of the Christmas vacation—was still hard to believe. He had given no hint of such a plan when they parted last term, and it was most unlike him to go off, in that way, leaving all the work, all his precious notes and files, like so much rubbish. She would have expected endless explanations and parting injunctions. Even Miss Frogmore and Miss Paine agreed that it was surprising, though they deplored his departure less than Lucy did. For some time now they had thought themselves perfectly able to run the drama school without any interference from Mr. Thornley.

"Well, anyhow, I've got to carry on," she said. "And I wanted to ask if you'd like the idea of putting on *Outward Bound* at the Institute theatre? You've often said what a nice theatre it is, and how wretched the hall is. I'm pretty sure that, as it's a town dramatic society, and most of the company from the Works, you could have it for nothing, or anyway for the cost of lighting and heating. And you could have it for all rehearsals, and I expect Emil would do sets for you. We don't put on a play in the Lent term."

She paused and looked at him enquiringly, but he said nothing.

"I thought I'd better sound you first," she said. "But if you like the idea I could ask Lady Frances. Do you like it?"

"No."

That was all. He offered no explanation. Lucy tried to keep her temper and asked if the hill was the difficulty. Did he think audiences would be deterred by the hill.

"Might do," he agreed tonelessly.

"Any other reason?"

He lit a cigarette before he answered.

"I don't reckon to pull your chestnuts out of the fire for you."

"What?" cried Lucy in astonishment.

"You're director. You're taking money, our money, to put on shows. All right, put them on. If you can't, then you're not up to the job, that's all I can say. Don't come running to me to do your work for you."

"Owen! I thought you'd jump at it. You were glad enough to play Hamlet."

"I wouldn't have done, if I'd seen what was behind it."

"What was behind it?"

"You know perfectly well what was behind it."

"No, I don't. All I know is that you've got some grievance so silly you don't like to admit what it is."

That stung him, and he let her have it. He accused her roundly of having schemed to get Thornley out. She had always meant, he said, to pinch the old man's job and the *Hamlet* production had been engineered to that end. Thornley had not resigned. He had been sacked at the instigation of detractors set on by Lucy. The whole town knew it, and everybody thought it a dirty trick.

As he spoke of Thornley his eyes blazed and he became very Welsh. He seemed quite to have forgotten that he had ever been caustic and critical concerning Thornley's productions. His Celtic imagination had endowed the old man with a posthumous halo— had turned him into a hero and a martyr. Thornley had dared to stand up to Lady Millwood, and Lucy, that scheming toady, had got his place.

"Oh," cried Lucy, outraged, "I did not!"

"Didn't you go creeping to her at Cyre Abbey, the moment she came back, before he could put his word in?"

"She sent for me. . . ."

"She wasss put against him in that hour. . . ."

"Who says so? Who says all this?"

"The whole town says it."

"Yet they never bothered to go and see Mr. Thornley's shows when he was here. If they had, perhaps he mightn't have thought his other work suited him better. Only when he's gone do they discover he ever existed!"

"This town iss waking up, let me tell you."

"I'm glad to hear it."

"And so am I. I wass a fool. I thought you were on the level. I didn't believe you were snooping for them, and spying for them, till I saw you with Lady Millwood."

"Do you mean Lady Frances?"

"I'm not on first name terms with her."

"Oh, don't be so stupid. She's not Lady Millwood. She's Lady Frances Millwood because she's an earl's—"

"Thanks, I know she's supposed to be an earl's daughter, and I couldn't care less. I've seen how you cringe to her, and that's quite enough for me. I fell for it like a sucker; I played your game for you and acted for you. But then my eyes were open. Oh, yes! When I saw you at the party, bowing and scraping before her, almost to your knees you went! Oh, my God! I wass sick and ashamed to see such servile gestures."

"And I'm sick to hear such servile talk!" flamed Lucy.

"This is not servile talk."

"Yes, it is. You talk like an underdog, and you are one. Couldn't you see those bows and curtseys were just for fun, to make the party go? No! You're so inferior, you imagine there must be some low motive in everything."

"There wass a low motive. . . ."

"There was not. But you can't understand *that*, because you've got a slave's mind, and you'll always be a slave . . . somebody's slave."

"You come here to insult me. . . ."

"You've insulted me. You've said what you think of me. So I'll say what I think of you. I suppose you're one of those idiots who think the Institute has been taken away from the town?"

"It's God's truth it has!"

"So what? What do you do about it? Go and get it back? Get your own shows put on at the theatre? Find out what you want to do with the Institute and keep on till you've got it done? Oh, no! That's how top dogs behave. You'd rather be overcharged for a wretched hall and snivel about how you've been done down. You'll always be done down, because you're naturally servile."

"We are the massters now. . . ."

"Not people like you. All you'll get is a change of masters.

You think there ought to be some nice kind Nanny, somebody like Mrs. Meeker, to go and get your lovely Institute back for you. You don't ask what she'd do with it, and you don't know. All you can do is to howl that you've been done out of your rights, poor little underdog! So Nanny Meeker will get its rights back for it, and keep them locked up in her cupboard."

Lucy paused, breathless and a little astonished at her own eloquence. Rees was astonished too. After a moment she went on, in a calmer voice but still violently indignant.

"You say the Institute shows are rotten? Very well, I agree, they are. You say the town has a right to better? Very well. But who ought to be seeing to it? You know more about good shows than anyone else in Ravonsbridge. If you were worth a hill of beans you'd be on the job. But no! Everything has to be given to you—handed to you, all done up in tissue paper and labelled *Poor Owen's Rights!* So somebody or other will always be able to do you down. You'll only have yourself to thank when you open the parcel and find nothing inside but a raspberry. Goodbye and thank you for the drink."

She jumped up and ran out of the café.

Owen sat looking after her with his mouth open. Well, he thought, mopping his face, there's a tartar she is! There's a proper young termagant!

He liked her the better for her violence. Had she kept her dignity, and answered his accusations with well bred restraint, he would never have forgiven her. In turning on him and abusing him she had admitted an equality which he was quick to appreciate. He had never wholly believed that she meant to pinch Thornley's job, but, being a Celt, he could get up a very fine blaze of indignation without asking for any clear proof. Suspicion was enough, and he luxuriated in the mood of the moment.

Their obvious quarrel had been watched with interest by their neighbours. Adamson, on his way out, stopped by Owen's table and asked who the lady friend was. When told, he sighed and observed that it burnt him all up to think of that place on the hill —rotting, wasted. His face shone with a cupidity so forthright that it had a kind of innocence as he mourned the fate of that great big hall, the biggest hall in Severnshire, standing empty. Pots of money, he declared, could be made out of a place like that, in spite of the hill, if it was properly handled.

"Know what I'd do?" he asked, putting both hands on Owen's table and leaning forward. "If I had that hall I'd put on a Walkathon. That's what I'd do."

"It'd be banned," said Owen.

"Not if it was handled right. In California they chain them. After two or three weeks, when there's only a few couples left in, they chain them, see? So if the girl faints the feller can't push her under the ropes, has to go on dragging her, see? Well, couldn't do that here. They wouldn't stand for it here, I agree. But at that, it'd go to town in a big way. I believe we'd have competing couples from all over the country, and the gate! Oh boy! Never been anything like it before, see? Novelty. Anyway, that's what I'd do."

"Not at the Institute," said Owen coldly. "It's supposed to be for art."

"That's right," agreed Adamson, gloomily straightening himself, "that's where it is. And that's why it's empty. Art! Well . . . be seeing you. . . ."

"Be seeing you," agreed Owen without enthusiasm.

The idea of a Walkathon in the Institute would have shocked him, had he entertained it seriously. But he was confident that such an idea could never be translated into fact. The Institute was meant for art. "They" would never allow it to be used for such an obscenity. He was sure of that without ever asking himself who "they" were.

2

Dr. PIDGEON, after months of neglect, suddenly remembered that he was senior music director at Ravonsbridge. He appeared at the Institute three times in one week, conducted the choir, conducted the orchestra, tore his hair over their inadequacy, and issued a command that they should all repair to Severnton for a concert in the Cathedral. Thither they went, on a Thursday morning in February, transported by a fleet of motor coaches across the hills of Slane Forest.

Lucy went with the choir for she was not wanted in the orchestra. Her performance on the bassoon, though improved, was not up to Pidgeon's standards. He had stopped them all in the middle of a bar to demand that that woman be forbidden to play that thing. Lucy relinquished the instrument with much relief, for she was growing to hate it. During her first term at Ravonsbridge she had been well content to hide in her attic at the Angeras', making noises like a sick cow. Now that her zest for society had revived she had better things to do in the evenings.

Immediately on arrival at Severnton they were fed and herded to the Cathedral where they spent the whole afternoon rehearsing and enduring the insults of Dr. Pidgeon who told them, when he dismissed them for tea, that a monkey house would have been more harmonious.

"It's his own fault," grumbled Bess. "He never comes near us, and Rickie sings so loud himself, when he's conducting, I don't believe he can hear what sort of noise we make."

Lucy laughed and wondered if the senior drama director, when appointed, would be as elusive as Dr. Pidgeon. No choice had yet been made; Mr. Thornley was not so easy to replace as Lady Frances had supposed. One or two people had been approached, so Hayter said, and had refused because Ravonsbridge was so far from London. It was possible that the post might remain vacant until the autumn.

This news was not wholly unwelcome to Lucy. She did not much like her ambiguous position, but she had a scheme for the Summer Term which she wanted to attempt before some new superior, suddenly put over her, should discourage or interfere with her. She had discovered in Slane Forest a natural amphitheatre, a circular grassy hollow, surrounded by trees and easily accessible from the road. A play at midsummer, begun at sunset and continuing under a rising moon, with spotlights among the trees, began to take shape in her mind, though she had not yet chosen the actual piece. It was possible, she felt, to have too much of Shakespeare. But she meant to bicycle over before the end of the term and inspect the site again; there were practical points to be considered, such as a car park, and the seating of an audience on the banks of the hollow. While she was there perhaps the right play would occur to her.

She had been thinking about it during the drive over and through most of the rehearsal. Pastoral plays did not as a rule attract her and she was surprised at her own eagerness to attempt this one. The place itself had inspired her—the sculptured antiquity of the great beech trunks and the emptiness of the grassy stage. She put figures upon it and asked herself why a natural background should always diminish human stature. They looked too small, too indistinct. Still without having settled on a play she decided to dress them in white and yellow, to have a crowded stage but few speaking parts, and to keep her principals as stationary as possible. It was only as she followed Bess out of the Cathedral that she thought of *Comus*.

Instantly the various ingredients which had already attracted her explained themselves; she must really have been thinking of *Comus* for quite a while. A little raised mound on the left of the stage was intended for the Lady's chair; a pool and some reeds, on the right, suggested an entrance for Sabrina. She realised why Purcell's music had been running in her head all day instead of the Parry *Motet* and Fauré's *Requiem*, which she was to sing at the concert. Much excited, she dropped behind Bess and turned into the cloisters for a few minutes to examine this discovery.

If she wanted Purcell she had no time to lose. Rickie would need to rehearse his orchestra. She must get all the practical details settled this term, and secure the approval of Lady Frances and Mr. Hayter. Round and round the cloister she strode, the hood of her coat drawn over her head and her hands thrust into her sleeves for warmth, pacing and pondering like one of the young monks for whom, long ago, that cloister was built. Three times she passed the spot where Melissa and Stephen had once debated the constancy of women. On her fourth round she saw a man walking in front of her. He had come out of the Chapter House and was going towards the gate into the Close. His walk was familiar. She would almost have thought . . . she was sure . . . she ran after him calling:

"Mr. Thornley! Mr. Thornley!"

He turned as she came up with outstretched hand.

"Why . . . Lucy!"

As he took her hand they peered at one another in the gathering dusk. But how much older he looked! How shrunken and shabby and sad! This was the mere ghost of the dapper little man at whom she had so often laughed.

"How did you come?" he exclaimed, and then remembered: "Oh, yes, the concert. I saw the poster. I suppose you're all here?"

"Oh," said Lucy, "I am so glad to see you. I've been wondering where you were. Are you, are you living in Severnton now? I hadn't realised—"

"Oh, no, no. I'm only here on business. My headquarters are in Bristol now. Bristol . . . yes. I've settled in Bristol."

"And are you very busy?"

"Oh, yes. Very busy. Very busy. But Lucy, my dear, how are you? How is . . . everybody?"

His voice shook a little, or she thought it did.

"Oh, everybody is very well."

For a few seconds there seemed to be nothing to say. Then Lucy burst out:

"Mr. Thornley, it was so dreadful to come back this term and find you gone. How could you go off like that without saying goodbye to us? Were you . . . were you angry with us for anything?"

"Oh, no! No . . . but it was a sudden decision . . . I . . . I was sorry I had no opportunity to say goodbye . . . so much to see to, you know. . . ."

"If I'd known your address I'd have written; I thought you'd gone abroad."

"Yes, my dear, yes. I'm sure you would. We always got on very well together, didn't we, Lucy? I always thought we got on so well. It's been delightful, running into you like this. But I expect you're in a hurry. You'll be wanting your tea."

The hint was plain, but Lucy stood her ground.

"Couldn't you give me your address now?" she begged. "There is so much I want your advice about. I'm quite at sea. I'm having to carry on by myself. You know they've not appointed anyone yet, in your place? I never expected all this responsibility, and no chance to get your advice."

Mr. Thornley sat down suddenly on the low wall between two cloister arches. The waning daylight fell on his face and she could see a small tear wandering down his cheek.

"Oh, Mr. Thornley!"

She sat beside him and put a timid hand on his arm. He blew his nose and presently he quavered:

"Took me by surprise, meeting you like this. The dear old place . . . I loved dear Ravonsbridge. . . ."

"I know," said Lucy. "I know."

She squeezed his arm, and when he had recovered a little she said:

"I've been very much distressed since you went. And puzzled. May I tell you? Will you advise me?"

"Yes, my dear girl, yes. . . ."

She collected her thoughts and told him everything, starting with her luncheon at Cyre Abbey. She touched on her conversation with Hayter, repeating as accurately as she could, all that had passed between them. Finally she described her quarrel with Owen Rees.

"All these things, taken together, worry me," she finished. "If it wasn't for those events last term, I shouldn't pay any attention to Owen. But it's made me very unhappy. Mr. Thornley—I don't want to enquire into your affairs, I know it's rather impertinent, but was there . . . was anything wrong . . . anything you didn't quite like . . . in the circumstances . . . the reason why you left us?"

He did not answer. He had been listening attentively and without comment. After a while he got up and put a hand under her elbow, telling her that she would catch cold if she sat there any longer. They must go and have a cup of tea somewhere. But not at the Crown, protested Lucy, getting up; the whole choir and orchestra would be there. He said that he knew of a nice quiet little place just outside the Close where they could talk in peace. As he led her out of the cloisters he pressed her arm affectionately.

"I'm very glad I met you, Lucy, my dear. Very glad indeed. I never could believe that you had anything to do with it."

"Did anybody say I had?" cried Lucy.

"It was . . . hinted to me. . . ."

"Who hinted it? Mr. Hayter?"

"Oh, dear no. Certainly not!"

"Then who? Just tell me and I'll—"

"No, no. . . . Wait now and listen to me."

They found his little tea shop and were soon sitting cosily over a fire, China tea, and muffins. He seemed to be embarrassed and unwilling to say more, but at last he broke out with:

"One must be just! One mustn't jump to the conclusion that it was a put-up job."

"Please, what happened?"

Staring sadly at the fire he tried to tell her what had happened. The whole thing was still such a grief, such a shock, to him that he could not put his story together very connectedly. It was constantly interrupted by interjections of amazement. He could not understand how Lady Frances had come to treat him so badly after so long standing a friendship. Why should she suddenly command him to relinquish all his outside work? It might be allowed that he should not have gone abroad without leave; he was ready to admit himself in fault over that. Perhaps he deserved reproof. But she had spoken to him, he said, as though he had been one of the students caught staying out after hours. He could not submit to so peremptory a tone.

Sometimes he declared that she had been turned against him, and that their misunderstanding had been deliberately engineered. And then he would pull himself together and warn Lucy that suspicions of that kind may be very unjust. He had no evidence which gave him the right to accuse anybody. He had behaved foolishly, and had only himself to blame.

It appeared that he had had an angry scene with Lady Frances just before he departed on his December lecture tour. She had been incensed by his complete disregard of all that she had already said. She forbade him to go on his tour and commanded him to drop all his outside work forthwith. He had been tempted to tender his immediate and unqualified resignation. But his great attachment, both to her and to Ravonsbridge, had restrained him. He did not commit himself, on that occasion, either by resigning or by promising to obey her.

He then consulted his old friend Mr. Garstang, who agreed

that he could not possibly submit to such dictatorial treatment, but was very anxious to keep him on the council. Between them they thought of a compromise. Why, Mr. Garstang had suggested, should Thornley not hold the post as part time director, as Dr. Pidgeon did? It would mean a reduction of salary, but it would enable him to combine the Ravonsbridge duties with other work and keep him on the council.

"The idea," he said, "appealed to me. It appealed to me very much. And I felt it was fair to Lady Frances, since I gathered that she thought I should not receive a full time salary unless I did full time work. I hoped it would mean promotion for you, which you quite deserved. You could have rehearsed productions and I could have come and helped you with the finishing touches. And you could have consulted me at any time. I decided I would do that. Since I couldn't be at the council meeting I wrote them a letter, resigning immediately on account of the pressure of my other work, and offering my services to the Institute as a part time director. I . . . I never dreamt . . . I thought they would jump at it. So did Garstang. He took it for granted they would. So did Hayter. I saw him, and explained my idea, and he seemed to think it was a very good one. I didn't mention to Hayter, of course, that I had had this distressing scene with Lady Frances."

There was a long pause. Mr. Thornley did not seem able to go on. At last, in a stifled voice, he muttered:

"They simply accepted my resignation and never offered me the visiting post. I couldn't believe it when I got their letter. But that's what they did."

"Do you know at all what happened at the meeting?"

"Oh, yes. Garstang was there. I saw him when I came back to Ravonsbridge at Christmas to collect all my goods and chattels. He was greatly distressed. He said . . . he told me . . . that, when my letter had been read, Lady Frances said at once that she liked the idea of a visiting director but that she thought they ought to get someone more . . . more distinguished than I am."

No comment on this occurred to Lucy. She made a little commiserating noise and presently he said:

"Perhaps she was right. Perhaps they can."

"But didn't Mr. Garstang speak up for you?"

"Oh, yes, I think so. Oh, yes, I'm sure he tried to explain. He told me he was just going to say he doubted if I should have resigned at all, if I hadn't expected to remain with the Institute in some capacity, when Hayter said the same thing, and told them he'd talked to me and that I'd written the letter quite taking for granted that I'd get the visiting directorship. But that seemed to annoy Lady Frances very much. She said: We can't be governed by what Mr. Thornley may take for granted. Or something like that."

"I expect Mr. Hayter put it in a way that annoyed her."

"Oh, I don't know. Garstang said he might have put it more tactfully. But he voted for me, you know. Hayter did. They put it to the vote, but it was five against Garstang and Hayter. Pidgeon and Coppard weren't there, of course."

"If I'd been Garstang I'd have resigned from the council," declared Lucy warmly.

"Well, to tell you the truth, I felt that a little myself at first. I thought: If I'd been in his shoes I'd have resigned; but then I remembered that I didn't resign over poor Grier, Haverstock's predecessor. I thought we treated him most unjustly over the music directorship. I said so. But I didn't resign. So why should Garstang resign over me?"

"But still . . . why didn't you try to see Lady Frances?"

"Perhaps I ought. But you know I was so hurt, so mortified, after all these years; I thought if she could treat me like that I'd better go. I collected my bits and pieces and left Ravonsbridge without seeing anyone."

When old friends quarrel, thought Lucy, there is not much to be done. The shock of finding that they can hurt one another destroys confidence. But she wished that these two had met. Something might have emerged which incriminated Hayter, who was, she believed, at the bottom of it.

"And who," she asked, "hinted that I had anything to do with it? You say you saw nobody?"

"Nobody except Garstang," admitted Thornley, looking flustered.

"But surely he didn't . . . why . . . he doesn't know me! I've never spoken to Mr. Garstang. I know him by sight of course."

"No. He doesn't know you, and I told him so. If he did he'd see it was nonsense."

"But what did he say? That I'd intrigued—"

"Oh, no, no, no! He merely thought you had friends who . . . I might well have been mistaken as to what he said. I was so confused and wretched that day, I may not have understood him. He merely thought you are such a favourite at Cyre Abbey . . . with the *whole* family . . . he thought pressure might have been brought to get you promotion. It was an impression that he got at the Christmas party."

That damned waltz again! *Charles loves Lucy.* Was she never to be forgiven for that one small lapse? She asked no more about Mr. Garstang and returned to the main issue.

"But don't you see what is happening, Mr. Thornley? The old resident staff are all going and are replaced by people who don't live in Ravonsbridge, or really know much about the Institute. And the resident staff are all very young and inexperienced and aren't on the council."

He looked startled.

"I hadn't thought of it," he said. "But now you put it that way . . . of course, Angera ought to be on the council. But I doubt if they'll ever have him."

"I think it's all a plan. I think it's all Mr. Hayter's doing."

"Oh, no, Lucy. You've no right to say that."

"I can't help thinking it. I'm beginning to see what he was after when he talked to me, that day, asking if I'd like to stay on if you fell under a bus. Because he'd have been in the soup if all the drama school staff went. If only I'd tumbled to it I'd have said: If Mr. Thornley goes, I go, and so will . . ."

She broke off, shaken by a sudden doubt. Would Miss Frogmore and Miss Paine have gone? How much had they foreseen? Had they really been very much surprised when they came back to Ravonsbridge after Christmas and found no Mr. Thornley? She remembered that Miss Frogmore had been short and dry about it. Perhaps she believed that Lucy's amazed regret was all humbug.

"Might I talk about this to some of the others?" she asked.

He was emphatic that she might not. Not a word. Not for the world. The chief fault had been his; he had managed the matter badly. He loved the dear old place and he could not bear to leave bitterness or strife behind him, after so many happy years. That, he confessed, was why he had decamped in such a hurry. He could not help feeling bitter himself and until he had got over it he did not want to meet anyone from Ravonsbridge. Nor must she allow this business to interfere with her own advancement. She must not quarrel with anyone on his account. He would reproach himself for selfishness if these confidences were allowed to affect her interests in any way. After all, her prospects were so bright . . . so bright. . . . Lucy could not help smiling slightly. The poor old man seemed to think that the senior directorship must be the supreme goal of any girl's ambitions.

His next sentence enlightened her. The bright prospects were not entirely professional. He looked almost coy as he added:

"I wish I'd seen you at the party, Lucy. Garstang said you were quite the belle of the evening!"

"Yes, I was," she said quickly. "I even danced twice with Mr. Millwood! Nobody can get over it."

"A very fine young man," said Thornley emphatically. "I've always thought him a very fine young man."

She declared that she did not like him much, at which Mr. Thornley smiled so complacently that she saw she had said the wrong thing. By his standards it was what a nice girl, a lady, ought to say if she were very much in love.

Her tea interval was nearly up. He paid the bill, took her to the Cathedral, kissed her and shuffled off into the night.

None of the others had come back yet; the Cathedral was dark and empty. A few lights were burning up by the chancel screen, where the choir and orchestra were to sit. In the nave the Norman pillars soared up into night. Lucy slipped into a chair and tried to arrange her ideas.

Mr. Hayter was getting the Institute into his pocket. Of that she was perfectly sure, though she could not guess his motive. But why did she see all this so clearly when none of her colleagues did?

I, she thought, might have seen nothing if I had not been outside it all for a time. I was almost outside life, that first year. Because of that I noticed a lot of things which would not have struck me otherwise. I got to know something of the lower town because

I went to read to Mr. Meeker, so as to get through those unbearable evenings. If I had come to Ravonsbridge in normal spirits I should not have seen these things. I should have gone with the crowd. I should have liked Mr. Hayter as much as most people do, and disliked Emil as much as most people do. That year has made a difference to me after all.

More lights came on. The choir was trooping in. She went up the nave and took her place beside Bess. Tuning strings hummed and echoed among the aisles and arches. The audience, emerging from the foggy night, shuffled and scuffled in chairs which squeaked unpleasantly when shifted on the stone pavement. Bess whispered that she had been a duffer not to come to the Crown.

"Why?"

"Because we all went."

This did not sound a very good reason, but Bess insisted that it had been a huge rag. She retailed the jocund antics at the Crown until a cleric appeared in the pulpit and began to pray. When that was over Dr. Pidgeon came in with the soloists and the concert began with a *Brandenberg Concerto*.

String music in a stone building is too piercing and vibrant; its delicacy is lost in a confusion of echoes. Lucy was soon wishing for the impersonality of an organ. She watched Dr. Pidgeon, who made faces of frantic disgust and managed to get ten times more out of the orchestra than poor Rickie ever did. His eye was everywhere at once. He would certainly know it if she or Bess or anyone in the choir missed an entry. She must concentrate.

The *Concerto* was over. The choir was on its feet. She thrust all other thoughts from her and ceased to be Lucy—ceased to be anything save part of this majestic ship which was about to set sail. Raising her eyes to Pidgeon she left the world behind her and existed only for Fauré until she was in the coach going home. Even there she was not quite on earth; the *Requiem* continued in her mind and any other reality seemed faint. Intense effort made her tired and sleepy. Tree after tree on the roadside flashed into vivid, theatrical relief, as the headlights of the bus swept onward, and then slipped back into night. Their coach was not very full. She sat on a back bench with Bess, who kept up a continual chatter, but she hardly heard it through the shifting veils of remembered music.

". . . Miss Tanner. You know! Does massage and electric treatment . . . has a place in Shotter Street . . . walked back to the Cathedral with her . . . great friend of the Plum's . . . Ianthe's latest . . ."

Sanctus! Sanctus!

The song of the blest floats on tranquilly for ever and ever, over the crystal sea, over the waves of harp music.

". . . Well, she did leave Ravonsbridge very suddenly last summer. That much is true . . ."

Sanctus! Sanctus!

". . . Cagey about what happened. But the Plum is convinced she was going to have a baby and then got rid of it, whether by accident or on purpose, don't ask. And that's why she's been looking so jolly ill—"

"Oh, do shut up!"

"I know. It's pretty foul, isn't it? I said to Miss Tanner: But you can't ever believe a word Ianthe says. So she said Ianthe hasn't said anything. It's all the Plum's idea. . . ."

Requiem aeternum . . .

". . . Simply no idea who the man is. Ianthe won't say."

Et lux perpetua . . .

"Don't you, Lucy?"

"I do wish you wouldn't talk. I want to think about the *Requiem.*"

"Mercy! Haven't we all thought enough about it this last week?"

"Not nearly enough. I've hardly begun to think about it."

"Well, but the Plum says he must be somebody in Ravonsbridge."

"Who?"

"The man. The father of this baby which I don't believe Ianthe ever had. I mean I don't believe a single thing of any of it. But Plum says he's a scoundrel and ought to be whipped. What do you think of that?"

"Oh, do stop talking, you cackling creature."

"No need to be rude."

"For God's sake stop."

"No need to be blasphemous either. O.K. I'll stop."

"Thanks. Sorry."

"Don't mention it."

Sanctus! Sanctus! . . . *Sanctus! Sanctus!* . . . *Sanctus! Sanctus!* . . .

3

LUCY'S AMPHITHEATRE in Slane Forest was carpeted with wild daffodils. She picked a great bunch of them before returning to the high road. The place was even lovelier than she had remembered and she was quite determined to put on *Comus*, if arrangements could be made for a car park.

For this she must depend upon Hayter, but she was sure that he would manage it, if he took to the idea. Parking in the forest, and motoring on side tracks, was forbidden. She had found a large level tract of ground beside the high road, only a few minutes' walk away from the amphitheatre, which would hold a good many vehicles. This might be used as the main car park. But a great deal of the equipment, the loud speaker apparatus, the vans with the spot lights, must be driven close up to the stage. Hayter would know whom to approach. He would pull strings. Somebody would get the concession for supplying deck chairs and campstools, somebody else would run a refreshment tent; leave to park would be forthcoming.

She wished, not for the first time, that she liked Hayter better, for he was an invaluable ally. A little artfulness, she supposed, is essential if anything is ever to be done. She was sure that Matt Millwood had been, on occasion, a little artful. But she was sure, too, that if Matt had been in Ravonsbridge there would have been no Hayter.

She sat on a fallen log on the high road, waiting for the bus back to Ravonsbridge and hugging her bunch of daffodils. *Comus* was going to be lovely; she could hardly wait till midsummer. As she waited she hummed idly:

"Spring shall come, come again . . ."

Suddenly everything went flat and her spirits came tumbling down. Comus was, after all, merely another job of work. It might be quite pretty, quite a success, but then it would be over, and then she would do something else, and then she would do something else, and then she would be old, and then she would die. Whither was she bustling so busily, year after year, and why did she bustle? What did she want?

It must be the spring, she decided. The darned old spring which was supposed to cheer people up, but which could make one feel lonely and wasted. Was she never to be wildly happy? Never give wild happiness to anybody? Spring came along and other people were happy. Other girls were married. Other girls went courting. Other girls had a tumble in the barn or at least got kissed. But not Lucy! Oh, no! Lucy merely bustled about looking for car parks and would go on doing that for fifty springs until she bustled herself into her grave.

> Then worms shall try
> That long preserved virginity . . .
> The grave's a fine and private place,
> But none, I think, do there embrace.

She shivered, as the words passed through her mind, and thought suddenly of McNab. Where was he now? Still probably in the ottoman where she had tossed him on that night which she had thought to be the last of her maidenhood. Poor little old McNab! And poor old Lucy, who had once been that artless child.

A Ravon Roadster came roaring through the forest, braked violently, and slowed to a standstill a little way beyond her. Its occupant climbed out and walked back. She had known that he would, as soon as she recognised the car. They had not met since the Christmas party and it was said that he had been in the United States. She watched him, as she sat on the log with the daffodils in her lap and her long legs stretched out in front of her.

"Can I give you a lift?" he asked as he came up.

"No, thank you," said Lucy. "I'm waiting for the bus to Ravonsbridge."

"I could run you back to Ravonsbridge in five minutes."

She shook her head.

"Better not," she said. "If I'm seen driving around in your car they'll all have their eyes on sticks. Have you forgotten the Christmas party?"

"No," said Charles, and sat down on the log beside her.

Sit on a log and wish for a man, thought Lucy, and along one comes. What a pity I don't love him. What a pity he is not *the man*. Such millions and millions of men in the world, and lots of them very nice, and I daresay *the man* is in the Antipodes.

"Lucy!"

Ho! Lucy! We're coming on!

"I was thinking about you as I was driving along. And then I saw you."

What does a girl say to that? Rickie could do better. My dear Charles, your brains is dead—and you with a First in Greats!

"One often does," she said. "Think of a person like that, I mean, for no reason, and then suddenly meet them."

"Yes," agreed Charles. "Or they telephone."

Imbecile! Melissa was talking through her hat about his love life; he can't ever have had any.

"Lucy! I wish you'd look at me," cried Charles in desperation.

She turned and looked at him and was moved by his expression.

"You'd much better not think of me," she said gently, "if it makes you unhappy."

"I know."

He had been trying not to think of her for months, with varying success. He was sure that he would do well to put her right out of his mind. She was lovely and strange and agitating, but he did not want to turn his life into a three ring circus.

"Were you . . . waiting for anybody. . . ?"

"Yes."

And if he's in the Antipodes, thought Lucy, he's just under my feet probably. Just several thousand miles beneath my feet, upside down, making love to an Australian girl. Oh! I could make a better world than this one with my eyes shut!

"Who?" demanded Charles, seared by jealousy.

"Unfortunately, I don't know," said Lucy. "They've got

rather a long way to come, and are taking their time about it. Do you hear a distant growling? That's my bus, changing gears on the opposite hill. It'll be here in three minutes, full of people with their eyes on sticks. So please drive on."

"Look at me again first?" he entreated.

She looked at him again. It was a shame that he should feel so miserable. Poor Charles! Leaning over, she kissed him, thinking that, if a kiss would cheer him up, no harm would be done, and feeling guilty about the *Blue Danube*.

"Oh, Lucy!"

He returned her salute with ardour. And how nicely!

Melissa was right after all, thought Lucy. He's had a lot of practice. And then she thought: *It's catching!* And then she was sorry that the bus would be coming so soon.

"You must go," she said pushing him away. "That's my bus just coming round the corner."

There was no time for him to get to his car again. He retreated into a thick screen of holly bushes just behind them. The bus came growling up, was hailed by Lucy, and stopped. In she jumped and it started again. When it had gone Charles emerged from his grove. The ground by the log was strewn with wild daffodils. In her agitation she had dropped and forgotten them.

Not until the bus emerged from the forest did Lucy begin to recover any sort of equanimity. The discovery that Charles, whom she did not love, could arouse such feelings made her wonder if she had ever known herself. But as her racing heart subsided, and her face grew cooler, she decided to blame the spring, and the thoughts which spring had put into her mind when he chanced to come by. Also he had, as Emil would have said, technique. She had never believed in it much before, since she was sure that nothing of that sort could evoke the tender passion she had felt for Patrick Reilly, hitherto her yard stick for love. Now she was bound to admit that it could evoke something, inferior perhaps, but far from unpleasant. She could not be sorry that she had kissed Charles, sitting on that log, for the next few seconds had been as good as a first class ski run.

She concluded that she must have a very sensual nature and was surprised at herself for not being shocked by this. But when she had got back to Sheep Lane, and made herself a cup of tea, she resolved to meet Charles no more. It was with something of an effort that she took this decision, for the mere thought of seeing him again made her pulses beat more quickly. But if so much could happen to her in two minutes, less than two minutes, she might, on some other occasion, completely lose her head. And that, she felt, would be treason to Lady Frances.

For it would be known. Even if she did not lose her head, some blasting publicity would be certain to fall upon any dealings which she might have with Charles. The Christmas party had taught her what to expect, and she knew from experience her own inability to conceal anything. However careful they were, some Ravonsbridge gossips would notice them together. Nothing would have power to wound Lady Frances more cruelly than a scandal connected with the Institute, nor could any scandal underline the failure of Matt Millwood's hopes more cynically. Contemptuous things enough were said about that mausoleum of good intentions. Matt's wife was accused of exploiting it in order to give the town's money to her toadies. But nobody had as yet found an opportunity for describing it as a seraglio for Matt's son.

If it were anybody else, thought Lncy, one might throw one's bonnet over the windmill, in a lonely and restless moment. But in this case no bonnet could be thrown without hitting Lady Frances in the eye, and she could not do this to a woman whom she so much liked and respected.

She washed up her tea things and forbade herself ever to think of him again, ever to let her mind rest on those moments by the roadside. It should be easy, for she had learnt how to rule her thoughts. And if he tried to see her she would tell him quite frankly why it could not be. He would be very unhappy, but not so miserable as he might be, later on, if he broke his mother's heart.

She began to frame sentences in her mind and then realised that she was looking forward to the delicious agitation of another interview. This would not do. This was thinking about Charles, which she must not do. She must let that occasion look after itself when it arrived, and what she had to say was very simple; she need not plan her speeches, in order to have an excuse for imagining replies from him. *She must not think about him.* She must get on with *Comus.*

The habit of concentrating was easy to her. She got on with *Comus* for an hour until a knock brought her to the street door. Charles again!

Help ho! My virtue! thought Lucy, so much flustered that she was on the point of giggling. But she might as well get it over now, as he was here. She conducted him to her sitting room in silence and shut the door. His first words so much astonished her that she sat down on a small hard chair close to the door, because her knees gave way and it was the nearest.

"Lucy! We must get married! You must marry me!"

"What?" cried Lucy, collapsing onto the chair.

"I've been thinking it over. I've been driving about. Ever since you left me. I've been driving about. I've been thinking. We must marry. I can't possibly live without you, and you . . . I believe you'd very soon feel as I do if—"

"But Charles! We aren't suited. It would never do. We—"

"I know. I know we aren't suited. That's what has been holding me back. But I've been thinking it over. There's no other way."

"But I don't love you," expostulated Lucy.

"Oh, yes, you do. Oh, yes, I think you do."

Lucy jumped up and evaded him.

"No, no," she said. "Sit down here, by the fire, and tell me calmly. You . . . you've taken me so entirely by surprise. Since this afternoon, of course, I . . . but I never thought for a minute you'd ever want to marry me."

"But will you?"

"I don't know. I don't know. I don't think I love you. I don't understand. I can't imagine us . . . married. . . . I can't see how you can imagine it."

He took the chair she pointed out to him, and she sat down opposite. After a moment of staring at her, he began again, more collectedly, but still with considerable agitation.

"I can see that we aren't suited, in a way. You are very talented, very gifted; you have a great career in front of you. A conventional marriage would never be enough for you. You'd loathe having to live at Cyre Abbey, for instance."

"I don't know that I should," said Lucy, surprised. "If that were all, I should like to live at Cyre Abbey."

"Oh, no, you'd be stifled there," Charles assured her.

I should go into the glass houses and eat the peaches, thought Lucy. And then she remembered that the Millwoods never ate the peaches, which were reserved for the Poor when they had shingles.

"Well . . . perhaps . . ." she conceded.

"Whereas, in London—"

"Oh, I hate London!"

"No, but listen, Lucy. I've thought it all out. You needn't give up your career. You could have your own theatre. I'll finance it. You can have your own theatre and put on any plays you like."

"I thought you said . . . marry you . . ." said Lucy, bewildered.

"Oh, yes, marry me as well. We'll have a flat, and I'll come backwards and forwards between London and Ravonsbridge."

"But why couldn't I live in Ravonsbridge?"

Charles was perfectly determined that she would not like to live in Ravonsbridge. He did not want her in Ravonsbridge where, he dimly perceived, she might join forces with his mother and badger the life out of him. He intended that all this vehement vitality, which repelled as much as it enthralled him, should be diverted elsewhere. He continued to talk about her gifts, her talents and her career for some minutes until she interrupted him.

"But Charles, you know you've got me all wrong. I'm not a career girl at all. And I'm not particularly gifted. And I'm not all that devoted to the theatre."

"You can't say that. Your work on Hamlet—"

"Was nothing out of the way. Just schoolgirl's work. You're deceiving yourself. Compare it with any really good production you've seen."

Charles visibly wavered and then looked obstinate.

"I think you did a very distinguished piece of work."

"I'm quite bright sometimes. I took the Ravonsbridge job because it was a job, and I do it as well as I can. I have to earn my living. But . . . but if I married, I'd want to be a wife."

225

A wife was just what Charles did not want, though he was resolved to marry Lucy honourably in the sight of God and man before setting her up in her theatre.

"If you can do so well, in such a short time, with the material you have here," he told her, "you ought to try your hand at something bigger."

"No, Charles. What on earth would I do with a London theatre? I wouldn't know the first thing . . . everybody would laugh. You must be demented. And I wouldn't like it. I wouldn't be interested. You talk of the material here : ... it's just that which does interest me."

"What? Owen Rees? And that girl with the accent . . . Kitty?"

"Not exactly. It's Ravonsbridge. It's trying to see how much can be done by quite ordinary people in a small place. You don't understand that?"

"No. I can't say that I do. Ravonsbridge is a provincial backwater."

"Your father didn't think so."

"And you've not been here two years. I can't understand this devotion to it."

Lucy pondered, crouched in the firelight, while Charles racked his brains for an alternative solution, should she really reject his plan.

"If it wasn't for this currency nonsense," he said regretfully, "we could have lived in Paris. You'd like Paris."

"There are some soft currency countries," suggested Lucy. "Australia and South Africa. You might park me in Cape Town or Melbourne."

"I'm not trying to be funny," said Charles, when he realised that she must be laughing at him.

"You mayn't be trying, but you're succeeding. You don't really want to marry me one bit. You want me for a sort of honourable concubine."

"Oh, no, no!"

"Oh, yes! But listen, Charles. Let me try to explain about Ravonsbridge, because that will show you the sort of person I am, and how little we should suit. You see . . . I was very unhappy when first I came here."

She paused and looked up at him. He nodded.

"You know about that?"

"Yes. My sister told me. Penelope."

"Oh, dear. I suppose a lot of people know really. It can't be helped."

"I'd known half the story already," he said. "I'd known that Mrs. Lucas snatched Reilly away from some young girl he was going to marry. It's one of the stories people tell about her. But I'd never heard the name of the girl. And I had had the idea that you'd been in love with a botanist."

"So he was."

"What? Reilly? I thought—"

"He'd have been a botanist if I'd married him."

Charles felt a slight tremor of sympathy for Reilly.

"Didn't it put you off me?" asked Lucy.

"No."

Yes it did, she thought, looking at him. Yet he's ready to marry me. He must want me very much in his way, poor Charles!

"Well, so I was unhappy," she repeated, "and this is the sort of person I am; I suppose I am very feminine, but I can't bear not to have somebody to love and work for. I'm the very opposite of a career girl, if you only knew. But I had nobody. So I suppose I kept myself up by making a sort of romance out of your father."

"Good God!" said Charles.

"I know it sounds hen witted."

"But you never knew him!"

"Mr. Meeker tells me about him."

"Oh, Meeker goes in for hero worship. My father was a great man, certainly. But he was human. He had his faults."

"I should hope so. But I was fascinated by his ideas for the Institute, trying to guess what they had really been, and trying to carry them out."

Charles frowned impatiently. The Institute bored him to frenzy; he had never sympathised with his father's ideas and the continual chatter about it, which pervaded Cyre Abbey, had driven him to loathe the very thought of the place.

"When quite ordinary people get together to do anything for its own sake," said Lucy, "they sometimes do something remarkable. That's what I had in mind with *Hamlet*. I knew it wouldn't be very much; nothing near to what your father wanted. But if something real and lively could be started, it might grow; and then if somebody great turned up, someday, they could make something great out of it. I . . . I wanted to serve your father by getting something started."

"If you'd prefer to run some amateur group . . ."

"No, no, no! I'm trying to explain the sort of person I am. If I marry a man I'll want to . . . to help him and use all my brains and capacities to help him, in anything he wants to do with his life. I'd be quite happy in a small town, or the North Pole, or anywhere, as long as I could share his life. But that's just what you don't ask, Charles."

"There's nothing in my life that could interest you. Very little in it interests me."

"I know. That's why we aren't suited. Honestly, now we've got it straight, I find it easier to say I won't marry you than—"

"Than what?" he asked quickly.

"Say I won't see you again. I was going to say that when you came in. It will only be the Christmas party over again, and people will talk, and that wouldn't be good for the Institute."

"Oh, damn the Institute."

Charles wished that a bomb would fall on the Institute and said so. He was growing angry with her and less in love than usual. The wild, strange quality in her, which so troubled him, was in abeyance. When he saw her sitting in the forest, with her tumbled curls and the flowers in her lap, he had felt that the world could not hold her equal. But now she sat beside the fire prosing away like a governess about the Institute.

His expostulations grew more and more halfhearted until he allowed himself to be convinced. If only he could always manage to remember her like this he would not suffer extremely over his rejection. He departed without attempting any more technique, for which Lucy was thankful. And on the doorstep he made a solemn little speech about hoping that she would let him know if there was ever anything that he could do for her.

When she had shown him out she made herself another cup of tea, sat down to write an account of all this to Melissa, and

228

realised that she must say nothing of it. It was a thousand pities to be obliged to suppress so entertaining a story, but it was not fair to laugh at Charles. He loved her as much, probably, as he was able to love anybody, and he had treated her very honourably, considering what his opportunities had been.

Nor was she perfectly sure that Melissa would applaud her decision. From the very first, in their earliest letters, there had been a suspicious interest in Terrific Charles. Melissa had laughed at him and called him the Eel, but it was not impossible that she might wish to see her friend established in affluence at Cyre Abbey. Yet she had married for love herself; had forsaken several noble matches for the sake of honest John. She would never have accepted Charles, though she might think that he would do very well for Lucy.

Our friends, thought Lucy, make compromises for us which they would not tolerate for themselves. They love us, but we are not quite real to them.

4

IANTHE'S BABY, though enthusiastically sponsored by Miss Plummer, was dismissed at once, and impatiently, by most people in the upper town. Some astonishment was felt at the matron for swallowing such a fable. But, upheld by confidence in her own intuition, she stuck to her theory for some weeks, until silenced by some mysterious compulsion. Report had it that she took the tale to Lady Frances and received such a flea in her ear for mischievous gossip that she was obliged to take aspirin on reaching home. Nothing more was ever heard from her on the subject, and Ianthe left Ravonsbridge soon afterwards for a visit to some cousins in South Africa.

But the story smouldered in the town, passing listlessly from ear to ear as Miss Tanner massaged the citizens through bouts of spring rheumatism. Scandal in a clergyman's family is always attractive. So very few people believed a word of it that the legend might have flickered out had not Angera displayed Ianthe's portrait at an art school exhibition, towards the end of the term.

The picture attracted a good deal of attention; within a matter of hours his paternity would have been a settled thing, could anybody have quite believed in the baby. To Miss Tanner the dates were a deciding factor. The portrait had been painted in April and May; the affair, if there had been any affair, must have been going on then for it was in late June that Ianthe had been obliged, so suddenly, so mysteriously, to leave Ravonsbridge. A good deal of discussion sprang up among people who liked scandal in a parsonage, people who liked scandal about artists, and people who did not like Jews. The tale crept to the lower town, collecting a good deal of material on the way, until patrons of Adamson's Café Bar were telling one another that Mr. Angera, up at the Institute, a Jew mind you, had seduced fifteen of his pupils.

These rumblings from the nether pit were not immediately audible up the hill, and did not check the extreme hilarity with which the Institute greeted so fantastic a suggestion. Had anybody believed in Ianthe's baby, had anybody supposed that anybody else could believe in it, the matter might have been treated more soberly. Had Mr. Thornley been among them his strong sense of decorum might have restrained them a little. Had such a slander, incredible though it was, fallen upon anybody else, some sympathetic indignation might have been felt. But Angera was universally disliked; he had boasted of his own sexual prowess, had poured contempt upon British lack of technique, had scolded them for British prudery. Nobody could help laughing. His fury, when the tale reached him, was too ludicrous. The gale which was to blow down so much about so many people's ears began with a guffaw.

Mr. Garstang chuckled over it as he trod his lonely path to the first council meeting of the summer term. For Angera was in a resigning mood again. He had flown into a tantrum about the gallery commission which his contract obliged him to pay on the pictures he had sold during the spring exhibition, among which was included the famous portrait. All the solemn farce of persuading him to change his mind would have to be gone through once more, and Mr. Garstang did not know how he was to keep a straight face when the subject came up. He trusted that most of the council might not be aware of the joke. Hayter would certainly have heard of it, but Colonel Harding lived out at Slane Bredy and the Millwood ladies never listened to gossip.

In any case, Angera's resignation came last on an agenda paper of inordinate length. Poor old Thornley used to complain that the agenda lists were too short and that all sorts of things were settled out of hand, by Lady Frances and Hayter, which should have been discussed by the council. He could not have said that now. There were nineteen items. By the time they reached Angera they would be too much exhausted to laugh.

A surprise awaited everybody in the council room. Dr. Pidgeon was there. It was the first meeting he had attended since his election, two years ago. He explained that he had come over to Ravonsbridge for a concert rehearsal and had thought that he might as well look in.

We shall be seeing Coppard one of these days, thought Garstang, and asked what had happened to Spedding, whose resignation from the council was listed as one of the nineteen items which they were to discuss. Hayter said that Spedding's partner was ill and that he was, for a time, so much overworked that he had been obliged to resign from several committees. He had written a letter to the council saying so. It was a temporary crisis. Later in the year he would not be so busy.

Garstang grunted. He did not like Spedding and was not sorry to see him go.

"But that leaves us two short," he said, "for we haven't replaced Thornley yet."

"The new drama director will have Thornley's place, I suppose," said Colonel Harding, "when we get him."

"I dunno. He wouldn't be resident. I think we should have more members who live on the spot."

The Millwood ladies here arrived with Miss Foss and the meeting began. Mr. Spedding's letter was read and regretted. In the bun shop it had been decided that he should not be replaced. He might be able to serve on the council again after Christmas and he had been such a good treasurer that it would be a pity to lose him. As for Thornley's successor, this place on the council was certainly to be kept for the visiting drama director. Garstang raised a plea for more local members, and was reminded by Hayter that, at the general meeting in the autumn, several new members might be elected by the town. Once in every five years the whole council retired and was re-elected again at a special general meeting of the electors of Ravonsbridge. So few people ever came to this meeting, and the re-election of the retiring council was so much a matter of form, that Hayter's remark caused a little surprise.

"Bless my soul, yes, there's a meeting this autumn!" agreed Garstang. "Five years go in no time nowadays."

"Yes, I'd almost forgotten," said Lady Frances. "But I don't see why the town should elect anybody new. They never have. Whom did you have in mind, Mr. Hayter?"

"Oh, nobody in particular," said Hayter. "But Mr. Garstang spoke of getting more local residents on the council. I don't know if _he_ had anyone in particular on his mind . . ."

He paused and looked enquiringly at Garstang, who shook his head.

"And it occurred to me," continued Hayter, "that some local names might be put forward, when the nominations come in, if there are any suitable people who are willing to join us."

"No, I don't know of any," said Garstang. "I merely think that, on principle, absentee members are a pity."

Everyone looked at Dr. Pidgeon, whose withers were unwrung because he had not heard a word and had been thinking of something else. But it was felt that Mr. Garstang had been tactless and the subject was dropped. The afternoon was hot and they had nineteen topics to discuss.

Colonel Harding and Dr. Pidgeon fell asleep. From time to time a poke from Mr. Poole roused the chairman to read out a new agenda heading. Most of the points raised seemed hardly worth discussion. They were genuinely things which Mr. Hayter might have settled without consulting the council; but he seemed to have made up his mind that they should hear every letter that anyone had written to him for the past six weeks, and after each of them there was an endless, desultory chatter. Nobody felt much impulse to prolong this tedium by asking questions or volunteering opinions. Most of the discussion was a duologue between Hayter and Lady Frances, in which she told him what to do and he begged her to consider alternative possibilities until the thing strung out beyond any human power to listen. Even a pension for a retiring furnace man took them twenty minutes though it was merely a routine matter. Hayter had to ask a great deal about it because he thought he could get them another furnace man and wished to be perfectly informed about the terms of employment.

The church clock struck four. Dr. Pidgeon woke up and looked at his watch. His rehearsal was at four thirty. Tish began to think of her train. If she missed the four fifty she would be obliged to wait until seven, and she had a child at home with a temperature. Lady Frances wished to go to church at five in order to see her kitchen maid confirmed, and she would have been glad of a cup of tea first. Lady Anne thought longingly of the ladies' cloakroom.

"Resignation of Mr. Angera," read out Colonel Harding, in obedience to a poke from Poole. "We'd better have the letter."

All those who were awake ticked off No. 19 on their agenda papers with a sigh of relief.

Angera's letter had been written early in the Easter vacation. He stated that he wished to resign his post and to leave Ravonsbridge at the end of the summer term because he considered that the gallery commission on the sale of his pictures was a fraudulent imposture.

As Poole read it the ladies began to collect their gloves and handbags, and Lady Frances gave judgment as soon as he had finished:

"Well, I think we agreed, last time, on the line we should take, if this sort of thing should happen again. We will accept Mr. Angera's resignation. It will give him a good fright. He'll have to apologise and stop behaving in this silly, childish way."

"But hasn't he written another letter, taking it all back?" asked Garstang. "He usually does."

"No," said Poole. "There is no other letter."

"He probably means to," said Hayter. "He wrote to me about an autumn exhibition. That looks as if he means to stay."

"Then he'd better hurry up and say so, with apologies," said Lady Frances.

"Perhaps," put in Garstang, "he thinks a letter to Hayter is good enough."

233

"He has no business to think that. He knows very well that he must address the council through Mr. Poole. We can't take into account any private correspondence he may have had with other members on the staff."

"He's so unbusinesslike," persisted Garstang. "He may not, even now, have grasped that. Have you got the letter, Hayter?"

Hayter shook his head and explained that he had not looked upon it as official, and had merely mentioned it as evidence that Angera really did mean to take back his resignation.

"Then let him do so," said Lady Frances, rising from her chair. "And I personally should like him to wait until the very end of the term before we let him know that we accept his withdrawal. I'm getting very tired of this sort of thing."

"Yes," said Tish, also getting up. "He needs a lesson."

"Then that's agreed?" said the Colonel, looking round the table. "We simply accept his resignation without comment?"

An extraordinary thing happened. Miss Foss spoke. Her colleagues, who had never heard her voice before, shared some of the shock which must have been sustained by Balaam.

"No-I-don't-agree!"

Having uttered these words in a single, panic-stricken breath, she seemed to be about to hide under the table.

Everybody stared at her in silence. Dr. Pidgeon, who had already got as far as the door, turned impatiently.

"You don't agree?" said Lady Frances at last.

Miss Foss remained sitting at the table, and Colonel Harding, who had begun to get up, sat down again. Mr. Garstang also kept his seat. But the others, having risen, stood about the room as if protesting at this further detention.

"No," whispered Miss Foss. "No. I don't agree."

"But why not?"

Faint but valiant, the answer came:

"I . . . I don't think there should be any question of Mr. Angera going·just now."

"But Miss Foss, we must draw the line somewhere. He has behaved so badly, with these continual, meaningless threats of resignation. We all agreed, last year, that we shouldn't let him off too easily next time he did it."

"I know, Lady Frances. But not just now."

"I think we've been very patient."

"Oh, yes, Lady Anne. We have. But *just now* . . . I . . . I don't think this is a very good moment."

What larks! thought Mr. Garstang. We're going to have it after all, and from Miss Foss, of all people!

"And why isn't it a good moment?" demanded Tish, with Ravonsclere determination.

Miss Foss was trembling and blushing but she managed to whisper the words:

"There should be no question . . . *just now* . . . of . . . of want of confidence. . . . We should stand behind Mr. Angera. . . ."

"I think," said Garstang, coming to her rescue, "that Miss Foss is referring to a stupid story, a ridiculous story, that has been going about. Isn't that it, Miss Foss?"

"Oh, yes . . . yes . . ." she breathed gratefully. "Most unpleasant."

"What story?" asked Lady Anne.

"Never heard of it," said Lady Frances.

"Oh . . . I know what you mean," said Tish.

"A fantastic story," said Mr. Garstang, "and perfectly groundless, I believe, coupling Mr. Angera and Miss Meadows."

"The greatest nonsense I ever heard," said Tish.

"Not the sort of thing that ought even to be mentioned here," said Lady Frances severely. "I always make it a rule never to listen to gossip anywhere, least of all here. It has nothing whatever to do with Mr. Angera's resignation and . . . I beg your pardon, Miss Foss?"

For Miss Foss had actually interrupted. She had muttered something. With an effort she repeated it.

"People will think that it has."

"Oh, no," said Lady Frances. "Why should people think anything? Why should anybody know that Mr. Angera has resigned? We shall say nothing, and if he's sensible he will say nothing. He'll write us a proper apology."

"But he's not sensible," said Garstang, who was regretting the departure of Thornley more than he had ever done.

"Then he must suffer for it."

Thornley would never have allowed this to happen! He would have got a written apology from Angera in time for the meeting. He would have protested against all this hanky panky with the agenda. He would have demanded that Angera's case should be heard earlier.

"Things get out. . . ." Miss Foss was whispering.

"Yes," said Garstang. "I agree with Miss Foss. Things do get out. This isn't a moment for the council to quarrel with Angera. I don't know of anyone who believes that ridiculous story, but some people will believe anything. It might be thought we'd been influenced by this yarn."

"But we are not dismissing him," argued Lady Frances. "It is he who has resigned."

"Then let's have him up here now, and ask him if he means what he says. Let's settle it now."

"Oh, no," cried Tish, who was getting very anxious about her train. "That would give him an even worse idea of his own importance than he's got already."

"I quite agree," said Lady Anne. "It's not for us to implore him to reconsider."

"He'll be very lucky," said Lady Frances, "if we accept his apology when we get it."

Colonel Harding looked at Dr. Pidgeon who was still hovering impatiently in the doorway.

"I can't see what all the fuss is about. Fellow has resigned. Surely he knows his own mind!" said Dr. Pidgeon.

"Hayter?"

Hayter murmured that he would prefer to take no part in any discussion which concerned the conduct of a colleague. He thought it would really be more correct if he were not present at all.

"Then Poole had better write . . ." began the Colonel.

He was interrupted once more by the heroic Miss Foss, who quavered a demand for a vote. So he asked them to vote on an immediate acceptance of Mr. Angera's resignation. Lady Frances, Lady Anne, Tish Massingham and Dr. Pidgeon raised their hands, as they stood poised for escape. Mr. Garstang and Miss Foss kept their seats as they voted against the motion. Mr. Poole was instructed to write to Angera accepting his resignation at the end of the current term. The council dispersed at high speed, barely pausing to bid one another goodbye.

"I expect it will be all right," said Garstang reassuringly, as he escorted Miss Foss down the stairs. "It doesn't really matter what idiots think, even if some garbled version does get out."

He was fascinated at hearing her speak and hoped that she would go on. But the unaccustomed effort seemed to have exhausted her and she could only shake her head. Then he thought he heard a murmur about "dear Mr. Thornley."

"Ah, yes," he agreed. "Thornley! We certainly miss him. I don't quite know why. But things don't go so well without him."

Miss Foss muttered again.

". . . A very kind man . . ." he heard. "Always very kind to everybody . . . very sincere . . . a very good man . . . my dear father used to say . . . good people sometimes make mistakes but . . . clever people much more dangerous."

Part 6

L'Affaire Angera

1

UNTIL MELISSA came to Drumby the workers at the research station believed it to be the deadliest spot in the British Isles. Too large to have the charm of a village, too small to offer any urban amenities, it scattered a litter of houses on either bank of a disused canal. There was no cinema. The branch railway line only produced four trains a day, two in and two out. A bus ran, at impossible hours, three times a week.

Nor was the surrounding country at all pretty. Heathy wastes and flat fields, intersected by ditches, gave way to a horizon which always looked a little too near. A few windmills struck an exotic note, but they soon grew familiar. Groups of cows standing motionless under a cloudy sky suggested Cuyp; not everybody cares for unmitigated Cuyp. In the summer there was little shade, in the winter no protection from the gales which swept in from the North Sea. The local population had the smallest vocabulary known to man: the researchers had never heard them say more than: "Ah . . . bor. . . ."

Yet some grandee had once built himself a house in this horrid place. It stood to the east of the town—Drumby Hall, with Palladian wings, cupolas, ornamental water, an orangery, a gothic ruin, a walled park and stone gate-posts surmounted by gryphons. The walls were now encrusted by barbed wire and a custodian stood between the gate-posts, who examined minutely the passes of everybody going to the house. For, behind the barbed wire and under that magnificent roof, John Beauclerc and his associates spent their days doing a deed without a name. Not even their wives were allowed to know what it was.

These lodged precariously in the meagre little town and led the life of a frontier station without the common bond of shop which is the breath of life to an isolated community. Outside the barbed wire no man spoke of his work. Yet there were very few who could speak of anything else. Parties at Drumby were silent functions and there was nothing to do in the evenings save drink at one of the locals, all of which were bad, to grumble and to bicker. Some wives had babies and some had affairs; but research chemists are a serious breed, not expert in dalliance, and the wanton wives were short of material. There were numerous feuds over lodgings and charwomen, and a few scares about spies.

Everybody was glad to see a new face. Melissa's face had a tonic effect on all the men while the women brightened at the sight of her clothes. She went to church, which nobody else had thought of doing, and made friends with the parson. Through him she dis-covered that several white men were living in darkest Lincoln-shire. Some of the natives danced and drank sherry, had tennis courts and could talk English. They had noticed that a crowd of disconsolate exiles was now wandering about Drumby, but had never thought it possible to make contact with any of them until introduced to Melissa; she was discovered to be "quite nice" and had reputable connections although her husband was one of "the Research People." Invitations were issued, not only to Melissa, but to others in the colony. The beginnings of social life were ob-servable.

Officers from the training camp up the line were now also to be seen in Drumby. Hitherto they had spent all their off time in Fenswick, which had a cinema, and had regarded anything to the east as a wilderness. But they took to coming in for little parties, of which there was a sudden spate. Wives cooked chicken in port wine, a recipe introduced by Mrs. Beauclerc, and took the bus to Fenswick in search of brie, because Mrs. Beauclerc had discovered a shop there which stocked imported cheeses, which she served with amusing salads. Also they bought material and made themselves hostess gowns and became much fonder of their husbands, because dissatisfaction had suddenly gone out of fashion. There was still very little to say, but everybody smiled more and those who grumbled acquired the outmoded air of people who use ancient slang. It was dowdy to be glum.

All this was quite unintentional on Melissa's part. She had not set out to reform Drumby. She was extremely happy for the first time in her life and her spirits were infectious. She was passionately in love with John. She had her own little red brick house, right on the main street, all fresh and sparkling with wedding presents. Not a cup or a saucer was broken as yet, nor had her chintz faced the laundry. She had time to polish her furniture a great deal and wash the lustres of her pretty candlesticks; she could eat what she liked and get up when she liked. She took great trouble over her little parties and became an accomplished cook.

John, escaping every evening from the barbed wire, could not believe that this was the same town in which he had lodged uncomfortably last year and thought so unpleasant that he dreaded having to bring her there. He would jump onto his bicycle and scorch back to her as fast as he could. Sometimes she would be polishing her goblets for a party, and sometimes she would be cooking his favourite supper dish of red cabbage in cider, but she was always smiling and always delighted to see him. So that for very perversity, in order to make her frown, he occasionally called her his dear little Pudding, which was not a gentlemanly thing to do, for he had promised that he would not, when, after much persuasion, she had explained this mysterious phrase in their wedding address.

So passed the autumn and the winter. At Easter she glowed so warmly that Mrs. Callow, the town gossip, predicted a baby. But it turned out merely to be a brother who was coming to stay. Hump's work was over and he was returning from Africa. The French government, alarmed at the spread of cattle sickness to richer territories South of the Dandawa, had taken over his research. For Kolo and his poor little tribe this was fortunate. But Hump, after four years of struggle, after considerable success, was coming home with no prospects and very little credit for all that he had achieved.

Melissa wept indignantly over the collapse of Humptopia, but she was overjoyed to see him again. He arrived in the highest spirits, able, as he always was, to live in the moment and find it satisfying. He was sure that he would get another job sooner or later. In the meantime he meant to enjoy himself, tease Melissa, like John Beauclerc, and flirt with the girls in Drumby. As all the other men were shut up behind the barbed wire every day he had unique opportunities. Within a week he had improvised a golf course for himself and his harem on a sandy common near the Hall, cured Mrs. Callow's chronic catarrh, and was said to be in love with a young sister who was staying with her. But his great gift to Drumby was the canal. He had taken a look at it in the train while on his way there, and asked if anybody sailed on it before he was out of the station. There was a rush for boats. Brightly coloured sails began to skim through the fields and frighten the cows, and at last Drumby discovered a topic for general conversation. Every man could speak of his boat.

Melissa thought her brother quite unchanged. He had put on weight but was getting it off very quickly. During much of the time in Africa his work had been sedentary. He had lived in a small mosquito house, six feet by four, made of grey netting, inside which, he complained, everything, himself included, looked as though it were in a tank of dirty water. His ecstasy at getting out of it, at moving freely in the cool air, made every day delightful to him. He was perhaps more talkative than he used to be. Kolo and Mary Lou had been congenial but for four years they had been his only civilised companions and he relished social variety. He would talk about anything to anybody and even managed to converse with the peasantry who seemed to understand him better when he spoke Dandawa. He maintained that *Ah bor!* was a Dandawa greeting too, but his translation of it varied according to his company.

He also read a great deal, for he had been short of books for a long time—mowing through volume after volume with the speed and force of a bulldozer.

By the end of the second week the odds had lengthened on Mrs. Callow's young sister. It was realised that Hump, though susceptible, was not a marrying man. This was bad news for maidens but not displeasing to wives and increased the competition for him. He had decided that what Drumby needed was a club—some building with a large room where the colony could meet in the evenings and where, as he explained to Melissa, "one could dance with all the girls." Everybody agreed with him but declared that no suitable building existed in the town. He found one, however. On the banks of the canal there was a disused warehouse which, with very few alterations, would be just the thing. The government, of course, would pay for these, if properly approached.

"Just say it's for drama," he told them. "That's the key word just now. Say you can't carry on at the Hall unless you are able to act plays and they'll fall for it. I know there's no money for houses or hospitals or a cure for the common cold. But there's plenty for anything really crackers. Plenty for drama. Believe me or believe me not, in the British Dandawa they'd got a chap going round teaching drama in the villages, yes, teaching it to people dying of hookworm. You paid him, I expect. But not our side of the border. The French aren't crackers where money is concerned."

His persuasive powers were so great that John eventually wrote in the name of the research workers to ask for a grant for a drama club.

For the rest of his stay Hump worked like a maniac over his scheme. He drew neat little plans for the alterations. A staircase must replace the ladder to the upper floor, which was to be the ballroom. Downstairs there were to be cloakrooms, a kitchen, and a buffet. He made John apply for catering and drink licenses. He went round to sales and bought furniture, curtain materials and a piano with only one note gone in the bass. He spent money freely and was convinced that the government would pay.

"If you work hard," he said to Melissa, at breakfast on his last morning, "you can have it open by the autumn. The girls had better start sewing those curtains at once. It occurred to me in the night that you'd better have a fire escape. The staircase will be narrow; if the kitchen caught fire while you were all dancing upstairs, you'd be grilled in no time. Can I borrow Crabbe to read in the train?"

John here appeared with the letters and burst into loud cries of astonishment over his share of the mail. Authority had taken to the idea that drama was necessary to chemical research and a grant would be forthcoming.

"Just what I told you," said Hump. "If you can't get cash for something sensible, say you want it for something silly. Go on asking for it for every reason you can think of until you hit on some nonsense that suits their nonsense."

"But won't we be bound to use it for drama?" asked honest John.

"Certainly. The girls can act some plays in the club. It's the sort of thing they like. What's your letter, Melissa? What has poor Lucy been doing now?"

Hump took a great interest in Lucy's doings, though he was very critical of her and generally asserted that she had better have done something else. He was always asking Melissa for more about Ravonsbridge.

"They're having a most sinister drama," said Melissa, looking up from the scrawled pages. "A regular Dreyfus case."

"And poor Lucy the leading Dreyfusard? I bet! What childish writing she's got! Calls herself an educated girl!"

"It's legible, which yours isn't."

"Only very primitive types are legible. Who is Dreyfus? And what is bossy Lucy doing about it?"

"She's not bossy," expostulated Melissa.

"I say she is bossy. Read it out. Bet you sixpence she starts bossing somebody before the end of that letter. Is Dreyfus our friend Emil? Thought so. Well . . . read it!"

Melissa read:

"Of all the horrible things that ever happened this is the bottom. Poor Emil has been sacked. He brought it on himself—one of his token resignations, but the council have accepted it and ignored the letter he wrote taking it back, because it was sent to the wrong person (to the villain Hayter!) which is crazy of them, for they'll never get anyone else so good. And everybody thinks that's only a pretext and it's really because of the Ianthe scandal. But I don't, because that would be so unlike Lady F."

"I call it unwomanly," complained Hump, "not to believe what everybody believes. What I say is, women ought to be clinging, dishonest little things. Don't you think so, John?"

John, who was still wondering if it was all right to take this government grant, said yes, caught Melissa's eye, and said that he had meant *no*.

"And nobody is doing anything about it."

"Aha! So Lucy will."

"If it had happened to anyone else there would be an uproar. But they don't like Emil. Still—nasty people have as much right to justice as nice ones."

"Another very unwomanly sentiment!"

"So though everybody says they're disgusted at the council half of them are glad Emil has got into a scrape, and is going, and the other half don't like him enough to exert themselves on his behalf.

"He's been to see Lady Frances and she said the Ianthe scandal had nothing to do with it. That's why I think it really hasn't. Lady F. would be more likely to do a strip tease dance than tell a lie. But he says he doesn't believe it and that he called her a liar! And he says he got it out of her that Miss Foss accused him. But you can't trust his account of anything. He's got it into his silly head that Miss Foss was his accuser.

"I talked to Mr. Meeker about it and he agrees it is a disaster, whatever the council's reasons may be, because the town is very much worked up and all sorts of wild rumours are going about. He says somebody ought to tell them what they're doing . . ."

"I see sixpence coming!"

"So I said *I* couldn't. I'm the youngest member of the Staff."

"Oh, come, come, Lucy! Don't let me down!"

"I wish one of the men would do something. Bossy women are so repulsive . . ."

"Too right, my good girl!"
"Hump! If you keep on interrupting I shall stop."
"No, go on. I'll be quiet. It's just getting really exciting. She's going to work on some unfortunate man."

"So I decided to talk to Mr. Mildmay, the librarian. He'd hardly heard about it; he mixes so little with the rest of us. So I was very scatty and feminine so as not to scare the poor old . . . er . . . man."

"Old what?" demanded Hump, sitting up.
"Man," repeated Melissa smugly.
He stretched out a hand for the letter but she withheld it admitting that the word was not man, and that Lucy was sometimes rather vigorous in her expressions, but that this was written only for another girl to see. Hump threatened to guess something much more vigorous than it probably was, but she said that could not be helped, and continued:

"When he took in the facts he was quite upset. I plugged Nancy Angera and how tough this is for her. Don't you think that's an artful line? I mean, men don't like it much when a woman preaches to them about honesty and justice—but if she's worried about another woman they pat her reassuringly and do what she wants. . . ."

"I say! I say!"

"So I appealed to his manly feelings and he ate it.
"He said it sounded like a bad misunderstanding that ought to be cleared up, and that he would speak to Lady Frances. I only hope he's got it all clear, poor old honey pie. . . ."

"Really honey pie?"

"Yes, Hump, really honey pie."

"Gal's gossip," said Hump, "is beyond any man's power to comprehend or imitate. It's perfectly unpredictable . . . the idiom, I mean."

"Theocritus captured it," said Melissa. "If you want to know how Lucy and I talk, read *Gorgo and Praxinoë*. Purely imbecile!"

"But no. That's the point. It's not *purely* imbecile. Go on."

"Oh, you interrupt too much. And there's not any more about that. The rest is about Lucy's summer clothes."

"I think I get sixpence."

"You can't say she was bossy!"

"She interfered. She pushed the honey pie into doing something."

"Yes, but in a nice, womanly, clinging, dishonest way."

Hump looked thoughtful and said that poor Lucy had better have stuck to her summer clothes.

"Personally," said John, who saw that Melissa was a little ruffled, "I respect her very much."

"Oh, so do I," agreed Hump. "I respect her like anything. But when I respect a woman I want to keep my distance, you know. I walk out backwards, making a low obeisance. Whereas, with an attractive woman the boot seems to be quite on the other leg. Towards her I rush."

"Oh, I'm sure," said Melissa. "Like the Hyrcan tiger. But don't you agree, Hump, that this is a sort of Dreyfus case?"

"Absolutely. *L'Affaire Angera*. One of those muddles which wreck dynasties. A lot more in it than meets the eye. I've a notion Angera is merely a stalking horse."

"I mean Mr. Hayter must know that this construction would be put on it. And he, I believe, is on the council. Why doesn't he speak up?"

"Oh, there's a cartload of monkeys around. But poor Lucy has got it coming to her if she insists upon smelling them out. It's a mug's game to be a *Dreyfusard*. You see! They'll all let her down. Honey pie will let her down. I'll bet he hasn't got his facts clear. Angera will let her down. He'll do something idiotic. Only idiots manage to get themselves badly treated. Rush in to champion a poor victim and you'll always take a toss over something silly that he's done; there's always something that weakens his case. I know. I've been through it all in my time."

"If you've done it, why shouldn't Lucy?"

"Oh, it's all right for a man. Part of his education. It doesn't hurt a man to make a fool of himself and come a smacker for the sake of truth and plain dealing. But girls should hang on to their dignity."

"I sometimes think you've never rounded Cape Turk," said Melissa in disgust. "I suppose that you think the girls (by which you seem to mean the whole female sex) had better stand by with balm and bandages while their men come smackers?"

"I think it's a good idea," said Hump. "Smackers aren't very nice. A man's more likely to risk a smacker in a good cause if he knows there's balm waiting for him."

"Ah, but we're supposed to be so dumb and dishonest we don't know a good cause from a bad one. We just apply balm to our man. Balm for the mobster. Balm for the martyr. It's all one to us."

"I didn't say that."

"Yes you did. You said that women ought to be clinging dishonest little—"

"That's all that most men want. There aren't many heroes."

"There doesn't seem to be one in Ravonsbridge. There doesn't seem to be any man who's willing to risk a smacker."

"No," agreed John thoughtfully. "Young Millwood doesn't sound like a hero."

Melissa shot him a furious look. She had drawn her own conclusions from a sudden silence concerning Charles in Lucy's letters, and had communicated them to John, but he should have kept them to himself. Had it not been for her frown Hump might not have noticed the remark. He pricked up his ears.

"Millwood?" he said. "The Eel? Where does he come in?"

"Melissa thinks—" began John.

"No, I don't," snapped Melissa. "I don't think anything."

"I should hope not," said Hump. "He'll never need balm, for I never knew anyone less likely to risk a smacker."

He reflected for a moment and a look of sudden anger crossed his face. He frowned too, and John, glancing from the sister to the brother, saw a likeness between them for the first time.

"I should hope not," repeated Hump. "She's a million times too good for him."

2

NOBODY HAD ever called Lady Frances a liar before. She had never in her life said what she believed to be untrue and she expected everybody to accept her word. The Poor told lies because they were oppressed. Ill bred people told lies because they knew no better. Ravonscleres never told them.

When Angera screamed the accusation at her she was more stunned than angry. To her, it was strange and incomprehensible rather than an insult. She searched her memory anxiously for any slip of which she might have been guilty, and recollected one small inaccuracy. She had told him that Ianthe's name had never been mentioned at the council meeting. Now she remembered that it had. She hastened to amend her statement; there had been a passing reference to local gossip, she told him, which she had instantly suppressed. She had refused to listen to a word of it. And by whom, demanded Angera, was this reference made? He challenged her to deny that it was Miss Foss. She would not answer him, but her start of surprise confirmed his suspicions.

Before the end of their interview she had made up her mind that he must certainly go. She could forgive him for calling her a liar—that she overlooked as a piece of foreign hysteria, but she could not tolerate the terms in which he was giving his opinion of Miss Foss. He must go. She would not have him at the Institute, and she would say so at the next council meeting. No apology or retraction could now mollify her.

This decision strengthened her determination to hear no more about town gossip, or listen to the plea that current slanders against Angera made it advisable to keep him. But the first anonymous letter, which arrived two days later, shook her a little. She was applauded for getting rid of a dirty Jew who took advantage of the young girls at the Institute. Anti-Semitism had always horrified her. But she burnt the letter, telling herself that she must endure misconstruction and do as she thought right. And she burnt the next, which abused her for sacking people who stood up to her in order to make room for her own favourites, asked where "all that money" went, and referred to the Angera case as a "dirty fascist job similar to Thornley." Eventually she burnt any letter of this kind without reading it. There was nobody with whom she could have consulted, for it was not her habit to take advice from her daughters. Charles always refused to listen to Institute affairs and nowadays flew into a rage if they were so much as mentioned. Hayter had given her to understand that he could not discuss the conduct of a colleague. In all her life since Matt's death she had never felt so discouraged and so lonely.

For the first time she had quite a distaste for the Institute and a reluctance to go there. But she pulled herself together, one day, and drove in; she had to settle the summer programme with Hayter and endorse the proposal for a performance of *Comus* in Slane Forest. And that, she told herself, would be something nice to which she could look forward. She thought it a delightful idea, if only the weather was good. Mr. Hayter was enthusiastic; he suggested a repetition during the summer festival, if the production was as good as it promised to be. No Institute production had ever before reached the festival standards. Ravonsbridge could be proud of itself, if Hayter's hopes were justified, and there would be notices in the London papers.

So pretty it will be, all among the trees, she thought as her car purred up Gibbet Hill. Pretty music, too! A real treat for us all and a change from Shakespeare, because one gets tired of Shakespeare, though one shouldn't.

A squalid tin erection on the top of Gibbet Hill caught her eye and shattered her pleasant reverie. After a fight, which had torn Severnshire in half, the Meekers were going to disfigure it with a horrible monument. She had done her best to prevent it, and so had every Severnshire magnate except Charles, who had shrugged his shoulders and said that no monument would be as ugly as a gallows. But a gallows, she had argued, can be removed more easily than a monument with a lot of untrue things inscribed on it. And now the thing was to be unveiled at Midsummer. The idiotic Mr. Finch was going to read some kind of service at the ceremony. Canon Pillie was far too weak with that young man.

She was feeling quite depressed again when she reached the Institute and climbed out of her car and was waylaid by Mr. Mildmay with the request for a few words in private. She went with him into his own little room, behind the library, and while she enquired after his wife's arthritis, she thought how old he was getting to look nowadays. But everybody was getting old, or dying or going away. Links with the past were snapping every day; hardly anybody was left who seemed to remember the old Ravonsbridge. How many years ago was it now since Matt had fished Mr. Mildmay out of some obscure library and sent him to buy rare books? A queer, dried up little man he had been even then, smelling like a book, and calling her your ladyship every time he spoke until Matt told him not to. Matt did that sort of thing so easily.

"She's not so good," said Mr. Mildmay, shaking his head over Mrs. Mildmay. "Not so good. She suffers a great deal."

"Has she got efficient help in the house? Perhaps I could help to get her a refugee maid."

"Oh, yes, very efficient," he assured her. "We have an excellent daily woman."

The daily woman was far from excellent, but the refugee maids produced by Lady Frances were feared in Ravonsbridge like the plague. To escape from such a threat, he plunged hastily into his subject, though he did not much relish it. He said that he had been asked to speak to her about Angera's resignation, at which she stiffened and became haughty.

"This gossip about his personal character," said Mr. Mildmay, growing flurried, "is most unfortunate. Nobody believes it; none of his colleagues believe it for a moment. If the council is influenced—"

"It is not," interrupted Lady Frances. "You may set your mind at rest about that, Mr. Mildmay. I never listen to gossip. Nor does the council. I don't allow it to be mentioned in my presence."

Mr. Mildmay shook his head slowly and felt that he had blundered. He had not been charged to reprove Lady Frances for

251

listening to gossip. On the contrary, he had meant to hint that she ought, on this occasion, to take its existence into account.

"It is felt to be a great pity that Mr. Angera should go," he began again.

"By whom?" asked Lady Frances stiffly.

"By . . . by some members of the staff."

He would have liked to say by the whole staff, but Lucy had been the only one of them to consult him, so that he did not feel able to speak for his colleagues in a body. Now that it was too late he wished that he had sounded some of the others before attempting to speak to Lady Frances.

"Which members? Who asked you to speak to me?"

"Actually it was Miss Carmichael."

"Miss Carmichael?"

"She . . . she's a great friend of Mrs. Angera's, you know. Naturally she is distressed . . . she asked me if there might not be some misunderstanding which could be cleared up. The whole thing seems to be so unfortunate."

"But what business is it of Miss Carmichael's?"

"She told me that it is widely believed, in the lower town at any rate, that the council has been influenced—"

"But why Miss Carmichael? She is not one of the senior staff. How did she come to make this request to you?"

"I'm so out of things . . . I never know what is going on."

"I still don't see that it was her business."

Mr. Mildmay looked round at his locked cases as if for inspiration. He felt that he was making a mess of it and letting Lucy down.

"She was troubled by these rumours, and so was I when she told me of them. I am the oldest member of the staff. I think that she acted quite properly."

"I can't agree with you. It has nothing whatsoever to do with Miss Carmichael, and I must say, Mr. Mildmay, I'm surprised you didn't tell her so. Nor do I think that her opinions need have been reported to me."

Lady Frances was so angry that she could not trust herself to say more. She turned without a word and went off to do her business with Hayter. But she felt that her pleasure in the prospect of *Comus* was likely to be spoilt by this extraordinary behaviour in the hitherto sensible Miss Carmichael.

Comus, however, was off. Hayter had changed his mind and was now against it. Upon careful consideration he thought the plan a little too ambitious. Reluctant as he always was to criticise or to check youthful enthusiasm, he thought that it might be kinder to put some slight curb upon Miss Carmichael. It was so easy for a girl in her position to get a swelled head. She was not really a senior director, but she was treated with such deference, nowadays, that she might be pardoned for having got the idea that she ranked with the older staff. Difficulties might arise, when a new senior director was appointed and she had to take a back seat.

"I quite see what you mean," said Lady Frances thoughtfully. "A snub now might prevent her from getting too big for her boots."

"It's very natural in so young a girl, brought forward so quickly," said Hayter. "One hates having to put the brake on. She's so delightfully enterprising, and I'm sure, if we save her from making mistakes now, she'll eventually do us all great credit."

Lady Frances agreed. A blue pencil went through *Comus*. Another Shakespeare, they decided, should be suggested to Miss Carmichael; *The Merchant of Venice*, said Lady Frances, had not been produced at the Institute for some time.

"And another thing," said Hayter. "I venture to suggest that for our next production we don't have recruits from the lower town. There is a little too much running up and down the hill with gossip of Institute affairs, I think."

"So one gathers," said Lady Frances grimly.

"Miss Carmichael means very well, but I don't think she's always discreet. I can't help feeling sorry that she goes so much to the Meekers."

"The Meekers?"

This name was anathema to Lady Frances, especially since the tussle over the monument.

"Oh, yes. She's down there constantly. She is not, I know for a fact, cautious in what she says. And of course she thinks she can

253

run the Institute better than any of us. It's my impression that a great deal of . . . er . . . recent gossip might be traced to that source."

"Where is she?" demanded Lady Frances wrathfully. "I'd like to see her at once."

"It's only my impression," said Hayter. "She may have said nothing that she shouldn't. But I think it's an intimacy which . . . well, at the moment, I regret it."

"I'll ask her what she has been saying. Please find her and send her here."

Hayter went off to fetch Lucy. He did not warn her that she was in disgrace and she thought that she had been summoned to discuss *Comus*. But as soon as she got to his office she saw that there was trouble. Hayter ushered her into the room and retired.

"Mr. Mildmay," said Lady Frances, "has been telling me, Miss Carmichael, that you think the council cannot manage its own affairs."

Oh, hell! thought Lucy. He's bitched it. But how like Charles she looks! They are alike. I've never seen her in a temper before.

"I was a little astonished," continued Lady Frances, "that he thought it necessary to let me know that. I've not sent for you on that account. But it has occurred to me that you may be publishing your opinions to people outside the Institute, and that is another matter. There is a great deal of unnecessary gossip going on in the town about Mr. Angera's resignation. Have you discussed that with anyone down the hill?"

"Yes," said Lucy. "I discussed it with Mr. Meeker."

"Mr. Meeker! Why?"

"I wanted his opinion."

"Can't you see what a disloyal and mischievous thing that was to do?"

"No. I don't think it was. He cares very much about the Institute and he was a great friend of Mr. Millwood's."

"Nonsense. They never met."

"But . . . they went to school together!"

"Oh . . . you mean the old man? The father?"

"Of course I do. Did you think I meant Dr. Meeker? Mrs. Meeker's husband?"

254

Lady Frances, by silence, conveyed that the manner of this answer was impertinent. Lucy coloured.

"I beg your pardon," she said. "But old Mr. Meeker is quite different. I've never discussed anything with Dr. or Mrs. Meeker. I hardly know them."

"It's all the same family. What you say will be repeated."

"Oh, no. I'm sure not."

"And you'd no business to say anything. I wish you could realise the harm you may have done. All sorts of foolish rumours seem to be going round the town."

"Excuse me, Lady Frances, but I didn't start them. It was because of those rumours that I spoke to Mr. Meeker."

"How did you know there were any?"

"Everybody knows. The students know, the staff know, my landlady knows . . ."

"The way to stop that sort of thing is to say nothing. In future I hope you'll be more careful. It is, in any case, no business of yours, you know."

Lucy looked miserably at Lady Frances and racked her brains for one of the many openings upon which she had pondered when she was wondering if she ought not to go herself to Lady Frances.

"Don't you think," she said diffidently, "that injustice is everybody's business? It hurts everybody."

"In this case there has been none."

"Oh, but there is. There is injustice to you and to the council. You are quite misunderstood. . . ."

"I think you can allow us to take care of ourselves."

"And there will be injustice to Mr. Angera," continued Lucy resolutely, "if he goes just now. He may have put himself in the wrong by resigning. But if he goes now it will be regarded as proof that the council believes that story against him, and it will be a slur on his character."

Lady Frances pursed her lips and made no answer.

"When you were my age," cried Lucy desperately, "and saw something which you thought was very wrong, didn't you feel bound to try and do something? I know I'm young, and young people shouldn't speak out of turn, but didn't you feel you had to, sometimes, even when you were my age?"

At Lucy's age Lady Frances had gone to prison for her principles. And she had never, at any age, kept silence when she saw something which she thought to be wrong. Lucy's words and aspect quickened that instinctive sympathy which had always existed between them.

"Don't you think," she said, in a kinder voice, "that in this case there are older people to whom it can safely be left?"

"Who is there? Mr. Thornley has gone. Dr. Pidgeon isn't here. Mr. Mildmay didn't know anything much about it till I told him. When he did, he agreed with me and said he would speak to you. He didn't disagree; if he had, I'd have piped down."

"You seem to forget that Mr. Hayter is on the council and is perfectly able to tell us what is going on."

Lucy was silent. She had decided to say nothing against Hayter. She would not be believed and such a step might injure Emil's cause. She must fight Hayter without accusing him.

"He, I think," said Lady Frances, "would have been a better person to talk to. And there must be no more gossip to people outside."

"Oh, no. I've consulted Mr. Meeker. I've got his opinion. I wouldn't want to speak of it to anyone else."

"Consulted?" said Lady Frances, with reviving irritation. "That's such nonsense, you know. How could he advise you?"

"I was wondering if I oughtn't to go straight to you or to Charles . . ."

"Charles?"

"To . . . Mr. Millwood."

Lucy blushed as she corrected herself. She had spoken thoughtlessly, and yet she would scarcely have known how to speak of him otherwise. She did call him Charles and he called her Lucy; she could not very well call him Mr. Millwood to the woman who might have been her mother-in-law.

This unfortunate slip ruined all chance of an understanding. Lady Frances was completely taken aback. She had thought that she understood Lucy and was beginning to sympathise with her. But this was a piece of deliberate ill bred impertinence quite inconsistent with what she had supposed to be the girl's character. She never imagined for a moment that they could be Charles and

256

Lucy to one another on so slight an acquaintance, though she had thought him attracted at the Christmas party. Such informality had been unknown in her young days and she knew little of modern manners.

"I see," she said coldly. "Well, you can set your mind at rest. I know that a great deal of responsibility has been thrust upon you lately—perhaps rather more than is good for a girl of your age. You mustn't let it make you conceited. That's all. I won't keep you any longer."

Lucy withdrew, in a transport of indignation, telling herself that Emil, Lady Frances, Mr. Mildmay and the Institute could all go to hell. Conceited! When she had taken such pains to be diplomatic! When she had tried so hard not to injure her cause by putting herself forward too much!

Hayter was waiting in the corridor and she saw at once that he knew it all. She would have marched past him but he detained her to express regret about Comus.

"Comus?" said Lucy in surprise.

"Didn't she tell you? I'm afraid it's been turned down. A little too ambitious, she thought. I'm so sorry."

Lucy stared at him and then laughed, for no reason at all except that a laugh might be likely to disconcert him.

A punishment for a naughty girl, she thought, as she returned to her office. A warning to keep off the grass. He knows what I'm after and he's warning me. If I pipe down and give no trouble I'm safe. If not, I'll be out on my ear. But I won't pipe down. No, I won't pipe down. I'll go to Charles. I'll spill all the beans. I'll tell Charles everything. It's Hayter or me.

There was nothing for it now but to come into the open and say what she thought of Hayter. She had already decided that, if she was driven to do this, she would go to Charles. She believed that he too had his suspicions, ever since the lunch at Cyre Abbey. To go to Charles was the last shot in her locker, and she must act at once, before Hayter, who worked fast, got another move ahead of her.

SHE CAUGHT a bus down the hill to the Works. She had not seen Charles since their parting in Sheep Lane, but one of the last things that he had said on that occasion had been to beg that she would let him know if there was ever anything that he could do for her. He had spoken very earnestly and she had no reason to suppose that he did not mean what he said. She needed his help now and she went to him without hesitation. He might not agree with her, might think that her suspicions were nonsense, but she expected him to be cordial, and had no fear that he would resent her sudden reappearance in his life.

This confidence sustained her through all the difficulties of reaching him. Barricades of gate men and secretaries enquired her business, telephoned to one another, left her waiting on benches, and sent her wandering through the endless labyrinth of the Works. So far was she from having ever thought of him as a millionaire and a motor magnate—as, in his way, terrific—that she was inclined to giggle at all this fuss. Had she strolled into the Vatican and demanded an audience with the Holy Father there could scarcely have been more astonishment. But at last, by sheer persistence, she achieved the ante-room of his office where a super-secretary was persuaded to tell the great man himself, through a house telephone, that Miss Carmichael, from the Institute, wished to see him immediately on important business. After a few seconds of respectful listening, this final Cerberus informed her, in hushed tones, that Mr. Millwood could see her.

A door was opened for her. She walked through it into a large light room which contained a perfectly enormous desk—the largest desk she had ever seen, with nothing at all upon its polished surface save a massive silver inkstand, a telephone, and a perfectly clean blotting pad. A formidable stranger was rising from behind this object and coming round to shake hands with her. He looked so much older and harder than the Charles she knew that she felt quite shy. Nor was he friendly. His greeting was perfectly civil. He shook hands. He asked how she did. He settled her in a chair on one side of his mammoth desk before returning to the other, but he scarcely smiled. His eyes were cold and watchful, as though he was on his guard. It flashed across her that he might think she had changed her mind and was now going to insist on marrying him. This idea would have been funny if she had not been so much distracted.

"I badly need your advice," she told him. "You are the only person who can tell me what I ought to do; you've always been very kind to me. Can you spare a few minutes and listen, while I explain?"

He thawed a little at that and said:

"Tell me."

Lucy told him. She spoke well for she had arranged her story beforehand, when she was considering what she should say if ever she should appeal to him. She gave him the facts clearly and in the right order, without digressions or repetitions. Having summarised her reasons for suspecting Hayter of some large scale intrigue, she outlined the Angera situation and ended with an account of her scene with his mother.

He listened closely and nodded from time to time. She felt that she was impressing him. She was also aware that her former power with him was gone. She got none of those agonised stares which had been wrung from him in Slane Forest. But this was as it should be. She did not want him to be in love with her, nor had she come to ask for anything personal. Her appeal, she felt, was in the public interest, and former passages between them had nothing to do with it, apart from a legacy of goodwill which might help them to co-operate.

So she talked on, pale and resolute and, in her anxiety to make her points, a trifle over emphatic. Charles watched her and reflected on the magnitude of his escape. He had never seen her looking so plain; in her haste to catch the bus she had not troubled to change her shabby old suit or to renew her make up.

"I believe," she finished, "that Mr. Hayter thinks I'm trying to put a spoke in his wheel, and means to get rid of me. So I decided to tell you all this first, before I'm sacked."

Charles was looking much more genial. He said at once:

259

"That's all right, Lucy. I'll look after that."

"Charles! Will you? Oh, what a relief! Then you think my suspicions about Mr. Hayter are not all nonsense?"

"Not at all. I think you're absolutely right about him. I've been watching him for some time."

"Then—"

He put out a hand to stop her.

"But you can set your mind at rest about Angera. He won't go. My mother was talking about it on the evening after the council meeting. They merely mean to give him a fright. If he apologises, they'll accept it. Of course, you must keep this to yourself. They don't mean to lose such an able man."

"They mayn't. But Mr. Hayter may."

"Oh, no, I don't think so. He can't want to sack the best art director they're ever likely to get. I admit I think you're right about him in the main. He's pocketing the Institute as fast as he can."

"Then he should be stopped."

"Oh, I don't know that it's such a bad thing. It was deplorably run before he came and he's made a great many improvements."

"But he's an underhand schemer. Your mother would throw him out if she knew what he's really like."

"Believe me, it's the way most committees are run."

"I can't believe it. Here is all this ill feeling, getting worse every day, and Emil more and more likely to do something silly, and Mr. Hayter could stop it by a word to your mother any time. I believe he's doing it on purpose. I believe he wants people to think your mother is unfair."

"Isn't that rather hysterical?"

This accusation is always annoying. Lucy flushed.

"No, I'm not. A bad man oughtn't to have power. And I hope you'll stop it."

"I? You hope I'll stop it?"

"You're president. You could talk to Emil and make him come to his senses and write a proper apology. You could talk to your mother and get her to have a special council meeting to re-instate him, before things get any worse. If she's obstinate you could over-rule her; you could talk to the chairman, to Colonel Harding, couldn't you?"

Charles said nothing. He was getting a unique opportunity of looking at Lucy's eyes and was not enjoying it. His geniality vanished. She thought she must have been too domineering.

"I'm sorry. I expect there are better ways of doing it. You have the experience; you'll know."

"I see," he said at last. "That's why you've come? To tell me that I must interfere?"

"No! To tell you certain facts and my conclusions. You might have thought my conclusions were wrong. But you've said you agreed. And in that case I wouldn't think anybody need have to tell you that you must interfere."

There was another pause. She cried:

"You said you would! You said it was all right and you'd look after it. I thought you meant you'd put a stop to all this. What did you mean?"

"I'm sorry," said Charles. "I didn't understand. I thought you came because you were afraid you'd lost your job and wanted me to intervene."

"Oh, no! I only meant that was why I came in such a hurry. In case I vanished through a trap door like Mr. Thornley, without having a chance to tell you all this."

"I would have exerted myself to see that didn't happen, though I rather think you've brought it on yourself. But more than that I'm not prepared to do. I don't interfere with Institute matters. I never have."

Lucy could not speak for a few seconds. She had not thought it possible that he could take her view of Hayter and think no action necessary. He continued:

"I've always thought it a most ridiculous place. It gives my mother something to live for and that's all that can be said for it."

"Beneath your attention, I suppose?" said Lucy, recovering her breath, "a poky little town like Ravonsbridge. Nothing short of the Cabinet appeals to you. You're sore because this country doesn't ask to be Prime Minister, but you won't stoop to a job that's under your nose. You let a mean crook grab the Institute that your father meant for the people. You let your mother be deceived. Why . . . you aren't fit to run a kindergarten!"

Charles looked at his wrist watch with a long suffering air.

"Don't pretend you're busy," stormed Lucy, "because you're obviously not. What you do in here all day I can't think, unless you polish that inkstand. You've told me yourself that you're never *allowed* to do anything."

He still would not answer her. He merely looked at her with a kind of detached astonishment, as though asking himself how he could ever have found her tolerable.

"I suppose you think I oughtn't to have come here, after . . . after—"

"I can imagine better taste."

"Oh, taste! It must be a great consolation to have taste, when your life is so boring. Well . . . I won't interrupt you any more. I'll leave you to sit behind this ridiculous object tastefully doing nothing."

Lucy jumped up with a gesture so vehement that her handbag burst open and fell upon the floor. Its contents were scattered widely over Charles' beautiful carpet. She had to go on her knees to collect them. Charles, after a slight hesitation, took the long journey round his desk and came to her aid. Together they crawled about in search of hair pins, pennies, lipstick, powder, a comb, a pencil, matches, cigarettes, several used bus tickets, and a lot of toffees wrapped in paper. Lucy giggled angrily at this anticlimax, but Charles, even on his knees, maintained an expression of frigid distaste, especially when he handed her the toffees.

"Thank you," she said, when they were on their feet again, "it's all very undignified, I'm sure."

He opened the door for her and she took herself off, miserable for a great many reasons. She was furious with him and in despair over the Institute, but the bitterest memory was that of the toffees on the carpet. She told herself that it would be all the same a hundred years hence. Someday she might be able to think calmly of Emil, Hayter, Charles and Lady Frances. But she was sure that she would never, not if she lived to be a hundred, be able to remember those toffees without blushing.

4

THE NEXT day, however, was a good day—a day which sent her sanguine spirits soaring. It appeared that most of her colleagues had also come to the conclusion that something ought speedily to be done, and that her fears had not been as peculiar to herself as she had supposed.

Feeling on the staff had been shifting steadily in favour of Emil. The strongest impulse was undoubtedly compassion for poor Nancy, but there were other motives. Among the seniors there was a growing impression that the council was liable to be misled, that Lady Frances had lost touch with the Institute, and that Hayter could not be entirely trusted to set her right.

Mr. Mildmay, though unworldly, was not a fool. Upon reflection he became convinced that Lucy had been perfectly right to consult him, that he had been justified in his intervention, and that he ought not to have allowed himself to be shut up in so peremptory a manner. He consulted Miss Frogmore, who was next to him in seniority, and found her very ready to second him in any effort on Emil's behalf which he might be disposed to make. She did not like Emil, but she liked the behaviour of the council less. She had expected to join it, on Thornley's departure, and considered that she had been slighted. Her assent was warm when Mildmay suggested that Lady Frances, nowadays, seemed to know very little about the staff.

Together they determined to call all their colleagues to an information meeting in the library on the following day. Means of conveying to the council their point of view on l'affaire Angera were to be discussed. Angera was to be invited but not Hayter, on the grounds that Hayter's membership of the council might put him in an ambiguous position.

They met, and their hardest task was to bring Angera to reason, force him to write a proper letter to the council, withdrawing his foolish resignation, and persuade him to hold his tongue about

Miss Foss. This, for some time, he refused to do. He asserted mysteriously that he had friends in the town who would see him righted, and that it was the council which would be sent packing. But at last, with a very ill grace, he yielded.

A round robin was then composed, addressed to Colonel Harding, in which they expressed their esteem for Angera, their hope that his apology would be accepted, and their desire for an early council meeting to settle the matter, on the grounds that the present state of affairs was very damaging to the Institute. There was some talk among the bolder spirits of a mass resignation should this request be ignored, but this was felt by the majority to be a move which the occasion did not warrant. It was agreed that nobody should bind himself, but that Mildmay should write an unofficial letter to the chairman stressing the urgency of the matter and hinting that they had this weapon in reserve if the council persisted in ignoring them.

To Lucy it seemed that the battle was as good as won. Charles had assured her that the council really wished to keep Angera and an early meeting would forestall any further follies and misunderstandings. Such a proof of solidarity from the staff, moreover, might mean a general turn for the better and a check to the influence of Hayter.

For a week she was able to believe that all would be well. But, when a fortnight had passed with no rumour of a council meeting, she began once more to worry. Colonel Harding had acknowledged Mildmay's unofficial letter in a pleasant but non-committal note, and that was all.

Three weeks went by. Lucy grew frantic—the more so because nobody else would admit any cause for anxiety. Nobody wanted to believe that the staff had been snubbed, since to do so would have been to acknowledge that they had put themselves into a very difficult position. If it had not been for Lucy, who insisted on counting the days, they need not have noticed how time was passing. Her white face and sharp nose began to irritate them, and Rickie at last took it upon himself to read her a lecture.

"Honestly, Lucy, you're letting it get into an obsession. Everybody says so. Nobody else is worried."

"Then they ought to be."

264

"Don't be hysterical. Pull up your socks and think of something else. That's the only thing to do when you've got something on your mind."

"You're so awfully good at doing that yourself, aren't you, Rickie?"

"Yes," said Rickie complacently. "When I was going through that bad time, about Melissa, I had to do it."

Lucy burst out laughing, felt better, and rushed off to report this latest Rickie-ism to Melissa. It was some time since she had found anything funny to tell Melissa, who needed to be cheered up because Hump was returning to Africa. He was working for a while in Paris before joining a party sent by the French government to the Dandawa. Melissa was in despair at losing him again so soon, and because she thought he was being exploited.

Though what Melissa knows about despair, thought Lucy, when she had finished a lively letter, wouldn't fill half a sheet of note paper. It's just a word one uses. It ought to be reserved for people like poor Nancy, waiting and waiting for good news that never comes, and being driven out of the few senses she ever had.

She remembered, with a pang of guilt, that she had not been to see Nancy lately. She ought to have gone much oftener, during these grinding weeks of suspense. But the house was so squalidly cheerless, Emil so moody, that a visit was something of an ordeal. She braced herself to go that evening and console her poor friend. That Nancy was by now beyond reach of consolation had not been perceived by anybody in Ravonsbridge, and the sight of the baby, asleep on the stairs, did not startle Lucy as much as it might have done in any other household. The child had never led a very regular existence. She carried him up to his cot before joining Nancy, who was sitting, as usual, in her dirty kitchen, staring at nothing.

"I've just put Brian to bed," said Lucy cheerfully. "He woke up for a minute, while I was undressing him, and said: Has God got teef?"

Nancy picked at a knot hole in the kitchen table and presently said that she thought she would go to Kidderminster.

"To your mother?" asked Lucy. "For a holiday?"

"She has a little business . . . well, it's newspapers, you know and sweets and tobacco. . . ."

265

Nancy's voice trailed off. She picked at the knot hole and then added:

"Do you think Miss Foss really did it?"

"What? Invented that story? Of course she didn't."

"She would always look after baby. So I think I'll take baby to Kidderminster. In case it gets too much for me, I mean."

"A change would be very good for you."

"Emil thinks it was her."

"Miss Foss? Nancy, it's ridiculous. Who was it put such an idea into his head?"

"I used to work in a café, only Emil doesn't like it to be known. That's how we met. He came in one day and I served him and we got talking. She didn't like it. She didn't like me marrying a foreigner. But she's very fond of baby. She'll look after baby. He ought to be looked after."

He certainly ought, thought Lucy, remembering his precarious slumber on the stairs.

"But what I say is," murmured Nancy, "they ought to put Ianthe's name on the banners too."

"What banners?"

"Only Emil doesn't like me going there. They don't get on. They never did. Not the first time I took him home, oh, must have been a week before we were married. Whatever d'you want to marry him for? she said. I said: I love him."

Nancy sighed and then looked up enquiringly, as if anxious to know that Lucy understood.

"I know you do," said Lucy gently.

"That Ianthe, she's been up to her tricks ever such a long time. Why, last summer she was. Tried to make up they'd done something when he was painting her. No he never, I said. I know Emil. He never. I'll go to Mr. Thornley, I said, and he'll stop you saying such wicked lies. And he did. He sent her right away. But she came back . . . oh dear, oh dear! She came back. And it's her they ought to show up, only she's gone away again. It should be all written up on the banners, when they have the procession."

"Nancy, what on earth is this? Who is going to have a procession and banners?"

"It's a secret, because of Mrs. Meeker."

"Mrs. Meeker? Is she mixed up in it?"

"No. If she knew she'd stop it, though she's on Emil's side. I ought to be thinking about supper, I suppose."

Nancy rose and stooped to light the gas oven. The back of her neck was very dirty. She could not have washed it for quite a long time. Though a slattern in her housework she had hitherto kept herself and the baby tolerably clean.

"Basil Wright," she said, coming back to stand by the table. "He writes pieces for the papers. He's in the gas works."

"You mean there's going to be some kind of demonstration?"

"To show up Miss Foss," said Nancy nodding. "Emil's students are going to paint the banners."

"Merry Christmas!" exclaimed Lucy in exasperation. "But it'll ruin everything! Where is he? Where's Emil?"

"I don't know. He's out."

"Then I must wait till he comes in. I must speak to him at once. Nancy, can't you see that it's a crazy idea? Do please help me to persuade him. Get him to stop it!"

"But I love him!" said Nancy, staring at her solemnly.

"I know. So you must want him not to be so silly."

"I don't want him any different."

Stooping again, Nancy turned off the oven, which had been roaring away all this time. She seemed to have forgotten her idea about supper.

Lucy averted her eyes from that dirty neck in a spasm of pity and disgust, but it did not alarm her. Mental derangement, she imagined, becomes apparent in screams, frenzy, delusions. She was not aware that complete disintegration could take place so quietly.

The outer door opened and slammed. Hasty steps crossed the hall and went into the living room.

"That's Emil!" exclaimed Lucy. "I'll go and speak to him."

A burst of Wagner greeted her as she sailed in to the attack. Emil had turned on the wireless and was crouching beside it. He looked round and signed angrily to her not to disturb him.

"I'm sorry, Emil. I must speak to you now. It's urgent."

"Later please. It's the last act of *Tristan*. I'm furious to miss so much. I've been running all the way home."

"I can't help that. This is vital. Nancy's been telling me a fantastic story about processions and banners."

He started and scowled.

"She had no business to say anything," he snapped.

"Thank heaven she did! Turn that thing off. We must have this out."

"But it is Flagstad singing."

"Not just now. It's only old Mark maundering."

"In a few minutes it will be the *Liebestod*."

"Yes and I shall shout at you all through it, if need be."

He tuned the wireless down and knelt, half listening to it and half to her, while she pointed out the folly of his behaviour and reproached him for letting his colleagues down.

"They laughed at me and poked fingers at me," he growled. "What have they done for me?"

"We wrote that letter. . . ."

"Vich is not answered. It doesn't do anything. For nothing have I humbled myself and creeped to the council. My friends in the town, also, are very angry with me for deserting them. Basil Wright is only now saying to me how I have been used. You don't do it for me, only for yourselfs. Because you are afraid for your own jobs."

"All right," said Lucy, firing a shot at random. "I shall go and spill the beans to Mrs. Meeker."

Emil spun round with a jerk and forgot Wagner for a moment.

"Ach Lucy! Please! You mustn't do that. You don't understand. It would be bad for Basil Wright."

"Much worse for you, it could be."

"She would be very angry. By her, everything must be correct. And for now they don't quarrel. I think it's politics. For now he is working with her."

"I shall go to her unless I'm sure this crazy business has been called off."

"But that's all right. It's been called off."

"What?"

"Since I was so stupid, to listen to you and write that letter to Poole, I've told them we can't have this procession."

"Why on earth didn't you say so before?"

"Why should I? It wasn't your business."

"You're sure it's off?"

"Quite sure. Don't please tell Mrs. Meeker. She will be less sympathetic for me and she will quarrel with him."

"Emil, do you swear it shan't happen?"

"I don't tell lies. My students also I have forbidden. It's a great disappointment for them."

He turned up the wireless again and settled down to listen as though the episode were over.

Lucy knew that he was not a liar. She gave a sigh of mingled relief and exasperation. All this panic had been for nothing. She was turning to leave him when the first notes of Flagstad's *Liebestod* pierced the forlorn room like a shaft of light. Then she stood spellbound by the door, unable to go.

Fury and bewilderment, care and doubt, fell away from her as note serenely followed note. It was as though she had suddenly emerged from a tunnel, clamourous and dark, into a strange, lofty landscape. She came back and sat on a stool by the hearth.

Emil turned to smile at her, their late altercation completely forgotten. The pure voice floated on, rose, sank, soared, and carried them away over the mountains.

Not singing, not singing, thought Lucy, with tears rolling down her cheeks. More than singing. This voice goes on always, always, behind all the other voices; for all men must suffer and all men must die.

The door creaked. Nancy's vacant face peered in at them. Emil, who had risen and was pacing the room, went to her and drew her down on the sofa beside him. She leaned against his shoulder with a contented sigh.

We die. We were born to die. We are what we are: "*the sentient target of death.*" But, before we die, we speak.

Motionless the three of them sat in the summer twilight, as they had often sat together in the old days, when Lucy lived there. When the voice sang no more, she stole quietly away.

5

Mr. GARSTANG was both diverted and relieved when he got his copy of the staff letter. This time, he resolved, there should be no hanky panky, and he waited impatiently for his summons to a special meeting. None came. After ten days he rang up the chairman, and learnt that no special meeting was to be held. Lady Frances was against the idea. The staff letter would come up at the end-of-term meeting in July.

"But is no reply to be sent before then?"

"Oh, yes. I've written to Mildmay, telling that the letter is under consideration."

"Well," said Garstang. "I wish you'd consulted the rest of us, before deciding against a special meeting. Her Ladyship isn't the entire council."

"There are difficulties. I can't tell you on the telephone."

"Then I'd like to come and see you."

"Certainly. Any time."

Colonel Harding lived near Slane Bredy and Garstang to the west of the new town, on the edge of the Welsh hills. It was a signal mark of Garstang's anxiety that he took the trouble to drive seven miles in order to find out what had happened. He had been upon the council for fourteen years but he had never before exerted himself to so great an extent. He was angry at what he believed to be another Hayter victory.

"Lady Frances," explained the Colonel, "is furious over that staff letter. She thinks it was all got up by Miss Carmichael."

"Oh . . . why?"

"I can't think. The girl had signed it, of course, along with all the others, but Mildmay seems to have been the moving spirit. I don't know why she has such a down on Miss Carmichael."

Garstang thought that he knew why, and smiled.

"But what's worse," continued the Colonel, "is that she's now decided to get rid of Angera. We're not to accept his apology. He's to go."

"I shall fight that," said Garstang, "tooth and nail. We were distinctly given to understand that we were only holding out for an apology, and that there's no question of his really going."

"She's changed her mind, and she can always carry the meeting. Lady Anne and Mrs. Massingham will back her up."

"I've not changed mine, and I'm sure Miss Foss will back me up. I shall get hold of Pidgeon and Coppard and tell them they must come. That'll be four against three."

"Pidgeon's away. Be away till mid-June. And you'll never get Coppard in term time. If you want a fight with the Millwoods it'll have to be in July. A meeting now won't do Angera any good."

Garstang saw that this was true, but deplored the implied insult to the staff.

"Yes," agreed the Colonel. "I'm a bit worried over that. Mildmay wrote to me unofficially and hinted how very strongly they feel; in fact there was a veiled suggestion that they might resign in a body if we don't do something quickly, one way or the other."

"Good Lord! We can't have that happening!"

"Oh, I don't really think there's any danger. I had a word with Hayter."

"Oh? Did you?"

"He said there'd be no resigning when it comes to the point. He's sure he can manage them, though he thinks Miss Frogmore ought to be on the council. He says they'll hang on to their jobs when they've had a little time to think it over. I gather he's encouraging them to think."

"Even Mildmay?"

"He couldn't afford to resign. Got an invalid wife, and too old for any other job."

Mr. Garstang did not like the sound of all this, but he did realise that nothing could be gained by pressing for an early meeting. He would do better to mobilise his forces for a battle in July.

He waited until Dr. Pidgeon came back, and he then drove over to Severnton one evening, dined Pidgeon and Coppard at the Crown, primed them with some excellent Burgundy, and explained the position. Both promised to attend the next meeting, in July, and to support him in his fight to keep Angera. They could scarcely do less, with so much Burgundy inside them, though they grumbled a little at the impending exertion and could not understand why the council had dwindled so much, or why Thornley and Spedding had not been replaced. Garstang found that he could not explain that, but he was able to convince them that the ladies (bless their hearts) had got the council into a scrape and that it was time for all good men to come to the rescue.

It was a most successful little dinner, though Mr. Garstang regretted the brandy which topped it off when he went to get his car out of the Crown garage. It was most unlikely that he would run into anything, for he was a careful driver, but if he did there might be questions which he would not have cared to answer. Not that Coppard and Pidgeon were any better; the convivial manner in which they were strolling off, arm in arm, down High Street was delightful to see.

He got himself with safety out of Severnton and into Slane Forest. He was feeling genial and deedy, and so much pleased with himself that his imagination toyed with new campaigns. This little dinner was but the first move in a successful routing of Hayter. As soon as Angera was reinstated there must be some agitation for elections to the council. Sensible recruits must be found, who would join the Garstang party. And a pension must be voted for poor old Mildmay. It was a shame that the old man should, after so many years of faithful work, be subjected to rudeness from his employers—should have to keep his mouth shut or starve. On this point there would be no difficulty with Lady Frances; she would see it at once, when she had calmed down, for she was the last person in the world to penalise those who ventured to disagree with her. But, as a matter of principle, the whole question of staff pensions ought to be considered.

I may not often go on the rampage, thought Mr. Garstang with a chuckle, but when I do, I'm a corker. Hayter may be a very clever fellow with the ladies, but now he's up against me.

It was a beautiful midsummer evening and Slane Forest was silvered with the rising moon. Every prospect was delightful until he came out of the dip by Slane Bredy and saw Gibbet Hill looming above him with the red flare of a bonfire on the top of it. Then he remembered a distasteful circumstance. That abominable monument had been unveiled during the afternoon with speeches, hymns, prayers, folk dancing and every other foolery which the Meeker tribe could devise. All decent people had, of course, kept away. But he saw, as he took the hill road, that quite a large crowd must have attended, for the grassy turf at the top was littered with leaflets and ice cream cups. Quite a number remained, shouting and swaying in silhouette against the fire. There was the blare of a band; they were dancing. On all the rest of the way the road was dotted with groups returning to Ravonsbridge, and he had to drive very carefully. A police car, which came tearing over the hill with screaming sirens, scattered them to right and left, and suggested trouble in the town. Bound to be trouble, thought Mr. Garstang, blowing his horn, where that cow of a woman is concerned. She brings all the riff raff in Severnshire up here and expects them to sing hymns.

He swung cautiously down the hill. Ravonsbridge lay peacefully below him, the scattered lights, the spire, the massive bulk of the Institute, and the gulf of the Ravon valley beyond, stretching away to the Welsh hills and a lingering sunset. It was a slow journey. The returning groups were rowdy, larking and pushing one another all over the road, and not at all inclined to get out of his way. The crowd grew denser as he reached the town and there was such a mob at the bus terminus that he could scarcely get through. He crawled at a foot's pace into Market Square, where he was obliged to stop, hemmed in on every side by swaying people. There was a strange noise going on, a clamour of screams, shouts, cat-calls and a sort of music, as though people were banging on tin pans. He had just realised that something unusual must be happening when he heard another sound; the sharp crash and tinkle of broken glass. All round his car the people were exclaiming:

"Black faces. . . ."

"They got black faces, see?"

"Fellers dressed like girls. . . ."

"They got a guy! See? They got a old guy. . . ."

"It's the Reds. . . ."

"Look! Look at the banners. . . ."

"It's the Rebeccas! You know . . . the Rebeccas. . . ."

"See what it says? Down with Millwood?"

"Oh, Mum! I don't like it! I don't like it!"

273

"Sillee! It's only a old Guy Fawkes. . . ."

"The Rebeccas, they had black faces. . . ."

Rebecca riots? Men dressed as women? What wind from the past was this? Garstang peered at the innocent gaping faces pressed round the car, babbling an old wives' tale. He opened the roof and climbed upon the seat to see better as a fresh crash of glass mingled with the din. He caught sight of a fierce black face under a woman's straw hat trimmed with daisies. Then he was petrified by the sight of his own name. The square was full of heaving banners and one, swinging round, displayed its legend before it tilted again.

DOWN WITH GARSTANG

Another blackened face came into view, caught his eye, and shouted something. Then, the banners shifting, the horrible little corpse of Miss Foss appeared, strapped into a chair and swinging wildly over the heads of the crowd. She was wearing her well known black beehive of a hat and from her mouth issued a huge yellow bladder bearing the words:

THE POISON TONGUE

Just as he realised that it was not a corpse, but a guy, a soft, nauseating mass hit him squarely on the mouth and nose. He ducked down into his car again, retching and choking, to discover that he had been hit by a rotten tomato. The people round the car were now beginning to protest, to cry out angrily, to scream, as fresh crowds, running from the bus stop, pushed into the square and swept them off their feet. Crouching down over the steering wheel he was violently sick.

"Garstang!"

Colonel Harding was looking into the car.

"Get out and help us. They're breaking Miss Foss's windows."

"Where are the police?" gasped Garstang.

"We're the police," said the Colonel, displaying a Special's armlet. "They telephoned to us at Bredy for help. Come along. . . ."

Garstang found himself hauled out of his car and linked in a line of men who were forcing their way through the crowd. Must keep my elbows down, he thought, must protect my ribs. He fainted, but must have remained upon his feet, because when he came to his senses again he was aware of a slackened pressure and found himself shouting, as the others shouted:

"Make way there! Police! Make way! Get home! Go home!"

The crowd was thinning. In front of him was Miss Foss's neat little house with every window broken.

Mechanically he told several people to go home, which they were all doing as fast as they could, stumbling over the banners which had been flung down on the cobbles. Many of the women were sobbing with fright. He could not see the Colonel or any of the Specials, anywhere, until he found a farmer from Slane Bredy who wore an armlet and was bending over a huddled woman on the pavement.

"Where are the regular police?" he asked.

"Most of 'em were up on the hill, I reckon. It was there they looked for trouble. This lady's hurt. We must take her to Orson's; they've got the first aid there."

Between them they raised the moaning woman and supported her across the square to Orson, the chemist's.

"Where's Colonel Harding?"

"Gone after 'em up Shotter Street. When they heard us coming they gave us the slip, but it's likely the chaps from the station might have caught them the other end."

Orson's was full of indignant, clamourous people. Some Red Cross workers were arriving. Nobody seemed to be badly hurt but everyone was much shattered. Mr. Orson hurried up with sal volatile for their charge, exclaiming:

"A h'outrage! A h'outrage!"

In general he talked like a B.B.C. announcer, but the shock had revived the speech of his youth.

"But what was it? Who was it?" asked Garstang, wistfully eyeing the sal volatile, but not liking to ask for any.

"Students from the Institute, so they say."

"They come from the Institute," cried a woman. "Well, they come down Church Lane. I sor 'em."

"There's a child been trampled to death."

"A h'outrage!"

Garstang went back to the square. It was almost empty, but the Colonel had returned and was talking to some men by Miss Foss's front gate.

"No sign of them," he was saying, when Garstang came up. "They all got off before we could lay hands on them. How many would you say there were, Purdie?"

"Thirty or more, sir. They came into the square down Church Lane. They'd got their faces blacked and girls' clothes, and I reckon some of them were girls too. They'd got banners. Something about the Institute. They were singing and creating. We thought it was the students out for a lark . . ."

He broke off as the door of the house opened. Dr. Blake came out with Miss Foss and her elderly maid. Both the little old women were crying quietly. They crossed the square and vanished into the bank manager's house.

"What a bloody shame!" exclaimed another man.

"She came to the window to see what the noise was," said the first man. "Couldn't seem to understand it was her own windows till she got half a brick almost in her face."

A policeman appeared from Shotter Street with the news that three of the rioters had been caught and were down at the station. Colonel Harding turned to go with him but paused to examine a banner which lay on the cobbles at his feet.

"Just look at this!" he exclaimed.

Garstang joined him and read:

JUSTICE FOR ANGERA!

"Good God!"

"Yes," said the Colonel. "Well . . . we'd better get along to the station."

They went off up Shotter Street. The square was now deserted save for an ambulance outside Orson's. The Swan had wisely closed its doors. The moon sailed high over the roof tops and shone on torn banners, on shattered glass.

6

No CHILD had been trampled to death. Nobody had even been seriously hurt. The broken windows were quickly mended. Only three of the art students had been involved in the outrage. But everybody knew that Angera would now have to go.

He was summoned from Kidderminster, whither he had gone to see Nancy who was said to be ill there. Little progress was made in clearing up the mystery which shrouded the whole affair. The three students refused to give the names of their associates or to reveal who had instigated and organised the demonstration. They did say, however, that Angera had forbidden it and that they had acted without his consent. This did little good to his cause, for it was proof that he must, at some time, have known that such a scheme was in the air or he could not have forbidden it.

It was clear that most of the rioters had come from the lower town. Only two were arrested. One was a garage hand and the other a van boy from the M.M. They too maintained an obstinate silence. They denied having broken any windows. One said: "I never threw anything in Mrs. Frost's windows." The other said: "I saw Mr. Foster's windows smashed but I did not do it." Both thought that the guy had been "Lady Millwood." They said that they had thought it was only for a lark but that they would not give their mates away. Their stupidity, in allowing themselves to be caught while most of their fellow rioters got away, suggested that they really knew very little.

As soon as Angera arrived the council met and called him to account. He seemed to be quite stunned and, though his statements were confused, they were made calmly, without protest or self justification. He admitted that he had known of the scheme beforehand and had at one time encouraged it. Later he had called it off and forbidden his students to take any part in it. He named Basil Wright as the instigator but this clue, when followed up, led to nothing. There was no evidence whatever to implicate Wright;

at the time of the riot he had been dancing with Mrs. Meeker on the top of Gibbet Hill; he could bring fifty witnesses to prove it. Mrs. Meeker, who was as much shocked as anybody, regarded this attempt to vilify her partner as a personal insult.

The meeting was short. Angera was told that his resignation must stand and that he had better go at once. He agreed listlessly and withdrew. Nothing remained to be done save expel the three students and pass a vote of sympathy for Miss Foss who was said to be suffering severely from shock.

The whole Institute was aware that a council meeting was in progress, and the fate of Emil was a foregone conclusion. But one issue had yet to be decided; the staff had not debated the line to be taken over the rebuff they had had from the council. Events suggested that they had been perfectly right in asking for an early meeting, and that a prompt reinstatement of Angera might have averted this disaster. They were in a strong position, but they had not met to discuss it, though each one had reached a private decision.

Lucy rehearsed the duel in Kings Meads. Miss Frogmore explained the difference between Aou! and Oh! Miss Paine taught five girls how to sit on a low sofa without hitching up their skirts. Bess hunted through the library catalogues for a lost book and Mr. Mildmay deciphered a marginal note. Rickie traced the history of the *Tierce de Picardy,* while Harry Dent and Mrs. Carstairs, each closeted with a pupil, discoursed on bowing and consecutive fifths. But all of them kept looking at watches and clocks, for at half past four they would meet for tea in the staff common room and the future would have to be discussed.

Lucy was the last to arrive for she had wanted to finish her scene and thought it bad for the students to see that she was in any particular hurry to get away. She had expected to hear quite a babel of voices, a debate in full swing, when she got to the common room, but she walked into a silent assembly. They were all there, drinking tea, and nobody was saying anything. Then she saw the reason. Emil was with them; he was sitting a little apart, in a window seat overlooking the Ravon valley. She took a cooling cup of tea from Bess and raised her eyebrows. Bess shook her head and turned down her thumbs. Lucy went over to Angera and said:

"I'm sorry, Emil. It's all been a mess. . . ."

He turned and gave her a sad look. She realised how many undeserved disasters these mournful dark eyes had beheld before this final catastrophe which he had undoubtedly brought upon himself.

"Thank you, Lucy," he said quietly. "Now you have come I wish to say something."

He stood up and addressed the room with the mild voice of extreme fatigue.

"First I want to thank you all for what you have tried to do. I was a fool. I see that now. But since Thornley went I couldn't feel I had any friend here. This has been my fault."

There was an awkward murmur of sympathy and compassion.

"For the second: I want to warn you. I've said so many stupid things perhaps you won't listen. But this is not stupid. It was not stupid when I said that this council is going once. That will happen unless something is done very, very quick. There is a plot. I have been used."

He looked round to see if anybody understood him. Lucy said:

"I think that too."

"For you," said Angera, "that will be bad unless you guard yourselfs. These people will use you only. They won't care for you any more than they cared for me."

"But what people are you talking about?" broke in Miss Frogmore. "Who are these mysterious people?"

"That I don't know. But it's necessary now you act. You should ask for Mr. Thornley to return. There is no senior director; the place is open. You are strong now. You could demand him. These bad things didn't happen so much when he was here. You should ask now. Please forgive me. I know it's very funny for me to tell you what to do. I've become quite sensible now that it is no use to me or to anybody else."

He hesitated for a moment and added:

"Please! I wish you all great happiness and good luck."

He made them a little bow and went quickly out of the room.

"Well," said Bess, "I do think, under the circs, that a lecture from Emil on sensible behaviour is *not* indicated."

"But I think he's quite right," said Lucy.

"What?" cried several voices. "A plot?"

"Yes. I think there was some very clever organisation behind that business last night. I think ill feeling is being deliberately worked up so that the council will go in the autumn."

"I shouldn't die of grief if they did," said Miss Frogmore. "They've made a pretty good mess of things."

"Yes, but who would we get instead?"

"You don't understand, Lucy. You've never been at a meeting where they re-elect the council. Hardly anyone comes, and they're all people like Mr. Orson—staunch Millwoodites."

"They have to prove they're on the electoral roll to get a voting card," explained Mr. Mildmay. "That's rather a bother. Very few people take the trouble."

"And the council resigns?" asked Lucy.

"Yes, but somebody has always nominated them for re-election. Nominations have to be in a week before the meeting. Again it's only friends of the Millwoods who bother to send in nominations."

"You don't think this business may have shaken the Millwood prestige a little?"

"It might. But the dissatisfied faction are just the sort of people who would never trouble to get cards."

"I still think," persisted Lucy, "that somebody very efficient is behind it all. Somebody who might see that people do bother to get cards."

"I wish you wouldn't talk in this mysterious way," said Miss Frogmore impatiently. "You're as bad as Mr. Angera. Have you anybody in mind?"

Lucy decided to burn her boats.

"Yes, I have. I think Mr. Hayter is behind it all."

There was a general gasp.

"What?" exclaimed Miss Paine. "Not the riot!"

"I shouldn't wonder if he didn't know about that too."

"But you're crackers!" expostulated Bess. "He's on the council himself."

"Oh, he'll be re-elected," said Lucy, "whoever else goes off."

She paused and waited for more comments, but none came.

Bess and Rickie were obviously astounded. But the others . . . none of the others was surprised. And they were watching her warily, as if they were a little afraid of her, yet, at the same time, sorry. Because, if she must say these things, she would have to go, and none of them intended to go with her. She sighed and added:

"But he's talked you all round and persuaded you that it's better to take no notice of the way the council has treated us."

Rickie was the first to find an answer to this.

"I don't mind admitting that I've discussed it with him," he said. "But I deny that he talked me round. I merely feel that there's no point in resigning after the way Emil has let us down."

"Absolutely crackers!" agreed Bess. "I'm sorry for Emil. But really . . ."

"It isn't a question of Emil," said Lucy. "Mr. Mildmay! You don't think it's a question of Emil, do you?"

Mr. Mildmay put down his tea cup and shook his head.

"No," he said. "It's a question of our position. We were clearly in the right. We've been most contemptuously treated, and I think it's deplorable that we should sit down under it. I would like to resign but . . . frankly . . . I can't afford to do so. My wife's health . . . and at my age another post wouldn't be easy to find. I have discussed it with no one, Miss Carmichael. But I'm afraid I spoke hastily when I talked of resignation, at our last meeting. I was carried away. . . ."

"I don't look at it in that way at all," said Miss Frogmore. "They've behaved badly, I agree. But I don't think Lucy has any right to put it all onto Mr. Hayter. I can assure you that he's not at all satisfied at the way we've been treated. He's going to see that this sort of thing doesn't happen again. He's going to insist that we are better represented on the council. Colonel Harding quite agrees. One of us should be on the council, who can explain our point of view."

"I wonder who he has in mind!" said Lucy.

Miss Frogmore reddened, and exclaimed:

"I think the whole matter had better be dropped. I personally would prefer to forget Mr. Angera and everything to do with him, and I'm not at all sure that our intervention wasn't a mistake. If some perfectly innocent person, who has always behaved well, receives unfair treatment, the case might be different."

This was echoed by Harry Dent and Mrs. Carstairs, who both insisted that the present occasion was not a good one. But the staff must assert itself as soon as a better chance was offered to them.

"If Mr. Hayter ever offers you a better chance," said Lucy, "I take back all I've said about him."

"I simply can't see why you've got your knife into Hayter like this," broke in Rickie. "He's always been very nice to you and he got you the job here. He's always ready to help any of us. Look what he did for me about the broadcast!"

"Oh, yes," agreed Lucy. "He's always been nice to me. If I was clever I think I could be senior director."

"Yes," said Miss Frogmore, "you could. And you're simply throwing it away."

"Umhm!" agreed Lucy. "I'm resigning. I'm leaving at the end of the term."

There was a clamour of consternation and protest, from which the voice of Miss Paine emerged:

"But you can't! You can't! It puts the rest of us in such an awkward position."

"We should all act together," urged Harry Dent. "Either resign in a body, or stay on in a body. I think you should abide by what we all decide."

"But I couldn't stay," said Lucy, "after I've come out into the open and said what I think about Mr. Hayter. There isn't room for us both on one staff."

"Oh, we'll all forget what you've said," promised Mrs. Carstairs. "But don't force the issue like this."

"No," said Lucy. "I can't stay. I don't see any future here. He's a crooked, unscrupulous man who oughtn't to have any power, and he's going to get a lot more. We're all going to be completely at his mercy. But of course it's different for all of you, if you really trust him. I don't."

She turned to leave them. Before she reached the door Mr. Mildmay exclaimed:

"I'm so glad! If I were your age, Miss Carmichael, I think I should do the same. I think you take rather too gloomy a view of the future. I hope you do. But I'm sure you are acting rightly in deciding to go."

"Meaning that the rest of us are not?" demanded Miss Paine sharply.

"Every man must decide for himself, Miss Paine, what he'll sell for his bread and butter. Miss Carmichael is not prepared to sell what we are selling."

Lucy smiled at him and left them to it. She was sure that every word of this debate would get round to Hayter by some means or other, and hoped that Mr. Mildmay's opinions would not cost him too dear. But she did not believe that they would if he behaved with submission.

That her decision might put her colleagues into a quandary had not occurred to her, and for the first few minutes after she left them she was so angry that she did not care if it did. On reflection, however, she resolved not to implicate them in the grounds for her resignation. She would not announce that she was going because the staff had been improperly treated, for that might cause repercussions—enquiries, during which they might be forced to forswear themselves and humbly to aver that no slight had been put upon them. They were determined not to go. Hayter knew it, and he would lose no chance of engineering their cautious retreat into a total capitulation. She thought she might thwart him best by resigning because she did not like her ambiguous position—burdened with all the responsibility of a senior director and none of the prestige. She had been told that this would only last until Easter, but there was no prospect of a new appointment and she had real grounds for discontent.

When she had finished her day's work she went in search of Emil and met him coming out of the art school. They turned together into the garden and took the long shady walk over the top of the hill. She wanted to tell him of her regret and remorse for her part in the disaster; for she felt now that she had been wrong to laugh at him in the early stages of the scandal. The mockery of his colleagues, the sense of being friendless, had probably driven him to seek the sympathy of people like Basil Wright.

He said abstractedly that it did not matter, and they talked for a while of Thornley and then she confessed to him that other load

283

on her conscience: her responsibility in bringing Ianthe back to Ravonsbridge. Again he said that it did not matter.

"Without Thornley I should do something stupid; if not this, then something else. So then it is a muddle, and the council is blamed. Ianthe was only an occasion."

"Why do you think Mr. Thornley was got rid of?"

"Because he was the only sensible person on the council. Hayter is very clever, Lucy. He does nothing. Nothing at all. Nobody can say it is his fault. But he is now the only one who can stop them from doing stupid things. Comes a stupid thing that is convenient, and he does not stop it."

"But what will you do now, Emil?"

"This evening I go back to Kidderminster, to Nancy."

They sat down on a bench overlooking the valley where the town ended and the fields began again. All the Ravon valley must have looked like this once, with the dotted farms and the river winding among water meadows and the blue ranks of the hills to the west. Lucy was very fond of this view, and often strolled along to it after her day's work. But this must be very nearly the last time that she would see it. Soon they would both be gone, having lived through so much in this town, and the hills would always be there, and other people would sit on this bench and talk, but Lucy and Emil would be gone, and their memory would fade from all the circle of the hills.

"Nancy is mad."

His voice was so low that she could not be sure of the words. She turned to him with startled eyes:

"What? What did you say?"

Emil stretched out his long, capable hands in front of him and looked at them intently.

"They have had to take her away . . . to a hospital for mad people. . . ."

"Emil!"

A train came puffing out of the town below. The smoke rose over the roofs. It vanished behind the gas works, and then reappeared among the fields where the line ran beside the river down to Gloucester and the world beyond the hills.

"I was afraid," whispered Lucy. "I was afraid."

"She must be taken care of, you see."

"But she'll get better, Emil. They'll cure her. They're so clever nowadays."

"Perhaps. I don't know."

He was still looking at his hands as he continued:

"Perhaps it was some disease that would have come even if I had been kind husband. That too I don't know. I only know . . . that I was not kind."

"She always loved you. I'm sure she still does."

"You don't need to tell me that."

Lucy watched the train puffing down the valley until tears blurred the view.

"She's like a little baby now," said Emil. "Like a very little baby for whom everything must be done. She must be fed and washed and dressed, and she doesn't speak. And all this must be done by people who don't love her. So you see, I'd have to go in any case. I must find some home where she can be with me and where I can do all for her, like that."

"Oh, she'll get better."

"I can work. I can keep her. And with my hands I shall do all for her. With my hands. No stranger shall touch her. Even as she is she will know, I think. My hands won't be strange hands. . . ."

He held them out and frowned at them. Lucy knew that he would do as he had said. He had failed Nancy in the commonplace demands of life, but many a better man could not have given her what he offered now.

"Oh, she must get better!"

He smiled at her.

"That we must hope. If she is better I shall write that good news to you. If I don't write, you will know it's not good. And please tell nobody about this."

They walked together back to the Institute and she undertook various commissions for him, for his household effects must be packed up and sent to Kidderminster. He showed more method and practical sense in making these arrangements than she had ever discerned in him before. He left Ravonsbridge that evening. She never saw him or heard from him again.

7

A MONTH later she departed herself. Mr. Hayter was so very co-operative about her resignation, so ready to agree that her position was not comfortable, and so alert in getting her a glowing testimonial from the council, that she doubted very much whether she had managed things well.

Her relations with her colleagues, during the rest of the term, were not quite easy. Rickie and Bess tried to make her change her mind. All, save Mr. Mildmay, resented what they felt to be an implied rebuke in her decision. But memory was already beginning its beneficent work of transformation and by the end of the term most of them were able to think that she was leaving because she did not like the job. The awkward affair of Emil must find some place in the lumber room of their minds, thrust out of sight, where it need not often be scrutinised, and a dust sheet thrown over it. To each it had been a drama in which he or she had been the central figure. That Lucy had foreseen more, had urged more effort, than anybody else, few would have allowed. On the whole, Miss Frogmore came to be remembered as poor Emil's champion. She had called the meeting and talked more than Mr. Mildmay. But Emil had let her down.

Lucy went on a grey and windy day, feeling almost as solitary as when she came. But a surprise awaited her at the station. Owen Rees was at the ticket barrier and explained that he had come to see her off. She was taken aback, for she had said nothing of her departure to anyone outside the Institute, not even to Mr. Meeker.

"How did you know I was going?"

"Things get about."

"They certainly do. But how did you know what train?"

"I rang the taxi office to find when you'd ordered a taxi. Do you always have so much luggage?"

"Only when I'm leaving a job."

"Where are you going now, then? Have you another job?"

"Not yet. I haven't the least idea what I'll do."

He helped her to pile up her luggage on the platform and then said:

"We're all very sorry you're going, Lussi. It's a wicked shame they should sack you."

"Sacked! I wasn't sacked. I resigned."

He insisted that she had been sacked because she stood up for Angera. The whole town said so. And he looked mutinous when she begged him to contradict the story. A fine indignation over the sacking of Lucy was hard to relinquish. She realised that her departure might well be turned into another stick with which to beat the council, and besought him so earnestly to see that the truth was known that at last he gave in.

"O.K. I'll tell them you couldn't stand the place."

"No, no, don't tell them that."

"Then why are you going?"

"Here's my train!"

"Stand you back and I'll get you a seat."

"Take care of that basket. It's got my tea set in it."

The train came puffing in half empty, so that he did not have to be as deedy on her behalf as he would have liked. But he stowed away her possessions for her, and then stood beneath her carriage door while she leaned out and talked to him.

"Give my love to Aunty," she said.

"Come again?"

She had to explain rather lamely that it was a joke; a parody of what people said when parting at railway stations. He looked mystified but laughed obligingly.

"Someday," he said, "you'll come back."

"No. I don't think so. No. I'll never come back."

As she said the words she saw Charles Millwood rush through the ticket barrier. He scanned the train, caught sight of her, and hurried up.

"I . . . I came to see you off!" he exclaimed.

"How nice of you," said Lucy. "I think you know Owen Rees."

Charles and Owen scowled at one another and muttered uncordial greetings. Owen kept his place firmly in front of the carriage door so that Charles had to talk over his shoulder, explaining that he had only learnt of her departure that morning and had hastened to Sheep Lane, to find her gone. Lucy began to enjoy herself a little. If Owen had not been there, Charles would obviously have jumped into the train and travelled to Gloucester with her. She did not want him to do so, but it was amusing to watch him deciding that he could not. Also it was amusing to be seen off by the two people who had most right to be offended with her, for she had been inexcusably rude to both.

"You know," she said suddenly, "you two ought to compare notes. You'd be surprised."

Before she could say more the train gave a snort and moved. They stood back. Owen ran beside it, waving, until he was left behind. Charles turned away.

The little houses slid past, and then the gas works, and then the fields. The valley curved. Ravonsbridge vanished. But the Lump on the hill still dominated the scene. As the valley wound and the hills changed places, it kept appearing and reappearing, each time a little smaller, a little more indistinct. Lucy hung out of the window to see the last of it. The smooth hills, the woody hills, waltzed and revolved, but she could not be sure which was her final glimpse because she was crying.

Part 7

The Lincolnshire Handicap

1

Melissa to Hump.

17 High Street,
Drumby, Lincs.
Sept. 14.

YOUR CLUB opened last night with great éclat. Much was said, much was ate, much was drank, including your health. The dancing floor is so resilient that I fear it is unsafe; one day, no doubt, we shall all fall through. But you will be in the Dandawa and will merely raise your eyebrows when you read of the disaster, in some old greasy newspaper which has lit into your hands by chance.

The fire escape will do nicely for couples sitting out in the summer, when we mean to have a lighted barge on the canal outside, and drinks and all. This is our organiser's idea. We decided we must have one full time paid organiser, and do the rest of the work in volunteer shifts. We give her £5 a week, which is not much, but all that we can afford. She does the catering and gave us a magnificent supper last night and very good drinks; (John got the licences through, by following your unscrupulous advice) very cheap, for what it was, and made a small profit. I enclose a list of eatables and prices, to show you the sort of thing. The *vol-au-vents*

289

were miracles—every one gobbled up. Shrimp and mushroom. She made them herself in the club kitchen before the party, being a genius at pastry.

She is devising various agreeable entertainments, including a pantomime at Christmas and a masked ball on New Year's Eve. And she has already sorted out all the cliques—the bridge clique, the musical clique, the charade clique, etc., and allotted them different evenings, so that no one clique can dominate the club and make it boring for the rest.

I can assure you that the club promises to be a startling success. John still worrries about having got the money for *drama*, but I am sure they will all be better chemists if they enjoy themselves a little. It must have affected their work to hate Drumby so much. But he says what if some official arrives and demands evidence of drama? Organiser says she can fix up a rehearsal at a moment's notice—just a few of "the girls" wandering about with books, and we'll tell him it's our forthcoming production of *Love's Labour's Lost*.

I must tell you that John has given me a dog. I will leave you to guess (a) Name. (b) Breed. I shall not mention this animal again because people with dogs should be reticent about them.

You ask in your last letter why I don't ride? I do. We have found a farm near Breenho which supplies horses, but we are keeping this to ourselves. Selfish? I think not. We have done a lot for Drumby and must have some private pleasures. It's a Lincolnshire tradition that anything done by the Beauclercs is immediately done by the whole population, and I don't care to ride with a cavalry regiment. So we are secretive and take our riding things to Breenho in a suitcase. This has already caused speculation to Mrs. Callow, who has done everything except ask me point blank why we vanish from Drumby at intervals, for a few hours, with a large suitcase. I believe she thinks we have secretly had a baby and have put it out to nurse at a farm and take clothes to it. Because it's so strange of us not to have one after fifteen months! What a thing!

Hump, dear, can't you come to see us before you go to Dandawa? Must you really be in Paris all the time till then? Surely you could fly home for a week end? Think of all the years before we meet again! And not everything can be said in a letter.

Could you, sometime, let me have Crabbe back? I have tendered this request before. You borrowed him in May.

No date or address.

Cocker spaniel. Collins. Sorry about Crabbe. I left him in the Metro by mistake. Would you like Racine instead? A better poet. I'd come if I could, sweet Rose of May, but I'm on to something here that I really can't leave and I'm afraid it will keep me till I sail. Why can't you come here? *Who is this Organiser?* You've suggested a most formidable possibility. If she is who I think she is, I won't have her in my club. But you can't have done this to me? Are there two girls like that?

Melissa to Hump.

Drumby. Sept. 20.

How well you understand me in some respects! Collins is a cocker spaniel, golden. A very ordinary middle class dog, as our mother might say. *Parlons d'autre chose!* In other respects you are dumb, crass, mutton-headed and an egotist. Going to Paris wouldn't be at all the same thing as having you here; John couldn't go. But I will, if there's no other chance of saying goodbye to you.

I do not want Racine. I want Crabbe. I have got Racine and I do not like him and I was made to read him at school and I can only remember one sensible line (besides the one we all know, about Venus entire) which is:

L'Hymen n'est pas toujours entouré de flambeaux.

Wait till you find that out for yourself! Then you'll be sorry you wouldn't come when your sister called. It's so unlike you to say you *can't* do anything. You always do what you like, and always have. I never heard you say can't before.

The club organiser is my friend Lucy Carmichael who came to stay with us this summer, and about whom I have ceased writing to you because you said she sounded a most unattractive girl. She left Ravonsbridge in July. John loves her as he ought, though I think he was at first afraid she might be going to live with us. But we've got her lodgings in a cottage next door to the club.

Of course the job isn't nearly good enough for her. But we hope she may marry. Drumby is well stocked with unmarried chemists, all of them very brilliant and sure of a future, and never was anybody like her seen here before, except myself, for looks, wit and chic. The competition is brisk. John and I, who have become very horsey in our conversation, call it the Lincolnshire Handicap. I prefer Mr. Birkett, the man who upset your boat, so I'm sure you'll remember him. John favours a blackavised Scot called McIntyre, entirely devoid of charm, but much respected by all the men behind the barbed wire. Lucy however wastes far too much of her time with two infants called Cobb and Brett, new since your time, far too young and too poor to marry, who lark about with her and help her to wash up at the club. I'd have told you all this long ago if you'd been nicer about her.

Hump to Melissa.

Paris. Sept. 26.

I knew it was bossy Lucy! And you expect me to come to Drumby! You come on to Paris and I'll take you to see the Morgue if you're good.

Birkett did not upset my boat. I upset his. He has adenoids and I hope she marries him. Why did she leave Ravonsbridge? Did they run her out of town? And what about l'affaire Angera?

I can't buy Crabbe in Paris. The French have never heard of him.

If you should go to London you might look up Pattison who will remember perfectly who you are because I've been talking to him about you; he was over here last week for some medical conference. He put the eels in Millwood's bed. Now he's a full fledged gynaecologist, 357 Harley Street, but has got whiskers which I think a mistake. He'd love to see you again and will take you out to dinner if you ring him up. I believe our mother keeps spies in Harley Street, so it doesn't do to be seen ringing doorbells there.

Personally, if I was a girl, I shouldn't part with my money to any of them. If I was a girl I'd remember that the watched pot never boils, and put myself down to ride in a gymkhana at Easter —sort of thing it's going to be a nuisance to have to cancel. But then I'm dumb, crass and an egotist, and don't share our family trait of crossing rivers before I come to them.

God bless you. Keep me posted in the racing news. What are the odds on the Lincolnshire Handicap?

Lucy to Mrs. Carmichael.

2 Canal Cottages,
Drumby, Lincs.
Oct. 10.

How I have neglected you! But the club is really very strenuous. They have given me a little cripple car in which I can drive about and collect provisions. It's always breaking down, which takes up a lot of time.

First before I forget: can you find and send my riding breeches? I don't know where they are but they must be somewhere. Alan (Birkett) says he can get me a horse; I don't want to poach on the Beauclerc horses, but he has found another farm, down by the sea.

I am writing the club pantomime, very primitive and topical, the All Low in rustic imbecility but "they" will like it. It's about what we women think happens behind the barbed wire. Joe Cobb is to be the Fairy Queen. That gives you the tone. It's a rest not to have to be intellectual for a bit. We had a property horse once, didn't we? What has become of it? It would be useful for the pantomime. If it's still extant you might send it with the breeches.

Melissa dotes on Collins, but always speaks of him disparagingly for fear we shall think she is sentimental. But I think it was just a little tactless of John. I mean when a husband decides that his wife isn't going to have a baby he always seems to give her a puppy, and I'm almost sure that Melissa has worked herself up into one of her panics that she is probably barren. She is not quite as happy as she was; I know that by her mannerisms. She has become very fastidious and Jane Austenish again—more like what she was when I first met her in Oxford. It is her façade against secret anxiety.

In her family everything is always expected to go wrong. And in Drumby every bride has a baby within a year; you can see them all speculating over poor Melissa and deciding it's intentional, which I'm sure isn't the case. And I expect that reacts on her nerves and pushes her back into the state of doubt and insecurity which she has only just learnt to shake off. People think her so happy and placid, but she is really a mass of nerves, superbly controlled.

Mother, you know all about such things—need she worry? I mean, if a couple who want a baby don't start one in 15 months is that anything to worry about? Not that I'd ever have a chance to discuss it with her. She never speaks of anything that really worries her to anyone; I shouldn't be surprised if she hadn't even discussed this with John. The only person she's *quite* at her ease with is Hump, I imagine, and he'd be no use over a thing like that. I'm sure he's very nice, but he sounds the sort of insensitive extrovert who would never guess anything unless it was shouted at him through a megaphone.

I have a slight prejudice against Hump, partly because they are all so boring about him here, especially the women, who say: Oh, my *dear!* Hump! *Oh!* . . . and languish. And I must say he sounds rather bossy. I said so to John one day and he seemed to think it very funny. He got the *fou rire* rather solemn people get when once they start laughing. He went hooting into the kitchen and told Melissa and then *she* started! I could hear them cackling and cackling so I put my head round the door and said: My wife and I roared! Which is what Mrs. Callow's husband says when retailing the dreariest joke. I don't know why they thought it so funny.

Well, I must stop.

No, I'm going on because a letter from you has just arrived, which I must answer.

Darling, darling, darling Mother, please don't worry and fuss so much! I know it's a poor job, and doesn't lead anywhere, and I ought to be getting on with my career. But I don't want to leave

Drumby just yet. I'm having a lot of fun and I want to pick myself up and pull myself together a little bit, before launching myself on life again. The tornado at R. in the summer was so shattering; I still can't think of Nancy and Emil without crying, and can't free my thoughts from it all, somehow. But I promise I won't stay in Drumby for ever, though I can see M. and J. hope I will; they want me to marry behind the barbed wire and settle down here. But the chemists leave me cold. If I could fancy anybody it would be Larry Quinn from the Breenho camp, but he is violently Irish and one Irishman in a girl's life is enough, don't you think? Besides, I'm sure his intentions are strictly dishonourable. But he's more fun than a chemist.

But I have a sort of instinct to stay here for a bit and not try to rush my life. Haven't you ever had the same feeling? As if you were at a loose end, but something was telling you to keep quiet because something important was soon going to turn up which would change everything? I keep feeling that, I don't know why. I can't think what it would be. Perhaps I'll get a call to be a missionary.

Melissa to Hump.

Drumby. Oct. 10.

I have put myself down for a gymkhana in the spring. Jumping. I'm sure Pattison's whiskers are a mistake. They wouldn't inspire confidence.

I don't exactly know what happened over l'affaire Angera, for Lucy won't talk of it. But I gather it ended in some tragedy so dire that her own resignation was a minor evil. Angera came to awful grief, I imagine. Perhaps the poor man went mad. I don't know.

Racing News: Stop Press. Birkett scratched. He fell off his horse and made such an unconscionable fuss about it that Lucy was quite disgusted. McIntyre scratched. He emerged from Scots dourness to Scots sentimentality at the club and sang a dreadful song called: *Oh Lay Thy Loof in Mine Lass!* As Lucy says: We don't know what a loof is and we never want to. Cobb and Brett still on the course but they don't count. A dark horse called Quinn is moving up, a dashing captain from Breenho who rides like the devil. I can't bear him.

Bess to Lucy.

12 *Shotter Street,*
Ravonsbridge,
Severnshire.
Nov. 12.

This is to tell you a most surprising bit of news. You'll never guess. *Lady Frances has been turned off the council.* What do you know about that? I still can't believe it somehow. But they all are, all the Millwoods, Mrs. Massingham and Lady Anne I mean, and Colonel Harding and Mr. Garstang too. Miss Foss died. Did you know? About a month ago she caught a cold and had bronchitis.

I must tell you how it all happened. It was quite dramatic and a shame you weren't there. Well, it was the general meeting and the first shock was when we got in the hall. It was packed! But packed! Because generally hardly anyone comes. So I sat next to Mrs. Carstairs and she said have you seen the list of nominations? Some very strange names! Mr. Finch, my dear. Not a joke. *And he was elected.* But I'm going on too fast. I said who'd elect *him?* Who are all these people? So then Mr. Orson—you know—the chemist in Market Square—he was sitting just behind—and he said they've caught the Millwoods napping. Most of these names were only sent in on the last day.

So then the council trooped up onto the platform and King Charles took the president's chair and I could see his face getting longer and longer when he took in what the hall was like. He got so green before the end I thought he was going to be sick on the platform. But we all said it was awful for him to have to sit there and see his mother humiliated, all the family really. So then he made an opening speech and they hardly clapped at all, and then the council climbed down and sat in the body of the hall while the voting went on. So the ballot boxes went round and everybody voted and Mr. Poole and the counters went away and counted. By the way, they are saying Mr. Poole is a *snake*—he knew all these masses of people had applied for voting cards, quite different from other years—but he never let on, so it was a surprise for the Mill-woods.

So while we waited, Mr. Hayter gave his report on the festival, and he *is* popular. They cheered *him*. But he was a bit tactless because he finished by saying that he must now make way for the other directors, and of course there are none, my dear—Emil gone, Thornley gone, you gone, and Pidgeon had cut the meeting so there was nobody but Rickie! You'd have screamed. He went on and on about intimate opera and nobody listened and after 20 minutes, about, he turned to King Charles and said sorry have I had 10 minutes? And Charles, green as grass, said no carry on.

So then Poole came in with a poker face and handed the list of the new council to Charles who had to read it out. And all the time, of course, we were expecting to hear Lady Frances Mill-wood's name, and when he'd finished I thought he must have and I hadn't heard it. Till Mrs. Carstairs gave a sort of gasp and said there must be some mistake. You could hear people saying that all round, while all this stamping and cheering was going on. But Mr. Orson said oh no there's not and got up and went to where Lady Frances was—a lot of people did that—old Ravonsbridge people —they just went and stood round her while the new council was getting up onto the platform. You should have seen Mrs. Meeker's hat! Did I tell you *she* was on? Oh they went prancing up, ever so pleased with themselves, except the Frog—she was put on at the beginning of this term you know, and was one of the ones who were re-elected, and she stood in the hall just staring and staring at Lady Frances till they called to her to come up, and then she crawled up after them as if she didn't like it a bit, and never expected to find herself with such a crew.

So then Charles made a speech—he was supposed to welcome them but he didn't, he just said that the town was evidently in favour of changes so he thought it was time he resigned his presidency and rushed off the platform and took Lady F. by the arm as if he meant to drag her out of the hall. But she wouldn't go! She hobbled up the hall and started climbing up on the platform. Oh you could have heard a pin drop! Miss Paine said afterwards she thought she was going to hit Ma Meeker! But when she'd got up 2 steps she turned and made a speech—quite short and very nice really, not sore at all—saying how her husband had always believed in changes or something like that and how she looked forward to the future work of the Institute and how we ought always to be proud of it. And thanked everybody for their help and co-operation all the years she's been on the council. She was so sort of gentle and friendly that I began to wonder if it was really all right after all—not something nasty I mean. And then she went down and went out with all her family, but everybody rose as she went out and cheered her and cheered her, and Mrs. Carstairs began to cry —I hadn't realised she was so popular.

So then we had a lot of hot air about how wonderful the Institute is going to be now!—20 minutes from Ma Meeker and Mr. Finch just as bad. Mr. Mildmay is terribly upset, but I can't see that it's going to make much difference. Our jobs will be the same.

A funny thing—Mrs. Carstairs says you said it would happen. Did you? I don't remember you did. *Emil* said so but we all thought he was cuckoo. Send me a line if you're above ground, but if you're dead don't bother.

Lucy to Mr. Mildmay.

Drumby. Nov. 14.

I have heard from Miss Turner of the changes on the Institute council and her letter has grieved me very much. She doesn't tell me several things I'd like to know, so I venture to ask if you'll be so very kind as to tell me what you can about it. What really happened? Who is on the new council?

I am so distressed for Lady Frances; her whole life was devoted to the Institute. I can't think what she will do without it, or it without her.

When I got Miss Turner's letter I felt quite like Mr. Thornley when I met him once, after he left us, and he said: "I loved dear Ravonsbridge." I suddenly saw it all so clearly, and Slane Forest and all my friends there. I shall never forget it. I would so much appreciate a letter from you if you could spare the time.

Mr. Mildmay to Lucy.

7 Church Lane,
Ravonsbridge,
Severnshire.
Nov. 16.

You have been much in my mind of late. I will try to tell you what I can, though I think it will be some time before one realises all that has happened, and there are certain details which we may never know.

The new council is as follows:

Re-elected. Mr. Hayter, Dr. Pidgeon, Mr. Coppard, Miss Frogmore. Also, one might say, Mr. Spedding, who was up for election again after a temporary absence, which, luckily for him, took him off the council at the critical time.

Newcomers. Mrs. Meeker, Mr. Finch, Mr. Basil Wright, Major Harris, Mrs. Strong, Mr. Carruthers, and Mr. Davis.

Of the names which may be new to you, I can only say that I know nothing whatever of Major Harris. Mr. Carruthers is on a great many committees, I believe he's on the County Education Staff. Mr. Davis is from the Works and is said to be going into politics. Mrs. Strong is the wife of a Nonconformist minister in the new town and is interested in child welfare. They may be very good sort of people but I'm afraid I have a prejudice against them, for I feel that they must all have been aware that their election was due to a certain amount of double dealing.

I have had a chat with Colonel Harding since the meeting. He says that it was all engineered—that all these new names were added to the nomination list at the very last moment. If the Millwoods had, in the ensuing week, launched a regular campaign, and whipped up all their supporters, there might still have been hope, though I fear the unfortunate events of last term had done much to shake their popularity. But they were quite unaware of the strength of the attack. Hayter and Poole never breathed a word of this unusual application for voting cards. Not until the meeting did anyone realise what had happened. The hall was packed with people, *bona fide* voters, who have never been near the Institute before or taken the least interest in it. I have an idea that they were recruited by four or five anti-Millwood cliques, each working to put in a nominee but that these groups had not much in common, and that the integrating element was Hayter. I imagine that the new council has cause to be grateful to him, but it may be possible that not all of them expected such a complete coup d'état.

I am really very sorry for Miss Frogmore. I think she was dissuaded from resignation in the summer by an offer of a place on the council and that she sincerely believed she could do better service to her colleagues by accepting it. But of course she envisaged the old council, and hoped to be in closer touch with Lady Frances and Colonel Harding. I think the poor lady is appalled by her present position and I doubt if she will be with us much longer.

In this connection, my dear Miss Carmichael, I should like you to know that my own position is much more satisfactory than it was. I can retire when I please, as the old council, at their July meeting, voted me a small but sufficient pension; I believe Mr. Garstang urged it. It is a great standby to me to know that this has been done, for I do not know how long I shall continue here. My own department is not likely to suffer from much interference, but I don't think I can remain upon the staff with Hayter. Not that I don't blame myself a little for what has happened. For some years now I have been half aware how things were going; but I shrank from interference and buried myself in my own work, telling myself that in this way I was serving my old friend, Matthew Millwood, and that it was not my business to take part in "politics." Now that his "Athens" is delivered up to this Cleon I feel that I have, to some extent, betrayed him.

I don't know if Miss Turner has given you an account of the actual meeting. I cannot. It was intensely painful for anyone who remembers, as I do, the foundation and the opening of the Institute. I thought, more than once, of the opening ceremony in that hall, and the psalm that we sang:

Peace be within thy walls, and plenteousness within thy palaces;
For my brethren and companions' sake I will wish thee prosperity.

300

We heard it again, not a month later, in such stunned grief, when we buried him. And we had the same lesson: Ephesians 4 vv 11-15. It was not any abstract philanthropy which inspired him in this undertaking; it was his warm, heartfelt affection for the people in this town, his brethren and companions.

But did Miss Turner tell you of the beautiful little speech that Lady Frances made? I don't know how she was able, immediately after such a shock. It is proof of how much more the Institute, and his memory, mean to her than any personal consideration. She completely ignored, rose above, the insult to herself. It took everybody by surprise. Till that moment the atmosphere had been revolting; a kind of jeering, triumphant undercurrent in all the applause. But she was so dignified. When she began: "I want to say goodbye . . ." one could feel the change. I think she never, in a lifetime of devoted work, did more for Ravonsbridge than she did then, in that two minutes. She turned a brutal occasion into a civilised proceeding and made it possible for everyone to behave decently.

I suppose the majority of people in that hall had scarcely ever seen her before and had not the least idea what she is really like. I felt that they were startled, uncomfortable, and a little ashamed. When she had finished, Hayter got up, nodding at Spedding to do likewise, and giving the signal to the whole hall to rise and cheer her to the echo. I don't think that man ever makes a mistake. He had lost a lot of ground during those two minutes, and the rest of the people on the platform would probably have sat looking foolish while she went out. But the cheering relieved the discomfort and, I expect, gave many present an impression that they were doing her some belated kind of justice.

So many are indignant that I sometimes hope for a reaction. We have got these people for five years, but a vacancy might occur and pressure might be brought to get her onto the council again. Her speech has left the door open for friendliness and co-operation. Her son's behaviour did not. His resignation was furious and abrupt, and left us in no doubt as to his feelings. But the humiliation of the whole business must have been unendurable and was intended to be so. It was intended that the Millwoods should be so much surprised and provoked that they would commit themselves in some way. No strategy could, I think, have saved them. But Lady Frances was saved by her great natural *goodness*, which impelled her to do the right thing.

I think it will be a comfort to you to know this, for much that I have written will distress you. And it is a comfort to me to write to you, for there are not many who feel about it quite as I do. You would be surprised how little most people seem to care. There is indignation on behalf of Lady Frances, but no sense of shame at the unworthiness of the whole transaction, no real grasp of the implications.

Thank you for writing to me, my dear Miss Carmichael. My wife joins me in sending you our kindest regards.

Owen Rees to Lucy.

> 275 Dawson Avenue,
> New Ravonsbridge,
> Severnshire.
> Nov. 17.

I hope you are well and have got a good job. This night last year we opened in *Hamlet*, which is why I am writing, though it seems longer, doesn't it?

Lucy, there have been some big changes at the Institute, as I expect you have heard. Personally I could not care less; you know what I said about it, especially after last summer. But I was surprised when I heard about the elections and I do not see how the new lot is an improvement. Why can't they elect some people who know something about art etc? I do not see why Harris should be on—he is in cahoots with Adamson and helped him snitch the Drill Hall. Might as well have put on Adamson himself, everyone knows anything Harris does Adamson is behind it. And if they had to have some one from the M.M. there is plenty who know more about art than Hugh Davis.

And I was really sorry about Lady Millwood. I think she had a right to be on. Lucy, I keep remembering her at the Xmas party; I suppose she will not be hostess any more. It is rather pathetic. But:

> What's Hecuba to him or he to Hecuba
> That he should weep for her?

Do you remember I made you cry on that line? And you were shocked when I said I was not too sure who Hecuba was—I thought she was the same as Dido. So we had quite an argument about acting.

Well Lucy send me a line if you have time. Or are you too busy telling the fellows off? I shall not forget the Café Bar in a hurry. You should have seen yourself—if looks could kill! Which reminds me—what did you mean *compare notes?* Did *somebody else* get what for beside me?

It is 7 p.m. Curtain up a year ago. You were in the wings and you gave me a scarab for luck. I have got it still. I shall never forget that night. It was great.

Melissa to Hump.

Drumby. Dec. 18.

This is a Christmas letter, unilateral as usual, for I don't expect to hear from you. I have some good/bad news. I shan't be able to go to Paris in January so shan't see you before you sail. John is making a most unheard of fuss about my going all alone and has got the cretinous old doctor here to back him up and threatens an appeal to Mother if I rebel! And I've got to cancel that gymkhana, so I really have nothing to look forward to and I'm perfectly miserable. Hump, how do you come to know so much about "girls"? There's something not right about it, in an ostensible bachelor. But I try to believe that it's just *me* you understand. That gymkhana idea was pure magic. Instantaneous!

We are very busy with the club pantomime. No racing news. Lucy just larks about with Cobb and Brett and rides with Quinn so often that people are beginning to talk, which I regret. She is a little moody and unsettled. She has had letters from Ravonsbridge which have upset her, though, as far as I can gather, they only prove how right she was. The Institute seems to have collapsed and she was very wise to get out in time.

303

Oh Hump I am so very happy and so very wretched that I shan't see you. Can't you, *can't* you, come?

Charles to Lucy.

Cyre Abbey,
Severnshire. Dec. 24.

My Dear Lucy,

I want to tell you that the Christmas card you sent to us has given enormous pleasure to my mother. It always makes her happy to hear from people who have worked for the Institute. And this was an inspired choice of yours; she does not care much for pictures generally, but that *Simone Martine* is a great favourite with her. It is a lovely thing; the best they have in the Uffizi, don't you think?

I know she will be writing to you herself, but it has occurred to me that you must be longing for news of her and unable to get it. I remember, with some remorse, your great affection for her and feel that I ought to have written before to tell you how she got through the shock that we have all had, for the news of it must have distressed you.

Other people will doubtless have written to tell you of what happened at the general meeting. Of course we all realised at once, when we arrived at the hall, that something of the sort was going to happen. But we never expected that my mother herself would not be re-elected. She tells me that she was in great doubt and dismay, when the voting was going on; she foresaw that her old colleagues would go and that she would have in future to work with a set of people whom she did not know or did not like. She could not be certain of her duty in the matter, or what my father would have wished her to do. So that the final blow came really as a relief. She realised that the choice was out of her hands.

She made a little speech before leaving the hall. I was sorry that she did; I was afraid that her motive would be misunderstood and that these people would think she was trying to conciliate them. But she is quite sure that my father would have wished it.

We got her home and I was very anxious about her. I thought she stumbled a little as we went down to the car. To tell you the truth I was afraid of a stroke. But she recovered in a wonderful way. She went to bed as soon as we got home, and when I went up later to see her she was very cheerful, sitting up in bed drinking egg nog out of a little silver cup which my father always used, and reading the Bible.

Since then she has hardly ever referred to the Institute, though she insisted upon going with my sister to the Nativity play and to the Christmas party, which I thought unnecessary. Penelope tells me that none of our old friends were there, but that she and my mother were very cordially received by several members of the new council.

The thing which has most distressed her was a visit we had from Haverstock, just before the end of the term. He came to ask for her intervention in some trouble he has had with the council and could not seem able to grasp the idea that she has now no power to intervene.

But I think she is enjoying herself very much this Christmas, for all my married sisters have come with their families. It is years since we have had the house so full, and her seven grandchildren are a great joy to her.

My dear Lucy, I don't know where you are or what you are doing. I'm sending this to the Institute office which must have a forwarding address. But, wherever you are, I hope you are very happy. It was like you to send that card.

Yours affectionately,
C.M.

Rickie to Lucy.

278 Kings Road,
Richmond, Surrey.
Dec. 26.

Thank you for your Xmas card. I'm afraid I didn't send any this year. As a matter of fact I wasn't in the mood.

I am staying with my Aunt.

I am getting fed up with the Institute. I would leave if I could hear of anything else. Do you know of anything? I have written to the B.B.C.

It's this new council. Hayter says he can't do anything with them. I can't get anybody to back me up. Pidgeon is resigning. I went and saw Lady Frances. She says she has nothing to do with the Institute now, which is rot, the founder's wife must have some say, I should think. Most of the people in our orchestra have always been amateurs. They played because they thought it was rather jolly to be in an orchestra. We only paid the leaders and the soloists. The whole idea was that people played because they liked playing. If everybody has got in future to be paid at Union rates, look at the cost of rehearsals! I don't get the idea that all voluntary work is wrong because some people can't afford to play for nothing. The Institute was meant for amateurs.

I ran into Ma Meeker in the quad and tried to make her see. She said only rich people can afford these expensive hobbies, playing in orchestras. But that's rot. Our orchestra isn't rich. My 2nd fiddle is a railway porter. People grow roses and play darts in their spare time, nobody thinks they ought to be paid for that. Why shouldn't they play in orchestras? But she says every voluntary worker takes a career out of the mouth of somebody who needs a job. Well, there aren't enough professional musicians here for that to apply to. She says it is the principle.

Anyway I'm absolutely fed up and that's why I didn't make the effort to send any Xmas cards.

Hump to Melissa.

Paris. Dec. 26.

I've been so busy I forgot it was Christmas till I got your good/bad news. Dare I say how tremendously pleased I am? Or are you now occupied with a new set of gloomy forebodings? What's wrong with happiness, and why are you so much afraid of it?

You are the only girl in my life, more or less, and I'd come and scold you into placidity if I wasn't afraid of losing this African job. But I smell a plot to squeeze me out of it, which I mean to foil if I can.

I'm so sorry about poor Lucy's Institute. No comfort at all to her to have been in the right. I found a piece in Wordy William which sums it up; like your Miss Bates he always "says everything."

> By superior energy, by more strict
> Affiance in each other, firmer faith
> In their unhallowed principles, the Bad
> Have fairly earned a victory o'er the weak,
> The vacillating, inconsistent Good.

2

"IF IT wasn't for you, my dotey dear," said Melissa crossly to Collins, "I should be inside my nice warm house by my nice warm fire reading a nice warm book."

Collins gave her a glance of reproach as he plodded beside her along the bleak high road. He did not seem to like a north eastern gale in his face any better than she did. The iron frost, which had held Drumby for a week, had depressed both of them quite enough. They had believed themselves to be cold until this wind arrived to teach them the true meaning of the word.

"I believe it's all a myth that you like exercise," grumbled Melissa. "But you're a man and men are slaves to myths. You bark and jump about when I get your lead, because they told you at school that all Regular Dogs like walkies, and you've firmly believed it ever since, mutt that you are. How can this be advisable for man or beast?"

She said no more because the wind gave her toothache. She regretted the cowardice which had prompted her to choose the south west road out of the town, where she had the wind behind her and could put off the horror of facing it until the second half of the walk. But she had hoped to get a lift on the way back from Lucy who had, she knew, gone in that direction to collect some eggs. They were to spend the afternoon in the club, as soon as Collins had had his walk, preparing it for the New Year's Eve party.

The air was full of noise, the scream of the wind and a deep drumming, as though the waves which thundered on the waste beaches, ten miles away, were audible over the fens. Sometimes she turned and walked backwards so as to get her breath and to wipe away the tears which froze on her lashes. But Collins had not the sense to do this; she tried to think of a dog walking backwards and could not remember ever having seen one. There was not even a hedge to protect them, for the road ran slightly raised through the fenny fields.

Presently, on one of her retrogressive interludes, she saw hope arriving. The cripple car was bucketing along with surprising agility for anything so decrepit. It drew up with a scream of its ancient brakes and Lucy put her head out. The wind blew all her curls straight backwards, making her face look very narrow, and her voice was inaudible. Melissa tottered with Collins to the rear door.

"I said you'll have to come in in front," screamed Lucy. "The back is full."

There was scarcely room in front for Lucy, Melissa, Collins and the gears, but the car was agreeably stuffy. It smelt of petrol and kippers.

"Oh, heaven! Oh, bliss!" gasped Melissa, as they bucketed off again. "What is all that in the back?"

"Eggs, beer, kippers and a barrel of smoked oysters."

"Smoked oysters? What fun! But aren't they fearfully expensive?"

"They're a present to me really. But I can't eat a barrel of smoked oysters all by myself. I thought I'd brighten the club supper with them."

"Who gave them to you?"

"Larry. And he gave me a bottle of rum too. I shall hang on to that. We might stop off at your house on our way through the town and have some; it would warm us up before getting to work at the club."

"Rum? Oysters? Lucy, are you sure he means to do right by you?"

"I'm sure not."

"A nice girl wouldn't accept."

"Not pearls or a cabochon emerald. But oysters . . . think of seagulls, Melissa. They always offer shellfish to their flames when they go courting."

"Seagulls are nicer than Captain Quinn."

Melissa was becoming seriously perturbed by Captain Quinn. Drumby was talking. Nobody supposed that he meant to marry Lucy, yet they were constantly together and Melissa suspected him of the kind of vanity which likes to vaunt a conquest. As long as Drumby believed that he had prevailed, he would probably be quite content, though Lucy took his oysters and kept him at arm's length. Such an impression would inevitably damage the club, which would lose its *cachet* if run by a rackety girl who might or might not be Quinn's mistress.

On their way through the town they drew up at 17 High Street, fought their way into Melissa's house, and made themselves rum cocktails.

Lucy is getting rather hard, thought Melissa. I suppose she is really very lonely. Why isn't she married, when she is so beautiful?

Lucy's beauty had stood up to the inclement day better than her own had. She alone in Drumby had escaped a red nose. She sat on the hearthrug, sipping her rum, with the firelight on her bright, wild hair.

"I really bar Quinn," insisted Melissa.

"You're drinking his rum."

"There are plenty of nice men in Drumby. Why pick up with a garrison Lothario from Breenho?"

"Because he doesn't fall off his horse."

"I believe you're still moping over Ravonsbridge. I can't understand it. You weren't so very happy there."

"One gets ties with a place one has been unhappy in."

"It's time you got ties here."

"What sort of ties?" asked Lucy dangerously. "You're cross with me, I believe, because Birkett came to nothing. He was quite struck with me. 'Some of those little attentions and encouragements, which ladies can so easily give,' would have fixed him."

Melissa laughed, mollified by the quotation.

"Well, I did my best," protested Lucy. "I plastered his bottom

309

when he fell off his silly horse, after which he seemed to take against me. You weren't so anxious for me to fix people at Oxford."

"Ah, but we're both older."

That was the trouble. They were older and the current of time had carried them in diverging ways. The Lucy-Melissa partnership had broken up and, though still exceedingly fond of one another, they were aware of it. As girls they had exerted an important mutual influence and each might have turned out a little differently had they never met. Melissa had gathered courage from Lucy's gay vitality. Lucy had learnt to discriminate as well as to enjoy. Now, for the moment, they could do no more for one another, though it was possible that at some later stage in their lives they might again be able to pool experience. Each had traversed her own range of emotional territory during the past two years. Lucy had been obliged to rely on herself while Melissa had learnt to rely on John. Lucy was less confident than she had been, Melissa more so. The last wish of Melissa's heart had been granted; she was with child and perfectly happy. But Lucy's heart was unoccupied, since the sorrowful ghost of Patrick had ceased to haunt it. Friends lodged there and enjoyed its generous hospitality, but no one called it home.

They sat in silence, each musing on this suspension of their intimacy and its causes, until Lucy said, in a gentler voice:

"But what ties do you mean then?"

"Oh, Lucy, friends. You made friends in Ravonsbridge. Why not here? Everybody likes you, but you don't seem to care for anyone as you did for the people in Ravonsbridge."

Friends are not made on purpose, thought Lucy, nor is affection mixed like a rum cocktail.

"Give me time," she said with a sigh. "Perhaps there will come to be people here I care for as I did for Lady Frances and Owen and Rickie."

"Owen and Rickie! I never supposed you gave two thoughts to Owen and Rickie!"

"Nor did I, till I got letters from them and realised what idiots they are and how nice. But I'm happier about Lady Frances since Charles wrote. She had all her grandchildren for Christmas."

310

Melissa sat up. *Charles wrote?* This was the first she had heard of it. She had given up all hope of Charles.

"I didn't know he'd written," she murmured.

"Oh, yes. I sent them a Christmas card which turns out to be more classy than I knew. I picked it out as the prettiest in the tray, but it's a *Simone Martine*, my dear, and the best thing they've got in the Uffizi."

"Oh, the Annunciation?"

"Yes, it was an Annunciation. How cultured you all are! I thought the Botticellis were in the Uffizi. Surely they're better?"

"So he wrote to thank for the card?"

Lucy pushed the hair out of her eyes and looked suspiciously at Melissa. Then she grinned.

"Yes, my dotey dear, he wrote to thank for the card. Now we must get along to the club or we'll never be ready."

She jumped up and ran out into the wind, laughing at Melissa's look of horror. For Melissa had believed that her sentimental maunderings to Collins were never overheard.

"The wind is dropping," said Melissa, as she climbed into the cripple car again. "John says if it drops there'll be a thaw."

"Oh, plague, I hope not," said Lucy. "We're going to take the train to Brattle tomorrow and skate the whole way back to Drumby on the canal, with the wind behind us."

"Who is we?"

"Me and Cobb and Brett."

"Not Quinn, I hope?"

"Oh, heavens, no. He's not to be told anything about it. He'd be a terrible bore on an expedition like that. 'Och! just let you catch hould of me hand, acushla! It's after getting toired ye'll be.' "

"Oh, Lucy! How can you like him?"

"I don't like him. I've said so."

They parked in front of the club. Lucy unlocked the door, which she left ajar for Cobb and Brett, who were arriving later with more drinks. Having carried in the kippers, eggs, beer and oysters, they went to the upper floor to finish the decorations. Lucy had painted beech branches white and stuck on cellophane leaves. Melissa exclaimed in admiration.

"Do you really think they're nice?" asked Lucy. "I want the

room to look like a glass forest; it costs nothing and looks festive, but I was afraid you'd think it rather Woolworth."

"I think it's most effective."

"If you'll finish putting them up, I'll put the pantomime props away."

Lucy picked up the property horse and the fairy queen's wings and took them down to the lower floor. Melissa, working with the branches, could hear her moving from the kitchen to the buffet, as she prepared for the evening's supper. Outside the window there were shouts from children sliding on the canal. The wind was undoubtedly dropping.

Presently footsteps came along Canal Lane. There was a knock at the door, and Lucy called from the kitchen:

"Come in!"

They came in, a little uncertainly. Cobb or Brett? thought Melissa. Then she heard Lucy come out of the kitchen, and a gasping cry:

"Charles!"

Charles? thought Melissa. What Charles? Can it . . . it can't be!

"Oh, I am so glad to see you!"

What a thing to say to a man, reflected Melissa crossly. Lucy will never get married unless she can manage to learn a little duplicity.

She made a move to go downstairs but was checked by Lucy's muffled voice:

"Hi . . . no . . . Charles . . . please . . . I only meant I was very glad to see you. . . . How is your mother?"

Melissa, trapped in the upper room and unable to help hearing every word, began to walk about the floor very heavily. She commended Charles for explaining himself in a mutter which was far more difficult to catch than Lucy's bell-like exclamations. But they did not seem to notice her footsteps and presently Lucy was audible again, more clearly than ever, as if disentangled from the muffling obstacle.

"But I've nothing to forgive!"

Mutter, mutter, mutter.

This is impossible, thought Melissa, and went across to the radio.

"But it's odious of me to have been in the right," wailed Lucy, "and very generous and noble of you not to mind it."

Melissa switched on the radio to its loudest volume. A stentorian voice boomed through the club:

". . . MANY MANY MILLIONS OF YEARRRS AGO. AS THE GAHSES CONDENSED AND THE SAIRRRFACE OF THE AIRRRTH HARRRDENED . . ."

This really did startle the couple below. The muttering ceased. Lucy's excited face appeared up the well of the ladder stairs and Melissa switched off the radio.

"Charles Millwood is here!" announced Lucy.

"How nice!" commented Melissa. "Is he staying long?"

"I don't know," said Lucy and called down the stairs to ask Charles if he was staying long.

Charles, below, was heard to say that he did not know either.

Melissa suggested that Lucy should take him to Canal Cottages for tea. She could herself, she declared, finish the preparations for the party, especially if Cobb and Brett were coming to help her. And she went down to shake hands with the blushing Charles who had now realised how much she must have overheard. Very sweetly she reminded him that they had met once in Severnton and she found his hat for him, which had rolled under the buffet table, probably when Lucy hurled herself into his arms.

"When Cobb and Brett come," said Lucy, "make them get the clinkers out of the stoves and fill up all the anthracite buckets. The eggs must be boiled hard and all the anchovy stuffing is on a plate in the pantry."

She went off with Charles. Melissa began to lay the buffet table, distracted by a variety of emotions. On the whole, relief predominated. She need not have tormented herself over Lucy's future. It was apparently settled. And how nobly settled! Cyre Abbey and the Marsden-Millwood millions! Drumby had nothing to offer which could compare with that. This obsession with Ravonsbridge had turned out well; Lucy could go back there in triumph, and how she would boss them all about, to be sure, as soon as she had got used to being rich!

But there was another voice in Melissa's heart which refused to be silent, though she tried not to listen to it. She did not really like Charles Millwood, though she had toyed with the idea of this marriage for two years, ever since his name appeared in Lucy's letters. She had wanted the triumph and security of it for her friend, if only he had been a different young man. But, if Lucy loved him, she told herself, that did not signify, and there was no reason for supposing that Lucy did not love him. She would not marry him unless she did.

But not as I love John, whispered that uncompromising voice, and not as she could love, if she met the right man. She's lonely and she doesn't know what to do with her life, and I daresay she's fond of him, and he is very much in love with her. And isn't that better than knocking about with Quinn? But not as good as she ought to have. She ought to love him as I love John. She will never know . . . never know . . . what happiness, what bliss . . .

Brisk steps rang on the road outside and the odious Quinn himself appeared in the open doorway. He saluted Melissa gallantly and she gave him an icy smile.

To ask one pretty girl where another might be was not good technique. He adopted a roundabout method:

"All alone? Couldn't I help ye now?"

"Yes," said Melissa, "you could."

He advanced, ready to have some fun over laying the buffet table, but she explained that he must rake the clinkers out of the stoves and fill the anthracite buckets. A little crestfallen he complied, while she thought of several more things which he might do, all of them arduous and unpleasant. She kept him very hard at work for more than an hour, allowing him to suppose that Lucy might be arriving at any moment, and evading his questions about tomorrow's skating party. He seemed to have got wind of the scheme and to be nettled at being left out of it. Melissa hoped that tomorrow might see him entirely off the course.

Lucy and Charles sat over the fire, in her small sitting room, and tried simultaneously to explain themselves. Charles wanted to tell her why he had come and she kept interrupting to beg that her ardent greeting might not be misunderstood. She had been very pleased to see him. She was very fond of him. She had been so much delighted to see somebody from Ravonsbridge that her feelings had run away with her. But he must not suppose that she had changed her mind. She was not going to marry him.

"I haven't asked you yet," said Charles at last.

"No. But you're going to."

"Er . . . yes. But I want to explain what led up to it."

"Charles, dear, that won't make any difference."

"It might. And in any case you'll be very pleased, I think, with some of my news. I got your address from Owen Rees."

"Did you? Oh, Charles! Have you been comparing notes?"

"Yes. We have. We've had a long talk. After which I decided to come here. Do you mind if I go back a bit?"

"No. Have some blackberry jelly."

Charles explained that he had taken a long time to forgive her for being right. The sudden news of her departure had shaken him, and he had rushed off to the station that morning on an impulse, not knowing what he meant to say when he got there, but meditating some kind of apology. The intrusion of Owen, however, had made him angry and he had gone home, vowing to put her out of his mind.

"So you should," said Lucy. "Though I'd rather you didn't forget me in anger. But we're not—"

"I've talked it all over with my mother. . . ."

"Oh? She knows you've come?"

"Yes. I've told her everything. She sends you her love. She hopes I'm going to bring you back with me."

He broke off to look at Lucy's eyes, which were so beautiful when she was thinking of anyone whom she loved.

"Oh, Charles, now you're here you can tell me; was it Ephesians IV she was reading in bed, that night after the meeting? I did so want to know."

"I really couldn't say," said Charles in some surprise. "I think it was an Epistle. Why?"

"I'm sure it was. They had it at the opening ceremony you know, and at your father's funeral. I think it entirely explains everything . . . why she made that speech."

Lucy jumped up and snatched a Bible from her bookshelf.

She found the passage, while Charles stared at her as though she were a spring in the desert.

"That we henceforth be no more children," she read, "tossed to and fro, and carried about with every wind of doctrine, by the sleight of men, and cunning craftiness, whereby they lie in wait to deceive: But speaking the truth in love, may grow up into him in all things, which is the head, even Christ."

She looked up to see if he understood and met an adoring but uncomprehending gaze.

"It's the only thing to do against cunning craftiness," she said. "Speaking the truth in love. But did she say anything more to you about it, when you went up to see her that night?"

"She did a little. She talked about it very calmly and judicially. She said she was beginning to see that she had been to blame and had made great mistakes, but that she meant not to try to think it all over until the first shock had worn off. She quoted some Canon or other who prepared her for Confirmation, to the effect that self blame can be as egotistical as self praise. She said that any work worth doing is greater than we are, and that we must not overrate our importance to it, either for good or ill."

"That's true," said Lucy. "And we are sure to praise or blame ourselves for the wrong things, anyway. Mr. Mildmay says your mother's last speech was the best thing she has ever done for Ravonsbridge. But I'm sure she doesn't know that. She probably thinks she looked after the soap and towels in the cloakrooms very well. What else did she say?"

"I can't remember. Oh, yes . . . she said that if we are doing God's work badly it is taken away from us, which I thought very pathetic. She quite clearly believes that the Institute is God's work and that He takes a personal interest in it. Her religion is a great support to her, of course, but it's completely childish. She has exactly the same ideas, I imagine, that she had when she was confirmed at fifteen. I refrained from saying that it was rather odd of the Almighty to hand His work over to Hayter."

"Oh, but He didn't," said Lucy. "I don't know about God's work. But the Institute could have been a . . . a vehicle for that impulse there is in people to get together and work for a better life. It failed to be, so Hayter has got it. But the impulse is still

316

there, it's always there, and it will break out in some other form . . ."

She stopped, realising that he was not attending to her.

"But what about Owen?" she asked.

Owen Rees had turned up at Cyre Abbey on Boxing Day, demanding to see Charles, in a very mysterious and conspiratorial manner. It was impossible, apparently, that he could ever be seen speaking to a Millwood at the Works. He was in a state of furious indignation, for he had approached the Institute in the hope of getting the theatre for his operetta and had been quoted terms which were far beyond anything which his little company could afford.

"I told him," said Charles, "that I couldn't intervene. If he's dissatisfied with the council he must go with his friends to vote them off at the next general meeting."

"He'll never get that into his head," said Lucy. "Of course he ought to be on the council himself. But he thinks everything should be looked after for him by some people he calls 'them.' "

"I think he's waking up to it a little," said Charles. "He told me what you'd said, and how right you were. And then . . . well then we began to compare notes."

"Oh, Charles! You told him about me and the toffees?"

"What toffees?"

"I spilt toffees all over your carpet."

"Did you? I'd forgotten."

"Thank goodness! I never shall. What did you tell him then?"

"What you'd said and how right you were. After which we became much more friendly—more at our ease. In fact I've never been able to talk so freely to anybody of . . . anybody like Rees, before. We owed it to you that we could, I think."

"You mean you began to like each other?"

"Why, yes, I suppose it was that, in a way. He has the darkest suspicions of some of the council—so dark I'd think he was exaggerating if I didn't remember what has happened already. He thinks they mean to turn the Institute simply into a money making affair. There is already talk of hiring out the buildings for all sorts of rallies and conferences. The art school has been closed. I daresay the music and drama schools will go too. They'll never do

317

more than cover their own expenses. It's the buildings which would bring in money, if ably exploited. And then Rees thinks they mean to get up a citizens' petition to change the Constitution by Act of Parliament and divert this money to purposes outside the Institute. Of course, the line would be to use it for all sorts of amenities in the town, but the greater part of it would go into private pockets."

"But everybody who wants to oppose that idea must get together now!" exclaimed Lucy.

"That's what we think," said Charles, "and what we mean to try to do. It's not easy for us to work together, situated as we are. But we're going to keep in touch with one another and do our best. The first step we took was to consult another crony of yours —old Mr. Meeker. I said I'd like to talk it over with him sometime, and Rees, who is a headlong fellow, insisted on doing it at once. So I drove over to Ravonsbridge and called on the old man and invited him out for a drive. I took him to Cyre Abbey where he and Rees and I had a long discussion."

Lucy bounced on her chair with delight, and then sighed to think of the time wasted. If only these three had got together two years ago so much more might have been saved.

"Meeker's advice," continued Charles, "wasn't very palatable to either of us. He said we ought to do our best to support his daughter-in-law, who is on the council now, you know. He says she's an awful fool but an honest woman and that these sharks will use her, hoodwink her, and throw her out when it suits them. He also says that Mrs. Strong is a very decent sort of woman, and Finch quite harmless. The sharks are Hayter, Spedding and Harris. Carruthers is a nonentity out for an O.B.E. Wright they believe to be a Communist. About Davis they were cautious; I'm his employer and I suppose they didn't want to commit themselves. Meeker says we must mobilise public opinion in support of the more honest members of the council, or we shall see them thrown out and replaced by sharks. Rees thought that fearfully tame; he's all for cloak and sword drama. And I must say that close co-operation with Mrs. Meeker doesn't much appeal to me. But my mother has paved the way. She went, you know, to the Christmas party,

318

and she said that Mrs. Meeker really did seem to be making efforts to be civil and that Mrs. Strong was very nice indeed."

"Mr. Mildmay," said Lucy, "hoped they'd get your mother back quite soon. Well, go on. This is thrilling."

"Why then Owen asked if we couldn't get you back. He says you are quite a heroine. Apparently there is some legend you were victimised."

"But how could I come back? They'd never appoint me to the drama school again. Hayter would see to that."

"I pointed that out. And Rees stared at me and asked if I hadn't come to the station to persuade you to stay, that day you went away. So I said I'd thought of getting into the train and going with you to Gloucester. And he said: Man! Why didn't you?"

"Yes," said Lucy. "Why didn't you?"

"I don't know."

She sighed impatiently.

"I think," he said, "that both Meeker and Rees guess how I feel about you. After they'd gone I thought it all over and decided to come to you. I thought perhaps you might feel differently if you knew I was determined to get this business put right. Because I am determined, whatever answer you give me. I'm not going to let those crooks get hold of a property that my father intended for people like Rees. I'll do my best but I'd have much more chance of success with you to help me. You make friends so easily. I don't. Personally my idea is to buy off Hayter; I don't know how much he expects to get out of it all, but, if some more promising opening turned up elsewhere, I shouldn't think he'd stay in Ravonsbridge, and I believe they'd fall to pieces without him."

"Oh, but that's cunning craftiness."

"I know; it wouldn't build up the kind of confidence and friendliness we'd need before we can get a decent council. I feel we need you for that. I haven't told my mother about all these plans. But I have told her that I love you and want to marry you and she is very much pleased. So . . . so I've come to ask you if you won't come back . . . and pull us all together . . . and make me so happy that I hardly dare to think of it?"

Lucy sat staring at him in agonised perplexity. His appeal moved her and she was delighted at the turn of events in Ravonsbridge. But she had been aware, more than once during their talk, of a want of sympathy between them. And his failure to jump into that train annoyed her. He would always be like that—never be able to get into or out of trains save in the most conventional manner.

"You are . . . you do love me a little," he said.

"Yes, I do, Charles. But I don't know if it's enough."

"Then don't turn me down now. Think it over. I can see you're hesitating. . . ."

She was hesitating. To send him away in the cold, disappointed and pledged to a task which she herself had urged upon him, seemed very cruel. With one word she could make him so happy and nobody else wanted happiness from her. She asked where he was staying, and he told her that he had got a room at the Lion, the best of the bad Drumby hotels.

"I'll try to think it over tonight," she said, "and let you know tomorrow. But I've a feeling that . . . that a marriage one has to think over is probaby a mistake."

"Oh, no. Most people don't think nearly enough."

"I didn't have to think twice . . . before."

"But that ended rather sadly, didn't it?"

"Ye-es. And perhaps one doesn't care like that a second time. I don't know . . . I must try to think."

"This evening, could you dine with me at the Lion?"

"Oh, I'm afraid I couldn't possibly. I've got this party at the club. I ought to be back there now. But you'll come, won't you? It's a masked ball. Everybody is to come disguised, and take off their masks at midnight."

"I have no disguise, I'd better not."

"Oh, borrow a sheet from the Lion and come as a ghost or something. You can't sit all by yourself there on New Year's Eve."

Charles said that he would rather do that than dress up in a sheet, and, when she pressed him, he became annoyed with her. He had forgotten how little sense of dignity she had. During the long cold journey to Drumby he had often wondered how he should spend the evening—had seen himself in bliss or in despair or still racked by suspense. But he had never expected to be told to dress up in a sheet and cut capers with a lot of chemists.

Did he, *did he*, really want to marry Lucy? She had put on her coat and fur lined boots and was preparing to go back to the club. But before she could open the street door he caught her to him and kissed her angrily.

"I believe you rather hate me," she murmured.

"I'm not sure that I don't. But I can't live without you."

"Oh, dear . . . well . . . I don't know. I don't believe we suit . . . I still don't . . . but I hate to see you so wretched. . . ."

She pushed him away and ran back to the club, stirred by his kisses but still exclaiming under her breath that they did not suit.

3

THE GLASS forest glittered very prettily, with lights among its branches, and by ten o'clock the upper floor of the club was crowded with masked dancers. The only member to refuse disguise was the sombre McIntyre, who changed the dance records.

The women took the occasion more seriously than the men, who had mostly dressed up under protest and refused to disguise their voices. A few who had, or believed that they had, some gift for mimicry, observed this rule and were applauded by the wives who, to a woman, squeaked and growled until identities were established or their throats grew sore.

Most of the revellers, remembering how dreary last New Year's Eve had been, thought it a good party and were pleased with the club which they had all laboured to secure. But Mrs. Farraday, the newest bride, who intended to cut out Mrs. Beauclerc as the social leader of Drumby, thought it all too dim for words and would have organised a counter-attraction had she dared. But Melissa was too popular and there was no getting Larry Quinn away from La Carmichael; nothing could be done until she was reinforced by other newcomers who might also disparage the club because they had not known what Drumby could be like without it.

"I wanna skate and I'm gonna skate," said a cowboy to the

Venetian lady with whom he danced, "and I'm gonna skate with you, baby. Will ye be starting from Brattle now?"

"Since you aren't coming it doesn't matter where we start."

"Ah, but I'm coming. Who's the boyo in the blue coat?"

"How should I know?"

"Ye've been peering at um ever since he came."

"Who brought him?"

"Mrs. Fothergill. She's dancing with him now."

"Is that Mrs. Fothergill?"

"Sure it is. Didn't you know she was coming as Nell Gwyn? Will ye stop turning to look at the man!"

The tune changed to a lively gallop and all couples spun apart for a Paul Jones. The Venetian subsided into the arms of a cardinal.

"I see you've brought Charles," she said. "Where did he get those clothes?"

"They're some Melissa has for a Regency charade she's getting up. They fit very well, don't they?"

"They're magnificent. But what happened? Did you go to the Lion and persuade him to come?"

"I went round and asked him to dine with us and we persuaded him to come, during dinner."

"Oh, John, how very nice of you. I tried to get him to come but he was stuck about it. Why is Melissa Nell Gwyn? I thought she'd got a Spanish dress."

"She changed with Mrs. Fothergill for fun. So many people knew what they were going to wear. They're alike in height and build."

"I know one person who's been deceived already. But, John . . . do you . . . do you like Charles?"

"What? Oh . . . er . . . yes!"

"What did you talk about at dinner?"

"You."

"Oh!"

"He, he, he!" tittered the Pierrette to the Regency Buck. "I think you're marvellous. How do you do it?"

"Do what?"

"Put on that marvellous voice."

"I'm not putting on any voice."

"He, he, he! I know who you are all the same."

"Who am I?"

"Mike. You're not sore because I danced with Larry?"

"Oh, no."

"But you see I really think it's tough on Larry. La Carmichael is a bit of a bitch, I do think."

"I beg your pardon?"

"He, he, he! Ay baig your pahdon! Why ever did you say you couldn't act? Well, you know how she's led him on and led him on and taken all she could get out of him, and now it seems he's out on his ear. She promised to go out with him tomorrow and now she's going skating with Cobb and Brett. He's livid. So I'm going to get Denis to give Cobb and Brett a special task up at the Hall tomorrow so they won't be able to go. And Larry's going up to Brattle instead, and that'll teach La Carmichael a lesson."

"Very kind of you."

"I don't mind doing poor Larry a good turn, though I think he's crackers, mind you, to want to go skating with her."

"Which is he?"

"Haven't you spotted him? The cowboy, dancing with Mrs. Fothergill in that Nell Gwyn affair."

"I thought that was Mrs. Beauclerc."

"Oh, no. La Beauclerc has gone all Spanish."

"You needn't keep up that mutter for I know who ye are," said the cowboy to Nell Gwyn. "You're Mrs. Fothergill. Who's the man in the blue coat you're after dancing with?"

"You'll know at midnight."

"Ah, you're very crushing. Will I hide in a coke buckut and feed meeself to the flames? Would that melt ye?"

"Not at all. The stove is too hot already."

"And who saw to that? Who raked out the cinders this afternoon? Who brought up the coke? Meself. You'd have no party at all, at all, if it wasn't for Melissa and me. Didn't we spend the day entoirely getting it all ready?"

"Melissa?"

"Och, yes. Just the two of us. Just Melissa and meeself."

"I didn't know you called her Melissa."

"Ah, sure I do. She's not half as stand offish as you might think, when ye get to know her. Ah, bad luck to ut! Here's Paul Jones again."

"If Paul Jones hadn't struck up that minute," cried Nell Gwyn, collapsing into the arms of her cardinal, "there would have been one cowboy less in this club. He's unspeakable! How could we ever let such an object into the club? How can Lucy endure him for a moment?"

"I daresay he's at his best on a horse."

"Where's . . . oh, good! He's dancing with her at last. Now do tell me what you think of him. I haven't had a chance to ask."

"Do you really want to know?"

"I'm longing to know."

The cardinal put his mouth close to her little ear and whispered:

"A solemn ass."

"Oh, no!"

"Well, that's the impression he made on me."

"He's a bit pompous, certainly. But think of the agitating position he's in!"

"But what is the position? Are they engaged or not?"

"I think not, though when I sent them off to tea this afternoon I thought it was as good as settled. But he wouldn't be staying on if she'd refused him, so I suppose it's all in the balance. I think he's very nice."

"No, you don't. You always used to call him the—"

"Ssh! If Lucy marries him we'll forget about that."

"You want her to marry him?"

"Ye-es. Yes, I do."

"Why?"

"I think it would work very well. He's an introvert and she's an extrovert, and that's supposed to be a good mixture."

"Nonsense! Lucy isn't an extrovert."

"John! She's the complete extrovert. Always organising."

"I don't think it's her nature. She has a strong effect on people, but that is because they affect her. I don't think she'll be happy unless she marries a man who dominates her."

"Who could? Barnum?"

"Mike!" said the Pierrette to a buccaneer. "But you can't be! Oh, my God!"

"Why all this alarm and dismay!"

"Then who on earth . . . where . . . oh, my God! He's dancing with La Carmichael. Oh, this would happen to me!"

"But what's happened? I don't get this."

"See that man in the blue coat? I thought he was you. And I told him . . . Oh, my God!"

"Lucy, who is Larry?"

"A Captain Quinn. He comes from the Breenho camp."

"Nice man?"

"No. I say Charles, did you have a nice dinner? Did you have a nice time with Melissa and John? Do you like them?"

"Oh, I do, very much. Lucy! Have you done any thinking yet?"

"No, Charles, I haven't. I can't, till this party is over and I get home."

"I wish I knew just what all this thinking amounts to."

"I wish I did. There is something I know I ought to see clearly and I don't. I must think more about your mother."

"I sometimes wish I was an orphan. It's always either my mother or my father . . . what have they to do with your feeling for me?"

"It was so very nice of you, really generous of you, to write to me about her."

"This dance seems to be over. You'll have the next one with me, won't you? I've hardly danced with you at all yet."

"Oh, yes, and we'll have a waltz. Mr. McIntyre! Put on a waltz this time."

Waltzing with Charles was glorious. Lucy had forgotten how well partnered they were and how intoxicating it could be. If marriage could but have been a prolonged waltz she would have accepted him on the spot. But surely I love him, surely I do, she thought as she drifted round the room in his arms. He excites me and I am fond of him, because he wrote me that letter. I used not to be fond of him, but now I feel a real affection for him, since he wrote me that letter. Passion is not enough unless one feels affection, but I am fond of him, though I see his faults.

People were looking at them curiously. It seemed that they could never waltz together without causing a stir. The news spread through the club that the man in the blue coat was a stranger and a friend of Lucy Carmichael's. The Pierrette was frequently obliged to call upon her Maker and demand why this sort of thing should happen to her.

"I think it's a case all right," whispered John to Melissa.

"Yes," said Melissa. "She's lost to the world. She ought to be downstairs making the punch."

But when the waltz was over Lucy came to her senses a little and ran off to the kitchen. Charles sought the sympathetic company of Melissa to whom he confided the strange business of Cobb, Brett, Brattle, Larry and the task at the Hall. He wanted to know what it all meant.

"It's that odious little Mrs. Farraday!" exclaimed Melissa angrily. "Larry is this Captain Quinn who is pursuing Lucy with no justification whatever. He evidently wants these boys kept at the Hall while he goes skating with her himself. I imagine they are bottle washers for Mr. Farraday, who could keep them at work tomorrow if he likes, though it's supposed to be a holiday. He's mere putty in the hands of that wife of his."

"Then Lucy had better be warned not to go."

"Why don't you go with her? John could lend you his skates."

Charles was silent.

"You do skate?" asked Melissa in surprise.

He did skate, but not well, and he disliked doing things badly. He reflected that even if Lucy accepted him she might still want to go skating, and his look became gloomy. Melissa feared that he might be jealous of Quinn. There was no knowing what gossip that horrid little woman had repeated.

"I want," said Charles suddenly, "to go back to Ravonsbridge tomorrow and take Lucy with me."

"Oh!" cried Melissa, "if only you could!"

"You think that?"

"I'm sure it's the only way to manage her—to be very decisive and determined."

"She could stay with my mother at Cyre Abbey till . . . we could be married in a week."

"Oh, yes, oh, yes. Get it over. Get it settled."

He had never mentioned before that he wished to marry Lucy but they both forgot that he had not.

"We could manage perfectly here without her," declared Melissa. "It was always understood that she could leave at any time, if a better job turned up. She has got us started; we could manage till we'd found somebody else."

This aspect of the matter did not trouble Charles. The Drumby club was nothing to him. He was engrossed in his perception that, if he was ever to marry Lucy, he must do it immediately; she might accept him, after that waltz he was almost sure that she would, and then change her mind because he would not go skating with her.

"It's a great thing that you're on my side," he declared.

"Oh, I am, I am," said Melissa. "With Lucy it's got to be like that. In a week or not at all. I'll do everything I can. Here she comes with the punch. I'll wish it for my New Year's wish. When the clock strikes twelve I'll wish that Lucy shall be married in a week."

She rose and went across to John by whom she wanted to stand when they greeted the new year. Lucy with an escort of helpers was handing round the glasses of punch. McIntyre had removed the dance records and turned on the radio. The Westminster bells rang out through the clamour and exclamations as everybody took off his mask. Not much surprise was felt, for most disguises had been thin, but Charles was scrutinised with considerable curiosity and Captain Quinn had a bad moment when he realised that Nell Gwyn was not Mrs. Fothergill.

Ding-dong, ding-dong! went the bells, as husbands and wives drew together and a circle was formed. Charles, abandoned, looked round for Lucy and saw her at the other side of the room between Cobb and Brett. Ding-dong, ding-dong . . . the bells faded and the voices sank and silence fell upon the club, as they waited for Big Ben.

John took Melissa's hand. They thought of what the new year would bring to them.

BOOM . . . BOOM. . . .

I wish that Lucy shall be married in a week, thought Melissa. I wish she shall be happy . . . happy . . . as happy as I am . . . in a week. . . .

BOOM . . . BOOM . . . BOOM . . . BOOM. . . .

All over England, people are listening, thought Lucy. Mother and Stephen at Gorling.

BOOM . . . BOOM . . . BOOM. . . .

A beastly cross-country journey, thought Charles. Much better hire a car from Fenswick and drive her down.

BOOM . . . BOOM. . . .

I ought to have wished she should be married to *him* in a week! But that's only a detail!

BOOM!

A chorus of "Happy New Years" broke out. Wives and husbands kissed and then a good deal of indiscriminate kissing went on. People who disliked one another felt a temporary warmth. Glasses were raised, punch was drunk, and hands were crossed for the ritual song. Charles looked longingly at Lucy who was still monopolised by Cobb and Brett. Strangers on either side of him were extending hands. He crossed his own and took them, still wondering about the best route from Drumby to Slane Forest.

> Should auld acquaintance be forgot
> And never brought to mind?

Lucy had not sung it since the party at Ravonsbridge and it seemed suddenly to her as if the Drumby club and all these people had faded away; she was back in the Institute hall, in that other circle, and face after face flashed before her inward eye. Lady Frances, Colonel Harding. Ianthe, Mr. Mildmay, Mrs. Mildmay, Rickie, Mr. Hayter, Wendy, Owen, Emil, Nancy . . . Emil . . . Nancy. . . .

With my hands I shall do all for her, like that. Even as she is,

328

she will know. They will not be strange hands. And that, thought Lucy, is love.

She whispered a word to Cobb and Brett and slipped out of the circle. She ran downstairs and out into the frosty night, back to Canal Cottages where she could think and be alone.

There was not so very much thinking to be done. There was only truth to be faced and accepted. She blew up the ashes of her fire and put on a log and sat down to review life in that sublime, relentless light which played upon Emil and Nancy. She did not love Charles; she did not feel for him one tenth of what she could feel, what she must feel, for the man with whom she should share her life.

His desire would die, when once it had been gratified, and her own response would die with it. Their sympathy over the Institute was only temporary, only an accident. Other issues would arise, and they would quarrel as bitterly as they had once quarrelled in his office. He would be icy and obstinate, she furious and frustrated. Even when he had been telling her of his plans with Owen, and she had been most tempted to go back, she had found herself thinking: *Then I could keep him up to it.* She could not go back. Ravonsbridge was behind her and the time had come to go on to some other place. If it was her lot to be lonely, she must endure that. In Ravonsbridge she had known Lady Frances, who had loved Matt Millwood, and drank out of the little cup that he had used, and tried to speak the truth in love, because his living self was still with her. In Ravonsbridge Emil had sat looking at his hands as the train went down the valley.

Love is an invisible sun, she thought. It is shining down upon us all the time. It is not of us. We don't know where it comes from. But sometimes, when it shines through a life, like hers, like Emil's, we know that it is divine. And there is nothing of that between Charles and me.

As the long winter night wore on she wrote to Charles, telling him that she could not marry him and begging him to go away without seeing her again. She took the letter up to the Lion early in the morning and gave it to the night porter.

329

4

THE THAW was coming. The frost still held but the north east wind no longer whistled in from the coast. It had shifted to the west. The clouds had softer edges; grass, plough and stubble took on a greater variety of hue.

Most people in Drumby spent New Year's morning in bed, recovering from the party and enjoying their holiday. But John was one of the few who had to go up to the Hall for an hour or two. He hurried away after an early breakfast, promising to be back for luncheon and apologising for being so hard worked. Next year he would arrange things better.

"Next year," said Melissa gloomily, "we shall be wheeling little Buttinski about in his perambulator. There'll be no days off next year. We shan't even be able to go to the club."

"We'll get a sitter-in for them," said John.

"Them?"

"If we're going to be pessimistic, don't let's spoil the ship for a ha'porth of tar."

John no longer took everything she said very seriously. Hump had taught him to laugh at her a little. When Melissa shoots a line, Hump had once told him, don't protest or argue. Take it up and embroider it. She shoots a line to hide her feelings from herself, not you.

He went off to the Hall and on his way home he met Lucy, Cobb and Brett, running full tilt to catch a train, their skates swinging from their hands. The sight of his two juniors did not surprise him, though he had heard Melissa's indignant account of the Farraday-Quinn plot to keep them at the Hall. He had never believed that they would be kept, but he had been too discreet to say so, for he had formed the habit of never mentioning the smallest detail, even to Melissa, of what went on behind the barbed wire. Mrs. Farraday might undertake such a mission, but

Mr. Farraday was not in a position to oblige her. Cobb and Brett were not his bottle washers.

"We're just off to Fenswick," called Lucy.

"I thought it was Brattle."

"It was. But the wind has changed, so we're going up the line, not down."

She was looking very happy and gay in a short red skirt and a red leather coat. John wondered why she should be rushing off to skate with Cobb and Brett when she was supposed to be in love with the solemn ass. Where was the fellow?

The fellow was in the Beauclercs' sitting room, drinking their best sherry and receiving sympathy from Melissa. He had called to return the blue coat and remained to tell his sad story. Lucy had refused him. She had sent a letter which came up with his early morning tea, begging him to go away and not to see her again.

John was unfairly prejudiced against Charles and even snorted at the tea, though he had some every morning himself before he got up. Melissa made it from an electric kettle beside their bed. But to share a wife's tea, he felt, is one thing; it is quite another when a bachelor solemnly orders it the night before and causes a chambermaid to bring it up to him. He was so contemptuous over the tea that he was not very compassionate towards the anguish which accompanied it.

Melissa, however, was warmly compassionate, though in her heart she would have thought more of Charles had he kept his disappointment to himself. But he was consulting her, and few women are proof against the temptation of explaining their sex to a man. He wanted to know whether he should go or stay. If he went, of course he could come back, for nothing would induce him to desist in his suit. But did Melissa think he should stay and force another interview, or did she think he might have a better chance if he raised the siege for a while?

Melissa implored him to stay. A letter written in the middle of the night, after an exhausting party, could not, she said, be taken seriously. She was anxious that it should be disregarded for she had made up her mind that Lucy loved him. Also she believed that Cobb and Brett were at the Hall, that Lucy was going alone to Brattle, and that she would be ambushed there by Quinn. If Charles were suddenly to appear, and rescue her, there might be a very pretty reconciliation. Prompt, manly behaviour was likely to appeal to Lucy.

"But . . ." interposed John.

Melissa frowned at him. She wanted no words from that quarter. She would have liked to despatch Charles on his knight errantry before John came in to throw cold water on the idea and suggest, by his *buts*, that a more sensitive lover would accept his dismissal, respect Lucy's wishes, and go away.

"There is only one train to Brattle, the 1:30," she told Charles. "Lucy will certainly take that—"

"But—"

"—And start skating from a wharf close to the station. I imagine that if Captain Quinn really means to thrust his company on her he'll be waiting there."

All right, thought John. I won't say *but* any more. I'll leave them to it. I've tried to tell her twice that Lucy has gone to Fenswick, and all I get is an old fashioned look.

"John can lend you his skates."

"No, I can't," said John. "I'm going skating myself this afternoon."

Charles said hastily that he could buy skates in the town. The cosy atmosphere of Melissa's sympathy had been quite dissipated by her husband's demeanour, which suggested that Lucy's affairs ought not to be settled for her in this high-handed way.

"I'll take a car to Brattle," said Charles, getting up, "and if she doesn't want to skate back with me she can say so. Otherwise I'd have no means of getting back."

A thoroughly ill-tempered mouth, thought John. Lucy will have a sorry life of it if she takes him. A peevish fellow who mistakes obstinacy for firmness. Why! I should never have treated Melissa like this. If she had said no I'd have taken my medicine and gone away and tried to get over it. Let him go to Brattle. Let him go and cool his heels there with Quinn! I don't see why Lucy's afternoon should be spoilt.

He escorted the guest to the door and they parted rather coolly. When he returned to the sitting room Melissa was all ready for battle. So he said nothing save to ask when lunch would be ready. Melissa replied that she must now cook it. They took the sherry glasses into the kitchen and he washed them while she made a cheese soufflé. Still nothing was said. During lunch they discussed the party. Melissa was extremely pleasant, as was her way when ruffled. But an unspoken argument was going on between them all through the meal.

If Lucy is in love with the fellow, she'd have accepted him.

You don't understand women.

Yes I do. They're very like men, only sillier.

You were ungracious. I was ashamed of you.

I'm not the fellow's Nanny.

Scowling like that over the sherry decanter!

Simpering because he asked your advice!

It was not until they were drinking coffee that the dispute became vocal. There was one question to which he could not imagine Melissa's answer.

"Why," he asked suddenly, "do you think Lucy refused him if she wants him? It's not like her."

"Oh . . . I think it's the money."

"His money, you mean?"

"Yes. After all, even for these days he's oppressively rich. A girl like Lucy needs to be tremendously in love before she'll marry a very rich man. If he hadn't a penny I think she'd know her own mind."

"Now I wouldn't have thought Lucy ever considered the money one way or the other. I've never met anyone less conscious of money than she is."

Melissa knew this to be true. It had struck her at Oxford that money meant nothing to Lucy. Her allowance had been very small but she seemed to enjoy an independence which was rare, even among richer girls. Anything which she badly wanted she got; what she could not get she seemed very well able to do without.

"Lucy," she said, "has got rather a noble character really. And that makes her do stupid things."

"I agree about her character," said John smiling. "And therefore I think we should let her do as she pleases."

"Oh, no, John. People with noble characters ought to be certified. They never attend to their own interests. Look at Hump! Look how he's been exploited! So cracked about his cattle fly he lets other people get all the credit."

"They have a different idea of their own interests. They want the best or nothing."

"So they get nothing."

"Very often. But they aren't so disappointed as we would be, if we got nothing. The best seems to them so much more worth while than any compromise they could have had."

"But life is nothing but a compromise," argued Melissa.

"For most of us. But it's a good thing to have a few noble characters cropping up. Not for anything they do, so much, as for their challenge to our values. They force us to compare our good with their best. They see the best and say *Hi!* And make straight for it. They don't see all the pitfalls and barbed wire that frightens us. They may never get anywhere. It's their *Hi!* that matters. It forces us to look at what they've seen."

"Well, I'm not content to leave Lucy hung up on barbed wire all her life. I hope she'll take a rest from being noble, and marry Charles, and devote herself to Ravonsbridge."

"But she's probably done all she could do in Ravonsbridge. She went and said *Hi!* I don't gather that anything else she did was particularly sensible or effective. And I notice that you agree there's nothing noble in marrying Charles."

"But I'm quite sure she's really in love with him. You didn't see her when he arrived yesterday. I did. I believe they'll come back from Brattle engaged and very grateful to me for pushing them into it."

"And I," said John, "am quite positive they won't."

"What will you bet?"

"I never bet on a certainty."

"I'll wager half my dowry."

"Darling, you can't, and a good thing too. It's all in the hands of trustees."

"I'm going to get out a bottle of the champagne my father sent us. I'm perfectly convinced it will be needed."

"That's all right as far as I'm concerned. I never mind drinking your father's pop."

334

"You'll drink it on your knees. You'll drink it in a white sheet."

Charles went back to the Lion and rang up his mother who reproved him for wasting money on an unnecessary trunk call. He explained that he would be staying in Drumby for some days.

"You could have said that on a postcard."

"I thought you'd want my news."

"Have you got any?"

"Yes. I've asked her."

"And she said yes?"

"No. She said no."

"Then why are you staying in Drumby?"

"I'm hoping she'll change her mind."

"Why should she?"

"Girls often don't know what they want."

"Lucy Carmichael does. You'd much better come home."

"I'm not going home without her."

"Don't be childish. You've no right to pester her. Come home at once. Goodbye."

There was a ping as Lady Frances hung up.

Charles pondered for a while and then thought that he would take her advice. He did not like skating and did not much relish this farcical drama with Quinn. He decided that he had better withdraw for a while, mobilise his resources, and renew the attack when the weather was milder.

5

THE SUN came out as the skating party emerged from the wharves and gas works of Fenswick. They congratulated themselves on having seized the day, for the ice would scarcely be safe for very many more hours. The green fields, the reed beds, and the alders were waking from the rigid death which had held them for a week. During the gale, flocks of gulls had flown inland; now they flashed silvery through the dark trees as they returned to the coast.

Cobb and Brett were very young and they liked Lucy because she was the only girl in Drumby who did not make them feel inferior, callow and poor. She was always ready for a lark. She did not mind that their boat leaked and she paid for her own ice cream. They skated on either side of her, holding her crossed hands, as the benign west wind blew them home, and they all sang:

> "You'll never get to Heaven on roller skates;
>   You'll shoot right past dem pearly gates . . ."

The canal ran through fields to a horizon which had gained in distance since the thaw began. They knew it well, for in summer they had often sailed their boat from Drumby to Fenswick and back. They knew the reed beds, where swans nested and herons fished, and all the low bridges where a road or a cart track crossed the canal. These were a nuisance to sailors for the mast had to come down, and there was a pleasant spice of risk about skating under them. All three had to bend nearly double as they shot under a bridge; upright, they would have cracked their heads against the arch. To maintain speed and to bend at the very last minute was part of the game.

> "You'll never get to Heaven in a rocking chair!
>   De Lawd don't want no slackers there . . ."

Lucy was extremely happy. Her companions were so genial and uncomplicated; they had not begun to grow up. They thought the club was faultless. They were still enraptured by their own performance in the pantomime. She could not have wished for better skating companions; the wind, the swift movement, the gulls in the sunshine, were enough for them and enough for her.

Fenswick dropped away behind them, a smoky blur. They came to some flooded and frozen water meadows through which the canal ran, as it ran across the reed beds, on a levee. The ice was good here and the three of them, tired of skating straight forwards, scrambled down the embankment onto the meadows to cut fancy figures. They tried to do impossible things and frequently fell down. But Cobb and Brett, who had an infantile capacity for never tiring of any amusement, persisted, until Lucy began to fear that they would never get back to Drumby before nightfall. She urged them to come on. At last, climbing up the embankment of the levee, she went on herself.

Much as she liked Cobb and Brett she enjoyed being alone still more. The light was so beautiful and the emptiness of the landscape so satisfying. Their raucous shouts soon died away on the meadows behind, and she flew on to where the ground rose again. The canal ran through a little spinney of hazels and past a farm yard where a child was feeding chickens.

Soon it would be spring again, with catkins on the hazels and the first lambs in the fields. And oh, thought Lucy, how beautiful it all is! "How beautiful the earth is still, for thee how full of happiness!"

Her restlessness was all gone. She loved Lincolnshire. A bliss, an ecstasy, came to her, which she had known constantly in childhood but which she had thought to be lost. It came again, that overpowering joy, from the fields in the yellow winter light it came, from the huge sky, from the hard ice beneath her ringing skates. She wanted nothing more of life than the moment held, and she was sorry when the sheds of Breenho camp came into sight on her left, across some brick-fields, and she knew that she was halfway home. But she did not stay for the others, though she slowed a little and listened, in case they were coming. She could hear nothing except a cow lowing in a field and a train which rattled tranquilly beyond Breenho and paused at the camp halt.

After the halt the line curved and ran for some way beside the canal. Lucy quickened her pace, determined to see how far she could get before the train overtook and passed her on its way to Drumby. She made a bet with herself that she would first reach a place where a road crossed the canal and the railway line by a high bridge. After that the canal curved away again. She skated on, as fast as she could, and presently heard the train come rumbling up behind her on the slight embankment which raised it above the level of the canal. It caught her up while she was still a long way from the bridge; she must have quite misjudged her pace. And then it passed her, though she still tried hard to race it. The engine passed her, whence the fireman leant out to grin at her, and then several carriages full of schoolboys coming back to their homes down the line from Fenswick Grammar School. Clusters of them hung out of the windows to watch her losing race and wave to her. She wondered to see them there in holiday time, and then remembered that there had been a football match on the Grammar School ground. She waved back but did not slacken her pace until the whole train was past and she knew that she had lost. On it went, getting smaller, with its plume of smoke above it, towards the bridge which spanned the canal. And then, just before it reached the bridge, it stopped. She remembered that men were working on the line and railed at fortune that they had not been a little nearer to Breenho; an earlier stop might have given her the race.

It only paused for a few seconds but, in that brief interval, she saw somebody jump out onto the track and scramble down to the canal bank as the train moved on again. He sat on the grass beside the canal. As she came up she saw that he was putting on skating boots. He looked up and smiled at her as she flew past him, a hopeful smile, but not so hopeful as to be impertinent.

She had not gone many yards before she heard the ring of skates behind her. He shot past, his head thrust forward in a determined way which reminded her of someone, and she heard herself cry out *Hump!* even before receiving the conviction that this must be Hump. Nobody else would have jumped out of a train quite like that; and, though he was a man, he was also the boy in Melissa's snapshot.

He did not turn but checked in one movement and skated backwards till he was level with her.

"Oh, back-checking!" cried Lucy. "Oh, you are good at it!"

"Did you call?" he asked politely, falling into line beside her.

"Yes. You're Hump."

"I know I am. But thank you for telling me."

"Does Melissa know you're coming then?"

"No, she doesn't. Who are you?"

She felt a sudden reluctance to tell him and immediately become poor-Lucy-jilted-at-the-altar. He would inevitably think of her as that. She said:

"I thought you knew everybody in Drumby."

338

"So did I. But when I saw you from the train I thought—she wasn't here before when I was here before. But then you waved, so I thought I must know you."

"I wasn't waving to you. I was waving to the boys."

"What boys?"

"The schoolboys coming from the match."

"Oh."

"Why did you get out of the train?"

"Wanted to skate."

"But what about your luggage? Hadn't you any?"

"A boy in my carriage said he'd put it out at Drumby."

"You made up your mind very quickly."

"He said we might stop at the bridge, so I was all ready. We'd been discussing it ever since we saw people skating on the canal."

"People? Did you see two men?"

"Yes. Do they belong to you?"

"Well, they started with me."

"They looked like chicken chemists but they're new since my time. Who are they?"

"They're called Cobb and Brett."

"Cobb and Brett?"

Hump remembered these names in connection with the Lincolnshire Handicap and inferred that this must be bossy Lucy. He reeled with surprise. But why would she not own to it Because, he surmised, she's afraid I shall remember that stupid business of the wedding; she probably thinks that's all I know about her. How boring that must be for the girl!

"I wish you'd been here last night," said Lucy. "We had a very good party at your club."

"Admirably organised I'm sure," suggested Hump.

"Oh . . ." said Lucy, blushing slightly.

Hump smiled, stretched out his hands, and took hers crosswise. They skated on.

"Melissa will shriek for joy," said Lucy.

"Melissa does not shriek."

"She will today. She thought she wouldn't see you before you went to Africa."

"Oh . . . Africa is off."

339

"No! What happened?"

"They found they could manage without me."

This was not entirely unexpected. Melissa had been right. He had been summoned to Paris to have his brains picked and the African job had gone to the colleague who picked them.

Lucy, indignant, gave his hand a sympathetic squeeze.

"Thank you," said Hump complacently.

"I know so much about you," explained Lucy in some confusion. "I can't feel I've only just met you. But oh . . . I'm afraid Melissa will be very unhappy about this."

"Oh, that's all right. I've got another job. I'm going to Texas."

"What? In America?"

"Umhm! Heidenstrasse Research Foundation. Fellow there who read my report on the work in the Dandawa. Gruber he's called; working on cattle diseases; knows an awful lot and wants me to go out there for two years to work with him on ichneumon parasites. We've been corresponding for some time; he's first rate, and the Foundation will pay me a screw. I couldn't want anything I'd like better."

"But how lovely to go to Texas!"

"Why? Have you been there?"

"No, never. I was never out of England. But I always wanted to go to Texas because of its name. The Lone Star State."

"Oh, but that's because—"

"I know that. Don't start 'that's becausing.' It *is* a perfectly lovely name."

"Fair as a star when only one is shining in the sky?"

"Yes. Do you like Wordsworth?"

"Sure. Read him from cover to cover."

"Melissa never told me that."

"She couldn't tell you everything about me."

"No. But she's told me an awful lot."

"Same here. I think we'd better wash out what she's told us and start clean, or we shall get muddled."

"I'm glad you like Wordsworth."

"Yes, but you know I always think that 'fair as a star' business is rather a doubtful compliment. Now if I was to write a poem about a girl I'd say what a performance she gives when *all* the stars are shining in the sky. That would show I had some standard of comparison."

"It sounds like a poem about yourself and what a good judge you are. When do you go to Texas?"

"In three weeks."

"Oh! . . . That's not very long."

"No. It's not."

It was a very short time, if he was to take this mettlesome creature with him to the Lone Star State. She would need a passport, and an American Visa . . . and a wedding ring.

Why on earth did I think I shouldn't like him? wondered Lucy. I like his voice. It's much quieter than I expected. Why did I imagine him always shouting and ordering people about like a film director with a megaphone?

"Are you sailing?" she asked, "or flying?"

"Sailing. I've got a berth in a cabin with three other men," he said thoughtfully.

Which was another complication. No end of things had to be done in these three weeks. Normally, thought Hump, I'd have allowed three weeks to educate the girl up to the idea of marrying me. But I can't stay here longer than a week. I've got to get busy. If Melissa had only told me. . . .

Melissa had told him, again and again. It was not Melissa's fault that no man ever believes a woman when she tells him that another woman is charming. It was not Melissa's fault that she had never been able to convey to him the particular enchantment of Lucy's eyes, her mouth, her young energy and her quick, soft voice. He had to see all this for himself before he could overlook the chilling fact that he already respected Lucy like anything. Having seen it he felt not a second's hesitation.

He began to skate very fast indeed for he was in a hurry to get to Drumby where the speediest piece of work that he had ever undertaken lay before him.

Lucy liked the pace at first, though she could never have made it alone. But after a while she grew dizzy and had to protest.

"Oh, please . . . I can't go so fast."

"Sorry," said Hump, slowing.

"You go on. You must be dying to see Melissa."

She tried to drag her hands away, but he held them firmly and said that he was not in all that hurry. Drumby, its red brick strangely lit by the setting sun, was cropping up on the horizon. He realised that he was in no hurry at all. He did not want to get to Drumby. He began to skate at a snail's pace.

"I think Cobb and Brett are catching us up," said Lucy.

"Oh, are they? Do you want them to?"

"No."

The pace became brisker.

"I'm enjoying this very much," suggested Hump.

"Oh, so am I," said Lucy. "Just before the train came I wished I could go on for ever."

A sudden pang of compassion assailed Hump—almost of guilt. She had been perfectly happy by herself. He had seen that in his first glimpse of her. All alone and perfectly happy, flying through the wintry fields. And now he had come tumbling down the bank, wanting to shatter this solitude, wanting her never to be happy again unless he was there. It was, he felt, rather tough to be planning to sweep her off her feet in a week. It was hardly fair to a girl who could manage to be happy, all alone, in spite of so much sorrow, defeat and humiliation. I must never forget it, he told himself. If she comes, I must never forget what she gave up for me.

Unconsciously he began to skate very fast again and Lucy gasped:

"Please . . ."

"So sorry. I don't know why I did that."

"You were thinking of something you mean to do next week."

"Yes, I was. How did you know?"

"It's what I always do. If I think of something in the future I begin to run. The only way to do anything the right pace is to concentrate entirely on the moment."

He took a quick look at her and decided that her mind, anyway, was on the moment. She seemed to be intent upon skating. And so she was. She was sure that she liked Hump very much and felt as easy with him as though he had been an old friend. Since he did not, obviously, think of her as poor Lucy, she did not much mind what he thought of her. He must like her or he would have taken the opportunity she offered to go on ahead.

"Is this right?" he asked.

"Rather too slow. I like going fast, as fast as ever I can. Faster than I can, if possible. With you I can go much faster than I did alone."

He concentrated upon a pace which should carry Lucy without alarming her, and presently hit on the right momentum. Freeing his left hand, he stretched an arm behind her shoulders, in a rigid bar, so that she could not fall back. Drumby, burnished, its windows glittering in the sunset, rushed towards them.

"Oh!" cried Lucy, in manifest ecstasy, "this . . . is . . . simply glorious. I never enjoyed anything so much in my life!"

Wonderful how far you can get, thought Hump, if you concentrate on the moment. So far as she's concerned I'm merely an auxiliary motor, but she's taking a trial canter down the course, though she doesn't know it.

A tawny blob was trotting along the tow-path and a solitary skater emerged from a cluster of cottages on the edge of the town.

"Here's John and Collins," said Lucy.

"Is that Collins? Poor little brute!"

"Oh, he's not a poor little brute. Melissa's quite soft-headed about him."

"Yes. But his nose is going to be put out of joint."

"Is it? Oh. . . ."

John came skating carefully towards them; with the setting sun full in his eyes he did not see who they were until they all met, when he was so much surprised that he skated into the bank and fell down. Hump and Lucy broke the outboard motor formation and helped him to his feet.

"Yes," said Hump, "me! I hope you've got a bottle of my father's pop left."

"Yes," said John. "We've got one out. . . ."

And then he began to hoot with laughter.

"Joke?" suggested Hump.

"Melissa's on the bridge by the club," cackled John. "She . . . she's looking for Lucy. She's expecting to see her come from Brattle!"

"But who'd go to Brattle with the wind in the west?" cried Lucy.

"Wrong at the start," agreed Hump.

They all three went on, Lucy crossed-hands between John and Hump, and Collins bucketing along the tow-path. As they shot past the cottages the sun set, and a bloomy, frosty twilight advanced from the sea.

Melissa was on the high hoop of the canal bridge, just beyond the club, where steps led down to the ice. But her back was turned. She was looking anxiously in the opposite direction, hoping to see Lucy come from Brattle in quite other company. They shouted, but she did not turn.

Lucy remembered a favourite story of Mr. Meeker's and how he had stood once in Slane Forest, looking the wrong way, till he heard his friend come singing up the hill. She lifted her voice and sang in the rosy dusk:

> "Go fetch to me a pint of wine
> And fill it in a silver tassie;
> That I may drink before I go
> A service to my bonny lassie."

Collins barked. Melissa turned. Melissa shrieked as the three who shared her heart checked their swift flight, slowed down and came to rest at the bridge.